Belinda Alexandra's bestselling books have been published around the world, including the United States, Spain, France, Germany, the United Kingdom, Turkey, Hungary and Poland. She is the daughter of a Russian mother and an Australian father and has been fascinated by world culture and travel since her youth.

She lives in Sydney with her three black cats and a garden full of interesting wildlife. Her hobbies include flamenco and belly dancing, piano and foreign languages. A lover of all creatures, Belinda volunteers with several animal charities.

www.belinda-alexandra.com

www.belinda-alexandra.com/blog

belinda_alexandra_author

BelindaAlexandraAuthor

hellobelindaalexandra

Also by Belinda Alexandra

Fiction

*White Gardenia*

*Wild Lavender*

*Silver Wattle*

*Tuscan Rose*

*Golden Earrings*

*Sapphire Skies*

*Southern Ruby*

*The Invitation*

*The Mystery Woman*

Non-fiction

*The Divine Feline: A Chic Cat Lady's Guide*

*to a Woman's Best Friend*

*Emboldened: On Finding the Fire to Keep*

*Going When All Seems Lost*

# *The* FRENCH AGENT

## BELINDA ALEXANDRA

**HarperCollins***Publishers*

**HarperCollins**_Publishers_

Australia • Brazil • Canada • France • Germany • Holland • India
Italy • Japan • Mexico • New Zealand • Poland • Spain • Sweden
Switzerland • United Kingdom • United States of America

HarperCollins acknowledges the Traditional Custodians
of the land upon which we live and work, and pays respect
to Elders past and present.

First published in Australia in 2022
This edition published in 2023
by HarperCollins_Publishers_ Australia Pty Limited
Gadigal Country
Level 13, 201 Elizabeth Street, Sydney NSW 2000
ABN 36 009 913 517
harpercollins.com.au

A catalogue record for this book is available from the National Library of Australia

ISBN 978 1 4607 5852 6 (paperback)
ISBN 978 1 4607 1231 3 (ebook)
ISBN 978 1 4607 4497 0 (audiobook)

Cover design by Christine Armstrong, HarperCollins Design Studio
Front cover images: Woman © Rekha Garton / Arcangel; Eiffel Tower by
   Geoffroy Hauwen on Unsplash
Back cover image by istockphoto.com
Author photograph by Elizabeth Allnutt
Typeset in Bembo Std by Kirby Jones
Printed and bound in Australia by McPherson's Printing Group

*For my family*

# PROLOGUE

*London, May 1943*
*My beloved Diana,*
*It breaks my heart to write this to you, because I know it will
cause you grief. You have stood by my side in all things, and I
cannot forget the brave face you showed when we said goodbye
on the wharf in Sydney. It is the memory of your courage that
has kept me strong.*

*At the time we thought the separation would be brief and
the battle easily won. But the war that spreads like an evil
stain across the continent is reaching its darkest hour and now
requires the greatest sacrifice of all of us who believe in a civilised
humanity. You'll understand that, won't you?*

*I write to tell you that I am leaving for my most dangerous
mission yet, and if all should not go well, promise me that you
will not allow your sorrow to be prolonged. Your disposition
has always been so cheerful, your zest for life so inspiring, and
your ability to overcome challenges so valiant. You cannot allow
anything to deprive you of your spirit, for our dearest Freddy
must always be your first concern.*

*We had four wonderful years together, and my heartfelt wish was always that I would return to you to continue where we left off, and to see our son grow into a young man.*

*Do not feel sorry for me if I don't come back. It is simply that God had another plan for me and I trust in His mercy that He will watch over my dearest wife and son. Please know that the time I spent with you has been the happiest in a joyful and privileged life. It will be you and Freddy that I will be thinking of until my last breath.*

*Until we meet again, on earth or in heaven.*
*Your forever faithful husband,*
*Casper*

# CHAPTER ONE

*Paris, February 1946*

Sabine Brouillette's apartment was cold, much colder than it had been during the war when she had been warmed by the hope that tyranny could be defeated and life could be beautiful again. Her chilblained fingers hovered over the saucepan. The flame on the burner she was using to heat the water could go out at any moment. Utilities, along with bread, coffee, oil and sugar, were still rationed for everyday Parisians, while across the river fashion houses were staging shows again and the automobile industry was producing cars based on German design. Wan't that what General de Gaulle had said should happen? *The days of weeping are over. The days of glory have returned*. France would rise again.

Sabine took her coffee and hunk of dry bread to the dining room. The long table was made of walnut and had seating for ten. She placed herself at the end and stared out at the view of the slate rooftops of Saint-Germain-des-Prés. She was only thirty-six and still had plenty of life ahead of her. Her dark hair had grown back to its pre-war lustre and her olive skin had plumped out again. But ever since she had come back from the camp, she had felt as though she was living in a state of suspended animation. She was waiting for something – or someone. But for what? For whom? Everyone who mattered was dead. The apartment had once been filled with people and music. Now it was like a grave, the air frozen, the lopsided books on the shelves untouched, the grand piano covered in dust.

Sabine squinted through the doorway at the instrument. The day France mobilised, she had been teaching tiny Hélène Rosenfeld to play Rachmaninov's 'Lilacs'. Now Hélène, her mother, her sisters, her entire family were lying dead in a ditch somewhere in Poland. It was hard to believe that Sabine had once instructed young slender hands – and pudgy eager ones – to play Chopin's nocturnes, Schubert's sonatas and Debussy's lilting 'Clair de Lune'. But she had been an entirely different person then. Four years of living by nothing but stealth, fear and a determination to rid her country of the enemy had altered her. There was nothing in her makeup that had any resemblance to the former Sabine Brouillette – once a highly sought-after piano teacher, once a devoted wife and mother.

Her neighbour, Madame Chout, said Sabine could play again if she really wanted to, that she could adapt the music to accommodate her crippled left hand. But Sabine didn't trust a word Madame Chout said. It would be too painful to pick up the sharp pieces of a shattered life. It was better to move forward, to become somebody else. Besides, if Sabine could gather enough evidence, she was going to have Madame Chout arrested as a collaborator. She took a sip of the bitter coffee and imagined the immaculately coiffed matron being carted off to prison for her crimes. The picture made Sabine smile, her first in a long time.

*

It was starting to snow outside but Sabine was loath to take the Metro. She didn't like being underground and she hated crowds. It was better to risk the icy streets than to be crammed shoulder to shoulder with her fellow citizens all the way to Place Victor Hugo. She locked her front door and wheeled her bicycle down the steps to the foyer. The concierge, Madame Rouzard, came out of her office and gave Sabine a friendly smile.

'You look nice today, Madame Brouillette. You have colour in your cheeks,' she said.

Sabine watched Madame Rouzard's stout legs climb the stairs to the second floor. The steely seventy-year-old had hidden Jewish women and children from the Gestapo. It was Madame Rouzard who had coaxed Sabine away from the window ledge the day she decided that a life without those she loved wasn't worth living. *If you are still here, it is because God has a purpose for you,* she had told her. *France needs women like you to rebuild it. You will do so in memory of all those you have lost. Do it for them.*

Sabine mounted the bicycle and headed in the direction of Rue de Buci. She took a different route to work each day. It was an old habit she couldn't shake. Despite the rationing, there was still a line of shivering people waiting outside a bakery, and the shelves of the shoe store next to it were empty. The once bustling Quai Voltaire was as sedate as a country road, its only traffic bicycles and noisy, foul-smelling petrolettes. The Germans had taken the cars, buses and trucks when they left.

The misshapen fingers of her left hand weakened her grip on the handlebars and the road was slippery. She wobbled and narrowly missed a man driving a goat cart. He swore at her and shook his fist.

'*Pardon, monsieur!*' Sabine called back to him over her shoulder. She slowed down, having no intention of falling off and breaking her neck that day. Not while the Nuremberg trials were in progress. A kiosk displayed the headlines. The full extent of the atrocities was finally being exposed. The court had been shown films of the concentration camps. Yet the men in the dock demonstrated no guilt. They even complained that the accusations against them were unjust. But Sabine knew they were already condemned because nobody loved the theatre of perceived justice better than the Americans. It was the thought of the other monsters, the ones who were slipping away, that kept Sabine up at night. For Madame Rouzard had been correct when she'd said that God had a purpose for Sabine. She didn't believe she had any part in building a new France, but she would avenge the old one and all those who had perished trying to defend it.

\*

Sabine passed the Haussmann buildings of Avenue Victor Hugo with their cream-limestone façades and intricate ironwork balconies and came to a stop outside number 43. The building had been used as a Gestapo office during the war and nicknamed the 'Villa Bömelburg' by the Resistance members after the head of the Gestapo in France. It was now the offices of the branch of the French secret services responsible for hunting war criminals and collaborators. Sabine parked her bicycle next to the others lined up outside and made her way through the tall wooden doors, nodding to the guard before taking the stairs. For the first month she worked with the Department for the Investigation of Enemy War Crimes she had been haunted by her memories of her own interrogation. It was the spring of 1944 when the Gestapo struck the *Pianiste* circuit, the Resistance group her family had set up after Marshal Pétain's cowardly capitulation. One by one the members fell like dominoes. They were arrested, tortured, deported and shot. Hitler termed it *Nacht und Nebel* – Night and Fog. His opponents were to be made to disappear in such a way that no one would ever know of their terrible fate. Sabine was the only survivor.

Her desk was at the far end of the department, crammed between two filing cabinets and a window. She made her way through the thick haze of cigarette smoke towards it.

'*Bonjour*, Sabine,' Agent Brodeur said without looking up from his typewriter.

The rest of the male agents gave her a curt nod. The other female agent, Juliette Vignes, pretended not to see her. The war had made Sabine aware of inconsistencies in the way people presented themselves – the slightest false note in a story, the tiniest movement of someone's eyes. Juliette's nails were painted bright red, and her stockings were sheer. Her shoes didn't clack like everyone else's, so it was safe to assume they were leather. For a long time, Sabine had suspected that Juliette Vignes had collaborated, or at the very least been involved in the black market. Everyone in the section was supposed to be a former member of the Resistance, but Sabine didn't trust any of them. There had been few true patriots in those early, dangerous days of the war. Most of her countrymen had been content to throw roses to the invading German tanks, as long as they could get on with their lives. The Resistance only swelled in numbers when the Germans began deporting young men and women for forced labour, and when it seemed clear that Hitler was going to lose the war. Joining the Resistance at the last minute was a way to cover your tracks if you'd been in bed with the enemy.

Sabine sat down without taking her coat off. Government offices weren't any better heated than private apartments. The files on her desk were systematised but there was nothing orderly about her work. She opened a file and stared at the photograph of a woman clutching a child in front of a German firing squad. Seconds after the photograph was taken, the woman and child were dead. She studied the men holding the rifles. Most of them would have had wives and children at home, but she never saw any trace of regret in the expressions of these killers. She leaned back in her chair and stared out the window. Investigating war crimes was like delving into the mind of evil. Every evening, when Sabine went home, she took a bath even when the water was freezing. She had to wash that evil off herself.

She sensed Juliette's gaze on her and turned around, meeting the agent's sour expression with her own stare. Juliette must have suspected that Sabine saw through her, or perhaps all this animosity was simply jealousy over the department supervisor, Robert Fortin, who always included Sabine in formal interrogations and never Juliette. He didn't trust her either.

'Agent Brouillette.'

Sabine turned to see Robert standing in the doorway of his office. He was wearing his winter coat but not for the same reason she was. He had never got over his wartime thinness and was self-conscious about it. He'd been a champion skier and quite a ladies' man in the 1930s, she'd heard. Even now, Sabine thought, if you looked beyond the weariness in his eyes and the frown lines, he was still attractive, with a fine nose and thick waves of black hair. But her observations were purely clinical. Sabine felt no desire for Robert. She didn't feel desire for anyone.

'Can I see you a moment?' he asked her.

She followed him into his office, and he shut the door behind them. Robert's desk, which was three times the size of hers, had so many files stacked on top of it that it was sagging in the middle like an old mattress. She sat down and Robert pulled a packet of *Gauloises* from the drawer. He offered her one, although he knew she didn't smoke. She'd heard that during the war, when cigarettes weren't included in women's rations, he'd always given his share away to his female comrades. She shook her head and he lit a cigarette for himself and sat down, looking at her. There was an intensity between them that was as ardent as if they were lovers. If Juliette had seen that look, she would have been jealous because she didn't understand that sometimes there were things between a man and a woman that went deeper than sex. Robert and Sabine were as wrathful as each other; they recognised each other's souls. Their job was to gather evidence, not to mete out punishment. They were not to behave as the mobs had immediately after the Liberation, settling scores with old enemies and shaving the heads of ordinary women and parading them through the streets. Even in the chaotic times of the war, the Resistance had followed a strict code of evidence before a traitor could be executed. But without having to elaborate on it verbally, Robert and Sabine had an agreement that if they had a strong enough case against a suspect, and due to the fecklessness of the legal system there was a chance the suspect would get away with their crimes, then that person might be eliminated and the death made to look like an 'accident'. Sabine had lured such a criminal to a hotel room last spring. Robert had stepped out of his hiding place behind the curtains and broken the man's neck. It was justice for the Jewish people who had given that gangster all their life savings, believing his promise that he would spirit them and their families to America, when all he had done was hand them over to the Vichy police.

'We are on a doomed mission,' Robert said finally, blowing out a long stream of smoke into the air. 'Our work is to be phased out. I learned it this morning – the French secret service will be reformed to concentrate on espionage and counter-espionage only. We are in a cold war now against the Soviet Union. Germany is our new ally.'

'The Jews won't forget,' said Sabine. '*You and I* won't forget.'

The vein in Robert's temple swelled. 'Sometimes I think you and I are the only two who will remember. The British and Americans have already moved on. Even the French want to forget all about the war and fill their lives with frivolity.' He gestured to the overflowing files on his desk. 'While you and I pore through these reports, sorting the probable from the improbable, and persecuting black-marketeers, policemen and whores, a whole other section of the French secret service is in Berlin right now recruiting former Nazi intelligence officers.'

Sabine pursed her lips. She was used to fighting for hopeless causes and wasn't ready to give up the battle. That governments were corrupt, politicians hypocrites and people generally apathetic was not news to her. 'The Nazi intelligence officers will have valuable knowledge of the Soviet Union's secrets,' she said. 'I don't place ordinary rank-and-file party members on the same level as war criminals.'

He leaned back and looked at her warily. 'What if I told you a branch of our services is negotiating with Ernst Misselwitz as we speak. He is sitting in a prison in Germany and is more than willing to give up names of collaborators that might be useful to us in exchange for his freedom. They would like you and me to work with him.'

Sabine flinched as if he'd bitten her. To work with Misselwitz was unthinkable, even if he could name collaborators. He was a former Gestapo agent responsible for the torture and death of hundreds of members of the Resistance, including members of her own circuit.

'Well, how do you feel about that?' Robert asked.

She tempered her bitterness. 'I don't believe they will disband us just yet,' she said. 'Not after the support for the Nuremberg trials. Our department is still useful for public relations, and as long as we have the sanction to hunt' – she met Robert's gaze meaningfully – 'we have a chance to serve justice.'

'You remind me of my wife, Sabine,' Robert said, with a painful grimace. 'She died with a gun in her hand.'

He rarely talked about his wife, in the same way Sabine rarely talked about her husband and child. Something in his tone unsettled her. That the French government was corrupt wasn't why he'd called her into his office. It was something else. Something she didn't already know.

'What?' she asked.

He regarded her for a moment and then stubbed out his cigarette. 'I don't want you to get emotional. When an agent gets emotional, they make mistakes. You are too precious to me to let you make any mistakes.'

'I don't feel anything anymore,' she said. 'Everything died in the war.'

Robert hesitated, then seemed to come to some decision in his mind. He picked up a file. 'An interesting piece of information has come from the military interrogators at Balingen prisoner-of-war camp,' he said. 'It seems a German cipher clerk has cracked to save himself. He has provided some vital information about the *Pianiste* circuit.'

Sabine's heart slowed to the point it almost stopped. The faces of people who were forever lost flashed across her mind – Jacqueline, Madeleine, Henri … Lucien and Pierre.

'I don't know if I should tell you,' said Robert, frowning again. 'This one is too close to home.'

'Tell me. What information has the clerk provided?'

Robert bit his lip and leaned forward. 'He has revealed who betrayed the circuit.'

Sabine kept her eyes fixed on his face.

'You were right in your suspicions that it was a double agent,' he continued. 'One who had direct contact with Berlin.

According to the cipher clerk, the messages the agent sent were always marked "Highly Reliable", indicating someone important, someone high up in the circuit.'

'So, has he revealed the traitor's identity?' she asked.

Robert leaned back in his chair. 'The cipher clerk was curious to know how Germany had recruited such a fine agent. He had a friend in the analysts' department and put that question to him. His friend answered that it was too dangerous to ask questions like that. But he did tell him the double agent's codename.'

'Which was?'

'The Black Fox.'

Sabine tried to picture the person but could only see the animal, creeping under the cover of darkness, sniffing for the scent of its prey. A black fox was rare in Europe. She had never seen one in the wild.

'Where is the analyst now?' she asked. 'I'll interrogate him.'

Robert shook his head. 'He's dead. He was killed in the bombing of Berlin.'

Sabine chewed her lip. 'But there will be records for the Black Fox in France. Where is all the information that was retrieved from the region's Gestapo headquarters?'

Robert pushed the file towards Sabine. 'When the British bombed the Château de Valois, the Resistance members who raided it did a rush job. They only had time to take files from desks.'

'They didn't search for a safe?'

'There wasn't time. They had to get in and out before the German reinforcements arrived.'

Sabine bristled. The Nazis were meticulous record-keepers. They kept track of their agents and informers. Rushed or not, failing to retrieve a safe from Gestapo headquarters was a grave mistake. It could have saved hundreds of lives.

'The safe might still be there. Under the rubble,' she said.

'I had our agents in Bergerac check,' Robert told her. 'They've had some preliminary digging done and they have sighted a safe. It will take them all day to get it out. I want you there tomorrow when it's opened.'

'I'll leave first thing in the morning,' Sabine said, scooping up the file.

Their eyes met and that familiar feeling of understanding passed between them. Ever since she had returned to Paris, she had been investigating the fall of the *Pianiste* circuit. Sometimes when a circuit was compromised it was because of carelessness on the part of a member bragging too much to friends or some other foolish behaviour, but most of the time it was because a member had been caught by the Gestapo and was persuaded to save themselves by denouncing others. When the demise of the *Pianiste* circuit came, however, the arrests were systematic, which implied the Gestapo had very detailed information. It could only have been the result of infiltration by a double agent. But as much as she had investigated the matter, as to that person's identity, dead ends were all that she had managed to find. Now her answer might be lying in a safe in the rubble of a former Gestapo headquarters.

# CHAPTER TWO

> *Gardening is about the future. One plants a seed dreaming of what it will become. It requires patience. It requires faith …*

Diana White leaned away from her typewriter and stretched her arms upwards, releasing the tension from her shoulders and back. Writing was as hard mentally as digging in the garden was physically. Each idea had to be lifted and examined individually, like the rocks of a dry-stone wall, to make it fit neatly into the text as a whole. She went to run her fingers through her hair before remembering it had just been set and the hairdresser had told her not to do anything that might put it out of shape. It had taken all her skill to tame Diana's mop of unruly chestnut curls into anything like a hairstyle from *Vogue* magazine. That meant no sweaty work in the garden, dusty housework, or even lying down to read a book. In the end it seemed that applying herself to her monthly gardening article for *Australian Home and Garden* was all she could manage.

'How do other women put up with it?' she wondered, standing up from her chair and looking out the open French doors to the garden. Each evening after working in her garden or someone else's, Diana soaked in a bath laced with Epsom salts and lavender oil, scrubbing furiously at her short nails to remove the dirt. She wore a wide-brimmed hat and gloves to protect her skin from the sun in summer and smothered her lips in lanolin to stop them chapping in winter. But that was the extent of her beauty routine. She was usually too busy to fuss about fashion and, although she would never say it to anyone's face, she thought powder and lipstick made women look like clowns. But today was a special occasion.

The shrill sound of the telephone ringing jolted her to her senses. She picked up the receiver and the commanding voice of Phyllis, her editor, came on the line.

'Are you ready, my dear?'

'I've almost finished the article,' Diana replied. 'I'll file it on my way to the port.'

'Not the article, silly. For Casper. It's not every day that a woman's husband comes home from the war.'

Diana was glad Phyllis couldn't see her flinch. Ready? She had been getting herself ready for Casper's homecoming ever since he'd returned to his native Britain to join the RAF six years earlier. Now their reunion after such a long time apart was near, she had been doing everything possible to distract herself until it was time to pick him up from the wharf.

'I'm excited, Phyllis,' she said. 'But I'm nervous too.'

'Nervous? What on earth is there to be nervous about? You should be grateful. There are many women in this country whose husbands will never come home – let alone in one piece.'

'I am grateful … It's just that …' Diana bit her lip. She glanced out the doors and saw Freddy tossing a soccer ball to Blossom. The pig was chasing the ball and then rolling it back to Freddy with her snout. Diana smiled at the scene. Freddy wasn't like she'd been at seven years of age, anxious and fragile. He was adventurous and imaginative. He saw the possibilities in things, including the idea that a pig could be as good a companion as a dog. 'Freddy was only a baby when Casper left,' she told Phyllis. 'I've shared with him millions of things about his father and shown him all the pictures …'

'Casper and Freddy are so much alike!' Phyllis interrupted. 'They can't help but bond. Don't even worry about that. They'll sort themselves out.'

'Yes, I'm sure.'

How could she reveal her deepest fear to Phyllis? Her editor thought she'd suffered through the war simply because she'd had to place blackout curtains on the windows of her penthouse apartment. But Diana had a niggling doubt that she hadn't been told the entire truth about her husband. When Casper was in training, he'd written to her constantly. Then, after that one mysterious letter about a mission – a particularly dangerous sortie he feared he might not return from – she'd heard nothing. The RAF told her he was missing in action. For almost a year she accepted the possibility that he might be dead, until she received word that Casper was in a British hospital, recovering from typhus after being released from a prisoner-of-war camp. But during his long convalescence, he hadn't written to her. A friend of his from his university days, Peter Todd, had corresponded with her about his progress instead.

'Now!' said Phyllis, with such emphasis that Diana's mind was forced back into the present. 'None of this ridiculous trouser-wearing of yours when you go to meet him. Casper will be very proud of all you have achieved – he's not one to be threatened by a woman's success. But no man wants to see his wife wearing pants.'

Diana glanced out at the garden again. Marilyn, her assistant, was pushing a wheelbarrow piled with rocks along the path that led from the creek. Even in her overalls she managed to cut a distinctive figure, with her close-cropped hair and steel-rimmed glasses. If Phyllis had only seen the two of them the previous day, sweating and grunting as they ripped out lantana and chopped down privet, she would have been scandalised.

'I assure you, Freddy and I will be immaculately turned out when we meet Casper at the wharf.'

'Good!' said Phyllis. Then, lowering her voice, she added, 'And be careful how you explain Marilyn to him. Lots of women shared places to cut costs and keep each other company while their husbands were away fighting. But not many decent, professional women have shared a place with ... well, someone like that.'

Diana stiffened. Marilyn was honest, kind and a hard worker. Diana wasn't put off by her gardening assistant's mannish appearance or her love for her pet pig. She herself was often looked at askance, simply because she didn't mind that ringtail possums had moved into her freshly erected dovecote, freely shared her fruit trees with the cockatoos and flying foxes, and usually wore pants. For someone who appreciated avant-garde art, Phyllis could be annoyingly conservative sometimes.

She said goodbye to her editor and sat down again at her desk. Her eyes drifted to the photograph in a silver frame. In it, Diana was wearing a tailored 'going away' dress suit. Casper, with a rose in his buttonhole, stood with his arm linked in hers. Behind them loomed the Eiffel Tower in Paris. It had been thrilling to honeymoon in France and visit all the places that were meaningful to her husband – from the farmhouse where he'd spent summers with his French grandparents, to the stately Sorbonne, where he'd studied literature. In those carefree days, they could not have imagined that only a few years later, Europe would self-combust.

She picked up the photograph and studied her husband's face. Life with Casper before the war had been so much fun. He was a brilliant scholar with a well-honed appreciation of aesthetics, but humble and easy-going in spite of it. Even going on a walk with him had been an exciting adventure as he'd move the conversation from one interesting topic to another. Peter had assured her in a jolly tone that Casper would soon 'recover his spirits' and plied her with stories of their student days together to reassure her.

Diana turned to the garden again. But who was Peter? Casper had mentioned him before the war, he'd even borrowed his boat to take her out on the Thames when they'd first got together, but she'd never actually met him. Was he hiding something from her by writing on Casper's behalf? Was Casper returning home paralysed or missing his arms?

Her eyes drifted to her notepad and two words jumped out
at her: *Lemons. Blackberries.*

'Oh no!'

Her visions of the worst possible scenarios were instantly
replaced by an image of Janet, Casper's sister, regarding her
in that condescending manner of hers. Diana rushed to the
kitchen cupboard to fetch her basket. She had completely
forgotten about the lemons and blackberries – ingredients for
one of Janet's stodgy desserts. As a concession for not coming
to the wharf, Diana had agreed that Janet could be responsible
for Casper's homecoming dinner. *Because if I leave it to you,* Janet
had told her, *my poor brother will be eating scrambled eggs on his first
night at home.*

Diana picked up her long gloves from the garden shed
and hurried along the flagstone path to the fence where the
blackberry bushes still ruled. But the beauty of the sun streaming
through the canopy of trees stopped her in her tracks. The
air wafting from the garden was warm and she was sure she
could smell the sunshine on it, the way she could smell it in the
bedsheets when she took them off the clothesline. She closed
her eyes to distinguish the other scents that blended with it, like
the notes of a fine perfume – sweet jasmine, the cinnamon-
like scent of the tea roses, the minty aroma of the narrow-
leafed peppermint gum. Phyllis had once asked her if it was
true that she could distinguish between gum trees before they
came into sight, just by sniffing the air. Diana had assured her
she could. The sharp citrus smell of the lemon-scented gum
and the strawberry sweetness of the red stringy-bark were as
familiar to her as old friends. It was this play of light and scents

that affected Diana right to her soul, which was why her garden designs incorporated so many Australian trees. She was not a lawn and rosebush landscape designer, and any client looking for that would soon realise they had the wrong person. But she was slowly making a name for herself for being able to combine the tame and the wild in perfect harmony, and there were people in Sydney and its outskirts who now boasted they had a 'Diana White garden' the same way someone might brag they had a painting by Tom Roberts or a sculpture by Norman Lindsay.

Diana reached the fence and pulled down her sleeves and put on her gloves to avoid being injured by thorns as she harvested Janet's darned berries. Some writers talked about having 'a critic on their shoulder' – a nagging voice forever chiding them that if they only tried a little harder, got up earlier, stayed up later, their work would be so much better. Diana didn't need one of those – she had Janet. Although Casper and his sister were the offspring of an English father and a French mother, instead of ending up a blend of the two cultures as siblings often did, they seemed polarised, with Casper embodying the best of both cultures and Janet the worst. Whereas Casper was polished and assured, Janet was brash and uptight.

Her sister-in-law had been put out that Diana had kept the land in Killara rather than selling it. *But why do you want to live out there?* she'd asked. *There's a lovely little bungalow for sale down the street from us.* Even less than Diana could imagine living in Janet's inner-city suburb – where the streets and the gardens were uniform, with the same identical pathways leading to the same identical front doors – could she imagine living anywhere closer to Janet than at least half an hour away by car. Diana had been delighted when Casper had agreed that as a condition of their marriage they would live in Australia. What she hadn't expected was that fussy Janet and her henpecked husband, Alfred, would come too.

She was reaching for a cluster of ripe berries inconveniently located in the centre of a bush when she heard footsteps scuffing up the gravel on the road that passed the house. Mrs Keener was shuffling towards her, walking stick in one hand and the lead for her beagle in the other. If Diana had been wearing her hat, she would have pulled it down low. Mrs Keener had been a matron when Diana was a child. Now elderly, she didn't seem to have kept all her marbles, but that didn't mean she wouldn't recognise Diana.

'Good morning,' Diana said politely, but kept herself obscured by the bushes to avoid further conversation.

She grimaced when Mrs Keener came to a stop.

'I don't know why they have come here,' the old woman said. 'They should have left it all alone. The garden was beautiful once, but terrible things happened here. It doesn't do any good to stir that sort of thing up.'

It wasn't the first time Mrs Keener had voiced such a sentiment, but her words were never spoken directly to Diana. It was always as if she was having a conversation with another person – an invisible companion. Or perhaps she was talking to her dog.

Diana inwardly willed Mrs Keener to move on. But the old woman continued. 'A woman died here. I remember the sound of the fire engine. But it was too late coming. Far too late. The house burned to the ground.'

Diana drew her hand back quickly. A thorny leaf caught on her sleeve like a barb on a wire fence. A terrible image filled her mind, and she opened her mouth, almost crying out. *Never think of that!* She'd worked so hard to block it all from her mind. Was it truly wrong of her to come here? To try to recreate the beauty that had been lost?

She picked up her basket and fled towards the house. It was a cottage with white painted walls, paned windows and a slate roof with dormer windows. It wasn't anything like the house that had stood there before, and that's how she'd wanted it. Her simple cottage was a refuge. As she approached the front steps, she caught a glimpse of the crepe myrtle tree in the centre of the turning circle. It had burst into lilac blooms overnight. Diana's eyes travelled from the crown of ruffled, showy flowers down the beautifully mottled bark of the trunk. When they'd first started working on the garden, Diana and Marilyn had found the tree strangled in morning glory. They hadn't been sure they'd be able to save it. But now it stood gracefully, strengthening Diana with its beauty.

Tears filled her eyes. The tree was the only remaining thing she had of her mother – the woman who had died in the fire.

# CHAPTER THREE

The morning mist hung over the forests and farmlands of the Dordogne valley like a dainty lace curtain. Green grass still covered the fields, but the trees were bare and ghostlike. Sabine leaned forward in her seat and stared out the train window. Each leg of the journey, each little station or empty village the train passed through brought back memories both bitter and vivid. She felt the creeping cold travel over her skin and the erratic beating of her heart as she recalled those moonlit nights, crouched in the freshly ploughed fields waiting for the drone of a British plane. It was a rugged existence for a young mother who had known only the cultured atmosphere of Paris. But Lucien had ancestral ties to the region and his parents had owned a vineyard on the banks of the Dordogne River. It was there that Lucien and Sabine had fled with baby Pierre when the German army descended on Paris. It was there in the rustic kitchen with the smells of garlic and fresh butter wafting around them that the family and neighbours had gathered to express outrage at Marshal Pétain's decision to surrender. And it was there that they had listened to Charles de Gaulle broadcasting from London, urging the French people to resist.

*But has the last word been said? Must all hope disappear?*
*Is this defeat final? No! ... Whatever happens, the flame of*
*French Resistance must not be extinguished and will not be*
*extinguished ...*

Sabine was a piano teacher, Lucien a lawyer. The other inhabitants of the village were small-town professionals and farmers. Yet they set themselves against the most highly trained army in the world. Slowly and painstakingly, they sorted the courageous from the cowards and formed a chain of safe houses stretching from their village to the border. They helped downed Allied pilots get to the foot of the Pyrenees, where they would be able to cross into Spain and make their way from there to England. Sabine had taken some of the pilots with her by train, posing as the wife of a terrified man decked out in French clothes and not speaking a word of the language.

'Your ticket, please, madame.'

The conductor's voice interrupted Sabine's recollections. She reached into her purse as if to retrieve her papers before she realised that he was only asking for her ticket. The war was over. She was free to travel wherever she liked in her own country for whatever reason.

She handed her ticket to the conductor, who looked barely sixteen. His was the generation that would forget.

The conductor handed the ticket back and moved on. Sabine looked at the scenery again. *Free?* The memory of machine-gun fire sounded in her head, and she clenched her fists. She would never be free. Not until every one of those monsters was dead – and perhaps not even then.

The train passed by a tiny village with all its windows shuttered and not a single person out on the streets. For the first time in a long time, she allowed herself to think of *him*.

The rescued pilots had gone back to London with glowing reports about the efficiency and courage of the Brouillette family's group of patriots, which brought them to the attention of the British Special Operations Executive. SOE were developing a secret army in France for sabotage and subversion. They needed the help of citizens who could receive and distribute weapons and other supplies to the local rural Resistance fighters, the maquis, so they in turn could create havoc for the German army ahead of a planned Allied invasion.

One day when Sabine was at the markets, a woman she had never seen before brushed against her and slipped a note into her hand. *Destroy it straight after you have read it*, the woman told her before disappearing into the crowd. The note instructed Sabine to go to the women's lavatory at the station and find her instructions hidden behind the washroom mirror there. It was extremely dangerous to be involved in any sort of subversive activity. A German soldier had been killed in Tours and ten young men and women from a nearby village had been shot in reprisal. Yet Sabine went to the washroom and received instructions for the day and time to receive an SOE agent who was to be parachuted in to help the village set up a formal Resistance circuit.

By rights, Sabine should have been terrified on that still night when she'd waited by the lit kerosene tin in a field. Yet, as she watched Lucien and her neighbours wring their hands and strained her ears for the sound of an aeroplane, she had felt strangely peaceful. When the plane approached, a flap dropped in its belly, giving a glimpse of an eerie light within. Then six chutes fell out. One of the chutes would belong to the SOE agent, the others would be supply boxes. But it was difficult to distinguish one from the other in the dark. Lucien and the other men ran in the direction of the drops as the parachutes and supplies would need to be hidden quickly. Sabine stayed under the cover of a tree. Then she heard a warm, rich voice from the heavens.

'*Bonsoir, madame.*'

She looked up and saw a man gliding towards her from the sky. For a split second, a rising current lifted his canopy and he hovered above her like an angel before dropping to the ground. He released himself from his chute and swiftly gathered it up before turning around to look at her. His face wore a friendly expression, and he had the dashing good looks of a storybook hero. She wondered how she could discern them so clearly in the dark, but he seemed to be lit from within, luminescent, like a firefly.

Sabine never learned his real name. She knew him only by his field name and cover name, Christian Vidal. But he, Lucien and Sabine soon became an inseparable trio, organising landing fields for British airdrops, distributing supplies and couriering messages. When the Allied invasion was imminent the following year, they blew up bridges, railway lines and even a police station. The constant insecurity and danger they lived with – where the slightest slip-up could lead to arrest, torture and death – cemented them together. Only once did Christian ever break protocol and tell her something personal about himself. He had been watching her make an omelette for

Pierre in the kitchen and his eyes had misted over. *I have a wife and a son the same age as Pierre*, he said. *My son was barely a year old when I left to fly for the RAF*. Sabine felt a spark ignite in her, as if she were a piece of inert flint that had suddenly been struck. She finally understood that his serenity, that light she sensed in him, came from a complete acceptance of death in the aid of a noble cause. He was helping France and had left a wife and child behind to do it. In a world of horror, he represented the best of human nature. He represented hope. She would have done anything for him. *Anything.*

\*

The train pulled into Bergerac Station, where Agent Chareau was waiting on the platform for her. He was middle-aged, gaunt like Robert, and the only man among the crowd of women, all of varying ages but dressed identically in 'widow's black'.

'The garage is ten minutes from here,' he told her, taking her overnight bag and helping her down to the platform. 'We got the safe out this morning and brought it to the mechanic's by truck. The locksmith wasn't available so the best burglar in town is working on it.'

He related the last part about the burglar without irony. Sabine understood. During the war, some of the most ardent patriots had been prostitutes and petty criminals. She regarded them as more honourable than the 'upright' citizens of France who had been too consumed by their own welfare to sacrifice anything for a greater cause.

Together they headed through a warren of narrow winding

streets. Chareau walked with a limp and Sabine slowed her naturally fast pace to avoid embarrassing him. The town had the sleepy atmosphere of a peaceful medieval village, with its cobblestoned streets and half-timbered buildings. It was very different to the last time she had been there. But she still surveyed every doorway and shop window with suspicion, as if at any moment a Gestapo agent might leap out to arrest her. The people who passed them were ordinary-looking – a woman pushing a pram, a man on a bicycle, a priest in a black cassock – and yet she found the same question running through her mind as it had during the war: *Friend or foe?*

They arrived at the garage to find the mechanic standing outside, smoking a cigarette and staring at the slow-moving river. Chareau exchanged a brief nod with him before leading Sabine through a workshop reeking of grease and crowded with engine parts and old tyres, and into the back room. A heavyset man in his thirties was supervising a bald man drilling the safe. Chareau introduced the first man as his colleague, Agent Brun.

'He says it's a difficult one,' Brun told them. 'It will take at least another hour.'

While he spoke, he studied Sabine from head to foot with a squint in his eyes and a patronising smile. It was meant to intimidate her, but she kept her own expression impassive while taking in every detail about him. His face was fleshy and smooth. His trousers were neatly pressed and his shoes were new. There were no scars on his hands or face, and he didn't limp like Chareau or have deformed fingers like hers. If he'd been a true resister, which she now doubted, then the war had been easy on him.

Chareau invited Sabine to sit down at the workbench that had been cleared for them. He stared out the window at a barge moving down the river, but Sabine kept her eyes on the safecracker's hands as he diligently turned the dial. Before her fingers had been broken by the Gestapo, her hands had been noted for their long tapered elegance and naturally iridescent nails. During the war, those hands had been appreciated for their ability to mould plastic explosive expertly. In her lifetime, her hands had produced the most sublime music, rolled dough into Christmas cookies – and killed men.

A *click* sounded and the safecracker sat back, a satisfied grin on his face. He swung the door open to reveal shelves stacked with cardboard boxes with labels on them. Chareau took out his wallet and paid the man. After he left, the two male agents lifted the boxes out of the safe and placed them on the workbench. When they'd cleared the safe, they sat down at the table with Sabine. Brun pulled the first box towards himself and Chareau opened a notebook, ready to record the contents.

The process was painstakingly slow. Out of each box came the names of those who had collaborated with the Nazi occupiers – those who'd given information about Resistance activities, or who had denounced people who could have otherwise hidden their Jewish origins.

'François Corben, French, baker,' Brun read out, before picking up the next file for Chareau to record. 'Gabrielle Tarbarly, French, schoolteacher.'

Sabine listened with a knot in her stomach. It was disturbing how ordinary these people were. They had lived in the town all their lives, bought bread and cheese from each other, and sent their children to the same schools. Then, for money or out of jealousy, or perhaps simply a need to feel important, they had denounced their friends and neighbours to the brutal occupiers of their country. Chareau and Brun would deal with these petty collaborators; Sabine was chasing a bigger fish. Who was this double agent, 'the Black Fox'? Was he still alive? If he was, Sabine would set about tracking him down and she would certainly kill him herself. After what Robert had told her the previous day about the changes in the French secret service, she wasn't about to risk him being whisked away to work for the American CIA or British MI6 – or even, God forbid, the French secret service itself.

'Jean Rousso, French, pastry chef. Sylvie Gayraud, French, secretary,' Brun continued.

'I remember Jean Rousso,' Chareau interrupted. 'His patisserie was famous in my village. Who did he denounce?'

Brun opened the file and translated one of the reports from German to French. 'Denounced, Albert Rousso, ninety-four years of age, for possessing a radio and listening to BBC broadcasts.'

'He denounced his own father?' Sabine asked. 'What is the date of the report?'

'December second, 1942.'

They fell into a sober silence. In November that year, the Germans had made listening to BBC broadcasts a capital offence. Albert Rousso, despite his age, would certainly have been executed.

Brun glanced in Sabine's direction. 'What did you do for the Resistance?' he asked. 'Were you a honeypot for some Nazi officer? Did you seduce a German agent to reveal the enemy's secrets?'

Chareau cleared his throat and sent his colleague a warning look.

Sabine could have answered that she'd helped sabotage supply trains heading for the Eastern Front and blown up railway bridges. Instead, she cocked her head and asked Brun, 'How come you can read German so well?'

He tried to hold her gaze but couldn't and turned his attention back to the boxes.

*

After another hour of painstaking recording, Sabine began to fear that the Black Fox's file might not be among the papers after all. Perhaps someone had slipped it out before the château was bombed? The group that had conducted the raid after the building was destroyed was a sub-circuit of a larger network. Although it had a reasonable number of members, they were unregistered and untrained. Perhaps the Black Fox's file had been lost along the way? It could be mouldering on the side of a road somewhere or lying forgotten in some deserted barn.

She was about to give up hope when Brun suddenly read out, 'Codename – the Black Fox.'

Sabine's breath caught in her throat. For a moment time seemed to stand still. Here was the traitor who had destroyed everything she had ever held dear. Then the next words Brun said sent her world crashing down … again.

'British … SOE.'

CHAPTER FOUR

The summer day was disappearing under a blanket of thin grey clouds when Diana parked her utility truck next to Sydney's Royal Botanic Garden. She glanced at Freddy, who was looking smart in a shirt and tie, his thin legs in their long white socks dangling over the seat beside her. He was holding his sketchpad where he'd drawn a picture to show Casper. Everybody thought their child was a genius, but for a seven-year-old Freddy's use of correct proportion and perspective in his art was highly unusual. All his teachers described him as exceptional. In the picture, Diana and Marilyn were digging a flower bed. Blossom was in the foreground chewing on a dandelion weed. Freddy was next to her, patting her back. Casper stood away from them all, leaning against a tree. Diana had noticed Casper in a similar position in many of Freddy's drawings – remote, and with one hand clenched as if holding a secret object. While Freddy had captured the tiniest details of the scene with lifelike realism – a strand of hair falling across Diana's forehead, the deeply divided leaves of the dandelion weed – Casper's features were vague, and his expression was blank. It was a painful reminder that her husband and son had never bonded with each other. She hoped that they would be able to make up for lost time now.

Diana got out of the truck and opened the passenger side door for Freddy. 'Look, sweetheart, we can see the ship from here! It's already in its berth.'

They stood holding hands and watched the scene on the wharf. A crowd of people had gathered, waiting for the passengers to come down the gangway after completing their medical and customs formalities. It was not a military ship – most on board were civilians returning home or new immigrants. Diana let out a long sigh. As soon as she'd heard Casper was alive and well in England, she had wanted to go to him. But Peter had warned her that the trip was not only unnecessary, but potentially dangerous. *Passenger ships are still being sunk by unexploded mines bobbing in the ocean. Casper would never forgive me if I encouraged you to put your life in danger …*

For the past few weeks, she'd had a recurring nightmare that Casper's ship had struck one of the Japanese mines that had been laid along the Australian coast. Once she'd woken with a jolt, sure she'd heard the actual explosion. It was too horrible to contemplate that he could survive the war, and a camp, and still die short of Sydney. But now the ship was right there in front of her in the dock. Whatever the reason Casper hadn't written, he was now safer than he'd ever been in Europe.

Freddy squeezed her hand, keen for them to move on, but Diana needed a moment to let it sink in that the war was finally over, and Casper had survived. For the first time, a true feeling of excitement ran through her. It reminded her of the joy she'd felt on her wedding day in Paris, when she knew she was marrying the man who was right for her, and they were committing themselves to each other for whatever lay ahead.

\*

By the time they reached the wharf, the first passengers were already coming down the gangway. There were cries of welcome and happy tears as families reunited. Diana and Freddy passed a couple wrapped in a tight embrace. The man and woman said nothing but held on to each other for dear life. Diana wanted her reunion with Casper to be like that, a grand sweeping moment of emotion where words were unnecessary. But when she scanned the crowd and couldn't see him, she began to panic.

'Daddy!' Freddy cried out.

Her heart gave a jolt. Freddy was clinging to the trouser leg of a tall fair-haired man, but when the man looked up, it wasn't Casper. Diana's and the stranger's eyes met. The man shrugged apologetically, as if he could sense her anguish and regretted that he would have to disappoint her son.

'I'm sorry,' she said. 'My son was only a baby when his father left.'

The man nodded and tipped his hat before continuing on his way to greet two women whom Diana assumed were his wife and mother.

The crowd was beginning to thin, and still she could not find Casper. Then she spotted him standing near a crate of cargo. He was leaning against it, watching them, remote and apart as he'd appeared in Freddy's pictures.

'Casper!' she called out, waving frantically.

She pulled Freddy after her, dodging porters pushing luggage carts. Casper's expression remained blank. He was so still he could have been hewn from stone. Even when she and Freddy were before him, he didn't seem to recognise her. His skin had more lines on it than she remembered, and his blond hair was flecked with grey about the temples. But he was still Casper. Had time really made her so invisible to him?

'Casper?'

'Hello, Diana,' he said.

So, he had recognised her after all. Then why had he not approached her? She had imagined this moment so many times. In her mind, she'd kiss him on those lips that had always been soft and warm. But now she hesitated, like a child regarding a distant relative she wasn't quite sure of. She pecked him on the cheek.

His green eyes looked sad, as if the light had gone out of them. She noticed the way his clothes seemed to hang on him. The changes made her uncomfortable, and she quickly deflected attention to Freddy, as if he could somehow redeem this disappointing moment.

'Freddy, this is your father,' she said.

The boy stared at Casper with an open mouth but could not find his voice.

★

Diana watched Casper lift his trunk into the back of the truck and climb in the front passenger seat. *He's tired*, she told herself.

She'd waited for him for so long, another few hours of patience while he had a chance to eat something and get his land-legs back wouldn't make any difference.

She helped Freddy into the truck so that he sat between them on the front seat, and then placed herself behind the steering wheel.

'I don't think Sydney has changed that much since you left,' she said, starting the engine and pulling out onto the road. 'But I have a surprise for you.'

When Casper departed for Britain, he and Diana had been living with her aunt in her apartment in Rushcutters Bay. It was Aunt Shirley who had bequeathed the land in Killara to Diana. But Casper made no comment when, instead of heading in the direction of the eastern suburbs, they drove over the Harbour Bridge. He stared at the expanse of water, his mind on something other than where they were going. Freddy, normally so talkative, had gone quiet.

'Why don't you show Daddy your drawing?' she said.

Freddy opened his sketchpad but instead of showing the drawing to Casper, he began explaining it to Diana.

'This is you here, Mummy. And this is Marilyn in her big hat. See Blossom. She's eating the weeds you're digging up.'

Frustration began to strain at Diana's tolerance. It was Casper's fault that Freddy was so nervous. She'd expected that as soon as he saw his own son, he would have swept him up in his arms or given him a piggyback like she'd seen in the movies. Then she chastised herself for being so critical. Her husband was home from the war. He'd no doubt experienced horrors that were impossible to imagine. Other women were welcoming back husbands without limbs. Casper was all right. All he needed was a rest.

A wave of love for him swept over her. She leaned across and touched his arm gently as if to say, *You're safe. Whatever happened to you can't harm you now.*

# CHAPTER FIVE

Sabine sat in her hotel room in her underwear. The room was damp and chilly, but she was sweating. The documents Agent Brun had translated for her lay scattered across the bed. She hadn't eaten or slept for two days. Her stomach felt hollow, and her head was on fire. Every document seemed to confirm what she couldn't believe. It was Christian who had betrayed the circuit. He was the Black Fox. Only he could have known this volume of information about their activities and passed them on to the Nazis.

The telephone on the bedside table rang and she scrambled to answer it, knocking her revolver to the floor in her hurry.

'Robert?'

His voice came on the line. 'I've checked and rechecked, Sabine – there were no other SOE operatives in the *Pianiste* circuit apart from Christian Vidal. I'm trying to find out his real name, but, as you know, MI6 isn't always as cooperative as we would like. SOE has been disbanded and MI6 are busy nabbing the best of the agents for themselves.'

The floral patterns on the wallpaper blurred before Sabine's eyes. It was impossible. Christian would not have betrayed the circuit. Not him. 'It must have been somebody else. Maybe somebody claiming to be from SOE?'

Robert paused. 'How well did you know this agent?'

It was a question Sabine now found herself unable to answer. How well had she known Christian Vidal? Only enough to believe every word he'd said. Only enough to have trusted him with her life and the lives of those most precious to her. She sat back down on the bed. The hand holding the receiver began to tremble and she had to support it with the other.

'Why would someone from SOE turn double agent?' she asked. 'It doesn't make sense. He didn't have to come to France to risk his life.'

'Anybody could be turned, you know that. Everyone has a price.'

*Not us*, a voice whispered in Sabine's head. *Not you and I, Robert. And not Christian either.* For a terrifying moment she thought she was going to cry.

'We were arrested together,' she said out loud. 'We were taken to Fresnes Prison in the same van. He was shot. Why would they shoot one of their own?'

Robert didn't say anything, but she heard the rustling of papers. There was something he hadn't told her yet.

'What?' she asked.

'He's not dead.'

She frowned. 'I saw him being executed.'

'I don't know who you saw, but Christian Vidal spent the rest of the war in Fresnes Prison. He was not shot or sent to a concentration camp. Not like the rest of the circuit. Not like you.'

Sabine didn't move. She was no longer breathing.

'During the liberation of Paris, when the French retook the prison, Christian Vidal was sent to England to be treated for typhus and malnutrition,' Robert continued. 'According to information I have just received from the French Embassy in London, he had been recuperating in a British convalescent home before being discharged last month.'

Sabine pressed her fist to her forehead. The roar of flames burned in her head. She saw Pierre's angelic face dissolve into ashes. Her throat constricted as she let out a silent scream. Then everything went still again. Ice began to flow through her veins, starting in her feet and moving upwards until the chill reached her heart. It was as if whatever tiny spark of life she had left in her was snuffed out and now she was truly dead. She slowly lifted her head and stared at her gun lying on the carpet.

She had only one question left for Robert. She clenched the receiver and asked, 'Where is he now?'

# CHAPTER SIX

'We're not grand like the other houses in the street,' Diana told Casper as they drove past the stately Federation mansions with their gabled roofs and timber fretwork. 'It was difficult during the war to get building material – or even tradesmen for that matter. All the young ones were at war. So, Marilyn, two retired carpenters and I did it all. But I think you'll like the result.'

She turned the truck into the driveway. Unlike the neighbouring houses, which loomed over their sparse gardens of shrubs and rosebushes, the cottage Diana had designed was hidden away from the street under gently undulating foliage. Approaching through the trees was like discovering a delicious secret. When the house came into view, Diana glanced at Casper to see his reaction. But his face gave nothing away and she felt her spirits dampen.

She brought the truck to a stop and, not wanting Freddy to pick up on her disappointment, lifted him down from the vehicle.

'Go find Blossom, darling,' she told him.

Diana led Casper up the sandstone steps towards the front door of the cottage. 'This is our home now,' she said, ushering him inside. 'I kept all the walls and ceilings white to better appreciate the furnishings Aunt Shirley left us. And see here,' she said, indicating a pair of wingback armchairs with new brocade upholstery. 'A farmer in Berrima sold these to me. They had been sitting in his barn for years.'

Casper looked around the house, but not at all the details Diana was pointing out. Instead, he went back to the front door and locked it. Diana frowned. The anticipation of Casper's homecoming was giving way to a sense of foreboding. Perhaps she should have warned him, rather than surprised him, with their new location. But she hadn't wanted Casper to hear all about the house and garden second-hand from Peter. It had surprised the neighbours that Diana should decide to build her family's future on the site of an appalling tragedy, but she was sure Casper would understand. She turned away and fought back her tears. Restoring her mother's garden was a long-cherished dream of hers, and she rallied again.

'Come through here,' she said, forcing herself to sound cheerful. 'You'll like this.'

She led Casper through the narrow dining room to another room lined with bookshelves. Boxes containing Casper's books were stacked in the middle. When they'd lived in Aunt Shirley's second bedroom, those books had occupied every spare space on top of the wardrobe and under the bed. They had even piled them up to serve as bedside tables. *When we have a place of our own one day, I want a library*, Casper had told her. She could have used the space to make a larger dining room or an office for herself, but she wanted him to have his wish.

'I didn't unpack anything because I thought you'd like to do that yourself,' she said. 'I also didn't buy a desk, but I did see a rather lovely one from Maple and Co. in a shop in Lavender Bay that you might like.'

Diana realised she was prattling, and she detested prattlers. She waited for Casper to say something, but he remained silent. 'Do you like it?' she asked finally. 'You know it was the place …'

Casper caught the tremble in her voice and glanced at her, as if suddenly aware of her presence. 'It's very nice, Diana,' he said, in a feeble attempt at reassurance. 'It's in a good location. It's—'

'An elegant, leafy suburb in a bushland setting.'

Diana finished his sentence before she realised Casper was thinking something else entirely.

'*Secluded*,' he said.

Secluded? The word rattled around inside her head. That was a good thing, wasn't it? It was the word people used to describe an unspoilt beach or an island paradise.

Casper almost hugged the wall as he moved towards the window and peered out. 'But you haven't hung any drapes yet. People will be able to see into the house at night.'

Diana opened and closed her mouth, unable to fathom Casper's meaning. She'd designed the cottage so that every room had large paned windows looking out on some aspect of the garden. She had very few pictures hanging on the walls – she wanted the views of the garden to be living artworks instead. The leafy outlook was all the privacy she needed. She wasn't in the habit of locking the windows and doors. The way Casper was behaving, you'd think the house was supposed to be a hideaway for illicit activities.

She watched him continue to move around the room like a sleuth looking for clues. A thought nagged at her and she did her best to push it away. Casper had brought something back with him from the war: anxiety, fear, distrust – she couldn't pinpoint it exactly, but it was unnerving. She glanced out the window at Freddy, bouncing on his hopscotch squares with Blossom looking on. Then she turned back to Casper and hoped that whatever he'd brought with him, it wasn't contagious.

Sydney Morning Herald, *3 March 1926*

## SHOCKING TRAGEDY
### BODIES BURNED BEYOND RECOGNITION

*A house in the leafy suburb of Killara was the scene of a ghastly tragedy early this morning.*

*Shortly after 5 o'clock, the residence of William John Buchanan was found to be on fire. Neighbours alerted the fire brigade, but their efforts were thwarted by the heat of the blaze. After the fire was extinguished, the bodies of Buchanan and his wife, Margaret, were found. The heroine of the fire was Miss Shirley Donne, sister to Margaret, who managed to save her ten-year-old niece from the flames.*

*There are some peculiar features to the incident, the cause of which can only be surmised until a police investigation takes place later today …*

# CHAPTER SEVEN

After Diana had finished showing Casper around the house, she encouraged him to wash up and take a nap. In truth, she wanted to get away from him for a while to sort out her feelings. She sat down at her desk and listened to him pacing back and forth upstairs like a caged animal. She tried to calm the panic in her breath and stop the whispers in her mind telling her something was happening that she didn't understand and couldn't handle. Diana had read accounts in newspapers of the men who'd come back from the Japanese camps, men who screamed out from nightmares in their sleep. One of them had strangled his wife.

The sound of a car pulling into the driveway roused her. She stood and looked out the window. It was Janet and Alfred. Freddy skipped towards them and Alfred lifted him onto his shoulders. He was a roly-poly man with a boyish face that appealed to children. As Alfred bounced Freddy up and down, the boy threw back his head and giggled with delight. Diana's heart pricked. Her son was more comfortable with his uncle than he was with his own father. Through the garden arch, Diana spotted Marilyn disappearing with Blossom into her own cottage. Marilyn often joined Diana and Freddy for dinner but she eschewed other company, preferring a solitary life. It was a pity, Diana thought. She could have done with Marilyn's calming influence tonight. She opened the door and steeled herself before stepping outside.

'I've brought everything,' Janet said when Diana approached her. 'I prepared most of it in my kitchen, yours being so tiny. Help me take it all inside.'

Janet handed her a basket laden with knives and forks and passed two crates of crockery to Alfred. What irked Diana most about Janet was how she made her feel as if she was incompetent in the basics of life. Diana had cutlery of her own, she wasn't a savage. She might not have the same tastes as other people, but she appreciated everybody was different. Janet had to have everything her way all the time. Aunt Shirley had given Diana and Casper an exquisite mint-green dinner set that would have served perfectly for their meal, but Janet had declared Diana's choices in table settings as 'the sort of thing one might find in a convent'. Tonight's meal would be served on Janet's highly decorative dinnerware depicting amiable English country folk holding pitchforks.

'I got Casper the most darling cut-crystal sherry decanter for his welcome home present,' Janet told her as they made their way into the house. 'It will look perfect on the sideboard. Much better than that funny little ceramic vase you've got there now.'

Diana grimaced. It was true that she wasn't a great cook and preferred simple meals. Aunt Shirley had run her own art gallery and sent Diana to a girls' school where they provided hot lunches, because when her aunt came home late in the evening all she wanted to eat was an egg and salad sandwich washed down with a glass of champagne. But what Diana had missed out on in cooking lessons, she had more than gained from Aunt Shirley's sophisticated tastes. There weren't many girls at her school who could say they had rubbed shoulders with artists like Sybil Craig and Herbert Badham. That 'funny little ceramic vase' was an original by Klytie Pate. Yet somehow Janet managed to dismiss all that cultural education and regard Diana as some sort of naïve Australian peasant.

Once they were inside and the crates and boxes unpacked, it took all of Diana's diplomacy to stop Janet rushing up the stairs to foist herself on Casper. 'He's sleeping now,' she lied. 'He'll come down as soon as he catches a whiff of your delicious pie.'

She poured a beer for Alfred and settled him into one of the wingback chairs before submitting herself to Janet's orders about how to stir the custard on the stove. 'Don't overcook it and let it curdle,' Janet told her. 'I have such a deft hand at making custard that I never have to strain it. It turns out perfectly without that step for me.'

When dinner was almost ready and Casper still hadn't appeared, Diana went to fetch him. She found him in Freddy's bedroom, looking at the toy planes and Meccano sets. On the shelf above the bed were dozens of photographs of Casper holding Freddy when he was a baby.

'Freddy is very much like you,' Diana said, leaning against the doorframe. 'He's proud of you fighting for what's right. His schoolteacher, Mrs Macready, says you're the topic of all his compositions.'

Casper turned to her. His expression was harder than she remembered, yet she was sure she saw a tear in his eye.

'The house is very nice, Diana,' he said. 'You've done a splendid job with it all ... and with our son. I couldn't be more impressed.' Then more quietly, he added, 'I'm sorry about before. It's just all … so unreal. I dreamed of this day over and over again – the day I would reunite with my wife and son again. It's what got me through it all.'

Diana wanted to rush to him, to throw herself into his arms. She longed to hold him and be held tightly like the couple she'd seen at the dock. But she sensed that wasn't what he wanted just yet. She must approach her reunion with her husband with patience, she decided, and give him time and space to readjust to civilian life.

'It must be difficult to be back after so long away—'

'Casper! Diana! Everything is ready!' came Janet's loud voice from downstairs.

Diana grimaced and glanced back towards the stairs. Although she was the younger of the two, Janet bullied Casper almost as much as she did Diana. Yet Casper had always taken it with good humour. Would he be able to do the same now?

'Your sister …' Diana began. 'Well, she's missed you so much. She's been very kind to Freddy and was helpful after Aunt Shirley died. I couldn't tell her not to come tonight.'

Casper smiled, and for a brief second looked like his old self. Diana's heart leaped with hope. He straightened his sleeves and collar as if preparing himself for an ordeal, which was exactly how Diana was feeling. At least in that regard they were united.

She took his arm and gave it a friendly squeeze. 'I made the trifle,' she told him. 'With lemons and blackberries from the garden. All under Janet's careful supervision, of course, lest I accidentally poison somebody.'

# CHAPTER EIGHT

Sabine leaned against the window of her apartment and watched Madame Rouzard sweeping the courtyard downstairs. Before the war, Madame Rouzard had been like any other concierge in Paris, perhaps more cheerful and obliging than was generally considered the norm for a woman in her role. From her one-room apartment on the ground floor, she had noted people's comings and goings, sorted and distributed the mail, maintained the building, and collected the rent. She was known to be kind to children and animals, but stern with any resident who forgot to wipe their shoes on the doormat in the hallway. She had been like many working-class, childless widows in Paris – thankful to have a roof over her head, her health, a window box of petunias in spring, a bowl of café au lait in the morning and a plate of vegetable stew in the evening. It was only in the extreme conditions of the war that Madame Rouzard had distinguished herself.

When the Jews of Paris were being rounded up for deportation, Madame Rouzard woke the Kléber family and hid them in the broom closet on the ground floor. Then, showing remarkable sangfroid in the face of the French police, who were loading Jewish people onto trucks in service of the Nazis, she pretended the family had departed days before and had left no instructions about where to forward their post. Later in the afternoon, she had walked the Klébers past several German posts to the train station and waved them off to safety in the countryside, pretending all the while they were relatives who had come to visit. After that, Madame Rouzard became part of a network of citizens who risked everything to get their Jewish friends and neighbours to safety. And she had to perform her clandestine activities under the nose of another resident, Madame Chout, the wife of a petty French official, who frequently entertained German officers in her apartment on the second floor.

Once, when Sabine asked Madame Rouzard why she had taken part in such perilous activities to save people, many of whom she didn't know, the elderly woman had simply shrugged and answered, *It was the natural thing to do.*

*Natural for Madame Rouzard – not natural for everybody*, Sabine thought. She stepped away from the window and sat down at the piano. For the first time since returning to Paris from the camp, she opened the lid and brushed her fingers over the keys. But she could not bring herself to press them, certain that any sound the piano made would open parts of her that were full of wounds. Instead she breathed its familiar spruce-wood scent that conjured up images of the Austrian Alps, old leather and dusty books. To achieve the level of skill required to enter the Paris Conservatoire, Sabine had practised a minimum of four hours a day, and often ten or twelve, since she was a child. While her school friends were climbing trees, playing hide-

and-seek or sledding in the snow, Sabine had been up every morning before sunrise to practise scales and exercises. The piano was a precision-built instrument of wood, wires and hammers, but it had been Sabine's mental discipline, dedication and perfectionism that had given it a soul. She thought back to the last piece of music she had played before her interrogator ordered his lackey to break her fingers. In her mind, she heard the opening of Chopin's 'Nocturne in C Minor' with its faltering melody and dark, menacing chords. The piece was laced with grief yet was elegant, stately and achingly beautiful at the same time.

A knock at the door made her jump. She opened the three locks to find Madame Rouzard standing outside. She slipped a letter into Sabine's hand and leaned close to whisper, 'Monsieur Guillaume said to give this to you straight away.'

Monsieur Guillaume was a cover name Robert used. He must have organised her ferry ticket and fake passport to travel to London. Sabine thanked Madame Rouzard and went back inside. But the only thing in the envelope was a lady's felt glove and a note.

*You left this behind at the office. I know you suffer chilblains, so I wanted to return it to you quickly.*

Sabine turned the glove inside out and saw the message written inside:

*Champs-Élysées. Eight o'clock.*

He was directing her to the Café Colisée, a rendezvous the Resistance had used during the war. Why this extra caution? Had someone been listening in on their telephone conversation about Christian Vidal? The French secret service? They listened to everyone else, so why shouldn't they spy on their own? *I don't want you to get emotional. When an agent gets emotional, they make mistakes.* Had ringing Robert from Bergerac to tell him what she had found out instead of waiting until she got back to Paris been her first one? There was nothing she'd told him that couldn't have been said a day later. She had called him for comfort, and he had responded. She wouldn't make that mistake again.

★

At seven o'clock, Sabine left her apartment and walked in the direction of the Champs-Élysées. She was dressed like a woman going out for dinner, in a forest-green velvet dress covered by a narrow-waisted coat with a stand-up collar and a black halo hat on her head. They were clothes she had worn before the war when she and Lucien had gone out to meet friends or to a piano recital at the Salle Gaveau. For a moment, she felt his arm linked with hers, pulling her close. She was sure she caught the moss and lemon scent of his aftershave and the sweetness of his warm skin. Pinned to her chest was the sapphire and pearl brooch he had given her when Pierre was born. It was in the design of two robins guarding a nest with a single chick in it. When she wore it she felt her husband and child close to her, but it also renewed her pain. She wanted so desperately to remember them, but she also wanted to forget. Lucien had once said to her, *If something should happen to either one of us, then the one remaining must finish this thing.* When would 'this thing' ever be finished? When would justice finally be served?

She crossed the street. Her pace was leisurely, and she didn't glance over her shoulder or look around furtively. The first rule of evasion was to not act like someone who thought they were being followed. She had learned to use her sixth sense to tell if there was someone in pursuit. It was surprising how sharp survival instincts became when they were constantly used. During the war the world had been dark – the cities were deprived of their light and she'd had to learn to negotiate the forests of the Dordogne without the use of a torch. She had become like a nocturnal animal, able to sense objects around her without seeing them and adept at finding her way along mountain ridges with nothing but the moonlight to guide her.

Sabine arrived at the café, confident she had not been followed. Robert was sitting at a table with his back against the wall, the best position if you didn't want anyone sneaking up behind you. He was also near the kitchen, in case a sudden exit out the rear would be required. But when he saw her, his smile was relaxed. His eyes crinkled as he regarded her with affection.

'Good evening,' he said, standing to kiss her on both cheeks. 'You look splendid.'

The waiter took Sabine's coat and she and Robert sat down. They studied the menu, which was lacking in variety due to rationing – mushroom soup, stringed beans, mashed potato. Sabine used her peripheral vision to take in the other diners: a businessman on his own; a group of friends laughing merrily at each other's jokes; a married couple who barely looked at each other. She knew her caution was unnecessary – Robert would have assessed the place before he sat down.

'There are no Germans,' he told her, lifting his eyebrow ironically.

'I'm beginning to think war criminals are the least of our problems. Why the caution? Has one of our colleagues been ordered to watch us?'

It was not a frivolous comment. Given the nature of espionage, their section was likely to have a mole in its midst. At that moment, Juliette Vignes or one of the other agents could be passing on reports about the discovery of the Black Fox to the Soviets, ex-Nazis or even the intelligence services of France's allies.

Robert took Sabine's hand as if they were lovers engaged in an intimate conversation. It was remarkable that on a cold winter's night Robert had warm hands. In another place, another lifetime, they might well have been lovers.

'I think we might have uncovered something bigger than a mere turncoat,' he said. 'The lack of cooperation from British intelligence confirms it.'

He paused when the waiter came to take their orders. When the waiter left again, Robert resumed his explanation. 'I believe the British deliberately betrayed us in the war. They sacrificed us for their own cause.'

Sabine shook her head. 'They lost many of their own SOE agents. They shipped tonnes of arms into France that fell into German hands. Why do all of that? Simply because they didn't like de Gaulle?'

Robert released Sabine's hand and poured them both a glass of wine. 'The British intelligence service was not fond of SOE from the beginning. Intelligence-gathering and sabotage are antagonistic to each other. Although both rely on stealth, spies must always remain invisible. Saboteurs are eventually going to draw attention to themselves.'

'You think they let us be tortured and sent to concentration camps because of some departmental infighting?'

Robert pursed his lips. 'As soon as I start putting questions to British intelligence about Christian Vidal, there is suddenly a fire in SOE's records department and all files on that agent are lost? Don't you find that suspicious?'

Sabine tried to maintain the air of a besotted lover but it was hard to keep up. What Robert was telling her was unsettling. 'Can it really be true that the British secret service deliberately sabotaged SOE? Weren't they supposed to be on the same side of the war? Both fighting for jolly old England?'

Robert shrugged. 'The German intelligence service hated the Gestapo.'

Sabine sat back in her chair and thought that point over. Indeed, during the war some German intelligence officers tried to shield Resistance members from the Gestapo. They thought the Gestapo's brutal methods were a poor reflection on their country and German refinement.

'If MI6 had wanted to destroy SOE, then knowingly letting a German spy infiltrate one of the Resistance circuits without warning them would be a good way to go about it,' she said. Then looking at Robert directly she asked, 'Someone doesn't want us to find Christian Vidal, do they?'

Robert nodded. 'You have to be careful. This isn't as straightforward as it first appeared.'

'Then I won't approach the British government in London for information. I'll go to the convalescent hospital where

Christian Vidal was sent to recuperate. I can pretend that the French government wants to decorate him for his services to France. One of the doctors or nurses might tell me something.'

Robert took a sip of his wine then put his glass down. 'I don't think you should go. I'll send Agent Brodeur.'

Sabine recoiled. 'He's a coward. He won't see it through if it gets difficult.'

Robert frowned to remind her where they were.

She looked over her shoulder to check no one was listening before she continued. 'If there has been some sort of cover-up and we can get it before the courts, then everyone involved will be exposed.'

Robert shook his head. 'You'd have to get a British agent in front of a British court to have him tried for treason. This is not an official operation. I can't draw attention to it by sending a team with you. It's not as straightforward as you … "retiring" him. God knows, I'd prefer it if I could go with you.'

'Believe me, it will be my pleasure to "retire" him, but I need to know why he did what he did and who else might have been involved.'

Robert rubbed his chin. 'If we had known about the Black Fox six months ago, the French government might have put pressure on the British to bring him to trial. Your husband is considered a hero – it would have been a matter of French honour that justice be served. Now we are courting ex-Nazis, there is no honour.'

'I will put him on trial,' said Sabine. 'I will make sure he knows why I am retiring him and get the information I need from him.'

Robert shook his head. 'Just retire him quickly. Let that be your satisfaction. It's too risky for you otherwise. You have no leverage over him, and you'll have no backup.'

Sabine turned it over in her mind. Then she remembered the day in the kitchen when Christian had broken protocol and told her he had a wife and son. He might be a traitor and a liar, but given the way his eyes had misted over then she could believe his love for them was sincere.

'He has a wife and child. I'll use them,' she said.

Robert penetrated her with his gaze. 'You realise you might have to kill them all if you are exposed ... even the child?'

She understood his concern. She had no sanction to kill innocent civilians. To do so would be to go far beyond the role of an agent investigating war crimes, and the consequences for her could be great. She would be acting in a foreign country, so there would be no diplomatic immunity for her. She tried to put Robert at ease by appearing at ease herself.

'I'll avoid harming his wife and child,' she said, 'but I'll use them if I have to.'

Robert nodded, satisfied. But even as she'd said it, Sabine had difficulty making that promise to herself. Her own husband and child were dead. Why should she give a second thought to the wife and child of a traitor?

*URGENT MESSAGE FROM BERLIN*

*MY DEAR FRIEND. I MISS THE NIGHTS THAT WERE BLACK AND AM HAPPY WITH THE MEMORIES OF MY GARDEN VISITOR, THE FOX. SADLY, THE LADY FROM MAISON BROUILLETTE, WHO LIVES BY HERSELF AND WORKS IN MY FORMER LAIR, HAS DISCOVERED IT WAS THE FOX WHO KILLED HER BELOVED CHICKENS. SHE IS NOW HUNTING FOR THE FOX AND I FEAR THAT SHE WILL SOON DISCOVER THE LOCATION OF HIS DEN. ACT QUICKLY, MY FRIEND, FOR SHE IS YOUR EQUAL IN CUNNING.*

*THE FOREST WOLF*

# CHAPTER NINE

Janet greeted Casper as if he'd never been away. She pecked him on the cheek then seated him at the head of the table.

'I thought you deserved a hearty meal for your first night home,' she said, dishing out the potato and leek soup into bowls. She made a show of how small she thought the dining room was by squeezing herself between the chairs and the sideboard each time she had to get something from the kitchen, although there was plenty of room to go around the other side. But Diana's annoyance softened now she had Casper by her side.

Alfred leaned towards Casper and pointed to the stone chimney. 'You've got a capable wife,' he said. 'She built that chimney herself, you know. Not many women could do that.'

'You'd better get a professional to check it now you're home,' Janet said. 'It's not the sort of structure an amateur should attempt. It might collapse in the middle of the night.'

Casper shuddered. It was imperceptible to the others, but Diana noticed it. It wasn't because he doubted her building capabilities. It was something else. His mind was a million miles away.

'I'll put on some music,' Diana said. She went to the record player and selected an album by Charlie Parker. Casper had always loved jazz music. He was a man who absorbed life and had so many interests. Some of those books in the boxes in the library were written in exotic languages such as Hebrew and Sanskrit. She'd often thought there was nothing Casper couldn't master, once he'd decided to put his mind to it.

Diana returned to the table, patting Freddy's head as she passed him. 'Freddy can name all the tunes on this album,' she told Casper. 'We listen to it all the time.'

Casper looked up in interest at Freddy. 'Can you now?'

Freddy's eyes lit up at his father's attention. He was about to start reciting the list of songs when Janet interrupted.

'They've asked me to play the piano at church. Alfred has just bought me a new Beale.' She looked around the room. 'What this house needs is a piano. I'll give you my old one.'

Diana shook her head. If they had a piano in the house, she was certain Janet would insist on her tedious singalong sessions each time she came over.

'There isn't room for one,' she said quickly.

'Nonsense,' replied Janet. She pointed to the corner of the living room where Diana had her desk and typewriter. 'You could put it there.'

'But that's where I work,' said Diana.

'You could work here, at the dining table,' Janet insisted. Then with a sly smile she added, 'You probably won't be working that much anyway now Casper is home. Freddy will be expecting a little brother or sister soon.'

Diana bristled. It was too much, even for Janet.

Alfred diplomatically changed the subject. 'What is that picture you've got there on the wall?' he asked her, pointing to the watercolour of a sprig of eucalyptus blossoms. 'It's very good.'

'I did that,' Diana told him. 'It's one of a series I've been working on.'

Casper turned to look at the painting. Along with Aunt Shirley, he had been a champion of her artistic talent. Diana didn't just make sketches or line plans of her landscape designs. She painted everything in beautiful watercolours and presented the plan in a frame as a gift to her clients when the garden was completed. It was how she had earned her reputation as the landscape designer to the elite of Sydney at a time when people were planting vegetables instead of flowers. She would not have been able to thrive during the war otherwise.

'Do you like it?' Diana asked Casper. His eyes met hers and she sensed there was something he was desperate to tell her – or struggling to keep from her. Which was it? Before the war they'd been able to read each other's minds easily. Now that connection was no longer there.

Janet served the shepherd's pie along with a helping of minted peas, and Diana steered the conversation away from topics that had anything to do with the war. Instead, she asked Alfred his opinions about the upcoming census and the recent article published in the *Sydney Morning Herald* suggesting that the increase of motor cars, radios and drunks shouting obscenities in the early hours of the morning was turning Sydney into a 'noisy' city and causing families to flee to the suburbs for some quiet.

'You couldn't get much quieter than Killara,' Alfred said. 'The only thing you'll hear at night is the owls.'

When the trifle was dished out, Diana thought Casper was starting to look more like himself. There was colour in his cheeks and his body was less rigid. Then with one question, Janet made him tense again.

'When do you plan to go back to Sydney Grammar?' she asked him. 'I bet your students are keen to have their old language master back.'

A dark cloud passed over Casper's face. His expression hardened and his eyes turned black.

'My students?' he said, his voice strained and tight. 'My students were worked to death by the Japanese in Burma. They were starved and tortured. '

★

Despite Casper's morose mood during the rest of dinner, Janet prattled on about the wartime 'deprivations' Sydney had been subjected to, including the rationing of chocolate and Vegemite. She seemed indifferent to the horrors her brother must have witnessed. Diana tried to hurry things along by starting the washing-up before everyone had finished the trifle. It was a relief when Janet finally took the hint from Alfred that perhaps Diana and Casper would like to be alone. Even then it seemed to take ages for Janet and Alfred to leave, but not before Janet declared the evening a wonderful success and commented on how well Casper looked. 'It's as if you've been away on holiday.'

Now Diana stood before the mirror in the bathroom and wondered what it would be like to make love to a husband she hadn't seen for six years. She lifted her silk nightdress and examined the burn scars on her stomach. They had flattened over time and grown shiny and pinched. Her torso looked like a porcelain vase that had been broken and then inexpertly glued back together again. She'd kept the scars hidden all through her school years, not always an easy feat in the change rooms for swimming carnivals. Casper had assured her on their honeymoon that they did not diminish his desire for her. Would he still feel the same way now?

She covered herself again as the niggling doubt bit at her, as it probably did all wives whose husbands had been at war. Had there been other women during the years he'd been away? Was the change in Casper not so much due to the stress of the war, but because he was thinking of someone else? She shook her head and pushed the thought away. What good would it do to even contemplate it? He was with her now.

Casper was sitting on the side of the bed with his back towards the door when Diana entered the bedroom. He had taken off his shirt and was wearing only his singlet and trousers. His broad shoulders in the golden glow of the lamplight filled her with longing. She remembered how safe she'd always felt in his embrace, so loved and cherished. Night after night during the war she had gone to bed alone, thankful to be so bone-tired from her work that she would not experience those long moments of darkness before sleep came. For it was in those moments that her mind would turn to terrible scenarios.

The war was over, Casper was home and they would never be separated again. Those would be the things she would hold on to now. Whatever memories haunted him, she would help him to forget.

She stepped towards him. Her blood turned cold when she saw what he was holding in his hand. A pistol – long-barrelled and dark grey. A deadly, impersonal thing. Bile stuck in her throat. She couldn't believe anything as vile should be in the house – a home she had poured her soul into making a place of beauty. Her father had owned a gun – a shotgun that made both Diana and her mother jump with terror each time he fired it. Diana remembered her father picking up the rabbits, their bloodied bodies twitching. It was the suffering that haunted her, a horror she couldn't bear.

She moved around the bed to face Casper. 'What is that?' she asked, pointing to the gun. 'Why have you brought that into our home?'

He didn't look at her when he answered. 'For protection.' His voice was cold and distant, as if she were a subordinate he was giving a warning to, not his wife.

She watched in disbelief as he placed the pistol in the bedside drawer along with a metal tube that she took to be a silencer. She did not want that awful thing there alongside them in their bedroom. She wanted it out of the house and gone. What if Freddy should find it?

'Who do we need to protect ourselves from?' she asked. 'Killara is practically the countryside. People don't even lock their doors. You never felt you needed a gun in Rushcutters Bay with criminal gangs lurking in the streets only a few blocks away.'

Casper's shoulders stiffened. He took the gun from the drawer and stood up, placing it in his belt. 'I'll sleep downstairs if it makes you so uncomfortable.'

Diana's mouth quivered. In her heart she was a peacemaker; she would turn a blind eye to avoid an argument, as she frequently did with Phyllis and Janet. But Freddy's safety was not something she was willing to compromise. She said nothing as Casper brushed past her and out the door. Her eyes followed him. He was not the husband she had known. That man was gone and someone else had returned in his place. She was a stranger to this new Casper, and he was most certainly a stranger to her.

'Who are you?' she asked under her breath, before turning the light off and sinking down onto the bed. The churning feeling in her stomach and the panic in her veins were familiar. Too familiar. They sent her reeling straight back into her past.

# CHAPTER TEN

*Sydney, September 1925*

Diana stood at the edge of the garden, her face turned towards the sunshine, her eyes closed. She was listening. The soft spring breeze rustling the tops of the trees was her favourite sound, as delicate and moving as any human-composed nocturne or serenade. Her dainty red-brown eyelashes quivered, and she slowly opened her eyes. The air around her shimmered, and for a moment she thought she might have glimpsed them, the little spots of light – the garden fairies. Her mother had told her that life was not only made of the material things you could see but of the spaces in between, and that you had to be very quiet and very still to sense the magic that was always all around you. She inhaled the heady scent of the freshly blooming jasmine and listened to the symphony of the birds. She knew every one of their songs, from the screeches of the cockatoos to the warbles of the magpies, to the tiniest twitters of the fairy wrens.

'Diana.'

Her mother was calling, but not in the loud, fishwife-way that other mothers shouted to their children. Diana's mother only had to whisper her name and she would hear her. Her gentle voice flew like a tiny bird from the veranda and down the flagstone path, skimming the lily pond and low stone wall, whipping through the wisteria-covered pergola, and passing the golden honeysuckle and grevilleas before landing on Diana's shoulder and speaking into her ear.

Diana turned and took the meandering path back to the house. She had always known the garden was special, quite unlike the others in the street with their sweeping front lawns and topiary roses in diamond-shaped flower beds. It was no bigger than the others but was so lushly planted that it seemed as deep as a forest. There was always something new and beautiful to discover. But the house that appeared up ahead through the trees was quite another matter. It was smaller in size than the other mansions, but it was still showy, with a multi-gabled slate roof and grand formal dining room. It had kauri timber floors throughout and a wide double-arched central hall. But Diana always felt chilled in it and spent most of her time outdoors. The house was not her mother's doing.

Diana's mother was waiting at the bottom of the veranda steps, dressed in overalls and gumboots. Her pale eyes crinkled when she smiled and she rested her hand on her hip. In the wheelbarrow next to her was the crepe myrtle sapling that she and Diana had chosen at Swane's nursery together and were planting in celebration of Diana's tenth birthday. It was to be the centrepiece of the driveway's turning circle. A gardener came three times a week to help with the heavy work like digging, but Diana and her mother didn't want any assistance to plant this tree.

Diana had first come across crepe myrtles in the local park, where they formed an avenue of trees along the central pathway. Quiet and leafless in winter, she thought the cinnamon and green-grey swirls of the bark were as beautiful as the showy profusion of blossoms that burst from the branches in summer.

Diana took the handles of the wheelbarrow and pushed it towards the bed in the centre of the driveway while her mother carried the spade and trowel. When they reached the spot, Diana took the tree and then turned the wheelbarrow over so her mother would have something to sit on. While Diana pushed the shovel into the earth, her mother sang 'The Bonnie Banks of Loch Lomond' in her crystal-clear, lilting voice.

*The wee birdies sing and the wildflowers spring,*
*And in sunshine the waters are sleeping.*
*But the broken heart it kens nae second spring again,*
*Though the waeful may cease frae their grieving.*

It was a sad song, about separation, death and longing, but it sounded beautiful when Diana's mother sang it. She had grown up with her mother's singing and her stories of the Loch Ness Monster, fairies and other magical creatures.

When the hole was large enough for the plant, Diana looked up and noticed that her mother had a tear in her eye. It glistened and grew large, before spilling down her freckled cheek. Her mother often cried, but not always because she was sad. Sometimes it was simply that some moment of beauty had moved her – dragonflies hovering over the pond; filtered sunlight dancing on the garden path; the appearance of the first spring buds on the cherry blossom tree. Nature, to Diana's mother, was one miracle after another. Now that Diana was older, she was becoming sensitive to those moments too – when beauty touched you so deeply you could feel your heart swell with it.

Diana reached out and grabbed her mother's hand. In turn, she gently squeezed Diana's.

'You know that life is a cycle, don't you, my sweetheart?' she said. 'All things are born, and all things die. Other people are afraid of that, but you must never be. If you accept it, life will always be beautiful for you, even when it is sorrowful.'

Diana sat down and rested her cheek against her mother's shoulder.

'We are here to appreciate beauty,' she continued. 'When people forget that, they create strife and wars and all manner of ugly things. They destroy what is beautiful and precious instead of appreciating and respecting it.'

Her mother never did anything in a rushed or thoughtless way and Diana tried to follow her example. She stood and lifted the tree out of the hessian bag with a sense of reverence, then gently pinched its roots. Once it was in the ground, she watered it, imagining the roots reaching down through the damp soil to the centre of the earth.

'You must water this plant often until the roots become strong,' her mother instructed her. 'It is your duty. This tree binds us together. It will outlive me and when you see it, you will remember this day.'

They sat back and looked at the tree, their arms around each other. Another girl might have become fidgety and impatient, but Diana had learned to appreciate silence. The pauses between notes of music, the quiet of the stars, the way paintings spoke without using words. The birds in the bushland went silent when they sensed a predator approaching. Silence helped them stay undetected. It gave them a moment to consider what to do. Diana, too, had found that silence was the ultimate protection.

★

Later in the afternoon, dressed in a blue voile frock with pearl buttons down the front, Diana sat in the parlour with her mother, who had also changed from her gardening clothes into a dress with a polka-dot pattern and a sailor collar. At the sound of the gate opening, Diana jumped to her feet and peered through the gap in the lace curtains to spy the tall, elegant figure coming down the flagstone path. She carried a purse in one hand and a straw basket in the other.

'She's here!' cried Diana.

A moment later, they were opening the front door to the luminous presence of Aunt Shirley.

'Hello, my darlings,' she said, striding into the house in fashionable white canvas shoes with baby Louis heels.

She embraced her sister and pressed her cheek so firmly to Diana's that when she let go of her again, she had transferred some of her exotic Shalimar perfume to her skin.

'Happy Birthday,' she said. 'You are a grown-up girl now.'

Everything about Aunt Shirley was up to the minute. She wore a sleeveless pleated dress and a lace cloche hat, white like her shoes. She pulled aside the curtains and regarded the garden. A smile formed on her cupid bow lips. 'Every time I come here, this place looks more like paradise.'

Aunt Shirley was fifteen years older than her sister, but didn't look it. She approached life with the boundless enthusiasm of a child.

She reached into her straw basket and handed a red chocolate box to Diana's mother.

'You didn't have to,' Diana's mother said. 'I've baked a cake.'

'I like spoiling you both,' Aunt Shirley replied. 'You are my most favourite people in the whole world.'

Then she reached into her straw basket again and produced a large flat present wrapped in tissue paper and tied with a gold ribbon.

'For you, my clever sweetheart,' she said, handing it to Diana.

'Sit at the dining table and open it together,' said Diana's mother. 'I'll put the kettle on.'

'Where's Mrs Kent?' Aunt Shirley asked.

Her sister shifted on her feet and looked flustered. 'She's not coming anymore.'

Mrs Kent had been their housekeeper for as long as Diana could remember. When they'd lived in the smaller house three streets away, she came to clean, dust and cook every day. There had also been an ironing and washing woman who had collected the laundry on Tuesdays and Thursdays. Now they were in a bigger house, but Diana's mother had no help.

A look passed between Aunt Shirley and her sister. Diana had the feeling her aunt wanted to say something but checked herself. Aunt Shirley sat down at the table and patted the seat next to her to indicate Diana should take it.

'Open it,' she said, nodding towards the present. 'And then we shall have some of your mother's delicious cake.'

Diana had never seen such a present. The paper smelled of vanilla and patchouli, like Aunt Shirley's perfume. She tugged the ribbon and unfolded the paper to discover a book entitled *The Wildflowers of Western Australia* by Emily Pelloe.

Aunt Shirley flipped open the cover and showed Diana the inside title page. Opposite a brilliant watercolour of gum blossoms was a handwritten dedication from the author herself:

*To Diana,*
*Your aunt tells me that you are an artist too. Henri Matisse once said, 'There are always flowers for those who want to see them.' May you never stop looking!*
*Best wishes,*
*Emily Pelloe*

'Mrs Pelloe is a famous botanical illustrator,' Aunt Shirley explained. 'She was in Sydney last month, so I asked her to sign her book for you.'

Diana was filled with awe. The paper was thick and made a delightful swooshing sound when she turned the pages. Her eyes rested on a full-page sketch of different types of gumnuts. Some were cylindrical, others urn-, diamond- or cone-shaped – all meticulously sketched and detailed. Diana gazed at the pictures as if she was looking into another world. She was as captivated by the wonders of nature as another child might be by reading *Peter Pan*. Only the magical things she was seeing did exist and many of them were outside her front door. As Emily Pelloe had advised, she only had to look. Diana knew then that her future would somehow involve plants.

'The book is beautiful,' she told Aunt Shirley. 'I will treasure it forever'.

★

Diana's mother had baked a lemon pound cake. While Diana drank a cold glass of milk and nibbled a slice, she listened to her mother's and her aunt's tales of Scotland, in particular about Glasgow's famous tearooms.

'They were exquisite, weren't they, Margaret?' said Aunt Shirley, tilting her teacup towards her sister. 'You didn't have to have a lot of money to feel like a queen.'

'Indeed,' she agreed. 'They were oases in the middle of the city.'

Diana liked how her mother was when she was with Aunt Shirley. Colour came to her cheeks, and she laughed heartily. They giggled and ribbed each other like two naughty schoolgirls who had run away from the convent for the day.

'I wish you could have seen them, my darling,' Aunt Shirley said to Diana. 'You would have loved them. There were murals on the walls and chairs with high backs for comfort. The women's tearooms were decorated like beautiful cakes in pink, white and grey, while the men enjoyed the oak-panelled smoking and billiard rooms.'

'I remember the first time we sat in "The Room de Luxe" at Kate Cranston's tearoom to celebrate my birthday,' said

Diana's mother. 'It had a grand vaulted ceiling and the curved bay window looked out onto Sauchiehall Street.'

As the women reminisced, Diana imagined that she was stepping back in time with them. Dressed in an exquisite Edwardian gown with flounced sleeves and wearing a hat lavishly decorated with silk flowers, bows and tulle, she followed her mother and aunt through the double doors to the tearoom, admiring the Art Nouveau lead-glass panels as she passed. A waiter dressed in livery guided them across the plush carpet to their table, which was painted silver and covered with a white cloth. She sat down in a chair upholstered in rose-purple silk and let her ears be treated to the sound of the string quartet playing Brahms. When the waitress arrived with their tea selections, Diana lifted the willow-pattern cup to her lips and inhaled the floral scent of the Ceylon tea before taking a sip ...

The sound of car tyres on gravel had Diana sitting bolt upright. The sisters stopped talking and lowered their cups. Her mother's face turned ashen. Fear and panic ran over the trio as if they were rabbits who'd heard the click of a hunter's gun.

'I thought he wasn't supposed to be back until tomorrow?' said Aunt Shirley.

Her mother didn't answer. Instead, she grasped Diana's hand, her expression grim. 'Go to you room, quickly.' She grabbed the wildflower book and passed it to Aunt Shirley who put it back in her basket.

'Yes, go quickly! I'll keep the book for you,' Aunt Shirley urged Diana.

Diana did not want to leave, but she knew she'd better listen to them. She went to her room and huddled behind her bookcase.

'Hello, Bill,' she heard Aunt Shirley say.

Diana's blood pounded in her ears. It would be better with her aunt there, she hoped. Her father was a bully, but he was afraid of Aunt Shirley for some reason. Perhaps he didn't want her to witness his hypocrisy and that tempered his behaviour. Nobody would believe that handsome William Buchanan, with his angelic blond hair and neat moustache, was a brute to his wife and daughter. To the outside world he was the successful manager of the local bank. People looked up to him – the private school old boy. They came to his office seeking loans and overdrafts, sat in the leather chairs and made small talk with him about their wives and children. Diana had seen the photograph on his desk. It was a picture of her mother holding Diana as a baby in her christening gown. That's who people thought they were talking to when they spoke to William Buchanan – the doting husband and father, the backslapping golf partner, the man who sat in the front pew at church.

Diana lifted her eyes to the dent above her bed where her father had thrown the shepherdess figurine against the wall, smashing it to pieces. Her mother had brought the figurine all the way from Scotland. It had been a present from a much-loved aunt and she'd wanted Diana to have it. The shepherdess had been so pretty with her painted floral clothes. She'd stood on a patch of porcelain grass with a crook in one hand and a lamb at her feet. For as long as she could remember, Diana had woken to the sight of her friendly smile on her bedside table.

She'd always said 'goodnight' to her before going to sleep. The figurine had been a comfort somehow – a guardian angel. Diana had done nothing to provoke her father's attack. She'd been asleep when he burst into her room and began tearing her watercolour paintings from the walls.

She leaned her head against the bookshelf, which was empty except for the ragged volumes of the *World Book Encyclopaedia*. All the other books her mother had given her – including *The Wonderful Adventures of Nils*, with its cut-paper illustrations, and *Snugglepot and Cuddlepie*, with May Gibbs's drawings of Australian flora and fauna – had been ruined by her father in that fit of rage. Anything beautiful that Diana or her mother might enjoy became a weapon he used to hurt them.

Diana squeezed her eyes shut. She did not think of that man with the blond hair and blue eyes as related to her in any way. He was someone she kept as far from her mind as possible. He was nothing more than a beast and a destroyer of beauty.

## CHAPTER ELEVEN

After discussing the Black Fox and how to eliminate him, Sabine and Robert ate the rest of their meal in a comfortable silence. That was the way it was between them. They could deal with confronting situations and then afterwards slip into a mood with each other that was almost homely. Their secret life, their shared experiences and their reliance on each other gave them a sense of intimacy that few married couples shared.

Their dessert was apple compote with no sugar or cream, but the chef insisted on giving them a glass each of fine Cognac, which, as he proudly informed them, he had managed to keep hidden from the Germans during the occupation.

Robert paid the bill and they got up to leave. He helped Sabine with her coat and whispered in her ear, 'The passport and ticket are in your pocket.'

Outside, before they parted ways, he kissed her again on both cheeks.

'What's going to become of us, Sabine?' he asked, remaining close to her and straightening the collar of her coat.

The tenderness of this action caused Sabine's heart to ache. She would have liked to stroke his forehead or press herself against his chest to relieve the utter loneliness she heard in his question. What was to become of two people whose purpose was to avenge the dead? What future were they trying to build? Did anybody care? The fact that the war crimes department was at risk of being shut down was proof they didn't. But she could not give Robert the comfort he needed. He still had the vestiges of a real flesh-and-blood person in his ability to hope. She was a soul in purgatory. Her only allegiance was to those who had died. She could not enter a new life by acquiring different people to love without annihilating her past life.

'One day you'll find a good woman,' she told him. 'Someone who can give you peace.'

He grimaced at her gentle rejection. 'You know that it will only get worse, Sabine, don't you? This refusal of yours to let yourself be happy. Your insistence on deadening yourself to life.'

'You are a good man, Robert,' she persisted. 'You deserve to be happy.'

'And you, Sabine?' he asked, looking at her despairingly. 'Do you not deserve to be happy too?'

'No.'

His hands slipped from her collar to her shoulders. 'How long can you go on punishing yourself for surviving? Can't you forgive yourself?'

She shook her head. 'No.'

'Why not?'

Sabine lifted her eyes to his. 'Because if I forgive myself for my failure to protect my son, then I will have to forgive all the war criminals too. They failed in their duty to humankind. I failed in mine as a mother.'

★

As Sabine walked home through the dark and icy streets, she wondered if she had made a mistake in rejecting Robert. For a moment she allowed herself to think of a different path to the one she was now taking. Perhaps she and Robert could step away from the need to avenge the death of their friends and families, and accept that things had happened that were beyond their ability to change. They could find a place in the countryside together or move to another continent entirely, and create a quiet, peaceful life together. Even though she had loved Lucien and Pierre, there had inevitably been dull moments in family life when Sabine had wondered if she might have been happier if she had never married and remained independent. Now she would give anything to relive every single one of those ordinary moments.

When she reached her building and caught a glimpse through the window of Madame Rouzard sitting in her apartment with her cat on her lap, Sabine realised it was impossible for her to go in any other direction than the one in which she was heading. Despite the danger Madame Rouzard had dealt with in smuggling Jews, she had been able to return to her former life after the war. She had never stepped over that final moral boundary. She had never killed anyone. She had never snuck up behind a man and shot him in the back. When Sabine had first started her Resistance activities, she had been horrified at the thought of killing anyone, yet she had been proud the first time she did because it meant that she had not let her compatriots down and she had shown courage. *Sometimes a brutal war requires brutal methods.* Who had told her that? Then she remembered they were the words of Christian himself when he'd taught her how to use a grenade. It was Christian who had turned her into a monster. Now she was going to destroy him. Why should he live a happy life with his wife and child when the people he had betrayed were dead.

Sabine opened the door to her apartment and hurried to the bedroom, where she took off her clothes and hung them in the wardrobe. She replaced the brooch in her jewellery box, touching it reverently before closing the lid. Two robins protecting their nest. Sabine closed her eyes. When Christian had arrived in the village to help Lucien and Sabine create a formal Resistance network, Sabine had approached a neighbour she had always considered a courageous woman. But as soon as Sabine suggested she might help the circuit, her friendly expression had turned dark. She had clutched her youngest child to her chest. *What you are asking is impossible! I have my children to think of!*

Why had Sabine not made the same decision? Why had she believed that she had to fight for a higher cause? That neighbour's child would now be at school. He would one day be married and have children of his own. The neighbour had not paid the price Sabine had, and yet both women now lived in a free France.

Sabine lifted the hatbox from the top shelf of the wardrobe and was placing her hat back in it when she felt something in the tissue paper. She unwrapped the paper and discovered a photograph. It was a picture of herself and Jacqueline, her best friend from the Paris Conservatoire. It had been taken when they were both twenty years of age. They were wearing cotton sundresses and had their arms around each other's waist, smiling at whichever young man had taken the picture. Jacqueline had been a virtuoso harpist with a mischievous sense of humour. She was a daredevil who threw herself into life with gusto – riding, skiing, sailing, racing motor cars. She had come to stay at the house in the Dordogne with Sabine and Lucien and his parents that fateful summer when Christian arrived. Sabine pressed the picture to her heart, unable to look at the innocent expressions on their faces a moment longer. With their sun-kissed cheeks and beaming smiles, the two young women in the picture had no idea of the terrible fate that awaited them only a decade into the future. At the time, they had thought the biggest problems they faced were their music exams and choosing a husband from their many suitors.

Sabine put the photograph and hat back and placed the box on the top shelf of the wardrobe. She went to the kitchen and managed to coax enough of a flame on the burner to boil water for valerian tea. As she took the teapot from the cupboard, her mind turned back to Jacqueline. When Christian had arrived to organise the circuit, he'd brought a wireless set, but his operator was captured when he was parachuted into France later. Christian had immediately recognised Jacqueline for her courage and quick thinking and trained her for the role of wireless operator for the circuit. It was the most dangerous job but he said musicians made for natural signallers. Wireless operators were vulnerable to detection the longer they stayed on air. Their signals could be traced by German direction-finder vans. In the worst days of the war, the average life span of an operator was six weeks. Jacqueline had lasted much longer than that. At the time Sabine had attributed her longevity to her extreme skill and cleverness, but now she wondered if it was simply that with a traitor in the circuit, the Germans had been able to bide their time, waiting for the right moment to take down the entire circuit, rather than arresting one of them and alerting the others to go to ground. The rule in the Resistance was, if captured, to endure any torture for forty-eight hours before breaking. This would give the other members of the circuit time to hear of your arrest and abandon their safe houses, shut down letterboxes and destroy messages. Sabine had not broken, nor had Jacqueline. The last time Sabine saw her friend alive she had been so badly beaten and tortured that she barely recognised her.

The water boiled and Sabine sat down with her tea. She rested her forehead against the warm cup. She had once loved Christian Vidal, but she had no doubt that she would find it easy to kill him, and perhaps even his wife and child, if it came to that. All she would have to do was remember Jacqueline.

## CHAPTER TWELVE

The screech of cockatoos and rainbow lorikeets in the tree outside the bedroom window woke Diana. She stirred and rubbed her eyes. Out on the lawn the crested pigeons were cooing and the magpies were warbling their morning songs. There was never a need to use an alarm clock in summer; she had her avian friends to make sure she got up at sunrise. Waking up with nature always made her feel joyous anyway, as Eve must have felt when she lived in the Garden of Eden. But this morning, Diana was aware of an ache in her heart. Then she remembered what had happened with Casper the previous evening. She turned on her side and gave a start when she saw him in the bed beside her, his eyelids clamped shut and his breathing heavy with sleep. The drawer to the bedside table was still open but there was no sign of the gun. In its place was a copy of Goethe's *Faust*. He must have found it in one of the boxes in the library.

They had seen the play at the Wintergarten Theatre in Berlin while on their European honeymoon. It had been an enchanting venue, with plush velvet seats and a twinkling artificial night sky for a ceiling. That building was gone now, blown to smithereens with the rest of Berlin. She'd read about it in the newspaper and seen the pictures of the blackened shells of buildings and the orphaned children living like savages on the street. The pain in her heart clenched deeper. How terrible it must have been for Casper to fly sorties every night and bomb those cities where they'd blissfully travelled together a few years before. What must have been going through his mind when he helped destroy the music halls where they had danced the tango and the museums where they had stood in awe before great works of art? Not to mention having on his conscience the lives of the men, women, children and animals who had been reduced to ash by his actions. Her gaze travelled over Casper's form, once so familiar to her but now seeming to belong to a stranger. She reached out to touch him but stopped short of contacting his skin, lest she wake him. She had a terrible feeling that he wasn't quite real, and that at any moment he'd be called back to Europe and she would never see him again.

Diana slipped out of bed and went to the bathroom to brush her teeth and wash her face. '*Je me brosse les dents et me lave le visage*,' she said out loud to her reflection in the mirror, remembering the exact phrase as it had been written in her high school French textbook. *I brush my teeth and wash my face*. It was language that had first brought Diana and Casper together, when she'd attended a lecture he was giving in French at the Alliance Française, about the history of medicinal herbs in France. Aunt Shirley had sent her to Europe to finish her studies in horticulture by taking in the great artworks and gardens of the continent. She hadn't anticipated her niece would bring a husband back home with her. Early on in their courtship,

Diana had tried to break it off with Casper, believing it was impossible for two people who lived on opposite sides of the world to get married. He had looked her straight in the eye and answered, '*À coeur vaillant rien d'impossible.*' For a valiant heart, nothing is impossible.

Diana returned to the bedroom and leaned against the door, watching Casper's chest rise and fall with each breath. 'Impossible' was not a word she favoured either. Casper's letters before he went missing had always been warm. There had never been any reason to doubt that his heart had not been with her and Freddy at home. She thought of her encounter with Mrs Keener the day before. *The garden was beautiful once but terrible things happened here.* That Casper had savage memories, she had no doubt. She had hers too. She kept them tightly shut in a secret chamber in her mind. Would Casper ever be able to brush his aside and live a normal life again? Perhaps as in war, peace was something you had to fight for?

She stepped towards him and whispered, '*Après la pluie, vient le beau temps.*' After the rain comes good weather. Then she softly closed the door behind her and went downstairs.

★

Freddy was already dressed in his school uniform and drawing at the table in the dining room. He was an early riser, like herself. She rarely needed to drag him out of bed to get him to school on time.

'Good morning,' Diana said, smoothing down the hair at the back of his head, the part that somehow, despite his admirable self-sufficiency, he always managed to miss. She glanced at the drawing he was colouring. It was of the crepe myrtle tree. He had depicted himself holding her hand and staring up at some crimson rosellas perched on the branches. Blossom was nearby with Marilyn, but Casper wasn't in the picture at all. Diana's heart sank. She sat down beside him.

'It's quite a shock for your father to be home,' she told him. 'The two of you need to get to know each other again. He liked the model planes you made. He was admiring them last night before dinner.'

Freddy pointed to a corner of the drawing where there was an object he hadn't completed yet. 'That's a plane,' he said. 'Daddy's inside.'

Diana squinted at it. 'Indeed, it is,' she said, hiding her dismay. It appeared to her that the plane was flying away from, rather than towards, them.

She went to the kitchen to make Freddy's favourite breakfast of Weet-Bix with raisins and pineapple juice. Bacon was off the menu since Freddy had realised it came from pigs, and they usually only ate eggs at dinner. Diana made herself some Vegemite toast and a cup of tea. Australia's wartime rationing had been mild compared to Britain. Fruit and vegetables had never been rationed, although sometimes the supply was erratic and the prices high. Tea, butter, meat and tobacco rationing was what made people write terse letters to the newspapers, although in Diana's opinion the limits had been far from draconian. She had managed and didn't complain, having learned that in the Soviet Union during the German blockades, the starving population were eating wallpaper and boiling leather belts to make an edible jelly. They'd eaten their pets, and in some rare cases, each other.

She placed the food in front of Freddy and sat down next to him with hers. Her eyes ran over his sunny blond locks and peaches-and-cream skin. What hell those mothers in Europe had been through. What would it have been like to watch your children die and not be able to do anything about it? What would that do to your mind?

She listened for sounds of Casper stirring upstairs, but there were none. *Let him sleep*, she thought. Sleep was the best healer.

After breakfast, Diana walked with Freddy to school. Before he went in the gate, he turned and waved to her. With a flash of that cherubic smile, her heart melted. She waved back and watched him until he disappeared.

*

The cicadas were singing loudly when Diana stepped out into the garden, tying a scarf around her head. As a child she had sat for hours listening to the insects, noticing the contrast between the cicadas' loud pulsating crescendos and the grasshoppers' more musical mating calls. Her mother had told her that both ringtail possums and fairies made sounds at such high frequencies that they were inaudible to the human ear. Diana did not have her Scottish mother's gift for seeing or hearing fairies, but she was alert to the tiny shifts in the natural world. She sensed when the mauve jacarandas were about to bloom, that when the October sky turned a particular shade of ultramarine blue it was the midpoint of spring, and that the first blossoming of the Australian Christmas bush meant a heatwave was on its way.

Diana had not spoken to Freddy about the fairies – she felt unqualified compared to her mother. But she gave him the freedom to explore the garden whenever he wanted, believing that children needed to be away from the controlling influence of adults in order to develop their true gifts. His blossoming genius as an artist was proof that her intuition had been right. Maybe he had seen fairies and never told her, she thought whimsically. That would be all right with her. Everyone was entitled to their secrets.

She looked up to the bedroom window. Casper still hadn't stirred. She was half-tempted to call up to him, like Romeo to Juliet. There was a time when he would have thought that a great joke, but she wasn't so sure now.

The thump of Marilyn's pickaxe striking the earth near the creek brought her attention back to the task at hand. The plan for the day was to get started on planting the shrubs and groundcovers on the banks.

Marilyn greeted her with a nod and a smile when Diana arrived at the creek bank with a wheelbarrow full of seedlings.

'I didn't expect to see you until later,' Marilyn said.

'Casper is sleeping.'

'He's tired, I suppose.' Marilyn waited for Diana to say something more and, when she didn't, nodded towards the lower bank. 'I've measured everything out for you.'

Marilyn dug up the creek bank while Diana planted the bottlebrush and lilli pilli seedlings in rows perpendicular to the flow, and the groundcovers in clumps. Marilyn had once told

Diana that she liked to live alone because she wanted to be able to 'think her own thoughts'. The phrase had stayed with Diana. At first, she'd thought it an odd thing to say, as who else's thoughts could you think but your own? But after having Janet's voice in her ear all the previous evening, filling her with anxieties and dismissing her input, she now appreciated Marilyn's point of view.

The earthy, sweet scent of the soil and the bubbling sound of the creek calmed Diana's mind. After planting the rushes, she sat down with her notebook to record what they'd achieved that morning. Over the next few months, she would observe what plants survived and what plants didn't. The words for her next gardening article formed in her mind:

*One of my favourite species for creek-bank planting is* Waterhousea floribunda *– weeping lilli pilli. It's a versatile and fast-growing shrub that produces the prettiest of pink leaves, which eventually turn green as the foliage matures. The shrub produces clusters of white flowers that attract bees, and then it produces berries, which are appealing to native mammals and birds alike, as well as people who like to make jam with a slight tartness about it and the tiniest hint of cloves …*

The sound of a motor car had Diana looking up. She left her notebook on the rock where she'd been sitting and scrambled up the bank to get a view of the driveway. She recognised Harry Scott stepping out of his maroon Alfa Romeo. He was Phyllis's third husband and fifteen years her junior. Diana hurried towards the house before he could knock on the door and wake Casper.

'Harry!'

He turned and beamed at her with his straight white teeth. In his blue blazer and cravat, he was as dapper as ever. Out of all Phyllis's husbands — the previous ones being a cranky high court judge and a rather shady newspaper proprietor — Harry was her favourite.

'I'm sorry to arrive unannounced,' he said. 'But I was in the area.'

Diana resisted the urge to pull off her scarf and primp her hair. That Harry was handsome, with a high forehead and deep-set brown eyes, was not lost on her. Out of all the architects in Sydney, he was the only one designing homes that were innovative as well as beautiful. If Phyllis hadn't already nabbed him, and Diana wasn't so in love with Casper, she might have married him herself.

'Nonsense,' she replied. 'You're welcome anytime. You know that.'

He turned back to the cottage with an admiring eye. 'That's turned out rather well, hasn't it?' he said. 'Even if you didn't use my services to design it.'

Diana grinned. 'I think you're meant for bigger things,' she said.

'It sits beautifully in the garden, and you've positioned it perfectly.' Harry lifted his eyes to the second floor. 'Most people don't think enough about aspect and making the most of natural light. They build houses as if we were all living in England and every room is gloomy.'

'Come inside for a cup of tea,' Diana said. 'Casper is still sleeping but I can show you around downstairs.'

Harry shook his head. 'No, I won't disturb you. Phyllis told me your husband only returned yesterday. But I've had an exciting opportunity come up and I wanted to see if you were interested. If you are, then you can come to my office and we can discuss it in detail.'

'Well, I am intrigued.'

Harry returned to his car and took out a roll of paper. He spread it out on the veranda to reveal a map of Sydney and its outskirts. 'The government is expecting the population of the city to increase by over half a million in the next twenty-five years,' he said. 'So, a planning council has been created to decide what Sydney is going to look like in the future.' He moved his hand over the area west of the CBD. 'Part of that plan is to provide a greenbelt around the outer city. But I foresee a problem – only parts of the area put aside for open space belong to the government. Most of it is in private hands, which means it will probably be sold off for laissez-faire development that will result in ugly suburbs with no sense of order.'

Diana looked at the map. It was an enormous amount of bushland to be destroyed, and once destroyed it wouldn't come back.

'And you have a different idea about what the outer suburbs of Sydney should look like?' she asked, a smile forming on her lips.

He nodded. 'What I propose is to create houses that fit naturally into the landscape, so only a small percentage of that land would need to be cleared at all. The roads should also follow the natural formations that are already there. It would be a blueprint for creating a city with the most beautiful suburbs in the world. If they see my proposal, the government might be persuaded to buy those patches in the greenbelt back from private holders and develop them themselves.' He turned to Diana, his eyes shining. 'But I'm not familiar with the vegetation. I need someone who can analyse it for me and propose a way to integrate the natural bushland into my design.'

Diana's fingers tingled. 'You want me to help you with this proposal?'

'Not only the proposal,' he said. 'If we succeed, I want you on board as my partner to oversee the work.'

Diana felt as though she'd been lifted by a wave and put down again. To create a whole suburb of bushland gardens was something she'd secretly dreamed of but never expected to happen. She had long been dismayed by the constant clearing of bushland down to the very last tree. Sydney had the most beautiful setting of any city in the world and yet it was constantly blighted by ugly developments.

'What do you say, Diana?' Harry asked. 'Are you up for it?'

She looked at him. He was one of Sydney's most progressive architects and his desire that every suburb, no matter how humble its residents, be attractive and well-designed was a heartfelt one.

'I would love to do this,' she said. 'I've been waiting my whole life to be part of a vision for something so beautiful.'

Harry's smile grew wider. 'Come to my office this Thursday morning and I'll give you the details. We need to get onto this quickly.'

As Diana watched Harry disappear down the driveway, she realised she'd made a major decision without consulting

Casper. What she had agreed to would be a huge undertaking that would involve hours and months of work. A wave of guilt washed over her. She'd got so used to making all her own decisions that asking his opinion hadn't even crossed her mind.

Diana sat on the steps and took off her muddy boots. She would make a cup of tea and take it up to Casper now, then wake him and tell him the news. From the conversation last night, he hadn't seemed keen to return to teaching immediately. Perhaps he'd like to help her with her accounts or with sourcing the plants for her private jobs, which always took up so much of her time. Freddy went to Mrs Dalton's place straight after school four days a week, but Casper might be able to help take care of him too if Diana needed to work late. They'd been such a good team in the past; maybe Harry's proposal would be a way for them to find a renewed purpose.

She made the tea and went upstairs. But when she pushed the bedroom door open the bed was empty and the bedspread perfectly even and unwrinkled as if no one had ever slept in it. It was as though Casper had vanished into thin air.

## CHAPTER THIRTEEN

The sweet smell of almonds reminded Sabine of explosives. Before the war it might have hinted at her grandmother's *tarte Amandine* or *sole meunière* but now she associated it with the boxes of plastic explosives hidden in her bicycle basket as she'd ridden through German checkpoints. In the summer heat, the green plasticine would soften, and she was often terrified the odour would give her away. She scanned the reception room at the Helford Park Convalescent Home and realised the smell was coming from a cake box perched on the lap of a woman sitting near the door. She was wearing what Sabine had learned was referred to in Britain as a 'utility suit' – a jacket and skirt that could be worn with different blouses to change the look of the outfit, eradicating the need to waste fabric on too many clothes. It had been considered patriotic to wear one in Britain during the war. The French, on the other hand, could never view fashion in such a practical manner. At the outbreak of the war, women had been urged to keep up the morale of the French soldiers by always looking 'pretty and *soignée*'. When the Germans first occupied Paris, and were under orders to behave courteously, rebellion took the form of women wearing flamboyant hats and salving their wounded national pride by dressing as beautifully – or outrageously – as they pleased. All that changed, of course, when things got ugly. Still, Sabine had once shot a German sentry while wearing her favourite Lanvin suit.

She was wearing it now.

'Madame Allard?'

Sabine looked up to see a nurse surveying the reception area. She stood immediately. It was a reflex to respond to cover names quickly. Hesitation, in the past, could be fatal.

'Come this way,' the nurse told her.

Sabine followed her through what had clearly once been an elegant country house. It was spacious, with multiple doors coming off the grand oak-panelled hallway. Sabine had the unsettling feeling someone was walking behind them, but when she turned there was no one there.

'Madame, this way please,' said the nurse.

She followed the nurse up a staircase to the second floor and along a red-carpeted corridor. A door opened, revealing a ward of about twenty beds. A man in a wheelchair was sitting next to the bed of a burns victim. The patient's gnarled flesh had been smothered in ointment, with the result that he resembled a greased turkey. The man in the wheelchair moved his arm in a way that didn't seem natural. Then Sabine saw his hand, or rather the hook that had replaced it. She turned away, realising her own injury could have been so much worse.

'We are now a rehabilitation centre for amputees,' the nurse explained cheerfully. 'But until recently this was a convalescent home for prisoners-of-war recovering from infectious diseases.'

Through the French Embassy in London, Robert had been able to trace the path of Christian Vidal after his release from Fresnes Prison. He had been processed through the SOE office in Paris as one of their agents, but on arrival in England had regained his RAF status. It was, she supposed, a way to cover his tracks.

They reached a door at the end of the hall with a sign that read: *Administrator. Doctor C.H. Grosvenor.*

The nurse knocked and waited. Sabine tugged at her sleeve. She did not like to be standing at a door at the end of a long corridor. It made her feel trapped. But the man's voice that called out was not German, it was British – warm and proper. 'Come in.'

Sabine followed the nurse into the sunlit room. At a large desk sat a bespectacled man in a white coat.

'Ah, Madame Allard,' he said, rising to shake Sabine's hand. He nodded to the nurse. 'Thank you, Nurse Tucker. That will be all.'

The doctor offered Sabine a seat and the nurse closed the door as she left. 'I believe you are looking for one of our former patients,' the doctor said. 'And I think I know the gentleman in question.'

Sabine smiled. It wasn't easy to adopt a pleasant manner when she was hunting a war criminal, but her cover was that she was a representative of the French government, keen to award a courageous RAF pilot with the highest military honour, the *Légion d'honneur.*

'The man I am looking for was a bomber pilot who was shot down over France,' she explained. 'His crew were killed in the attack but he managed to parachute out and was picked up by the local Resistance circuit, who hid him. Unfortunately, the group was infiltrated by a traitor.'

Sabine took a breath. She was not telling Christian Vidal's real story, but the best cover stories were mixtures of fantasy and truth.

'He was sent to Fresnes Prison,' she continued, 'where he was brutally tortured by the Gestapo but refused to give the names of the Resistance members who had saved him. He was sent to Buchenwald and, despite the horrors he experienced there, still refused to denounce any of us.'

'*Us?*' the doctor asked.

Sabine lifted her left hand and rested it on top of her purse in full sight of the doctor. It was the hand that the Gestapo had taken such delight in mangling. The doctor's eyes took in the damage – the lack of extension of her thumb, the malalignment of her ring and index fingers, the drop of her middle knuckle. At first his look was clinical, but then sympathy filled his eyes.

'Did the Germans do that to you?'

'I was a member of the Resistance group in question,' she said. 'The Germans didn't like it when we didn't answer their questions. The French government sent me because I know the pilot's face well, but I do not know his name.'

Without hesitation, the doctor lifted a file from his desk and opened it. 'I believe this is the man you're looking for,' he said, handing the file to her.

Sabine's eyes fixed on the photograph. It was a shock to see him after all this time, but there was no question it was Christian. She glanced at the details: six foot two, green eyes, blond hair. Then her gaze fell to his name, *his real name*: Casper Julien White. His mother was French and his father was English. But then she saw his place of residence and gasped in surprise.

'He lives in Australia?'

Doctor Grosvenor nodded. 'Indeed. He's returned home already. You'll have to write to him. The RAF can probably help you with the address.'

This was a complication Sabine had not anticipated. She'd assumed he would be residing in Britain somewhere. It would take her six weeks to sail to Australia, unless Robert could pull some strings and get her on a 'diplomatic flight' for at least part of the way.

She looked at his marital status: Married to Diana Margaret White. One child, Frederick.

'Thank you very much,' said Sabine, rising.

The doctor stood as well and ushered her to the door. 'Your hand,' he said, 'it must cause you pain. A colleague of mine specialises in hand surgery. He's done marvellous work in repairing the malunion of fingers. If you don't mind waiting in reception a moment, I'll have my secretary type up a reference for you.'

'Thank you,' said Sabine, although kindness from others made her uncomfortable. 'I had a French surgeon look at it and he said nothing could be done, that it was impossible to fix.'

Doctor Grosvenor shook his head. 'I've seen worse come good,' he told her. 'It might take some time and courage, but nothing is impossible.'

Sabine's throat felt tight when she took a seat in the reception area. She really didn't think anyone would be able to help her, but it would look odd for her to rush off after such a genuine offer.

She had Christian's real name now – Casper White. She also had the names of his wife and child. What was she like, this Diana? For some reason, Sabine pictured someone blonde, cool and confident. An ice queen. Did Diana know she was married to a monster? But monsters often concealed their true natures well. Christian Vidal – she couldn't bring herself to think of him as Casper White just yet – had fooled her completely.

She closed her eyes and thought back to his arrival in the Dordogne. It was a night that would change the course of her life.

# CHAPTER FOURTEEN

*The Dordogne, May 1943*

With only moonlight to guide the way, Lucien drove the van across the arched bridge, while Sabine kept her eyes peeled for German patrols. Tomorrow, when the sun rose, she would show Christian Vidal – currently hidden behind crates in the back of the truck – the spectacular view of the village below, with its rustic shuttered houses and medieval church. Although she was Parisian through and through, it was a view she had come to treasure.

They passed the chestnut forests and acres of vines and travelled up the spiralling road to the farmhouse perched on a hillside. Lucien's father, Henri, was waiting by the side of the house holding a lantern. He opened the rear doors of the van and ushered Christian inside. Now that the British agent had parachuted into France, it was Lucien and Sabine who were responsible for helping him set up a proper Resistance circuit. They followed Christian and Henri into the kitchen, where Madeleine was stirring a pot of potato and bean soup, scenting the air with the smell of cloves and onions. The men sat down at the table while Sabine checked on Pierre, asleep in his cot.

She stroked his soft cheek, and then went to join the others in in the kitchen.

'Welcome to France,' Henri said to Christian, pouring a glass of his famous walnut-based aperitif, *vin de noix*.

Now that the light was upon him, Sabine could get a better look at their guest. He had a square, pleasant face with slightly hooded eyes and a straight nose. His mouth was wide and well formed, and his posture was erect but not stiff. He seemed like someone trustworthy and dependable – not the kind of person who would ever do you harm. As if to confirm what she was thinking, he glanced at her and smiled.

'Did you jump in that?' asked Madeleine, admiring Christian's suit.

He shook his head. 'No, we disposed of my flying suit along with my parachute. But I wore this under it. It was rather awkward to be packed like an overstuffed parcel in the plane.'

'A parcel sent from the English to France,' said Lucien, holding up his glass for a toast. '*Merci*, Monsieur Churchill.'

'But you look French,' said Madeleine, placing a bowl of the soup in front of Christian. She ran her hand over the sleeve of his suit jacket. 'This was made in France, surely? You don't get tailoring like this anywhere but Paris.'

Sabine's in-laws were from the capital. They had come to their ancestral home in the Dordogne to fulfil a dream of growing grapes and producing wines. But they were 'genteel farmers', not peasants, and Madeleine had never lost her eye for elegance.

'A French tailor in Oxford Street, London,' Christian replied. 'But the labels are all French. Before I got on the plane, one of the intelligence officers did a final check of everything. She went through my pockets to make sure I didn't have any British coins or laundromat stubs. I had to wear the suit for a week, and even sleep in it, so it didn't look too new.' He lifted his shoe and knocked the bottom of it with his fist. 'Wooden soles.'

'Well!' said Henri shaking his head. 'They think of everything. Even the fact nobody can get leather shoes, thanks to the Germans. And your French is perfect. Do you have your papers?'

Christian reached into his jacket pocket and laid his papers out on the table: his identity card, ration card, clothing and food coupons, his certificate of 'Not belonging to the Jewish race', and his exemption from compulsory work. The Brouillettes passed them to each other, murmuring their appreciation of British thoroughness.

'The British have done their research. But what do you know about the Dordogne? Do you know anything about wine-making?' Henri asked.

'I know the speciality of your vineyard is *vin paillé*, where you dry the grapes on straw mats for up to three months, and the final wine has hints of peaches and apricots.'

Henri clapped his hands with delight. 'Then I think you will pass as my nephew,' he said. 'You must excuse all my questions. But at the beginning of the war this village was helping British pilots escape out of France. Some were so careless they nearly brought us undone – speaking loudly in English outdoors, whistling at ladies, requesting British food and beverages at cafés. There was one pilot who simply refused to stay indoors. One day I woke to find he had disappeared.

Then I got a call from Marcel who owns the *bar-tabac*. "Are you missing an English pilot?" he asked me. "There is one sitting at a table now in a suit with pants and sleeves too short for him. He asked for something called 'bubble and squeak'.'"

The family burst into laughter and Christian shook his head.

'We can laugh now,' Lucien said, 'but at the time I almost shot him myself. There was a German battalion stationed in the next town and a *gendarme* who was a collaborator. He could have got us all killed.'

Christian's expression turned serious. 'I can assure you I will do all that I can to avoid that,' he said.

'We are happy to help,' Madeleine said. 'As winemakers we have many advantages. Our industry is considered "essential" to the war effort and our van has not been taken by the Germans for that reason. Before they occupied the whole of France, we had permits to cross the demarcation line.'

'Thank you,' Christian said, looking at each one in turn before his eyes settled on Sabine. 'I heard that the circuit is named after you, madame. The *Pianiste*? Britain has approved continuing to use the name.'

'My wife plays magnificently!' said Lucien. 'Tomorrow, after you have rested, she will play for you.'

'I noticed the grand piano in the front room,' said Christian.

'My mother-in-law bought it for me,' Sabine told him. 'It took four horses to bring it up the hill on a cart.'

'I needed something to make her stay for longer than a week at a time,' Madeleine said, smiling fondly at Sabine. 'So she can keep playing.'

Sabine reached for Madeleine's arm and squeezed it. She'd lost her father in the Great War and her mother had died the same year that Pierre was born. Henri and Madeleine were like second parents to her. The family was devoted to one another. Pierre could not have been born into a more harmonious household.

'I will show you to your room,' said Henri to Christian. 'Tomorrow morning you will see the magnificent view over the valley. Nobody can take you by surprise here. You are as supreme as an eagle.'

\*

Later, Sabine and Lucien lay in bed facing each other in the moonlight. Pierre was fast asleep in his cot beside them.

'I think Britain has sent us someone impressive,' Lucien said, stroking Sabine's hair. 'His manner inspires confidence. He has an air of leadership about him.'

'I like him too,' said Sabine. 'I hope the courier and wireless operator he says will follow will be just as inspiring.'

Lucien frowned. 'Are you sure you want to do this, Sabine? Perhaps you and my mother should take Pierre and go somewhere else. Leave this work to the men.'

'Where would we go? The Germans are everywhere. No, I belong by your side and I know Madeleine feels the same. Besides,' she added with a smile, 'haven't you heard that women make the best spies and saboteurs? We have the element of surprise on our side.'

\*

While waiting for his courier and wireless operator to arrive, Christian began to slowly and painstakingly expand the circuit. He started with those who had already proven their loyalty to the cause by helping the Allied airmen along the escape lines. Among the village's staunchest patriots was the mayor, who had wept openly when the Jewish families from the village were rounded up and taken away.

'I am shocked that such an outrage failed to stir the French people from their apathy,' the mayor told Christian when Sabine took him to meet him at his home. 'They complain endlessly about the British and yet sit around expecting them to do all the dangerous work in liberating us. The mayors of our neighbouring villages are all collaborators. One even refers to the Germans as "the friends of France".' The mayor's face turned dark. 'They are not our friends, Monsieur Vidal. They see France as a prostitute that they will use up and throw away when they are done with her. It makes me ashamed to be a Frenchman.'

The village priest, Father Alain, offered the church as 'a letterbox' – a place where messages could be left. 'I have never believed in fighting,' he told Christian, 'And I have wrestled many nights with my conscience about aiding sabotage activities. But each time I pray, I am given the same message – There comes a time when evil must be defeated by force.'

The baker and his wife, Josephine, were eager to do anything that would make life difficult for the Germans. Their acts of 'sabotage' so far had included daubing graffiti on German propaganda signs and adding urine to the bread they sold to collaborators. But they were aching to do something significant. Christian seemed impressed when Josephine demonstrated how she could make a copy of a key by pressing it into bread dough to form a mould. Several farmers offered their barns and cheese caves as weapons stores. Soon, Lucien was taking Christian around the countryside, looking for suitable drop sites.

Unlike professional agents such as Christian, the people of the village did not leave their normal lives behind and take up a cover identity. They went about their days as before, but now with a secret purpose. All of them, like Sabine, put their trust in Christian Vidal completely.

## CHAPTER FIFTEEN

After she and Marilyn finished their work for the day, Diana returned to the house to wash up before she went to pick up Freddy. She had hoped a bath would calm her nerves, but her mind refused to settle. She sank down into the tepid water and screwed her eyes shut. How could Casper vanish like that and not tell her where he was going? Didn't he realise that after these years apart she too might be anxious?

She heard the front door open and close and heavy footsteps make their way across the living room floor before coming to a stop. Diana's heart beat faster. She thought about the way Casper had crept around the house the previous day, as if he expected a murderer to jump out from one of the cupboards. His behaviour had not been normal. She'd never locked her doors in the past, and now she was lying vulnerable in the bath, she wondered if she should. But it was not the thought of an intruder that was making her stomach churn now. It was her husband.

She dressed and went downstairs and found Casper sitting in one of the wingback chairs, looking out at the garden.

'Hello,' she said.

He glanced at her then back at the garden. 'Hello.'

She waited for him to give her an explanation of where he'd been, but when none came she fought to keep her composure.

'It's hot today. Would you like a glass of water?'

'That would be nice. Thank you.'

Diana went to the kitchen and stopped in front of the sink. She had a strange, untethered feeling as if she were a leaf being twirled by the wind. A glint of light was shining in the window, and she caught her reflection in the glass. Her hair had sprung back into curly unruliness with the humidity and her cheeks were flushed from the fresh air. For a moment she thought she was looking at her mother. They had shared the same peachy complexion and chestnut hair, but it was in her eyes that Diana now noticed a startling similarity. She blinked and saw the same bewildered, hurt look that she had seen so often on her mother's face.

*He wasn't always like this, Diana. When he was courting me, he used to take me for drives in the country. We would swim in creeks and have picnics on the banks. He used to tease me about bunyips …*

Diana placed a bowl under the tap and ran it until the water turned cool. Then she took a glass from the cupboard and filled it to the brim. The warm afternoon air kissed her face as she tipped the unused water onto the herb garden. She stopped a moment to consider what she was feeling. Her childhood had been a lesson in walking on eggshells, where everything would be calm but you knew an outburst could happen at any moment – a ball of rage so volatile it would leave you breathless and terrified for days. She did not intend to live with that feeling now, and she would not accept that for Freddy –

not in the house she had so lovingly built with the intention of sending the ghosts of her childhood away. Her mouth set into a determined line.

She walked back into the living room and handed Casper the glass of water.

'I missed you this morning' she said, sitting down in the other armchair and doing her best to sound calm. 'You didn't tell me you were going somewhere.'

Casper didn't bat an eyelid. 'I saw that you were talking to someone, and I didn't want to disturb you.'

'Harry. Phyllis's husband.'

'I didn't recognise him.'

Diana found that hard to believe, given Harry's flamboyant dress sense, but she let the matter slide and stuck to her objective. 'Where did you go?' she asked.

His eyes drifted away from her towards the garden. 'I don't know this area well. I went on a walk to familiarise myself with it.'

Diana frowned at the strange choice of words. Casper had to 'familiarise' himself with the area? It sounded so formal, so clinical, as if he'd been on some sort of reconnaissance mission. But perhaps that was a manner of speaking left over from being in the RAF.

'There is a bush track at the bottom of the garden Freddy is keen to show you. He's been talking about the two of you walking it ever since he learned you were on your way back.'

A sad smile crept across Casper's lips. Diana's heart softened. In his expression she saw a glimmer of the husband she used to know. He'd been so excited when she had told him that she was pregnant. He hadn't expected to be away for more than a year, but as it turned out he'd missed the last six years of his young son's life. She couldn't even begin to imagine what that loss must feel like.

'I have to pick him up,' Diana said. 'Or you could do it and I'll make a start on dinner. Mrs Dalton is only a short walk away, or you can take the truck if you prefer.'

Diana realised she was pushing things along between him and Freddy, rather than letting them take their natural course. But Phyllis always told her that men needed direction from women in matters of the heart because they were otherwise clueless. Diana didn't think that could be true in Harry's case, and it certainly hadn't been the case with Casper when she'd first married him, but she'd do anything to get rid of the tense feeling in her stomach.

When Casper stood up and said he would go, Diana felt as if she'd won a victory.

'I'll draw you a map,' she offered, taking out a piece of paper from the bureau drawer. 'It's off the highway.'

'No!' said Casper, so sharply Diana flinched. 'Just tell me the directions. I'll find it.'

Diana gave him the directions then watched him head down the driveway. Why did Casper react so vehemently to her writing down the way to Mrs Dalton's house? She bit her lip. Perhaps she should have gone with him to get Freddy. It wasn't very responsible of her to put her son in the position of making awkward conversation with a father he barely knew, simply because she'd wanted to feel less uncomfortable.

\*

The dinner Diana prepared wouldn't have passed muster with Janet, but she was proud of her efforts. Following a recipe published during the war in *Australian Home and Garden,* she served stuffed eggplants and a potato salad made with beans and parsley from the garden. The mayonnaise was store-bought, but she made up for her lack of culinary finesse by laying out the Irish linen tablecloth and silver candlesticks Phyllis and Harry had given them as a wedding gift. At least the meal was an improvement on the cheese and tomato macaroni they might otherwise be having.

To Diana's surprise and delight, it was Freddy who kept the conversation flowing.

'Blossom is a Berkshire pig,' he announced as soon as they were seated at the table. 'She's actually a large breed of pig but looks small because of her short legs. Marilyn used to live on a farm. She knows all about them.'

At first Diana had been worried about Freddy's attachment to Blossom, and wondered if it had to do with him being an only child. She knew nothing about pigs when she and Marilyn saw the piglet tumble from the back of a truck bound for an abattoir. They had been buying manure from the farmer and rightfully should have returned the animal to him. But one look at the trembling creature's sad eyes and neither woman could do it. They hid her in a sack and brought her home. As soon as Freddy laid eyes on the piglet, he wanted to spend every spare moment with her.

'She won't be aggressive towards Freddy, will she?' Diana had asked Marilyn that first afternoon they'd spent building Blossom a pen and a 'piggy house'.

'Not this breed. They're fairly docile,' Marilyn assured her. Then a sly smile had crept over her face. 'Pigs are smarter than chimpanzees, you know. Which means they are more intelligent than most humans. Have you ever known a pig to start a war?'

Diana smiled at the memory of Marilyn's comment. Her wit could be acerbic at times, but also right on target.

'Blossom's such a clever girl,' Diana told Casper, passing him the salt and pepper shakers. 'Freddy has taught her some tricks. She sits on command and shakes hands. Now he and Marilyn are training her to run an obstacle course.'

For the first time since his return, Casper smiled with his whole face. His eyes lit up and his broad grin brought his expression to life. 'What a clever little pig, indeed,' he said to Freddy. 'Did you know Berkshire is a place in England? It's where Windsor Castle is situated. It's the palace the royal families have used as their residence since the eleventh century.'

Diana sat back with a sense of relief as Casper and Freddy talked about castles and moats and William the Conqueror, to whom Casper's family was remotely related. Although he'd seemed happy during the short time he'd lived in Australia, England and its history had always been an abiding passion of his.

*It will be all right*, she thought, looking from father to son. *It will just take time.*

★

After Freddy went upstairs, Diana cleaned the dishes while Casper dried them and put them away. She was grateful for the comfort that such a mundane domestic activity provided, but she was eager to talk. Where had he put that gun? She assumed somewhere safe. But she had so many other pressing questions, she wouldn't start with the gun. She'd ask about it later. Instead, she began with the question that had been plaguing her for months.

'Darling,' she asked, as she let the water out of the sink, 'why didn't you write to me from the hospital in England? Or from the ship? I was so terribly worried about you.'

She turned to him to see what he would say. But he only stared at the plate he was drying as if it held some particular fascination, and didn't say a word.

'Why was it always Peter Todd who wrote on your behalf?' she blundered on, her vexation getting the better of her. 'He was always very nice, of course. Always very civil. But I found it odd. And when I asked him why you weren't writing yourself, he never gave any explanation.'

Her words lingered, unanswered, in the silence of the kitchen. She sensed the gulf between them widen again.

'I was very ill,' Casper replied finally. 'I don't care too much to remember it. The headaches, the fevers and spasms … and the hallucinations. Peter visited me regularly, to keep my spirits up.'

He turned to her with such a cold look it sent a shiver down her spine.

'Is it really such a problem?' he asked. 'Peter is a loyal friend. His visits always cheered me up. I think his assistance is something that should be appreciated rather than questioned.'

Diana nodded, shamed like a child into silence. Something, a secret of some sort, hovered in the air between them like a dark cloud. She knew it was there, but not what to do about it.

Casper put the last dish back into the cupboard. 'I'm rather tired,' he said. 'I think I'll go to bed. Thank you for the nice dinner. I enjoyed eating fresh vegetables again.'

Diana did her best to smile when Casper pecked her on the cheek and made his way upstairs. She stood motionless in the kitchen, listening to the floorboards creak as he undressed. When all was silent, she walked into the dining room and folded the tablecloth and put the candlesticks back in the cupboard. She was about to head upstairs when her eye caught the photograph of herself and Casper in front of the Eiffel Tower. Those days had been full of laughter as they walked through the charming streets of Paris and planned their future. They had not foreseen a war that would change everything.

She thought of the time she'd first met Casper in London. She'd do anything to recapture the wonderful sense of optimism and adventure she'd felt then. But as she turned out the light, she feared it might be lost to her forever.

# CHAPTER SIXTEEN

*Westminster, London, April 1936*

Diana felt alive to everything around her when she stepped off the bus and saw Big Ben towering above her. The clock tower was taller than she had imagined it from the pictures she'd seen in books. It made her dizzy to look at its spire with the clouds moving behind it. She turned back to the street in front of her. It was congested with traffic, everything from double-decker buses and taxis to horse-drawn carts. People in shades of grey and brown tweed bustled about. The novelty of her surroundings delighted her and when she was approached by a man selling postcards, Diana bought three of Big Ben and two of the Abbey where the kings and queens of England had been crowned for centuries. There were buses and horse carts in Sydney too, and shops and streets, and people hurrying to work, yet in England, all these things were different. It seemed to her she was living in a Marjorie Sherlock painting, one that could be bright and bathed in colour one day, dark and sombre the next. The land was ancient in Australia but the buildings in Sydney sparkled in their Art Deco geometric designs and chrome finishes; in England, the buildings were grey with age, and even the windowpanes and doors seemed to be thick with layers of paint that went back hundreds of years. England was like a grand old lady – eloquent and gritty.

Diana looked at the slip of paper in her hands and headed in the direction of the pier. The sky felt lower in England than it did in Australia. It seemed to hang just above the rooftops of the buildings like a sheet on a clothesline dangling close to the ground. Charlotte, the girl she was sharing a flat with in Bloomsbury, found it amusing that Diana was so fascinated by everything, even the fog that had enveloped the city a few days after she arrived in January.

'It's a pea-souper,' Charlotte had said disdainfully. 'A killer fog'.

Diana had never seen anything like it, except perhaps the mists that lingered over the Blue Mountains on cold mornings. But those mountain mists were tinged with the sharp scent of eucalypts and fresh with nature, while the London fog was black, sinister and thick with the sulphurous smell of burning coal.

'It's extraordinary,' exclaimed Diana, who stared from the window of the bedsitter as the clouds of fog engulfed streetlamps and cars. 'It's as if it is the living embodiment of the grief the city has been feeling since the passing of the king.'

But there was no grief in the air now. It was April and the sun was shining and a soft breeze was blowing from the Thames. Diana felt jubilant and ready for anything. She normally wore flat-soled shoes and walked everywhere rather than catching buses. But today she was wearing court shoes with a slight heel and a smart knitted dress with a matching charcoal-grey coat. She was meeting Casper White, the interesting man she had encountered the previous evening at the Alliance Française. She hadn't intended to go to the lecture on 'The Medicinal Herbs of France', but Charlotte had a young man coming over for tea and Diana felt obliged to give them a few hours of privacy. The lecture, which was to be presented entirely in French, would be a chance for her to brush up on the language before she travelled to Paris the following month.

She hadn't anticipated there would be a large turnout for such a specialised topic and was surprised when she arrived at the lecture room to find it full of people of all ages. But then she hadn't yet experienced the charisma of Casper White and his ability to draw a crowd. The only seat left available was in the front row, directly in front of the speaker's lectern.

'Ladies and gentleman,' said the wispy-haired director of the Alliance Française. 'Monsieur White's lecture on air transport around Europe last spring was so popular that we are very pleased he has returned tonight to talk about the medicinal herbs of France, a subject he knows well, having had family interests in pharmaceutical products. Would you please join me in welcoming him.'

The audience clapped enthusiastically. Casper White stepped into the room from a side door and made his way to the lectern. His grey suit flattered his tall stature, and his blond hair was combed back to reveal a high forehead and green eyes. He looked the part of an English gentleman. With a surname like 'White', Diana expected he would speak French with an English accent, as had been the case with her high school French teacher. But when Casper welcomed the audience, his French was impeccably Parisian. Diana knew that because one of Aunt Shirley's best friends was from Paris, and when Diana spoke French with her, Linette constantly corrected her intonation and the way she pronounced some vowels.

As Casper described the beautiful nature reserve of the Plateau de Valensole and the history of lavender-harvesting, everyone in the room, including Diana, seemed to be hanging on his every word. Although his command of French was far superior to hers, Diana felt she understood him perfectly.

'The delightfully perfumed plant was first brought to France by traders from the Mediterranean, and it was found to adapt well to the climate of Provence, where it flourished under the dazzling sun and seduced all who came into contact with it ...'

He looked up from the lectern and their eyes met. Both smiled at the same time. Diana felt something she didn't understand shift in her. A blush ripened under her skin. She was sure his eyes had twinkled at her.

Diana stayed for the supper of tea and sandwiches afterwards and listened to the conversations around her. It seemed to her that everyone was talking about the new king and his paramour, Wallis Simpson.

'Kings have always had mistresses, but they haven't been so obvious about it. What on earth is he thinking?' said one woman to her companion, an elderly man who leaned heavily on his walking stick.

The man grimaced. 'No, she's a divorcee and an American. I don't think the new king cares much for his duties at all. I'd much prefer his brother on the throne.'

Diana lingered in the middle of the room, wondering if it would be rude to invite herself to join their conversation. But before she could open her mouth, the topic took a different turn.

'It's a dangerous tango we're dancing with the Germans,' the woman said. 'We can't seem to decide whether we are lovers or enemies. We appease them, then they appease us. But underneath it all there is a tension, a fundamental distrust.'

'There are plenty of fascists in this country,' the man replied. 'Not all of them are as obvious as the Mosley fellow, but with fascist leanings nonetheless.'

'Nazism has become a fashion,' the woman agreed. 'It does seem to be the rage among the social set.'

Diana wasn't sure that gossip or politics was what she felt like discussing and was looking about for another group to join when she felt a tap on her shoulder. She turned to see Casper White grinning at her.

'Let me guess,' he said in French. 'You are a chef and that's why the herbs of France interest you so much?'

Diana shook her head and answered him in English. 'If only you knew how appalling my cooking skills are.'

'A perfumer, then?' he asked, switching to English as well.

'No, not at all.'

'Well,' said Casper, pursing his lips. 'Am I going to be wrong again if I assume you are Australian? You're not going to tell me you're from New Zealand, are you?'

His attention triggered a delightful shiver down her spine and she laughed merrily. 'I'm Australian,' she said, 'And I enjoyed your talk very much. I finished my studies in horticulture last year. I'm here in England to study the gardens, and then I go to France to follow the trail of my favourite artist.'

Casper raised his eyebrows with interest. 'And who might that be?'

'Monet.'

'Ah,' he said. 'Claude Monet. No doubt because of his love of nature?'

Diana nodded. 'Monet's water-lily paintings are what made me fall in love with his art ...'

She was interrupted by the approach of the director of the Alliance Française. 'Excuse me, mademoiselle,' he said to Diana. 'But I must borrow Monsieur White for a moment. The Consul-General is about to leave for another engagement and I have promised to introduce them.'

Diana was disappointed that she wasn't going to be able to continue her conversation with Casper about Monet, but she nodded politely to both men. After they left, she turned and looked around the room with fresh eyes. Casper was one of those energetic personalities who infused others with his enthusiasm. She confidently approached a group of women standing by the stage and joined in their conversation about the author Agatha Christie, whose new book, *The ABC Murders*, was causing a stir among readers.

As she spoke with the others, she could see from the corner of her eye that Casper, while locked in what looked like a serious conversation with the Consul-General, kept glancing in her direction. She hoped they might be able to continue their own conversation, but time ticked on and the gathering began to disperse. She would have to hurry if she didn't want to miss her bus back to Bloomsbury. She was heading towards the door when Casper called out to her.

Her heart caught in her throat. She stopped and waited for him to approach her.

'I'm sorry,' he said. 'But I didn't get a chance to ask your name.'

'Diana Buchanan,' she replied, trying to maintain an air of composure while she was inwardly beaming. She would have been sorely disappointed to have had the evening end without speaking with him again.

Casper did not hide his delight and looked at her directly with a smile tickling the corner of his lips. 'If you like Monet, Miss Buchanan, then you must know he was fascinated by the Thames when he stayed in London. If you are free tomorrow, perhaps you will allow me to take you out on the river? I can show you some of the scenes he liked to paint.'

Diana watched as if caught in a dream as Casper took a pen and a piece of paper from his pocket and drew her a map of how to get to the pier and what number bus to take.

'I'll see you tomorrow, Miss Buchanan,' he said, not taking his eyes from hers.

When Diana caught the bus home, she settled into her seat and studied the map Casper had drawn for her. She wasn't sure if it was her imagination, but it seemed to still hold the warmth of his hands. The Houses of Parliament, the Embankment and other landmarks had been labelled in precise penmanship, but Big Ben's clock had been depicted as a smiling face.

Diana looked out the window as the bus passed Covent Garden. A billboard advertised the French play *Cyrano de*

*Bergerac*. She remembered her favourite line from the story. 'All our souls are written in our eyes.'

Diana had always loved the French language. She thought it was both beautiful and poetic. She'd received first prize for the subject at school and had continued to study it at night classes even when her hands were full with her horticultural studies. French was the language of artists and lovers. She glanced back to the map and smiled. If all those hours of study and practice had led to meeting such a captivating man, then she could not say that any of them had been wasted.

★

Diana arrived at the pier to find Casper waiting beside a river launch. He was dressed smartly in slacks, a white sweater and a navy blazer. The previous night he'd looked like an Englishman. Now he had the air of a French pleasure-seeker from the Riviera.

He spotted Diana approaching. 'Well, hello!' he said, nodding brightly. 'You didn't have any trouble finding the pier?'

'It would have been impossible with such a well-drawn map,' she told him.

He smiled and then looked about him. 'We have a slight breeze today and the sun's out. It's a perfect day for a river ride.'

The boat was about twenty feet long, with a varnished teak cabin and pristine white hull. Diana admired the brass fittings and the plate-glass windows. Then her eye travelled to the name of the boat, painted in bold black letters. *Elizabeth*. A tiny twinge of doubt pinched her. Who had the boat been named after?

'The boat belongs to my friend, Peter,' Casper said, noticing where Diana's attention had turned. 'We shared a room when we were studying at the Sorbonne. He's a terribly clever chap but falls in love at the drop of a hat. Elizabeth is his latest girlfriend. The one before that was Henny.'

Diana lifted her eyebrows. 'Don't tell me he changed the name of his boat from one girlfriend to the other?'

Casper climbed into the boat then reached out his hand to help Diana across. 'It's the third time the name of the boat has been changed, and I hope it will be the last. From what Peter has told me about her, this girl sounds special.'

There were two upholstered seats at the helm of the boat. Casper indicated for Diana to sit in the passenger one then placed himself at the wheel.

'Isn't it bad luck to rename a boat?' she asked.

Casper started the motor. 'Indeed, it is! I can't tell you what trouble it creates when Peter falls in and out of love. Renaming a boat involves a lengthy procedure if you don't wish to invite a lifetime of bad luck. First, you must thoroughly remove all instances of the boat's old identity before you can even say the new name out loud. And by remove, I mean you have to strip back any exterior lettering until absolutely nothing of it remains.'

'You can't just paint over it?'

'Certainly not!' he said with mock seriousness. 'Then after everything is removed you must perform a rechristening ceremony.'

'Just as well the same rule doesn't apply to painters,' Diana said. 'Artists redo old canvases all the time.'

Casper steered the boat towards the opposite bank, giving way to other pleasure craft, the river police and a barge with its sails billowing in the breeze. He glanced at Diana. 'We have precisely three hours before Peter wants his boat back to take Elizabeth on a picnic to Runnymede. So, you will have to tell me all about yourself in that time. It sounds like you're here on a grand tour? A woman of leisure and taste out to absorb the world?'

'Not quite "a woman of leisure",' Diana replied, watching the cloudy brown water of the river rush by. 'My Aunt Shirley and I saved hard for this trip. She's my guardian and owns an art gallery in Sydney. She believes travel enriches the mind, so she sent me to Europe before I begin my landscaping career in earnest.'

As she spoke, Casper listened attentively as if everything she said was delightful and fascinating. 'It all makes perfect sense,' he said. 'Of course you would like Monet. His love of the outdoors, his depictions of gardens and his use of light – which I believe you have more than your fair share of in Australia.' He pointed behind him. 'Look back to Westminster Palace. Do you recognise where I have brought you?'

Diana turned her head towards the North Bank. She knew that Monet had painted his views of Westminster Palace from his hotel window, and from a terrace at St Thomas's Hospital. But the spot Casper had brought her to was a close approximation.

'Did you know that Monet was enamoured of London's fogs?' Casper asked her. 'I've heard that's what he liked about London most of all.'

'There is something special about them.'

Casper pursed his lips as if trying not to laugh. 'They are ghastly and toxic.'

'What an unpatriotic thing to say,' Diana ribbed him.

'I can say it because I'm only half-English on my father's side,' he replied. 'My mother was French through and through. When I was young, we spent every summer at my grandparents' place in the south of France because my mother couldn't stand London in the heat. My father was a pharmaceutical manufacturer, so we were often in Paris as well. Tell me, don't you find the English drab and dowdy compared to the sunny Australians? Don't you think London a bit dingy? A bit Dickensian?'

'Not at all,' she protested. 'Besides, I like Charles Dickens.'

Then she saw from his smile that he was teasing her. 'The British can be a bit condescending towards those of us from the colonies,' she said, playing along with his joke. 'And a bit backward in their opinions. But other than that, I find them quite amiable.'

He let out a hearty laugh and she laughed too.

As they continued down the Thames, under the Tower Bridge and into the working section of the river with its docks and ports for overseas liners, Casper asked her questions about her life in Australia and her plans for the future. When he touched on the topic of her parents, he sensed her reticence and diplomatically turned the conversation to his own childhood. His parents, whom he'd been close to, had died when he was fourteen after contracting influenza in Italy. After that, he and his younger sister were taken in by his paternal grandfather, who had passed away the previous year.

'So, you see, we have similarities in our backgrounds,' he told her. 'Both of us have had guardians who've been very concerned with our educations.'

'What was your grandfather like?' Diana asked.

'A wonderfully brilliant man! He was a polymath and a polyglot,' explained Casper. 'He was fluent in six languages, and he had knowledge of many others. He had the most exceptional library.' He turned to Diana and smiled. 'I hope to have a library of my own one day, if I settle down.'

Diana made note of the last part of Casper's comment. She herself was deeply unsettled. She'd liked the girls at school but had not made any close friends. That's what happened when you were hiding an awful secret, something you could never tell anyone. It created a distance between yourself and others. The tragedy of her childhood made it impossible for it to be otherwise. But Casper's zest for life and natural empathy made her want to know him better.

'What do you do with yourself when you're not giving lectures at the Alliance Française or taking Australians on tours of the Thames?' she asked him.

Casper's eyes crinkled when he smiled. 'I'm a pilot, for Air France on the London–Paris route. And sometimes I fly in to Berlin.'

Diana's eyes opened wide with surprise. 'Really?'

She didn't know anybody who had been on an aeroplane let alone anyone who actually flew one. She associated air travel with movie stars and world leaders. 'How incredibly modern.'

Casper shrugged. 'Now that radio goniometry means planes

can be flown safely in all forms of visibility, it's not as daring as it once was.'

'So,' Diana said, tucking her windblown hair behind her ear, 'you like danger? What on earth would you do if you were to settle down?'

'Teach,' he answered without hesitation. He noticed the surprise on Diana's face. 'Seriously, I'd be quite happy in a roomful of schoolchildren teaching them the joys of discovering a new language. Each language you learn is like having another life, another personality. I'm English when I speak English, French when I speak French, and German when I speak German.'

Diana could see the truth in what Casper was saying. He did seem to change in some subtle way when he switched between English and French. She'd noticed it the previous night. Perhaps not a completely different person, and certainly not a 'Doctor Jekyll and Mr Hyde' transformation, but different just the same.

'So, you speak German as well?' she asked. 'As fluently as you speak French?'

'Yes. My father also did business in Germany, and it was one of my subjects at the Sorbonne.'

'Say something in German,' she said.

He thought for a moment and then said. *'Was der Löwe nicht kann, das kann der Fuchs.'*

'Which means?'

'What the lion cannot manage to do, the fox can. It is a German saying. It means that sometimes brains are better than brawn.'

Diana's mind travelled back to the conversation she'd overheard at the Alliance Française.

'What do you think of the Nazis?' she asked. 'I heard some people talking last night about fascists in Britain.'

But Casper didn't seem to have heard her. He pointed to something on the bank. 'That's the Royal Naval College,' he said.

Diana turned to look at the grand baroque buildings.

'Christopher Wren was the architect,' he told her. 'The greatest English architect of all time. And that central avenue between the buildings was not for any purpose other than to avoid obstructing Queen Mary's view of the river from her house.'

'I've read about Christopher Wren,' Diana said. 'He sounds a lot like your grandfather – an architect, astronomer, geometrician and scientist.'

'Indeed,' said Casper, looking pleased at her comment. 'I believe my grandfather would have been flattered by the comparison.'

★

When it came time to return to the pier, Diana sensed Casper was as disappointed as she was that their journey was coming to an end. The boat heaved as she was stepping onto the pier, and he grabbed her arm to stop her slipping. They looked into each other's eyes, each conscious that something wonderful was happening between them. She wasn't naïve enough to believe in love at first sight, but most certainly a bond had developed quickly between them.

Casper hesitated for a moment then said, 'If you're free tomorrow, there's a—'

'Yes!'

He chuckled. 'I haven't told you where I was intending to take you yet.'

'I don't care,' replied Diana, taking a piece of paper and pen from her purse. 'Just draw me the map. I'll be there.'

Casper took the paper and pen from her and started writing out the directions. 'Well, I'd never have guessed a young lady from Australia would be so interested in joining me to watch a pole-sitting competition. They say the champion managed to sit on a pole for forty-eight hours straight. Tomorrow night he's going for seventy-two.'

Diana grinned. 'I still don't care.'

Casper handed the paper and pen back to her. She saw he'd given her directions to a nightclub in Mayfair.

'Would you really have gone with me to a pole-sitting competition?' he asked.

At that moment, Diana felt she might go anywhere to be with Casper White, but she didn't say that. Instead, she told him in French that she would see him at the Astor Club the following evening and looked forward to it. She thanked him for the lovely ride on the river and gave him a final wave before heading back to the bus stop. As she walked, she did something that was not the custom in London. She looked directly into the faces of the people she passed and smiled at them. Her *joie de vivre* must have been contagious because a few of them even smiled back at her.

# CHAPTER SEVENTEEN

Sabine was having nightmares again. In her dream the shock of the freezing water forced the air from her lungs, as if her torso was being crushed in a vice. Brutal hands pushed her head further into the bath, slamming her skull against the hard porcelain. She dug her toes into the slippery tiles but could not get a grip. When her lungs were on the point of bursting, the Gestapo thug yanked her head up. She gasped for air, her body jerking with spasms of pain.

'Where are the weapons?' the interrogator asked. His voice sounded thin and faint through the pounding in Sabine's ears. 'Where is the wireless set? It is futile. Your fellow terrorists have already denounced you. They have told us everything.'

Despite her agony, Sabine almost laughed. If they had told him everything, there would be no need to do this to her. Forty-eight hours. She only had to hold out for forty-eight hours so Lucien, Jacqueline and the others would hear of her arrest and save themselves.

The interrogator waited for her to catch her breath, but when she remained silent, he nodded to the thug, who grabbed her by the neck and plunged her head into the water again.

This time she could not hold her breath. She inhaled and water rushed into her throat. The pain in her lungs was crushing. She felt herself fading away and lost consciousness …

*

Sabine's eyes flew open and she sat bolt upright in bed. She blinked as if surprised to find herself still living. Her hands instinctively moved around her throat and chest. Gradually her blurry vision cleared and the sight of the overstuffed armchair and tired-looking damask wallpaper reminded her that she was in a hotel room in England. It was a while since she had experienced such a vivid nightmare of her torture at the hands of the Gestapo. She'd hoped the dreams would have stopped by now. Perhaps they never would.

Rain was beating against the window. She slipped out of bed and stared out at the empty street. The lamp-post light was flickering. Rivulets of water ran down the middle of the street towards the overflowing drains. A rat appeared from a doorway across the road and scurried towards the hotel. Sabine looked away. She knew rats. She'd seen them crawling over the bodies of the babies that had been drowned after their birth at Ravensbrück. Sabine remembered the screams of the mothers and shuddered. What haunted her most was not what was inflicted on her, but on the people she cared about. She had trusted Casper White, and because of that they had trusted him too.

Sabine was drifting back to sleep when she heard the sound of soft footsteps outside her room. She sat up but did not turn on the light. Someone slipped an envelope under the door. She picked up her revolver and crept towards the sliver of light coming from the hallway. Her mind cleared and she realised she was overreacting – it was most likely a message from reception about breakfast. But as soon as she picked up the envelope, she saw that she was wrong. There was no hotel emblem on it. She swung open the door and, pressing herself against the frame, peered into the hall. But there was no one there. She closed the door again and locked it. Then she went to the window and looked out. There wasn't anybody in the street either. She called reception.

'Someone was outside my room,' she told the clerk.

'No, Mrs Allard,' the clerk answered. 'That's not possible. They would have had to come past me first and nobody is allowed on the guest floors after midnight.'

Sabine hung up the receiver and opened the envelope.

*Dear Madame Brouillette,*

*I must begin by informing you that I have been an admirer of your work for some time. There are certainly few agents – especially among the treacherous French – who have your tenacity. I have often thought that if you would just push yourself that little bit harder, you might well discover who was responsible for the collapse of the* Pianiste *circuit. It has certainly taken you some time.*

*Well! What a remarkable piece of good luck you have had in uncovering that safe in Bergerac! I must congratulate you on following your lead all the way to London!*

*I would like to encourage you by offering you some certainty. Do not entertain any idea that the Black Fox will be tried by the British government, and therefore spare his life should you corner him. There are those who were fully aware of his German sympathies and his role as a double agent, and they used it for their own purposes.*

*Before you head off to Australia, let me give you some inspiration for your mission. I think you will find this fact most interesting. Before the war and his marriage, Casper White was a pilot for Air France. His fluency in German meant he made many friends among the Lufthansa pilots. One of these introduced him to Karl Bömelburg at an air show. I believe you and your friends became well acquainted with the Gestapo in Paris, did you not?*

*Incidentally, I would look up that hand specialist that Doctor Grosvenor recommended. I've heard he is remarkably good.*

*Bon voyage et bonne chance!*

*Your friend in London*

Sabine stared at the letter. Its mocking tone rankled her. Yet she could not ignore it. Whoever had written it was aware of her mission, and his knowledge of Britain's betrayal of the French Resistance hinted that he was with MI6. Whoever he was, and whatever his purpose, he seemed pleased at the idea that she had succeeded in identifying the Black Fox. So what did that mean?

But the part of the letter that disturbed her most was about Karl Bömelburg. She thought that Christian Vidal – or rather Casper White – had been turned by the Germans into a double agent, and that his initial entry as an SOE agent into France had been sincere. A sick feeling gripped her stomach. If what the writer of the letter claimed was true, Casper White arrived in France with the intention of destroying the *Pianiste* circuit. From the day she and Lucien picked him up from the field and he'd sat in the kitchen eating Madeleine's soup and drinking Henri's wine, he'd had their downfall in his sights.

# CHAPTER EIGHTEEN

To Diana's dismay, Casper started a pattern of leaving the house in the morning and not returning until the evening. She watched his behaviour with ever-increasing bewilderment. She'd endured years of worry while he had been away. The dread of him being killed had constantly weighed on her mind. Sometimes she had been able to push it down – when she was playing with Freddy or working on a garden plan – but as soon as she stopped it would resurface. She had expected the heaviness in the pit of her stomach to go away when he returned, but now that feeling pursued her even more doggedly than before, like a salesman peddling something she didn't want.

Where did he go for all those hours? Was he spending them alone – or seeing someone? An old RAF mate, perhaps? If he didn't want to go back to teaching and was looking for some other work, why not simply tell her that?

She avoided listening to conversations about returned soldiers, but they seemed to be everywhere – at the grocers, at the hardware shop, even at the farm where Diana bought manure for the garden. Everyone had a story. Everyone seemed to know a man who'd found it impossible to adjust to peaceful life at home and had gone looking for conflict somewhere else in the world, or a man who had started drinking when he'd never so much as taken a sip of beer before the war, or a man who was beating his wife to within an inch of her life.

Janet, who must have noticed her brother wasn't quite himself, sent Diana cuttings from women's magazines full of self-righteous advice:

*It is the wife's job to make things right again. Society now calls on her to give up work outside the home and make it her full-time job to restore the man who has seen death and destruction on a grand scale. She must no more speak of her dreams and aspirations. It is her turn to sacrifice …*

It was so hypocritical it made Diana's blood boil. Janet had sacrificed nothing. After all the patience Diana had shown, now even more was expected from her? She was like a rag that had been wrung dry. She had nothing more to give.

One day, when she simply could not stand it anymore, Diana followed Casper. She saw him disappearing up the street when she was returning from seeing Freddy off to school. At first a feeling of helplessness came over her, but then she rallied. Didn't she have a right to know where he was going? Perhaps if she knew, she could better help him. She crossed to the other side of the street and pursued him, using the street trees as cover.

Casper reached the train station, and Diana waited by a postbox until he'd bought his ticket and gone down the stairs to the platform. Then she bought a ticket too from the change in her pocket and mingled with a group of women wearing sunhats and carrying beach bags under their arms.

The train arrived and Casper got into the first carriage. Diana stepped into the carriage behind, placing herself near the door between the two cars so she could keep her eye on him. But her task proved difficult because the track had some sharp curves and the train bounced violently as it took them. It seemed to her that Casper spent most of the trip dozing. When the train rattled over the Harbour Bridge, she wondered how far they would be going and whether he took the same route every day.

Casper got up from his seat at Wynyard Station and Diana had just enough time to slip off the train after him before the conductor blew the whistle for departure. She kept her eye on him as he was swept up the stairs with the crowd of smartly dressed men and women on their way to work. She panicked when she stepped out onto the concourse and couldn't see him, but then spotted him again at the George Street exit. She had to dodge people as she followed him up to Martin Place. He didn't look back once, but instead continued past the GPO and the cenotaph with the bronze life-size figures of a sailor and a soldier standing either side of it and the inscription that read: *To Our Glorious Dead*.

Casper continued through Hyde Park, striding past a young woman kissing a man in the khaki uniform of the Australian army. But he was far too young to be a returned serviceman. Diana guessed he must have been one of the guards who kept watch over the Anzac Memorial. *So many monuments to the dead*, Diana thought, *and yet we keep going to war*.

Casper reached William Street, and Diana found it difficult to keep her cover. She walked behind people, her head lowered in case Casper turned around. They'd been walking for over half an hour when Casper approached Kings Cross, the red-light district of Sydney. A lump formed in her throat. Was he going to a brothel? Was he going to a visit a prostitute to keep away his demons? But Casper passed by the Cross and headed down the hill to Rushcutters Bay, where he and Diana had lived with Aunt Shirley before the war.

When Casper reached the park where they had spent so much time, Diana felt a prick in her heart. She remembered lying on a picnic blanket – with Casper next to her and newborn Freddy between them – when the weather was hot and the apartment was stifling. She recalled sitting with him and staring out at the water the day before he left for England. The park held so many memories. Was that why he came here? To remind himself of who he used to be?

Casper sat down on the low stone wall that curved around the bay and dangled his feet over the water. Diana hid behind a fig tree and sat down on one of its enormous surface roots. Her feet were hot and blistered, and she slipped off her shoes. She peeked at Casper, who was staring out at the water, watching the yachts moored there bobbing in the gentle waves. She'd lived in Rushcutters Bay for almost twenty years. The sound of the yachts' riggings clinking in the breeze was as familiar to her as the salty smell of the harbour. She rested her head against the tree trunk and squeezed her eyes shut. Had she made a terrible mistake building the house in Killara? Should she have waited until Casper had returned? When he was overseas and thought of home, he would not have pictured the cottage in Killara. He would have had in his mind Aunt Shirley's quirky Art Deco apartment with its parquetry flooring and frosted glass doors. Although the floors creaked and the wonky windows didn't always close snugly, it had been a place of laughter and joy.

'Diana.'

She looked up to see Casper standing next to her.

'You aren't very discreet.'

She stood up and brushed off her dress. 'You knew I was following you? Why would you play such a game with me?'

'I'd prefer it that you didn't play such a game with me.'

Diana felt a flash of anger. 'You can't just wander off every morning without a word. Whatever reason you need to get away from me, I think I deserve to know.'

She wanted to say more but her voice caught in her throat. In truth, she had a more painful question. *Did you return home and discover that you didn't love me anymore?* But she couldn't find the words. She could not bear that she'd told Freddy a story that might not come true – a picture where he would have both his mother and father in his life. She saw the hurt in her son's eyes when Casper did none of the things she'd promised he would do, like teaching him to play cricket or building him a billycart. She could go on if Casper was honest with her and told her that he no longer loved her, but she couldn't bear it if he did not love their son.

She pleaded with him with her eyes, but he looked away at the water, thinking something over. Then he spoke in a voice that sounded very far away. 'When I see the questions written on your face, and the expectation on Freddy's, I don't know what to do. I've seen things … *done* things … you can't even begin to imagine. I'm not the man you're looking for when you search my face. He's not there anymore.'

Diana sensed his agitation. 'Casper, you're still my husband and I can see something is troubling you. If you won't talk to me about it, you're shutting me out of your life. You're turning us into acquaintances rather than partners.'

He grabbed her hands so tightly her fingers went numb with the pressure. It frightened her but she didn't want to push him away.

'No!' he said. His voice had an edge to it. 'What I want is for you to promise that you will never ask me.' He released her hands. 'Go back home, Diana,' he said. 'I'll do my best by you and Freddy. I won't go back to teaching but I will find something to do. Maybe in time we can try again. But I need you to understand that it will be different. Until then, leave me alone, please.'

He walked away from her, back along the path to Bayswater Road. Diana stood watching him, her stomach churning. She thought back to the cenotaph in Martin Place and the memorial in Hyde Park. Perhaps the war that had taken the lives of hundreds of thousands of men had taken her husband too.

# CHAPTER NINETEEN

Sabine stepped out of the kitchen, coffee pot in hand, and stopped in her tracks. The position Robert had taken at the window reminded her of the way Lucien would stand in that same spot, staring out at the rooftops and mulling over a legal case. Lucien had been shorter in stature and very Parisian in appearance, with a square face and light brown hair. His blue eyes were kind and intelligent and when his serious expression changed to a smile, it lit up the room. Robert was tall and broody-looking, with dark eyes like an Italian. They were different men, but with the same sense of moral justice. Sabine put the coffee pot down on the table.

'You'll have to excuse my poor hospitality skills. I haven't had a visitor in a while,' she said. 'It's chicory coffee. Do you mind?'

He shook his head. 'I am a poor guest. I wanted to bring you flowers, but there were none to be found.'

They sat down and Sabine poured the coffee. Robert's eyes travelled over the photographs of Lucien and Pierre on the sideboard, but he made no comment on them.

'I can get you as far as Laos on a government flight,' he told her. 'From there you can sail to Sydney.'

Sabine nodded. She had not told him about the letter that had been slipped under her hotel door in London. It was clear someone in MI6 was watching her. If Robert knew that, he would tell her not to go. Not only because it was dangerous, but because this other person might inform the Australian secret service of her mission and cause an incident. After all, she was undertaking covert activities in a friendly country. Australia had been an ally of France in both world wars. But she felt the letter-writer had his own grievance against the Black Fox and, rather than hinder her, he was keen for her to find him. She assumed it was a 'he' but kept her mind open to the possibility it was a woman.

Robert took a sip of the coffee. 'Now,' he said, his tone grave, 'I will give you my best advice. Casper White's wife and child will be your surveillance targets. You must *never* develop sympathy for your targets. Their wellbeing is not your concern. You may have to befriend them but you must always keep in mind that their sole use to you is to reach your kill target, Casper White. Your success will probably ruin their lives. You are not to think of that. You are only to think of your mission. Understand?'

'Yes,' said Sabine, not taking her eyes from his face.

'Once you leave France I can't help you,' he continued. 'We can't communicate. You will be on your own.'

'I understand.'

Robert clasped his hands and leaned across the table towards her. 'There is another question you must ask of yourself,' he said. 'Why did you trust Christian Vidal – or rather Casper White – in the first place? It wasn't simply because he was with

SOE. Think harder than that. How did he win your trust and the trust of the others? What deception did he use?'

Sabine stared at her coffee, searching for the answer in the dark places in her mind.

'Hold the answer in your head during your mission,' Robert said. 'Because whatever method he used that first time, he may use it to fool you again.'

Sabine raised her eyes to his. She doubted Casper White could convince her of anything, let alone his innocence. 'He killed German soldiers. He worked against the enemy. Wasn't that enough to believe him?'

Robert shrugged. 'If they were expendable, he could have got away with it. This is a man of extreme cunning. I gather that's how he earned his codename.'

★

After they finished their coffee, Robert stood up to leave. Sabine walked him to the door. He bent towards her, and she expected him to give her the usual kisses on the cheeks. Instead, he pulled her tightly against him and kissed her passionately on the mouth. She was so taken aback by his action she wasn't aware whether she had kissed him back or not when he released her.

'Good luck!' he said, his eyes sweeping her face one more time before he turned and rushed into the hallway.

Breathless, Sabine ran after him to the top of the stairs. But Robert did not turn back.

'*Au revoir, madame,*' she heard him call to Madame Rouzard before he left the building.

Sabine returned to her apartment and closed the door behind her. She went to the same window where Robert had been standing a short while before. Her heart was beating thunderously in her chest. Her mouth still tingled from the force of his kiss. She'd thought the obstacle of their pasts would stand like a wall between them, but Robert had smashed through it and given vent to his feelings. His passion had felt like love and violence combined. It had stirred something in her, the way lightning charges the rain and electrifies the air. But she would resist it. Her mind had to be totally on her mission. There was a possibility that she might not come back, and she didn't want Robert waiting for her. All sorts of things could go wrong. Casper White was a dangerous man.

She closed her eyes and thought about Robert's question. Why had she trusted Casper White so wholeheartedly? Her mind reached back to those first few months after he came to France. Then the answer dawned on her. She had trusted him without reservation not because he had killed Germans, but because he had risked his own life to save someone dear to her.

# CHAPTER TWENTY

*The Dordogne, June 1943*

Sabine was driving the van along an old secondary road and stopped at a crossroads to get her bearings. The increased enemy presence in the countryside these days made her fear being strafed on the road by German planes, as had happened to her and Lucien when they had tried to escape south with baby Pierre before Paris was taken. As if responding to her anxious thoughts, two German soldiers stepped out of the forest and were then followed by the rest of the patrol. She found herself surrounded. Fear rippled through her. In the past, the Germans would not have bothered with a woman driver, but with the escalation of Resistance activity in the region, they were being more careful.

The soldiers did not train their rifles on her. They weren't suspicious … *yet*.

The sergeant moved towards her window. 'Papers, please.'

She handed them to him, keeping her expression neutral. She was not carrying weapons or food for the maquis this time. But she was hiding in her underwear secret messages for Jacqueline to transmit to London, and in her bag, wrapped in a pair of silk pyjamas, was a new radio crystal and a bottle of *Je Reviens*. The crystal had come with one of the drops, and Sabine had bought the perfume on the black market when she'd made a trip to Paris, delivering messages to another Resistance group.

A farm wagon approached the crossroads, and the sergeant became more interested in what might be hidden under that hay than in Sabine. He gave her papers a cursory glance and waved her on. She didn't breathe again until the patrol was a good distance behind her. She glanced in the rear-view mirror and saw the soldiers prodding the hay with their bayonets. She was relieved when they found nothing and let the farmer go. During the early days of the war, hay wagons had been an effective way of moving Allied airmen between safe houses to help them escape. With the help of a funeral director and his hearse, Sabine had even managed to transport a pilot in a coffin over the demarcation line, all the way playing the part of the weeping widow.

Sabine brought the van to a stop in a grove of trees, where it would be hidden from view. She picked up the bag and walked the rest of the way to the farm.

The farmer's wife, Rosita, was feeding the chickens in the yard when Sabine appeared.

'There is a patrol at the crossroads,' Sabine told her. 'I'll warn Jacqueline.'

Rosita went into the kitchen to throw green leaves on the fire. The white smoke would warn any Resistance members in the area that a patrol was close by. Sabine knocked on the barn's side door four times. Jacqueline opened it cautiously then, seeing Sabine, quickly ushered her inside.

'I've just finished receiving. Help me pack up.'

Perched on a fruit crate sat the cumbersome wireless set that Jaqueline used to transmit the circuit's messages to London and to receive instructions from headquarters. While Sabine took down the long aerial which was looped over the stalls and roof beams, Jacqueline packed the transmitter in a metal box. Together they lifted the drinking trough and placed it to the side to reveal a secret door underneath. Jacqueline put the transmitter in the space under the door and then the two women lifted the trough back into position. Using water from some dairy pails, they filled it, although the horse and cow that usually occupied the barn were out in a field now that Jacqueline was using the building for transmissions. Anything that would add a degree of difficulty to discovering the radio set was worth it.

'There is a patrol in the area,' Sabine said. 'I came dangerously close to being searched.'

She opened her bag and passed Jacqueline the crystal, perfume and pyjamas.

'Thanks,' Jacqueline said, taking them and hiding them under a loose board in the floor. 'I'm fully immersed in my role as Musetta Arpin, the farm maid,' she said, screwing up her nose. 'I'm even starting to smell like a cow. The perfume and the pyjamas are for some sanity, and so I can imagine being Jacqueline again when this war is finally over.'

Sabine smiled. It was hard to reconcile seeing her friend in a faded cotton dress and apron. Her hair was unadorned and her shoes muddy. She did not resemble the chic young woman Sabine had studied with at the Conservatoire. Then, Jacqueline had lived with her parents in a grand apartment on the Champs-Élysées and had clothes designed for her by Elsa Schiaparelli and Madeleine Vionnet.

Jacqueline opened a battered tool box and produced two glasses and a bottle of wine.

'Did you see a detection van with the patrol?' she asked, pouring the wine into the glasses and handing one to Sabine.

'No, but the towns are crawling with them. They are getting more accurate too. Still, that patrol has made me nervous. We'll have to move you again soon. You've spent too long here.'

'A hotel with a bath would be nice,' said Jacqueline, sitting down on the crate and pointing to a milking stool for Sabine.

Her friend was joking but Sabine could see the strain in her eyes.

'Fancy having all those months of training and preparation in Britain,' said Jacqueline, cradling her glass, 'and then parachuting straight into the clutches of the Germans. How could that happen?'

Sabine grimaced. The fate of the two captured agents who were supposed to work with Christian was not a pleasant one to contemplate. 'We don't know,' she said. 'Careless talk. Money. A traitor. Christian thinks the reception group that was supposed to meet them may not have been as cautious as ours.'

They lapsed into silence. Then Sabine wrinkled her nose. 'It does smell like manure in here. You are made of stronger stuff than I am. But then they say the Palace of Versailles used to smell the same way.'

Jacqueline smiled and her dimples came to life again. 'I wonder what my grandfather would say if he could see me now – a wireless operator on a special war mission.'

'I imagine as a naval officer he would be very proud knowing that teaching you Morse code when you were a child had led to such great things.'

Jacqueline sighed. 'I don't think SOE much fancies me. London takes so long to reply. The other day it was over two hours.'

Sabine did not like the sound of that. She would have to speak to Christian. She had seen the wireless operator from the nearby circuit who had helped train Jacqueline. He was the only operator in the area at the time and was having to be on air for more than ten minutes per transmission, with the German detection vans constantly circling the town. The first time Christian and Sabine contacted him, he was sitting in his underwear in a boiling hot room at the back of a bar, his colt pistol by his side and his cyanide tablet perched on his lips in case the Germans sprang in on him.

'They don't know you,' Sabine told Jacqueline. 'You were trained in the field. That can't make them comfortable, but they have no right to be cavalier with your life.'

'It's because I'm French. They think we are naturally untrustworthy.'

'You transmit at twenty-two words a minute. The operator who was meant to join us did twelve. They should consider themselves lucky!'

Jacqueline topped up their glasses. 'I'd go insane if it wasn't for you, Sabine,' she said. 'For twenty minutes of my day I do something meaningful to help rid the world of the Nazis. The rest of the time I'm a sitting duck. My only contact with the outside is you. I don't even talk to the farmer's wife. Should we be caught, the less we both know about each other, the better.'

Sabine stretched out her legs. 'If I were a handsome man, then you would have another twenty minutes in the day to occupy yourself each time I visited.'

A slow smile broke out over Jacqueline's face. 'My darling, Sabine, you are naïve – or else Lucien is an exceptional lover. Two minutes is more the norm than twenty.'

'Really?' Sabine cocked her eyebrow. 'I promise you that after the war, you shall have as many two-minute lovers as you please. But doesn't the farmer have any sons that take your fancy? Sometimes it's the quiet ones ...'

The rumble of a vehicle entering the yard cut her short. Jacqueline's face froze. The engine shut off. Sabine edged her way to the window and peered out. Relief flooded her when she saw it was Florent, the farmer, returning from the market in his truck. Jacqueline sidled up to her. They gripped each other's hands and stayed in that position for a long time before either of them found the strength to speak.

'Do you know what's worse than the fear?' asked Jacqueline, her eyes turning dark.

'What?'

'The waiting,' she said. 'It's the not knowing exactly when and how you are going to die.'

★

When Sabine returned to her in-laws' farm, Madeleine told her that Christian and Lucien were waiting for her in the cellar. She took the stairs down into the labyrinthine underground cave and passed the racks where Henri had placed his new wines. He had labelled them deceptively and covered them with layers of dust. If the Germans raided his cellar they wouldn't find the best vintages, which were hidden behind a false wall, but these newer 'dummy' wines instead. Henri had even gone to the trouble of collecting spiders to cover the brickwork with their webs and disguise the wall's recent construction. There wasn't much Henri didn't think of when it came to preserving his collection. Lucien had inherited his father's penchant for attention to detail.

Sabine found her husband and Christian at the back of the cellar, sitting together at a wooden table and sharing a bottle of wine.

'There will be an airdrop on the fifteenth,' Sabine told them, conveying the message she had received from Jacqueline. 'We are to find a suitable field and report back to London.'

Christian nodded and indicated for Sabine to take a chair. 'There is something I have neglected to do, and I must do it now,' he said, taking out a revolver and placing it on the table. 'British agents receive extensive training. Now you are acting as my courier, I can't have you out in the field without the ability to protect yourself.' He pushed the gun towards her. 'I'll teach you all the skills I can, and I need you to be fit and strong.'

Sabine picked up the gun and felt its weightiness. She looked from Lucien to Christian and nodded. The Germans were everywhere now, rooting out the Resistance. It would be naïve of her to think she would never find herself in a life or death situation.

★

They couldn't fire real ammunition, as that would draw attention. To make up for that disadvantage, Christian left nothing else to chance when he put Sabine and Lucien through their daily drills. He did not allow them to hesitate or waste time adopting fancy stances.

'There won't be time for that,' he told them. 'Using a weapon at close quarters is a matter of split seconds.'

He trained them to point their revolvers at moving targets, always varying the distances and conditions, and firing two shots, in case the first missed.

'Two shots anywhere from the crotch to the head and you have put your opponent out of action.'

He trained them in poor light and sometimes in total darkness. He drilled them alongside the local maquis for attacks and counterattacks. He told Sabine to run rather than walk whenever she could. French women did not run as a rule, and so her fitness training had to be subtle. She would sprint to the washing line and back again. She pursued Henri and Lucien in the van when they set off for the market, pretending she had forgotten to tell them something. She chased Pierre around the house, which he thought was tremendous fun, and he would burst into peals of laughter. Even when Christian wasn't with them, Sabine and Lucien practised. After the dinner plates had been cleared from the table, they placed their revolvers in front of themselves and tested who was quickest to grab theirs and point it at their opponent. It was usually Sabine who won.

After they mastered their revolvers, Christian taught them how to use machine guns and other weapons. The first time Sabine picked up a grenade she was struck by its deadly potential. When it exploded it would send shrapnel into the air to claim the maximum number of casualties, but with its funny pineapple shape it could have been a child's toy. For a moment her mind flashed back to the apartment in Paris. She was sitting at her piano teaching Yves Dupuis to play Grieg's 'Arietta'. She could hear the melody in her head – sweet and clear, yet sad at the same time. Sabine had loved all her students, even the difficult and conceited ones like Yves. She'd had such a passion for humanity, and such a love of beauty. Who was that woman in her memory? she wondered. And who was this woman now, standing in a barn and holding a grenade?

★

One morning, Sabine and Christian were alone in the kitchen together. She was cooking an omelette for Pierre. Christian watched her for a while then said, 'Lucien's greatest strength is his ability to plan. He thinks calmly through all the details. He is an excellent tactician. But what you have, Sabine, is instinct. That can't be taught. I wouldn't want to meet you in a dark alley.'

Sabine smiled. 'I'll take that as a compliment, whether you meant it that way or not. I think instinct comes from motherhood. In my mind, I'm not defending myself but my family and friends. I imagine someone is trying to hurt my precious son. When I think of that, I'm capable of killing anyone.'

A faraway look came to Christian's eyes. 'That's what gets me through too. When bleak thoughts start to crowd in on me, I imagine my wife and son waiting at home for me.'

'So, you are married and a father?' asked Sabine, slipping the omelette onto a plate and cutting it up into small pieces.

Christian had told them so little about himself. That was part of his training in covert operations, she supposed, to reveal nothing of his normal life. He hadn't even told Sabine and Lucien his real name, although their daily training was creating a bond of friendship between them.

'I joined the RAF but was transferred to special operations before I saw any action. My first mission was in Marseille. That went well, so they sent me back here. My wife has no idea where I am.'

Sabine looked at him for a long moment. She remembered he had once told her that an agent's second mission into France was more dangerous than the first and it was not a requirement to accept it. She thought Christian represented the best, and most unselfish, of humanity.

He noticed her studying him and became self-conscious. Perhaps he realised he was tired and was talking more than he should.

'I'd better get going,' he said, rising from his chair.

Sabine took a rose from the vase on the table and handed it to him. 'Thank you for coming here,' she said. 'I want you to know that we appreciate it.'

★

The landing spot they chose for the next full moon was on a field not far from the farm where Jacqueline was stationed. In the moonlight, Sabine could see the shadowy trees around them. As well as Christian and Lucien, there were a handful of members of the local maquis. Two were French soldiers who had refused to surrender after the armistice, one was a veteran from the Great War, and the rest were simple farmers. After training alongside them, she realised what they were up against when facing the Germans. Their foes were well-equipped, had been drilled for years in preparation for this war, and were heavily indoctrinated in their belief that they had the right to invade countries and kill their citizens.

The hum of an aircraft sounded. *It's a Halifax*, Sabine said to herself. Christian had taught her to listen carefully for the differences between Allied and enemy aircraft. These days more British Lancasters were flying over France, and to Sabine their engines had a lower, more gentlemanly, pitch than the howling Nazi bombers. The reception committee moved into position with their torches to guide the plane for the drop. There was a quick flash of light from the undercarriage and soon parachutes were blossoming in the sky. The group moved quickly to collect the boxes and hide the parachutes. Sabine noticed how much more effectively they worked now Christian was with them. They had just loaded one truck when Sabine turned and saw a plume of white smoke coming from the direction of the farmhouse.

'Germans!' she said.

The group began to move faster. A figure burst out from the trees. Sabine and Lucien pulled out their revolvers but then recognised it was the farmer, Florent.

'The Germans are at the farm!' he said, panting. 'They have Rosita and the woman. They are searching the barn and farmhouse.'

Sabine's blood turned cold. 'Jacqueline!' She turned to Christian. 'We must do something!'

'How many are there?' Christian asked Florent.

'I didn't see more than ten,' he replied.

'Ten!' said Jacques, the leader of the maquis. 'We can't. It's suicide.' He looked at Florent. 'I'm sorry.'

Sabine started towards the farm as if she could tear Jacqueline away from the Germans with her bare hands. Christian grabbed her and pulled her back.

'I believe we can rescue the women,' he told the group. 'We have the element of surprise on our side if we act swiftly. I'm confident in your training. Be aggressive and we will succeed.'

There was something about Christian, some deep inner quality that commanded respect. As soon as he announced they were going to take action, everyone snapped into motion as quickly as if they were performing one of his training drills. While the maquis members, along with Sabine and Lucien, equipped themselves with their weapons, Christian gave his orders.

'You know your teams,' he told them. 'Sabine, you will go with Arnaud and attack the barn. Lucien will go with Romain's team and take the house.'

After that there was no more time for talking. Christian had drilled them all relentlessly, only now it was the real thing for Sabine and Lucien. As the group moved swiftly across the field towards the farmhouse, disconnected thoughts ran through

Sabine's head. She tried to remember if she had kissed Pierre goodbye. She wondered what Madeleine and Henri would tell him about his parents if they were killed. Then she recalled what Jacqueline had said about not knowing when and how you were going to die. She told herself to stop thinking about death, and to focus only on victory.

Christian stopped behind a low wall and indicated for the others to crouch down. From that position they had a view of the farmyard. A guard was standing over Jacqueline and Rosita. The women were on their knees with their hands behind their heads. From inside the farmhouse and barn came the sounds of furniture being overturned and dishes breaking. The wireless set was well-hidden. If the Germans didn't find anything, what would they do? Torture the women? Shoot them anyway? In that moment something clicked in Sabine. Her fear subsided and her heartbeat slowed. All she could think about was that she had to kill those Germans before they hurt Jacqueline.

The teams moved themselves into position silently. Sabine and Arnaud crept in the direction of the barn. Sabine took cover behind a barrel. From there she had a clear view through the side window and saw the broad back of a German soldier pulling objects from a cupboard. She aimed her rifle at him and quickly glanced over her shoulder. Arnaud was behind a tree. He nodded. He would give cover while she attacked.

Suddenly a burst of fire from Christian's machine gun rattled in the night air. Almost simultaneously Jacques' machine gun sounded. Sabine pulled the trigger of her gun and shot the German in the back. He collapsed and she wasted no time in running low towards the barn. She was in the dark, but she felt as though she had a spotlight on her and at any moment gunfire would tear her to shreds. She reached the side of the barn unscathed and pressed herself against it. Then she moved along the side of it, her back turned to the wall. She took a grenade out of its pouch and held it against her chest.

Shouts and gunfire were all around her. Sabine had no idea who was alive or dead, but she had one task and she kept her mind on it. Lifting her head slightly, she cast a brief glance through the side window. Four Germans were there, all of them now taking positions to return fire into the courtyard. She pulled the pin and threw the grenade inside. Then she crouched low, keeping her rifle ready for other threats. There was an explosion and a cloud of smoke. Piercing screams sounded from inside the barn as if hell had opened its doors. More machine-gun fire rang out, then there was silence. Sabine knew she should move but her chest was tight. She struggled to draw a full breath. Suddenly, strong arms lifted her off the ground. At first she thought she had been captured, but then she raised her eyes and saw it was Arnaud who was holding her upright.

'We must get moving,' he said.

They crept together around the side of the barn. Sabine could not bear to look at the carnage. She was aware of the body of a German hanging out one of the farmhouse windows and the dead guard lying in the dirt. But then she saw Lucien coming around the side of the house uninjured and that Jacqueline and Rosita were unharmed. The Germans were dead and by some miracle the maquis members had survived the attack. She gave a sigh of relief and knew that all the risk had been worth it.

'Good,' said Christian, stepping towards her and giving her a slap on the back. 'Now you and Jacqueline get the wireless. Hide it. Then go back to the farm. I'll meet you there later.'

He walked away to give instructions to the others. There were going to be consequences, Sabine knew that. The farm would be burned down as a reprisal and the farmer and Rosita would have to join the maquis in the woods now. She and Lucien might have to leave Pierre with Madeleine and Henri and go into hiding themselves. This was war, and she understood it much better now. The sacrifices were enormous. But tonight they had experienced a victory. Christian had risked his own life and inspired confidence in the people he led. He had proved that they would not always be defeated.

Jaqueline ran towards her, and they embraced.

'You came,' Jacqueline said breathlessly. 'I thought I was dead, but you came.'

Sabine grabbed Jacqueline's arm and they hurried to the barn. She averted her gaze from the dead Germans and together the two women pulled aside the water trough and retrieved the wireless set. It was an awkward and heavy thing to carry, but there was no time to expect chivalry and they would have to manage it on their own. As they made their way into the woods, Sabine looked back over her shoulder at the farmhouse. The men were moving on too. She could see Christian and Lucien disappearing among the trees. She was a true Resistance fighter now and Christian was her leader. She would do anything he asked of her, she was sure of it.

CHAPTER TWENTY-ONE

To ease her distress over the change in Casper, Diana threw herself into her work with gusto. Harry's office was in the same Italian palazzo–style building as the offices of *Australian Home and Garden* in the city. Diana took a moment to study its façade as if she was gazing at a wonder of the world. She'd always appreciated that the building was attractive, with its Florentine cornices and tall, arched windows, but now she looked at it with a more astute eye. If she was going to work with an architect, she needed to see buildings in a new way.

Harry's chirpy receptionist looked like a Hollywood starlet, with her perfectly waved hair and figure-hugging dress. 'Mr Scott is expecting you but he's on the telephone right now, Mrs White.' She held out a bowl of lollies. 'Would you like a Mintie while you wait?'

Confectionery had been rationed during the war and, as Minties were Australian, it would have been unpatriotic not to accept one in support of economic recovery. Diana unwrapped the lolly from the waxed paper and sucked on it while admiring the display of photographs of buildings that Harry had designed. In among the government offices and hotels was a private residence that caught her eye. It was a house in an L-shape with large windows that would make the most of Australia's long hours of sunlight.

'Diana! Good morning!'

She turned to see Harry heading towards her. He looked as neat as the hedgerows in an English garden. There was not a hair out of place on his head and his trimmed eyebrows were a work of art in symmetry.

'I'm sorry to have kept you waiting,' Harry told her, kissing her cheek. 'Please come to the drafting room.' Then turning to his receptionist he said, 'Two coffees, *Americano*, Miss Barker, please.'

Harry whistled Frank Sinatra's 'Coffee Song' as he led Diana past a group of draftsmen, two of whom were women. Diana already knew that Harry was egalitarian and always hired on ability rather than sex. Still, she was surprised to see that his desk was in the middle of the room and not in a private office.

'Your office is so modern,' Diana commented as he offered her a seat.

'Open plan is the way of the future,' he told her, placing a folder of sketches on the desk. He pulled out one of the drawings and showed it to her. Instead of separate rooms for living and dining, Harry had designed one space that could be adapted for multiple purposes by installing sliding doors.

'I wanted to avoid too many pokey rooms,' he explained. 'The sunroom can be closed off and become an extra bedroom or study if needed, and the side entrance means space isn't wasted with a passageway.'

'So simple yet so clever,' said Diana.

'The houses are to be built on a tight budget of twelve hundred and fifty pounds each,' Harry explained. 'I've included designs for some brick houses, but they will bump the cost up another two hundred and fifty pounds. It's not getting the bricks that's the challenge, it's the shortage of bricklayers.'

'These designs are attractive,' Diana said. 'They are charming and functional. I really should have consulted you when I was building my own house. I might not have needed that second floor.'

'You've done a fine job with your cottage,' Harry assured her. 'But the houses in this proposal must be as streamlined as possible. By creating outlooks onto the gardens and bushland, the houses won't make people feel they are living in a cramped space.'

'Nature is soothing to the soul,' Diana said.

Harry smiled. 'I couldn't agree more. In some of the outer suburbs, the signs of poor planning are starting to show. If you cut down every tree to clear the land, the residents and councils won't have the funds to replant them. If you build schools and parks on busy roads, children will be in danger of being run down. The government is in a hurry to get families out of the city slums and into the west, but if they don't provide enough attractive green spaces, they'll simply be creating a different sort of slum.'

Diana felt a ripple of excitement run through her. She was aware of the shortage of housing in Sydney. She'd read about flats that were meant for four people being partitioned off with plywood and now accommodating fourteen. There were people sleeping on balconies or in bathtubs, and in some places the landings were turned into makeshift bedrooms at night.

She and Harry would be helping to alleviate the problem and make slums a thing of the past.

'I can't thank you enough for joining me in this,' Harry told her.

'I think it is I who should be thanking you,' she replied. 'This is the opportunity of a lifetime.'

★

An hour later, Diana was in the birdcage elevator making her way to the *Australian House and Garden* office two floors up. Phyllis's throaty voice could be heard out in the hallway.

'We can't put the Brasso and the Silvo advertisements side by side,' she was saying. 'And Diana doesn't want the Flit advertisement near her article on winter vegetables.'

'Why not?' Diana heard Shelley, the sub-editor, protest. 'They're now making it with DDT. That stuff kills everything.'

Diana stood in the doorway of Phyllis's office and looked inside. The room was elegant chaos. A vase of white tulips sat on the desk along with copies of *Australian Home and Garden*, swags of fabrics, carpet samples, invitations to swanky parties, and products from advertisers, including everything from paint to lawnmower oil.

'Ants have a role in the garden, Shelley,' Diana said. 'And so do ladybirds and caterpillars. No caterpillars, no butterflies. Also, I don't believe a poison that "kills everything" should be anywhere near plants you intend to eat.'

Phyllis turned in Diana's direction and smiled. She was wearing a smart nipped-waist suit and puffing on a cigarette in a holder. She was in every way opposite to the grey-haired matronly stereotype of a woman in her fifty-fifth year. Always snappily dressed and with a trim figure, she had the inexhaustible energy of an adolescent girl.

'Ah, Diana the defender of forests and insects has arrived!' Phyllis said with a laugh. Then turning to Shelley, she said, 'Could you excuse us for a minute, darling?'

Phyllis moved a pile of layout pages from a chair so Diana could sit down. 'So, you've been to see Harry, have you?' she asked. She returned to her desk and began fossicking around in her drawer for something. 'No doubt he's won you over with his charm.' She found what she was looking for and waved a slip of paper at Diana. 'Harry's not the only person who can get you work,' she said. 'I met the most wonderful man at Marcia Manning's party last night. His name is Laurie Spencer. *Professor* Laurie Spencer. He's British, although he has been living in Melbourne for the past few years. He's just moved up here and bought a house – a beautiful Federation, as he described it. But it has no garden at all apparently, only lawn. He asked if I knew anyone who could create a garden for the house. I told him I had exactly the right person for the job.' She leaned over and handed Diana the slip of paper. 'I thought you could write a feature article about it for the magazine. Readers love "ugly duckling" transformations, especially when the owner of the property is a rather dashing bachelor.'

'So, he's "dashing", is he?' Diana said, shaking her head at her irrepressible editor. She looked at the slip of paper. Professor Spencer's house was in Wollstonecraft, not too far a drive from her home. She was going to be busy preparing for Harry's proposal, but she needed an income above what she earned for her gardening articles, as it would be months before she'd be paid for the project.

'I'll write to Professor Spencer and let him know I'm available,' Diana said. 'Have you seen Harry's designs, by the way? They are beautiful. Anybody living in one of his houses would be privileged indeed.'

Phyllis cocked an eyebrow. 'I don't want to discourage what you and Harry want to do but I've worked at this magazine for over thirty years, as editor for the past ten. And I can tell you there is no limit to bad taste. I've tried to instil in my readers an appreciation for things that are beautifully crafted, and for excellent design. I've encouraged them to save for the good and the lasting instead of the cheap and nasty. But I have been accused of being elitist and a snob. The house and garden editor of the *Daily Reporter* even said I was behind the times when I took her to task over her article on disposable tableware as the way of the future.' Phyllis leaned back in her chair and sighed. 'What I've learned is that most people wouldn't recognise good design if it hit them on the head. Do you think you and Harry are creating a beautiful suburb for … *the right sort of people?*'

Diana bristled. 'That does sound elitist, Phyllis, and rather horrid! Every person recognises beauty when they see it, no matter if they have money or not. Why do we make people live in ugly suburbs when what Harry is proposing is affordable?'

Phyllis shrugged. 'What I'm trying to tell you, my dear, is that beauty is in the eye of the beholder. You and Harry might discover there are quite a few people who think a bare block of land with a boxy house on it that's identical to their neighbour's boxy house is living the life of Riley.'

Diana grimaced. She didn't want to think that Phyllis could be right. How many times had she had to convince one of her own clients that a single gum tree wasn't going to result in a bushfire, or that native birds visiting the garden was a good thing? What hurt her most was when people failed to appreciate the beauty of the natural world and wantonly destroyed it.

'Well, before you get all caught up in Harry's project, make sure you write to Professor Spencer,' Phyllis said sternly. 'I told him I was seeing you today and I don't want another magazine snapping up the opportunity.'

Diana chuckled. Phyllis was extremely good at getting what she wanted, when she wanted it. She was sure that once her editor had set her sights on Harry, the man hadn't stood a chance.

★

Diana was still thinking about Phyllis with amusement when she stepped back out onto the street and began walking towards the laneway where she'd parked her truck. She turned a corner and a chill ran up her spine. Her heart thumped in her chest and her nerve endings sprang to life. The street was quiet and empty, but she sensed someone was watching her. She turned to look behind her. There was a shopkeeper leaning against a doorway, talking to a newspaper seller, but neither of them was paying her any attention. Diana couldn't see anyone looking out of the windows of the buildings around her. Yet the uncomfortable feeling persisted.

*You're imagining things*, she told herself, but increased her pace anyway. She reached her truck and yanked open the door before jumping inside. She glanced in the mirror again before starting the engine. Her hands on the wheel were trembling. She was sure she'd sensed a dark force around her, as if whoever had been watching her had been doing so with malice.

## CHAPTER TWENTY-TWO

Professor Spencer's home was a stately red-brick Federation mansion with freshly painted timber verandas and not a shingle out of place. Diana marvelled at it as she turned her truck into the gravelled driveway. It stood on half an acre of land that was nothing but lawn with razor-sharp edging around the paths and driveway. It must have had a garden once, yet it had been denuded not only of trees, but of every plant and flowerbed. Diana wondered why the previous owner would have done such a thing. A Federation house without a garden was like a naked woman put glaringly on display. The house needed some sense of allure and mystery to accentuate its charms.

Even the turning circle where she brought her truck to a stop had been deprived of its centrepiece. There should have been a circular flower bed with a specimen tree, or at least a small fountain. But all that remained was a low pedestal with an empty urn on it. She stepped out of the truck and glared at it as if personally affronted by this display of poor taste. Then, as she glanced around the grounds, she reminded herself that at least there was nothing to clear and that she could have a fresh slate with which to work. She turned to the tiled steps of the house, half-expecting that a butler and a bevy of staff might appear, but those days had gone with the Great War. *And thank God too*, thought Diana, otherwise she might have been expected to use the servants' entry. She wasn't wearing her overalls but a tailored dress that she hoped would convey the message that she was a serious landscape designer.

Suddenly, rousing opera music came from one of the open upstairs windows. The melody sounded familiar, but she couldn't place it. Trumpet blasts and rolling drums gave the impression of a grand display of spectacle with lavish processionals, choral numbers and special effects. When she had corresponded with Professor Spencer about meeting with him, his replies had been polite but brief. She'd imagined a quiet man in a cardigan and carpet slippers. This taste in dramatic music was unexpected.

She hoisted her folder of garden designs higher under her arm and pressed the doorbell, as curious now about her client as she was about the garden. A few minutes later a woman wearing an apron, whom Diana took to be the housekeeper, opened the door.

'I'm Diana White,' she told the woman. 'I have an appointment with Professor Spencer.'

The housekeeper led her to a drawing room and asked her to wait. The room was pleasantly cool, with a soft breeze drifting through the leadlight windows. It was mostly unfurnished, apart from two brown leather chairs by the fireplace. A picture leaning against the wall caught Diana's eye. Short thick strokes of paint captured the essence of a woman in Edwardian dress strolling over a bridge at twilight. It was in the impressionist style, but the artist's name in the bottom right-hand corner was unfamiliar to her: *P. Schwartz*.

'Do you like it?' a voice behind her asked. 'It has just arrived, and I haven't decided whether to hang it or not.'

She turned to see a man whose appearance matched his posh English accent. He was dressed in a checked shirt and tie and pressed trousers, and his hair was short at the back and sides with the length left on the top and brushed back. Long face, long neck, long body – Diana could picture him on a rowing team or taking a sprint around a track between lectures. His face, while not particularly young or handsome, was attractive, with a high, slightly furrowed forehead and golden eyes. But his most charming feature was his sweet, almost boyish smile.

'It goes with the age of the house,' she said. 'But sometimes it's better to have art that contradicts it. That's an observation from a design point of view, of course. In the end it's really a question of whether you like it enough to be looking at it every day.'

He stepped beside her so they were both facing the painting. The professor smelled of wool and leather-bound books. 'My area of expertise is the antiquities,' he said, with the air of a serious academic, 'and classical art movements that followed. Most of what I like can only be found in museums. Still, I don't believe one should limit oneself and I try to appreciate art of all eras and styles.' He turned to her and reached out his hand. 'I'm very pleased to make your acquaintance, Mrs White. When I met Mrs Scott, she gave such glowing reports of you that I was quite convinced by the end of the evening you were the only person who could fix the problem of my non-existent garden.'

'It's a pleasure to meet you too, Professor Spencer,' said Diana, noting that he seemed to have already made up his mind that she would do the work. 'Indeed, it is a mystery why the previous owner cleared the land. But sometimes people think not having a garden, or having a very sparse one, gives the house an air of grandeur or power. If that was what they wanted, they should have bought a Hollywood Spanish villa and not a Federation home.'

'Indeed, the house without a garden makes this place look like a mental institution,' he said. 'All it needs is the ubiquitous palm tree and people sitting around in white gowns to complete the picture.'

Diana flinched, unsettled by the unpleasant image. When he saw that he'd disturbed her, Professor Spencer's face turned crimson and he immediately apologised. 'I'm very sorry. I hope I didn't offend you, Mrs White. We British sometimes have a rather droll sense of humour.'

'I know,' she said, smiling to assure him that no offence had been taken. 'My husband is half-English and half-French. It took me a while to get used to his British love of the absurd, combined with his deadly serious views on what wine to serve with dinner.'

Professor Spencer's hearty laugh belied his shy manner. 'Oh dear, what a difficult combination!'

'My sister-in-law too,' Diana said. 'She came here at the same time my husband did, only she doesn't have a sense of humour at all.'

Professor Spencer's eyes twinkled. 'You certainly have your hands full! I make a solemn promise to show you only the good side of the English!' He nodded towards a pair of French doors. 'Shall we take a stroll outside?'

Diana followed the professor out into the garden. She could see what Phyllis had found so charming in him. He had that upper-class dash and wit that Phyllis would fall head over heels for, but also seemed so gentle. Diana only hoped that wonderful Harry wasn't going to be pushed aside for a new conquest.

'My mother was a gardening enthusiast,' Professor Spencer said when they reached the front gate and looked back at the house. 'I didn't inherit her green thumb, but I certainly appreciate the difference a beautiful garden can make.'

Diana opened her sketchpad and drew the outline of the roof. It was a gorgeously crafted house with terracotta chimney pots and Marseille-patterned roof tiles. There were even dragon gargoyles – not as popular with Australians as they were with Europeans, but a point of interest just the same. She would take her measurements later, but right now she wanted to get a sense of what would work well with the proportions of the house. The sun was so hot it was stinging her skin and she could feel a drip of perspiration run down her neck. She glanced at the professor's translucent English complexion and thought he wouldn't last ten minutes in the Australian sun. He would certainly want shade. Unfortunately, shade trees did not grow overnight, which was why she got so annoyed with people who cut them down without careful consideration.

'I'd like to put a eucalyptus tree near your gate,' she told him. 'It would give an immediate sense of place for the house. But it won't offer shade for five to ten years, and I'm not sure how long you intend to stay.'

Professor Spencer rubbed his chin. 'Now there's a question. It comes down to whether I want quick gratification or to leave a legacy for the future. As a man who appreciates art left to us from ancient times, I say let's plant for a legacy.'

He might have been Ali Baba declaring 'open sesame' to claim the treasures hidden in the magical cave for the effect his words had on Diana. Most of her clients were either businesspeople who had a lot of money and no time to think about their garden and so left everything to her to decide, or people who thought they knew a lot about gardening and treated her like a servant to do their bidding. But every so often there were people like Harry Scott – and she hoped Professor Spencer – who understood her sense of mission, her tremendous desire to create beauty that would endure.

'I'm pleased to hear you say that,' she said. 'But I'm saddened that you don't intend to stay. A garden isn't like putting down tiles or papering a wall, something that gives you instant satisfaction. A garden constantly changes and reveals its beauty over seasons and time. It's a living thing. It would be a shame for you not to see it.'

He raised his eyebrows. 'I didn't mean to imply that I don't intend to stay. It's merely that I approach the future with a sense of uncertainty.' His face clouded over. 'I guess we're all that way after the war. We can make plans for tomorrow but tomorrow may never come. Things often don't turn out the way we expect them to.'

She sensed the sadness behind his words. Whatever he had suffered, she felt she understood. Things with Casper were not turning out the way she had hoped, and her future felt very uncertain.

Noticing she was quiet, Professor Spencer changed the subject. 'It's very bland', he said, nodding towards the pathway. 'Is there something you can do to fix it?'

Diana was glad to turn her attention away from the war. 'You can see from the way the path curves, rather than going in a straight line, that the original intention was for specimen trees and flower beds to be planted in the bends. That way, guests would experience a pleasurable journey of discovery on their way to the front door.'

'What a charming idea!' said Professor Spencer. 'It's building anticipation rather than shooting like a bullet straight for the front door.'

'Exactly!' Diana laughed, enjoying his vivid imagery.

They moved down the path, stopping every so often so she could make notes about the trees she would use to create the best effects of light and shade for each season. When they came to the rear of the house, she stopped short. On the other side of the tennis court was a Victorian glasshouse with a domed roof. The wrought-iron frame was fashioned in Art Nouveau swirls. Jasmine had already taken over one side of it, and the whole structure, as ruined as it was, would be beautiful in spring.

'It's divine,' she said. 'It confirms my suspicion that the house was originally built with an elaborate garden in mind.'

Professor Spencer looked as pleased as Punch. 'I thought it might impress you,' he said, guiding Diana down the sandstone steps to the glasshouse's door. It was stiff and he put his shoulder into it. Once inside, Diana looked around with a sense of wonder. There were no plants left, save two large urns overgrown with ivy. The vines trailed across the tiled floor and up the sides of the glasshouse before disappearing through a broken pane in the roof.

'You could imagine that we have opened the door and discovered Sleeping Beauty,' whispered Professor Spencer.

Diana liked the atmosphere of make-believe he evoked. 'It's wonderful you have a glasshouse,' she told him. 'I don't use a lot of hybridised plants in my gardens, but it could be a lovely place to grow vegetables and seedlings.'

'I was thinking it might be a rather nice spot to take tea,' said Professor Spencer.

Diana walked to the end of the glasshouse and back. 'We could certainly convert it into a fernery.' She glanced at Professor Spencer and noticed his face was turning red and beads of sweat were forming on his upper lip. 'You wouldn't leave it as a glasshouse if that's what you want to use it for; it would be too hot,' she told him.

Professor Spencer took a handkerchief from his pocket and patted his face. 'Yes, I see what you mean,' he said. 'Why don't we return to the house for a cool drink? I'm afraid my English constitution is not up to this humidity.'

★

While sipping Pimm's garnished with cucumber and strawberries, Diana showed Professor Spencer some of the plans she'd made for other Federation houses. But rather than look at the lists of plants, he studied her watercolour plans with an appraising eye.

'My word, you are an artist, aren't you?' he said.

'Not quite Michelangelo, but I do enjoy it.'

He shook his head. 'Don't be so humble, Mrs White. What appears to be simple can take years to perfect. You can't have any hesitancy when you use a medium like this. You can't control and manipulate outcomes with watercolours.' He turned to her and smiled. 'I think your art says a lot about your personality. You're a woman who knows her own mind.'

Diana felt a prickle of delight run over her. She didn't mind the flattery one bit. 'If you don't mind me asking, how did you end up in Australia? Phyllis said you've recently moved up from Melbourne?'

Professor Spencer put down his glass. 'It's been a strange twist of fate. I set out on a lecture tour of Australia and New Zealand in 1939, intending to be away for only a few months. But then war was declared, and I ended up stranded here.'

Diana was on the verge of asking him why he hadn't returned to help in the war effort, as Casper had, but then realised the question might cause offence. There were many reasons people had for not joining the armed forces, and she didn't know him well enough to ask such a personal question. To her surprise, he offered his explanation freely.

'I couldn't join the armed services due to a congenital deformity of my spine,' he explained. 'I took a job serving at the Ministry of Defence in Melbourne. Then my London house was blown up in the Blitz and I decided that was as good a sign as any to begin my life again in a new country.'

'Oh,' said Diana, frowning. 'I'm sorry about your house. That's awful.'

Professor Spencer shrugged. 'Don't be. Things have worked out well for me. I got an offer from the University of Sydney to set up art history as a serious academic subject in their art department. They agreed to give me a free rein, something that would never happen at Oxford, so I moved up here.'

'What were you doing at the Ministry of Defence?' asked Diana.

'I worked in the records department. When it comes to meticulous cataloguing, you can't go past an art historian.'

Diana took a sip of her drink. 'I've often thought being an art historian might be a bit like being a detective. You have to be able to piece together all those clues.'

Professor Spencer let out one of his hearty laughs. 'Quite right. I was the child who always asked for a new jigsaw puzzle for my birthday.'

Diana felt so relaxed in the professor's company that she could have stayed with him the rest of the day and discussed art and gardens. But she had so much to do and assumed that he did too.

'It's been a delightful morning, Professor Spencer,' she said, rising, 'but I mustn't take up any more of your time. I'll need a couple of weeks to draw up a plan and quote. I can do the garden in sections or all at once, whichever you prefer.'

'All at once, I'd say,' replied Professor Spencer, standing up. 'I'm rather excited about the prospect.'

She took his hand and shook it. 'I am too.'

★

Diana turned her truck in the direction of the Harbour Bridge. She had the finished illustrations for her article on groundcovers and wanted to drop them off to Phyllis before she started on the plans for Professor Spencer's garden. She could have waited a day or two, but she was keen to discuss the professor with Phyllis. He was certainly a man who left an impression on a woman.

To her disappointment, Phyllis was out at a function, so Diana left her illustrations with Shelley. She had no sooner stepped back out on the street when she heard a woman call out to her.

'Diana!'

She looked up to see her former neighbour from Rushcutters Bay, Grace Simpson, waving and smiling as she ran towards her.

'Goodness me, it's been ages,' said Grace, tucking her thick mane of red hair behind her ears. 'I've been meaning to call you ever since you moved to Killara, but something always comes up. Has it really been a year?'

'A bit over,' said Diana. 'How are the girls?'

'Annie started high school this year,' said Grace. 'Can you believe it? Lucy is her normal mischievous self. And Freddy? Is he enjoying his new school?'

'It took him a little while to settle in but now he loves it.'

A slight knot formed in the middle of Grace's brow. Diana was aware of a note of tension between them. Grace's English husband, Howard, had joined the RAF along with Casper. But Howard had flown troops and equipment and had not been in frontline combat. Diana had not seen a death notice in the newspaper, but the lists were not always accurate.

'And Howard? How is he?' she asked, carefully broaching the subject.

'He came back last September. And Casper? Back home all in one piece?'

Diana nodded and Grace's shoulders visibly relaxed. She indicated a milk bar on the corner of the street. 'Come on, let's have a natter. We have so much to catch up on.'

*

The two women took a table near the window. The milk bar was new and everywhere Diana looked her reflection shone back at her from the polished chrome surfaces. The waitress took their orders for chocolate milkshakes, and Grace turned to Diana.

'We must really get together again with the boys,' she said. 'Those days before the war were so much fun. Do you remember how Casper and Howard were always up to some prank or another?'

'I do,' Diana said. 'I don't think either of us could ever open our umbrellas without being showered in confetti.'

Grace's mouth stretched into a laugh. 'Casper always had such an extraordinary memory for names and dates, didn't he?' she said. 'I wonder if that came from his pilot training.'

Diana nodded. She had to write everything down in a diary, but Casper could pluck dates and times directly from his brain.

'And I remember how he used to read spy novels whenever we went to the beach,' continued Grace. 'Howard was always ribbing him. Here was this serious intellectual, who was a walking encyclopaedia, spending his recreation time reading potboilers.'

'Well, not quite as bad as "potboilers",' said Diana. 'But he certainly did enjoy popular fiction.'

A picture of her husband on their honeymoon popped into her head. They were travelling on the train to Berlin. The conductor had needed to move Casper's bag and discovered it was extraordinarily heavy. 'Have you got rocks in there?' he'd asked Casper. To which Casper replied, 'No, just my favourite Joseph Conrad novels.'

'Is everything all right, Diana?' Grace asked her. 'You look sad. Have I said something wrong?'

Diana shifted in her seat. 'How is Howard *really*?' she asked.

Grace's cheerful smile dropped. She glanced at her hands. 'He came back very thin, but I soon fattened him up on lamb chops and fried chicken, all his favourites.' She played with her wedding ring a moment then frowned and added, 'He was very withdrawn at first. He always wanted to spend time by himself. The kids got on his nerves.'

Diana hadn't meant to start this conversation. Would it be disloyal to Casper to talk to Grace about his strange behaviour? She was desperate to know if how he was acting was … *normal* for a man back from the war?

Sensing she had a sympathetic listener, Grace continued. 'You know how small our flat is … but it couldn't have been noisier than sleeping in barracks with other airmen and having orders barked at him. So, one day I confronted Howard about how he was treating us.'

Diana leaned forward with interest. 'What did he say?'

'He apologised immediately,' Grace told her. 'He said that the flying had been nerve-racking – the responsibility for all those men. It was terrible to know that half of them wouldn't be returning and still have to take them. He told me he found it impossible to relax now that he was at home.'

Diana and Grace fell silent, feeling the weight that must have been on Howard's shoulders as if they were bearing it too.

'How is he now?' Diana asked after a while.

Grace grimaced. 'He's much better. I could tell something was playing on his mind. He was having nightmares and muttering in his sleep. So, I woke him up one night and asked him what was distressing him.'

Diana's whole body stiffened but she urged Grace on with her eyes.

'He told me about a surprise attack on his base,' Grace said, twisting her hands. 'A lot of men were killed. They had to …' she faltered, her lips trembling. 'He had to … his best mate … well, they had to collect what was left of him and put it in a bag.'

Diana gasped. She thought back to her conversation with Casper at Rushcutters Bay Park. *I've seen things … done things … you can't even begin to imagine.* If Howard, in his comparatively safe role, had witnessed such horror, what had Casper seen?

'He spoke to you about this?' she asked Grace. 'He actually told you? Casper has completely shut me out. He won't discuss what happened to him at all.'

Grace's eyes flickered with concern. 'A man can't keep such terrible experiences to himself. He needs to be able to confide in his wife.'

'Yes,' agreed Diana. 'A man should be able to tell his wife everything.'

She felt like a failure. Why wasn't Casper able to confide in her the way Howard had spoken to Grace? She remembered what it had been like living next door to the Simpson family. Grace seemed to be forever baking. The children were always neat with freshly ironed clothes and perfectly plaited hair. Perhaps Grace had been able to get Howard to talk to her simply because she was a better wife.

'Anyway,' said Grace, leaning back in her seat, 'as awful as it was to hear, it's much better that he confided in me. Nothing destroys a man or a marriage faster than war. I know that from my own father. He never got over his experiences in the Great War, and my mother and sisters, well, we all paid for it. I know the booklet says not to ask, but it just isn't right.'

'What booklet are you talking about?' Diana asked her.

'The booklet the RAF sent to all the wives and families. You know, about how to help your returned airman back into civilian life. You didn't receive one?'

Diana shook her head. 'Casper was in hospital for a very long time in England getting over typhus. It's all very mysterious. Nobody told me anything. I certainly never received any booklet.'

Concern washed over Grace's face. 'I thought you said Casper was all right?'

Diana couldn't stop herself now. 'It's not just the war he won't talk about, he barely talks to me at all. Sometimes I feel that he can't even see me … that he's looking somewhere else.' She bit her lip. 'Grace, do you think you could ask Howard to find out something for me? Could he speak with some of his old RAF contacts and find out what happened to Casper's squadron? If there was anything in particular that might have affected him?'

'Of course,' Grace replied, reaching out and patting Diana's hand. 'You know how fond Howard and I are of you both.'

The waitress brought their milkshakes and Diana and Grace turned their conversation away from the war to the neighbours who were still living in the apartment block in Rushcutters Bay.

'Does Mr Hartcher still play his radio so loudly that everyone in the building knows the cricket score?' Diana asked.

Grace laughed. 'He does. And funny Mrs Wattle wanted us all to dig an air raid shelter in the common garden.'

'Oh please tell me that didn't happen. Not after how long it took me to grow the frangipani trees!'

'No, we all staunchly defended your trees.'

When it was time to leave, Grace hugged Diana. 'Try not to worry. Sometimes it can take a long time to readjust. I'll see what Howard can find out and get back to you.'

# CHAPTER TWENTY-THREE

The art supply store on Castlereagh Street to Diana was like a toy shop to children. The endless selection of pencils, paints and brushes made her almost giddy with excitement when she entered. Professor Spencer's admiration of her garden plans had spurred her on to make sure her designs for him were especially well-presented. She wandered down the paint aisle, thrilled to see that the German-made watercolours that had been impossible to obtain during the war were back in stock, and was heading towards the pencil section when the shop bell tinkled and in came a middle-aged man pushing a younger man in a wheelchair. The young man's legs were missing below the hip. Amputees had become a common sight in Sydney since the soldiers had started returning. Diana exchanged smiles with the men as they passed her, but she noticed that the other customer in the store – a slender girl with her hair curled into enormous victory rolls – frowned at them.

'I couldn't get my son to study anything before the war,' the father told the clerk while he and his son waited for their purchases to be rung up. 'Now he's mastering the violin and painting like da Vinci. He's going to start a bookkeeping course next week.'

After the men left, the young woman went to the counter and said to the clerk, 'You would think getting his legs blown off was the best thing that ever happened to him.'

The clerk sniggered. 'Bookkeeping? Who's going to employ him? He looks like half a man.'

Diana, who normally scuttled away from public arguments like a startled crab, felt fury rise in her veins. She strode up to the counter. 'They are trying to make the best of a terrible situation,' she told the pair. 'I think it's admirable. What would you have the poor boy do? Spend the rest of his life staring at a wall?'

The young woman raised her eyebrows, not in the least bit shamed by Diana's rebuke. 'I can't see the point in people deluding themselves,' she said.

Diana trembled with rage. 'Men like him sacrificed everything to stop terrible regimes killing people in Europe and Asia, and you have the gall to deride him? He didn't get to go to university, or get married, or have children. He's lost years of his life as well as his legs!'

The store clerk lowered his eyes, chastised. But the young woman glared at Diana.

'What did any of that achieve? Japan blown to smithereens! Germany in ruins!' The victory rolls bobbed on her head as she spoke. 'If you're worried about racial supremacists, perhaps you should look to Britain and France and how they treat their colonies. What about the beatings and tortures of those who resist the oppression there? What about Australia and its White Australia policy …?'

*

Diana rushed along the street, feeling like a fool for having fled the art supply store and not having stood her ground. But she'd felt confused. Weren't the men and women who'd gone to war heroes and heroines? That's what Casper had been hailed as when he sailed off to fight the Nazis in Europe. He and Diana had sacrificed time they could have spent together, and Freddy had gone through his formative years without his father. And what for? So they could be mocked by a skinny girl sporting ridiculous victory rolls?

She stopped outside a bookstore to catch her breath. A feeling of utter pity for Casper overcame her. What horrors had he suffered? Maybe he would never be the same again. She glanced in the store window and saw a display of books by Eric Ambler, the British author who wrote gripping spy stories. Diana's eyes drifted over the titles and settled on *Epitaph for a Spy*. She didn't recall it having been published in Australia before Casper left for the war. Perhaps discovering his old pleasures would help restore Casper to himself. She pushed open the door and went inside.

# CHAPTER TWENTY-FOUR

Sydney was a shock to Sabine. She stared at it from the window of the taxi. It wasn't only the bright sunshine and the humid heat but the colours. Paris was a city of muted shades of grey, taupe and Prussian blue. Sydney, on the other hand, seemed to sparkle like its harbour. The women on the street looked like tropical flowers, dressed up in summer shades of canary yellow, sky blue and crimson. Food seemed plentiful too. Sabine gasped with incredulity as the taxi passed dozens of street vendors whose wagons were laden with fruit and vegetables. There were no lines of weary customers in front of any of them. Through the window of one shop, she saw tinned goods piled from the floor to the ceiling. Cars and buses were everywhere, with hardly a bicycle in sight. It was as if the war hadn't touched the city at all.

The taxi driver, a bleary-eyed man with an accent she could barely understand, informed her otherwise. 'Plenty of food,' he told her, 'but not enough manpower and places to live. We've got shortages of nurses, shortages of railway workers, shortages of houses. My wife and I and our four children are living in a converted stable for the grand price of a pound a week.'

Sabine had heard about the housing shortage from the passengers on the liner she had sailed on from Laos to Sydney. A doctor returning from war service had offered to wire ahead to book a hotel room for her until she got her bearings.

'I'm afraid I won't be able to find anything fancy,' he apologised. 'Those who can afford it are living in hotels and guest houses when they can't find permanent accommodation.'

Sabine stared at the expansive park full of palm trees and ponds that they passed on their way to the hotel. She rubbed her thumb over her chin. The accommodation issue was going to be a problem. She needed something secluded for her purposes. A hotel or a guest house would not do. She closed her eyes and exhaustion weighed her down as if someone had injected lead into her veins. If Casper White had been somewhere in England, the operation would have been far simpler. She and Robert could have done the surveillance and finished the mission in a week. Now, so far away from Paris, so far away from Robert and in an unfamiliar country, she wondered if she had bitten off more than she could chew. Robert had warned her that pursuing Casper White single-handedly was going to be difficult, but she was determined to see it through. The first thing Robert had said to her when she joined his department was: *There is no job in the world so lonely as ours.* She understood now how true that was.

'The government is talking about bringing thousands of displaced persons from Europe to fill the labour gap,' the taxi driver continued. He glanced at Sabine then back to the road. 'I don't mind if they're nice French ladies like you, clean and polite and able to speak English. But the other ones!' He shook his head ruefully. 'We don't want any Jews. I don't see why Australia should take the rubbish nobody else wants.'

Sabine's jaw clenched. The faces of the starving women and children who had shared her misery at Ravensbrück flashed before her. All those people sent to their deaths for no other reason than their race. The people the driver referred to as 'rubbish' were ordinary people like him. People who never hurt anyone or wished anything bad on anyone. No, that wasn't quite correct. The Jewish people Sabine had known in Paris were anything but ordinary. They were extraordinary musicians, doctors, academics – all highly educated and cultured people. After what had happened to them, she'd expected that the few who survived would be welcomed anywhere with wide-open arms. But clearly that wasn't the case. Even a bleary-eyed taxi driver barely able to articulate his words looked down on them. Sabine's heart felt like a stone. His attitude drove home how doomed her quest for justice was, and yet she knew she would never give up.

\*

The telephone book in the room where Sabine was staying was sticky and smelled like beer. Everything in the hotel had a malty fragrance about it, as if the sheets and towels had been washed in the Tooth's Lager she had seen advertised in the newspaper she had bought. *The beer of choice for the sophisticated lady.* She opened the window to let in some fresh air, and a sea breeze rustled the newspaper and blew her notes onto the lurid green carpet. It was unlucky that 'White' seemed to be one of the most common surnames in Australia, after 'Smith', 'Jones' and 'Brown'. The number of entries with 'C.J.' as the first and middle initials spanned several pages, but only a few of them included the wife's initials as well and that narrowed the choice of 'C.J. & D. White' to fewer than twenty. She would start with them. Unfolding the map she had bought, she surveyed the city. Somewhere in it was Casper White and she *would* find him.

She wrote down the addresses then stopped for a moment and glanced out the window. It occurred to her that she was using many of the skills Casper had taught her to now hunt him down.

*Why did you trust him?* Robert had asked her.

*Because he was noble. Because I thought he was the finest human being I had ever met*, she said to herself.

But he had been cold-blooded too. It wasn't until much later that she learned how ruthless Casper White could be. It was in May 1944, the day before she and Casper were arrested by the Gestapo. The order for the elimination of a civilian had supposedly come from SOE, but had it? Sabine never questioned Casper on anything. Now that she was an experienced agent she would have asked for some proof, but back then she had simply done whatever he asked of her. The face of a blonde woman with china-doll blue eyes emerged from the mists of her past. What had her name been? Then Sabine recalled it clearly. The woman she and Casper had murdered was a young secretary named Gisèle Babin.

# CHAPTER TWENTY-FIVE

*The Dordogne, May 1944*

Sabine could feel the throbbing in her temple as she waited with Lucien for Christian, who had been in Paris, to come and see them. Lucien got up several times to go to the window. She sensed death was drawing near but refused to believe it. She was exhausted yet alive. It was the war that was coming to an end, not her life, she told herself. The *Pianiste* circuit was still active and much larger than it had been even a few months ago. It was like a river with tributaries now, smaller sub-circuits feeding into it, creating a powerful force. The long-awaited Allied invasion of France was imminent. They would advance quickly; she was sure of it. Jacqueline, also a remarkable survivor, was receiving messages for increased supply drops so the circuit could step up their niggling small-scale attacks to more daring ones. In the last month, Christian had formed a small commando team, including Sabine and Lucien and select maquisards, and they had blown up railway lines, fuel reservoirs and powerlines. But each activity came at a cost. The Germans – desperate, vengeful, aware they were losing now – were more brutal than ever. In a nearby village, sixteen people – including three children – suspected of supplying food to the maquis had been locked in a barn and burned alive.

'The Gestapo know your identities,' Christian told them when he arrived. 'It's impossible for us to continue as before. We have to break up the configuration.'

He placed the new papers he had obtained on the table. They were remarkably good forgeries, Sabine thought. Christian must have made a useful contact in Paris. The Germans were now searching everyone, women included. But if her papers looked genuine that made her more confident she could bluff her way out of a tricky situation. Her name would now be Hélène, after her favourite student, and she would pose as Christian's wife when he met with the leaders of the various sub-circuits to coordinate their activities. Lucien was to go with Jacqueline to Sarlat, where they would pose as a couple visiting relatives. Henri and Madeleine were to take Pierre to a safe house in a nearby village.

★

On the morning they were due to leave, Sabine and Lucien stood in the vegetable garden holding hands. The cord that bound them to each other was being stretched tight.

'It's nearly over,' said Lucien, looking into her eyes. 'We only have to stay strong a while longer.'

His face had more creases than it did at the start of the war. She wanted to reach out and trace every one of them with her finger so she would never forget. They were both thin too. The farm hadn't been requisitioned and there was still enough food for them, but it was nervous energy that was burning up their flesh.

'Take care of yourself,' she told him. 'I don't want to be a widow.'

Lucien took her in his arms. 'We must do what we have to and then come back for Pierre.' He pressed his cheek to hers. 'If something should happen to either of us, then the one remaining must finish this thing.'

As close as the end was, Sabine suspected the longest months were ahead. There would be even more bloodshed, more danger and more suffering. She pressed herself against Lucien so tightly she could feel his heart beating against hers.

'We must go,' said Christian behind them. His tone was kind but urgent. The baker was waiting for them with his van. He would drive Sabine and Christian halfway to Bergerac. Then they would take the train the rest of the way.

Lucien turned and embraced Christian. 'Look after my wife,' he said, patting his back. 'I trust you like a brother.'

'I'll guard her with my life,' Christian promised.

Madeleine came out of the house holding Pierre's hand. A swell of emotion overwhelmed Sabine as she embraced her son. She looked into his sweet face. He had changed so much over the course of the war and now at five years of age she longed to be having conversations with him and sharing with him the beauty of music. Instead they were being torn from each other. But Lucien and Sabine had to fight for a world worth living in for their son.

'Your father and I will return soon,' she promised him. 'Until then be a good boy for *grand-maman* and *grand-papa*. Be brave.'

Christian helped Sabine into the baker's van and then climbed in himself. She felt shaky and frail when she waved goodbye to her family but willed herself to be strong. All that she had fought for these past few years was in those dear faces, now growing smaller as the van sped away. She would be nothing without them.

*

The tide of war was turning against the Germans, and they knew it. When Sabine and Christian arrived at the train station in Bergerac, the place was swarming with enemy soldiers. Christian had been ordered to coordinate the various maquis, which were now numbering in the thousands of men. But it was dangerous work. Soldiers with guard dogs were moving among the passengers climbing off the train and making random checks of documents and baggage. The Gestapo acted undercover and wore plain clothes, but Sabine had learned to recognise them as they often bore the demeanour of the thugs that they were. There were two of them near the ticket collector when she passed through, wearing wide-brimmed hats and long dark coats. It was the informers and collaborators, even more than the Gestapo, that she was wary of initially. They were the ones who gave tip-offs to the Gestapo, which would then be investigated with meticulous care. The collaborators were often better dressed than the general population, but the informers could be anyone – the friendly shopkeeper, the hotel maid, the woman who shampooed your hair. The manager of the hotel where Sabine and Christian were staying was with the local Resistance. 'I suggest you do what you need to and leave quickly,' he warned them. 'The town is swarming with enemy agents. Just yesterday there was a swoop and several arrests.'

Sabine and Christian weren't intending to stay the night. But it looked less suspicious if they came to town and booked a hotel, especially as they were posing as husband and wife. After they had met with the local maquis leader, they would be on the next train out of Bergerac. At least, that was their plan.

The meeting place was a house on the edge of town. As was the procedure for such a meeting, Christian and Sabine went separately to different checkpoints, from where a member of the local Resistance would guide each of them to the house. They set off as the sun was setting and turning the river a shade of grey-pink. Sabine found her guide, a petite red-haired woman, waiting for her outside a café.

'All our souls are written in our eyes,' said Sabine, using her pass phrase, a quote from *Cyrano de Bergerac*.

'A great nose indicates a great man,' the woman replied.

Sabine's guide said nothing further, but linked arms with her. They walked towards the river and then down a narrow street. While she adopted the demeanour of a woman out for a stroll with her friend, all Sabine's senses were on fire, and she scanned the doorways and alleys for enemy agents. She couldn't even be sure that her guide, whom she had never met before, was not leading her straight to the Gestapo.

They turned a corner, and the woman gave her a nudge towards the house in front of them and whispered, 'Good luck, madame,' before hurrying away. Sabine was relieved to see Christian open the door and wave her inside.

'My men are ready,' Bruno, the leader of the local maquis, told them. 'But I have a serious problem. The mistress of my lieutenant has threatened to denounce us all to the Gestapo.'

Panic pinched Sabine's gut. 'Why would she do that?'

'Because André has turned her over for another woman.'

Sabine gritted her teeth. 'Why can't your men keep their pants on! This is a war we are fighting! Where is your discipline?'

She looked to Christian, who had turned ashen in the face and was pacing the floor. 'Or at least if you must have liaisons, have them with sensible women, patriots for the cause,' he told Bruno. He averted his eyes from Sabine, but it was obvious that he was alluding to her. In the bleak situation, the idea that he held her in such high regard was a flicker of light.

The maquisard shrugged. 'We will have to kill the woman. I will organise one of my men to do it tonight.'

Sabine recoiled, horrified. 'You can't do that!'

'Hundreds of men's lives are at risk,' said Bruno gravely. He narrowed his eyes on Sabine. 'You and your family are in danger too. You know what the Germans are doing to resisters. Better one death than many.'

Sabine and Christian exchanged a look. She had no qualms about killing soldiers and members of the Vichy police, but this was something different. Christian rubbed his chin, thinking something over.

'I'll have to contact London,' he said finally. 'I must have permission for this sort of thing. SOE is a disciplined group. We are not a bunch of savages.'

★

It took two days for the message to come back from London. In that time, Sabine and Christian had kept up the pretence of being a married couple. They dined in restaurants full of Gestapo agents and collaborators. They shared the double bed in their room, politely turning their backs to each other when they undressed.

When Christian returned from collecting the message from SOE, he checked the door of the hotel room for eavesdroppers then told Sabine to sit down.

'We are to try to buy the woman off in the first instance, but, if that fails, we have permission to do "whatever is necessary".'

The implication made Sabine shiver. 'Can't the maquis hold the woman prisoner in the woods?' she asked.

He shook his head. 'They are men hardened by war. Prepared to fight but lacking in personal discipline, as we have already seen. If we handed the woman over to them … well, you can imagine what they would do to her. If she won't see reason, then we must follow through with SOE directions.'

They learned from Bruno that the woman in question, Gisèle Babin, went to the Café de la Place in the evenings. The waiter was with the *Pianiste* circuit, as was the local doctor. They arranged to be in the café when Mademoiselle Babin was there. When they arrived, Christian took a seat by the bar. Sabine looked at the waiter, who nodded to a young blonde woman wearing a fedora hat and sitting by the window.

'What an elegant hat,' said Sabine to the woman, sliding into the chair opposite her.

Gisèle glanced at Sabine with interest, but not alarm. She was extraordinarily pretty, with blonde corkscrew curls and china-doll blue eyes. It was understandable that the lieutenant's head might have been turned, but Christian was right when he said he should have selected a more honourable partner.

'Mademoiselle Babin,' Sabine began. 'It has come to my attention that you wish to denounce certain people to our enemy. I appeal to you as a Frenchwoman not to do such a terrible thing. France is on the verge of being liberated. So many of your fellow countrymen and women have risked everything for this moment. Please do not condemn them to death now.'

Gisèle's face pinched in annoyance. 'I'm not going to be treated like a fool by any man. If I wish to turn André in, that's my business.'

'And everyone else?' Sabine asked, repulsed by the young woman's arrogant tone. 'Their families—'

'That's their problem if they have broken the law. It's got nothing to do with me.'

Sabine paused and considered that Gisèle might be making an idle threat. There would be retribution towards collaborators once the Germans had gone. It made little sense to side with the enemy now when they were on the verge of defeat. The apathetic and traitor alike were scrambling to be part of the Resistance now.

'We can offer you money,' Sabine said.

Gisèle's eyes flashed and a nasty smile curled her pink lips. 'So, you are all frightened of me now?' she said, with a high-pitched laugh. 'Good! I don't want your money.'

Sabine's pulse quickened and her hands turned clammy. The young woman was not only arrogant but stupid. Before the war those qualities would have been merely irritating. Now they could be deadly. Sabine separated her squeamishness from her logic. She thought of Pierre's chubby face when she kissed him goodbye. Bigger things were under threat than Gisèle's pride.

'Please,' whispered Sabine. 'I have a young child. You will regret your position.'

She looked into Gisèle's eyes hoping for some change of heart, but the young woman continued to regard her with a haughty air.

Feeling as though she had a rock in her stomach, Sabine turned to Christian, who had been watching the exchange. She shook her head. His expression went from businesslike to icy. He nodded to the waiter, who understood the signal. The waiter poured three glasses of red wine. He placed one before Christian and approached Sabine and Gisèle with the other two.

'The gentleman at the far table wishes to make a toast to two beautiful ladies.'

Gisèle glanced at Christian with interest and smiled. She was used to being admired and flirted with, Sabine thought. Gisèle batted her eyelids, and her velvety lashes fluttered like butterflies. And like butterflies, she was not long for this world. The waiter placed the glasses in front of them.

'To France and beautiful women!' said Christian, raising his glass.

'To France!' repeated Sabine and Gisèle.

They drank the wine and Gisèle smiled triumphantly at Sabine. But her mouth twitched uncertainly as she sensed something was wrong. There was no turning back now, no chance for Gisèle to change her mind. The cyanide would take effect quickly.

'I'm sorry,' said Sabine, under her breath. 'There was no other way.'

Gisèle's body jerked. Her mouth flew open as she convulsed. Her eyes grew wide then rolled back in her head.

'No!' She struggled to say something else but gasped instead.

Sabine stood up. 'My friend is unwell,' she cried out. 'Please help. She is with child. Is there a doctor nearby?'

A murmur of alarm arose from the other patrons. Christian and the Resistance doctor rushed forward and made a great show of offering Gisèle assistance. Christian wrapped her in his jacket and the two men quickly bundled her off to the doctor's car, which was parked outside. People fainted or became ill all the time in France, either due to lack of food or illnesses caused by poor nutrition. So, after a brief moment of disturbance, most of the café patrons returned to their conversations. Christian placed Gisèle on the backseat of the car and held her down until she stopped moving.

The doctor got in the driver's seat and Christian hurried Sabine into the passenger side. 'Keep acting the part of the concerned friend,' he said. 'The doctor will issue a death certificate.'

Sabine couldn't bear to look back at Gisèle's body as the doctor pulled away from the kerb.

'Cyanide is quick, madame,' the doctor told her. 'It would not have been so for any of us had this woman gone through with her threat.'

What the doctor said was true. Sabine glanced back to the café where Christian was talking to the waiter. He was smiling as if nothing dramatic had taken place. It could have been good acting, but it unnerved her somehow. Maybe he was not the man she thought she knew.

# CHAPTER TWENTY-SIX

Freddy's eyes shone with excitement when Diana passed him the present to give to his father. 'It's a book,' she told him. 'Your daddy always loved reading. Let's go find him now.'

Casper was down by the creek, sitting on a wrought-iron bench. His face was serious and bore the frown of a man in deep thought.

'We've brought you a present!' said Freddy, eagerly taking a seat next to his father. 'It's a book Mummy thought you would like to read.'

Casper roused himself. 'Really?' he said to Freddy. 'A book?'

Diana stood in front of them and watched as Casper opened the brown wrapping paper and slipped the book out. She waited for a smile or some indication of pleasure, but instead of looking pleased, Casper stared at the cover as if frozen in time.

'It's about a man who goes to the Riviera for a holiday,' Diana explained, 'but ends up becoming a spy. It's been made into a movie.'

'I like to read too,' said Freddy, leaning in close to his father. 'My favourite book is *The Swiss Family Robinson*.'

Casper stared up at Diana. His face was grim. Something

was wrong. Something she didn't understand. Why was he looking at her like that? So strange and uncertain, like a man in a trance.

'What's wrong?' she asked. 'Don't you like the book?'

He stood up, his eyes blazing with anger. 'What are you trying to do?' he asked her. 'What is it that you want to say?'

His unexpected reaction sent her into a state of shock. 'You used to like spy novels,' she replied. 'You were always reading them before the war. I thought you'd like this one.'

A sob threatened to break in her throat, but she was conscious that Freddy was watching. She forced herself to stay calm. Casper glanced at Freddy and his face softened a fraction. He sat down next to him and put his arm around his shoulders.

'Don't worry, young man,' he said, trying to sound jolly but not succeeding. 'Mummy bought me a book about the war, which she knows I don't like to think about. Let's forget about that now. Why don't you tell me about this favourite book of yours, *The Swiss Family Robinson*.'

Diana looked on, humiliated. Casper had drawn an invisible cloak around himself and Freddy and shut her out. What right did he have to do that? What terrible mistake had she made? She stared at the book, now discarded on the bench.

'It isn't about the war,' she said. 'That novel was written before the war even started.'

She turned and hurried back to the house. She'd thought that giving her husband a present might make him happy. She wanted to be a pleasing wife, like Grace when she cooked Howard lamb chops. But her present hadn't pleased him at all. In fact, it had made him angry. Was that her fault or his?

★

'Off for another day of learning?' Casper called to Diana and Freddy as they stepped out the front gate the following morning.

They turned to see him rushing from the house. Dinner had been awkward the night before, Diana still fuming about the book before going to bed early. She'd not said anything to him that morning because she'd actually hoped he would go off by himself as usual. But now he was striding towards them. He reached the gate and ruffled Freddy's hair. Perhaps he was trying to make amends. She'd seen him speaking with Marilyn for the first time straight after the book incident, asking her about her pruning paste recipe and how things were going with the terrace garden. But it was all forced and Diana no longer had the patience for it. Her goodwill was hanging by a thread. Gone were Casper's easy laugh and the brilliant smile Diana had fallen in love with. Because of him, she could no longer behave naturally in her own home.

Casper glanced at her, as if sensing her resentment. He placed one hand on the gate and the other in his pocket.

'Well, be off with you both,' he said to them, with a grin like a model in a wax museum. 'I won't keep you.'

★

After Diana returned to the house, she saw Casper in the library unpacking his books. He was whistling and studying the spines before deciding where to place them on the shelves. When he saw her, he smiled but she pretended not to see him. There was something disturbing about him, although she couldn't say exactly what. His eyes? The tension in his jaw?

She sat down at her desk and took out her plan for Professor Spencer's garden, ready to soothe herself by focusing on her work. It would take some time to source all the plants on her list, but she could start with the fernery. She already had shadecloth on hand and a variety of ferns, palms and bromeliads. For container plants she had chosen a knotted breynia, which had lovely, variegated leaves, and an Australian indigo, which was one of the few native perennials. She also planned for a small pond and water feature for a cooling effect. She twirled the end of her pencil against her cheek, her creation growing larger and more splendid in her imagination. In keeping with the house, she would use traditional English plants such as roses, irises and petunias in the flower beds, and deciduous plants like Japanese maple, but she would put them all firmly in an Australian setting with native trees and shrubs around the border of the garden. She saw pretty pandorea and its bell-shaped flowers climbing up walls, deep blue dampiera draping over rockeries, and shady spots lush with native viola.

She took out another sheet of paper and heard the professor's resonant voice in her head – *I make a solemn promise to show you only the good side of the English!* She smiled and sketched him reclining in a wicker chaise longue and reading a book on Botticelli. Next to him she drew a trolley with a pot of tea and a tray of biscuits on it. Then she filled in his oblong face and recalled his unusual golden eyes. When the clock in the living room chimed noon, she stood and stretched. She tucked her plans away in a folder. It had been the most delightful couple of hours she'd spent in weeks. Then it all went to seed when Janet rang.

'Could you drive by here on your way to the magazine?' she said in her imperious, bossy voice. 'I have a household emergency.'

Diana sighed. It wasn't a request. It was an order. Janet had a habit of telephoning Diana and telling her to come over because of some 'emergency' to do with her garden. But when she had rushed to Janet's tightly clipped inner-city garden in the past, the only emergencies she discovered were that a perfectly harmless blue-tongue lizard had made an appearance or that Janet had discovered 'green caterpillars *with horns*' in her lemon tree. 'The blue-tongue lizard will keep down the snails,' Diana had told her, and as for the green caterpillars, where did Janet think the stunning blue triangle butterflies that pollinated her flowers came from?

'I'm not planning to go to the magazine for another fortnight,' Diana lied. 'Can you tell me what the problem is over the telephone? I'll be happy to help if I can.'

Janet did not answer her. Diana could imagine her sister-in-law's nostrils flaring at her refusal to drop everything and rush over on her command.

'Never mind, dear,' she said finally, her voice sharp. 'We had our neighbours over for dinner last night and I made far too many of my delicious pies. There's no room in our refrigerator and I thought you might like them. Casper's always loved my special pies. But I suppose I'll just have to let them go to waste.'

Although Janet was playing every guilty nerve in Diana's body like a violinist plucking strings, she sucked in a breath and resisted giving in to her manipulation. She was half-tempted to send Casper over to collect the pies – after all, they were for him, and he had less to do than Diana these days. But she knew that if Janet got involved in whatever was wrong with Casper, it would only make it ten times worse.

'I'm sorry about that,' Diana said firmly. 'But isn't the minister of your church a bachelor? I'm sure he'd appreciate the pies. Or he might know someone in need who could benefit from the gift.'

Diana was pleased with herself. Not only had she refused to be at Janet's beck and call, but she'd offered a perfectly reasonable solution to the issue. Janet loved to be useful, or at least be seen to be useful, and this gave her an opportunity to do something generous and be able to boast about it to everyone in her congregation on Sunday. But there was a price to be paid for rebellion, and Janet swiftly delivered it.

'Very well, dear. I'll follow your suggestion,' she said. 'By the way, Alfred and I noticed Casper didn't look happy the last time we were there. I've popped something in the post *you* might find helpful.'

*

Diana grimaced when she saw the envelope addressed to her in Janet's precise handwriting. She assumed Janet had sent some more of the articles she liked to clip from women's magazines in the guise of being helpful. Against her better judgement, she opened the envelope and found herself looking at a long article by the women's writer for the *Daily Reporter*, entitled 'Now He

Is Back Home'. The writer's tone was chirpy, encouraging …
and condescending:

> *It will take some time for you to get to know each other again.*
> *Expect some disappointments and temper your expectations.*
> *There will be changes. After all, you have both grown older*
> *since you saw each other last and have had different experiences.*
> *But, with patience, you will start to see glimpses again of the*
> *man you knew. When you do, treasure those moments. When*
> *he tells you a joke that makes you laugh, when he performs*
> *some act of kindness, be sure to praise him. It will remind you*
> *both of the best parts of yourselves.*
>
> *Don't pressure him for details of his battle experiences,*
> *don't smother him with attention, don't pester him with your*
> *own needs. Give him space and time to readjust …*

Diana sucked in her stomach as if she had been punched.
What did Janet or any of these magazine writers know of her
despair? She turned back towards the library. The door was
now shut, and no more sounds of books being unpacked came
from within. She would like to know what Casper was doing
in there. Reading? Writing? Staring out the window? She
pictured her sister-in-law sitting at her three-leaf dining table,
surrounded by her Toby jugs and Royal Doulton figurines,
feeling she had done her Christian duty as she sealed the
envelope. Had Janet taken her brother aside and asked him
how he really was? Alfred hadn't even offered to take Casper
out for a game of golf. They didn't truly care about Casper,
let alone Diana. With them, all their 'kindness' was token.

Their lack of empathy and true concern made her feel even more alone.

*

'I'd stop reading them if I were you,' said Marilyn, when she came up from the creek with Blossom and saw Diana shredding Janet's article before scattering it onto the compost heap. 'Your sister-in-law doesn't have an encouraging effect on you.'

Marilyn was probably the tallest woman Diana had ever known. She wore men's shirts and trousers because there were no ready-made women's clothes that would fit her. Next to Marilyn, Diana always felt like a child.

'The temptation got the better of me,' she said, patting Blossom's head when the pig pushed her snout against her leg. 'But you're right.'

They made their way down to the bottom of the garden where Marilyn had already dug the foundation for the dry-stone wall and laid the gravel. The stones were set out by size, the heaviest ones closest to where they would be laying them. Marilyn had come to Diana on a recommendation from Phyllis's sister in Bowral. 'Jane didn't intend you to steal her forever,' Phyllis often joked, after Diana's landscape business took off and she employed Marilyn full-time. Diana knew hardly anything about Marilyn except that she'd grown up in South Australia, and yet she trusted her more than anybody she could think of.

Marilyn pointed to Blossom to go to her 'rooting patch', the part of the garden that had been allocated to her to dig up and so keep her away from the garden beds.

'You have a well-trained pig,' Diana said. 'I don't think there is a dog in Australia that's more obedient and better behaved than Blossom.'

Marilyn picked up one of the large stones and started chiselling away some rough edges. 'I'd like to get her a companion, another female, if that's all right with you? Pigs are social creatures. She'll be lonely with us working away on that property in Wollstonecraft and with Freddy at school.'

'Of course,' agreed Diana. 'I'll help you build a bigger pen.'

Diana handed Marilyn the smaller stones when she pointed to the ones she wanted. There was no one who could build a better dry-stone wall than her assistant.

'You know you can join us for dinner anytime,' Diana said. 'Freddy misses you.'

'I figured you all needed some time together.'

Marilyn picked up a hammer to press the rocks into place. She hadn't been to horticultural school like Diana. Where had she picked up her skills? But Marilyn wasn't someone who talked a lot about herself. She was like a garden in many ways – you had to let her reveal herself over time. Only Marilyn's garden was very slow growing and sometimes Diana got impatient.

'You're always welcome to invite friends here if you want to,' she told her. 'I want you to think of this as your home too.'

Marilyn straightened and wiped the sweat from her brow. At first, Diana thought she hadn't heard her. Then she shook her head and answered. 'No, some of us are better alone.'

Diana bit her lip. Could that really be so or was Marilyn just saying that? Sometimes relationships could cause so much pain, perhaps it felt better to keep people at arm's length, even at the price of loneliness.

Blossom grunted happily from the rooting patch. Marilyn turned to her and smiled. 'Come here, girl.' The pig bolted towards Marilyn. She knelt and they rubbed faces together.

'I was married once,' Marilyn said. 'Back in Adelaide. It didn't work out.'

For a moment, Diana thought she might be hallucinating. Of all the things that Marilyn could have revealed to her, that was the one she least expected.

'I'm not suited to marriage,' Marilyn continued. 'I made a lot of people angry, but sometimes you have to face the truth.' She looked up at Diana. 'Sometimes, as much as you want something or as much as everyone else thinks it's the right thing, it's not on the cards. It's simply not meant to be.'

A lump formed in Diana's throat. Her mind began to race. 'How do you know something is not meant be – or whether it needs more time?'

Marilyn tilted her head. 'I guess the answer to that is how long you're going to allow yourself to be unhappy before you admit the truth.'

# CHAPTER TWENTY-SEVEN

'Aunt Shirley used to take me to the art gallery every Wednesday afternoon too,' Diana told Freddy as they walked through the Botanic Garden on their way to the Art Gallery of New South Wales, a grand sandstone building with massive Corinthian columns. 'I think she'd be happy to know we are keeping up the tradition.'

'I miss Aunty Shirley,' he said. 'She used to fall asleep with a book on her face.'

A smile tickled Diana's lips. It was funny what children remembered. 'Yes, she wasn't much of a reader, was she? She used to nap out on the sun-lounger with a book to protect her face from getting burnt.' She rubbed his hair. 'I miss her too. She adored you.'

Diana very much felt the loss of her worldly aunt. Aunt Shirley had always known exactly what to do in even the direst of situations. She wished she could talk to her now about what was going on with Casper. Diana had never thought of getting married before she met him. She had expected to live her life like Aunt Shirley – free and unfettered – and to devote her time to nature and art.

They stopped at the entrance of the gallery and Freddy turned his face upwards and smiled at her. She brushed his cheek with her fingertips. But without Casper there would have been no Freddy, and her son was everything to her.

A man in a faded brown suit and a hat with oily stains on it appeared from nowhere and lurched at Diana, muttering something she didn't understand but could guess the meaning of by the way he ogled her breasts. She grabbed Freddy and pushed him inside the gallery foyer and towards the cloakroom, doing her best to restore her composure. There seemed to be a lot of perverts hanging around the city these days. A dirty old man had exposed himself to her when she was walking through Hyde Park one afternoon. He'd jumped out from behind a tree and dropped his pants. Diana had frozen on the spot, transfixed by shock and disbelief, but an old woman nearby had come to her rescue and frightened the man off by beating him with her umbrella.

Fortunately, there were enough guards at the gallery to make Diana feel safe to be there with Freddy. She left her shopping bag with the cloakroom manager and handed Freddy his sketchpad and pencil box. 'You lead the way,' she said.

Diana liked to wander the art gallery with Freddy the same way she liked people to view her gardens, not necessarily having to go in a systematic order but moving where they felt inspired. This meant that the art gallery would be constantly offering them new surprises each time they walked through it, according to their mood.

Freddy skipped through the gallery, as excited as a child on an Easter egg hunt. They moved from the watercolours to the line drawings before entering the grand gallery of nineteenth-century European art. Freddy's eyes travelled upwards to the high ceiling with its long skylight. Then without hesitation he headed towards the painting at the end of the hall, which happened to be François Sallé's *The Anatomy Class at the École des Beaux-Arts*. It depicted a group of students listening to a lecture. The teacher was holding the arm of an artist's model, illustrating a point. Although the figures were dressed in the dark suits of the Victorian era, the picture had the atmosphere of a work from the Renaissance. The muscle definition of the model was detailed, as were the rapt expressions of the students, who could have been da Vinci, Michelangelo and Raphael.

'What do you think of that?' Diana asked Freddy. 'They are artists, like you. They're learning how to draw the human body.'

Freddy nodded his admiration and pointed to the human bones on the table in front of the lecturer. Indeed, they had the highest lighting in the painting, alluding to the title of the work. Even the background details of charts and the lecture room furniture were superbly done. No wonder the painting had pride of place in the gallery.

She turned and caught sight of a familiar-looking man studying a painting a few feet from them. She had to think for a moment where she had met him. With his long body and classical profile, he could have stepped out of one of the portraits in the gallery. She gave a little cry when she recognised him.

She took Freddy's hand and hurried towards the man. 'Good afternoon, Professor Spencer.'

The professor's face lit up when he saw her. 'Well, hello, Mrs White. What a lovely surprise!' His gaze fell to Freddy.

'This is my son, Freddy,' Diana told him. 'We come here every Wednesday after school.'

'Oh, how marvellous,' said Professor Spencer. 'What a wonderful thing for a mother and son to do together.' He beamed at Freddy. 'Now tell me then, young man, which of the paintings on this wall do you like the best?'

He put his hands behind his back and rolled on his feet, looking so much the part of the professor that Diana almost laughed. Freddy's eyes settled on the painting of the epic battle between the British soldiers and Zulu warriors that Professor Spencer had been admiring and he frowned. He put his hands behind his back too and studied the other paintings on the wall with great seriousness. Then he pointed to one of the smaller ones on the right. Diana and Professor Spencer stepped closer to see which one he'd chosen. It depicted a scene at a village school, where mothers had come to pick their children up at the end of the day. The women and children were in the sombre clothing of peasants and some of the children were barefoot, yet it was not a depiction of poverty but of happiness. The spectacle of children reuniting with their mothers and sharing stories of the day was so universal that, apart from the clothing, it could have been set anytime, anywhere. Diana read the title card next to it: *A Spring Day* by Friedrich Kallmorgan.

'What a delightful choice,' exclaimed Professor Spencer. 'I see you like the impressionists. I'm curious to know why you picked this one in particular?'

Freddy stretched his spine to stand taller. 'I like the clouds in the sky and the smoke coming out of the chimney – and the cherry blossoms,' he answered.

'Look here,' said the professor, lifting Freddy so he could see the painting better. 'The artist has given us clues to the time of the day by using shadows. The golden light and the fact the children aren't wearing shoes tell us it's warm outside. But see here, the smoke from the chimney conveys that it was still chilly in the classroom. Do you see how this painting makes us *feel* that it's early spring, not only with our eyes but with all our senses?'

Freddy nodded solemnly, taking in every word the professor said. He pointed to the path in the foreground of the painting. 'I like the dirt and the rocks,' he said. 'They look real.'

Professor Spencer put Freddy down again. 'Details are what makes a painting complete. Sometimes we look at a picture and miss all the individual clues. A good artist considers every detail, whether the viewer will notice them or not.' He indicated Freddy's sketchbook, which Diana was holding. 'Are they yours?' he asked her.

She shook her head. 'No, they're Freddy's. He loves to draw.'

'So, he's an artist, like his mother?'

'Much better,' Diana replied. 'I never had his talent so young.'

Professor Spencer straightened his jacket and looked at his watch. 'It must be getting on to afternoon tea. Would you and Freddy care to join me? I should like to see this sketchbook of his.'

★

Diana normally took Freddy to the Refreshment Room in the Botanic Garden, and when she explained that to Professor Spencer, he was happy to oblige.

'Freddy is very fond of the chocolate éclairs they have there,' she told him.

'Sometimes they have orange ice-cream as well!' Freddy piped up.

'Orange ice-cream!' repeated Professor Spencer. 'Well, who could resist that?'

When they entered the Refreshment Room, the smell of roasting coffee was intoxicating.

'You might like to try the "Vienna-style" coffee with whipped cream on top,' Diana told Professor Spencer. 'It's very good here.'

'Whipped cream!' he said, his eyes twinkling. 'Could you have chosen a better place?'

Diana was about to say that with his trim physique she couldn't imagine him consuming too much cream, but then she stopped herself. Would that come across as flirtation?

They ordered their drinks and sweets and Professor Spencer looked through Freddy's sketchbook with an appraising eye. 'These drawings are complex and well advanced beyond his age,' he told Diana. 'This one here of the colourful parrots is beautifully proportioned and vivid. Your son is more than talented. He is gifted.'

Freddy leaned close to Professor Spencer to see which picture he was talking about. Diana's heart melted at how comfortable Freddy appeared and how kind Professor Spencer was being.

'My aunt owned an art gallery,' she said. 'She recognised Freddy's talent and refused to let anyone give him colour-by-numbers or join-the-dots books in case that hindered his natural ability.'

'How fortunate he was to have had such an aunt,' Professor Spencer replied, continuing to admire Freddy's drawings. 'A child's art gives us insight into what they're thinking and feeling. Often their work expresses emotions that they can't yet put into words. They tend to enlarge things that are pleasant to them and leave out things that are not.'

He flipped to the picture Freddy had been drawing the day after Casper returned. Diana, Marilyn and Blossom were still standing under the crepe myrtle tree, but Casper and his plane were nowhere to be seen. Diana flinched. There was no doubt Freddy was hurt by his father's lack of interest. He hadn't been fooled one bit when Casper had tried to feign it by asking him about *The Swiss Family Robinson*.

Professor Spencer glanced at her, concern in his expression. She was relieved when the waiter arrived with their orders and she was saved from having to explain her reaction, and even more relieved when the professor turned the conversation to his garden.

'So, tell me, what have you been dreaming up for my property?'

His question worked like magic in cheering her up. She leaned forward in her seat. 'I've selected a eucalyptus tree to go next to the gate,' she said. 'A scribbly gum. Have you ever seen one of them?'

He shook his head. 'I don't believe I have.'

Freddy slipped the sketchbook from Professor Spencer's grasp and started a new drawing, leaving the two adults to their conversation. Diana took one of the pencils out of his box and began to draw a scribbly gum on a paper napkin.

'The scribbly gum is the iconic tree of Sydney,' she told Professor Spencer, drawing the outline of the tree's thick trunk. 'It has luminous silver-white bark. You could plant it anywhere in the world with a suitable climate, but what you wouldn't get if you took it out of Sydney are these ...'

She drew squiggles and twirls on the trunk, then showed the picture to the professor.

'The scribbles are made by moth larvae as they tunnel between the layers of bark. There are six species of moths that live in the scribbly gum bark, and each has its own distinct signature. The larvae hatch from their cocoons in early summer, at the same time as the tree blossoms with spectacular cream-coloured flowers. The moths fly up to drink the nectar and then fly from tree to tree, pollinating the scribbly gums. Nature works in a beautiful symphony together.'

She looked at her picture thoughtfully. The moths were so small that people barely noticed them. Humans went about their lives, oblivious to the magic all around them.

'Americans hang flags in their front yards,' she continued. 'Every garden in Australia should have at least one native tree to show our love for our country.'

Diana could hear her voice getting higher and more excited. She was afraid she might be sounding like a zealot and stopped herself. But when she looked up at Professor Spencer, he seemed enraptured by what she was saying.

'It really is the perfect legacy tree,' he said. 'You've put a lot of thought into it. We English can be very particular about our landscapes, and I think you are exactly the right person to show me what is unique in Australia.'

Diana smiled. 'When people don't appreciate nature, it hurts something deep in my soul. I could say what I've told you to some of my clients and they wouldn't understand. They'd simply wonder if such a tree would impress their friends or ask me if it will draw nutrients from their lawn.'

'Will it?' asked Professor Spencer, with a touch of mischief in his eyes.

'What other people think shouldn't matter. And in regard to the lawn, we're not going to grow grass right up to the tree,' she replied. 'My assistant has propagated a native grass from Western Australia that's perfect to plant under eucalyptus trees. It has silvery foliage and purple flowers. It's the Australian version of French lavender, only it grows in shade.'

Professor Spencer looked at her with interest. 'Tell me, where did this love of the natural world come from?' he asked. 'From your talented aunt as well?'

Diana shook her head. 'No, Aunt Shirley had many interests, but gardening wasn't one of them. My mother was the one who taught me to love nature. Aunt Shirley was her stepsister. My mother spent her childhood on a farm in the Highlands while Aunt Shirley grew up in Glasgow.'

'So, they were Scottish?'

'Yes,' said Diana. 'They couldn't have been more different. After my maternal grandfather died and my grandmother remarried Aunt Shirley's father, a widower, the two girls became the best of friends. They even emigrated to Australia together.'

'And your father?'

Diana's stomach tightened. She glanced at Freddy, who was absorbed in his drawing, and then back to Professor Spencer.

'I never like to talk about him.'

'I understand,' he said, with a nod. 'Let's change the subject. I was impressed by an Australian artist whose work I saw in the gallery. Margaret Preston. Her still life paintings are riots of colour and boldness, reminiscent of Matisse, but also show influences from Japanese art.'

Diana clapped her hands. 'Margaret was one of Aunt Shirley's best friends. I am very fond of her studies in oils of Australian wildflowers, and her ability to capture the subtle beauty of the bush.'

'I thought you might be,' he said. 'That's why I took a particular interest in her art.'

He looked directly into her eyes. She tried to hold his gaze but found she couldn't and quickly looked away.

The afternoon light was turning golden and Diana realised they'd been talking for over two hours. 'It's been so nice running into you, Professor Spencer,' she said. 'But I'll have to get Freddy home and start on dinner. I'll bring you the plan on Friday.'

'Please call me Laurie.'

'Diana,' she said, standing up a little too quickly and knocking her chair backwards to the floor with a loud bang.

Professor Spencer, or Laurie as she was to think of him from now on, stood up and righted the chair for her. Then he took her hand and squeezed it. 'Until Friday,' he said.

Diana and Freddy waved one more time at Laurie as they passed by the Refreshment Room's front window, then made their way back to the truck. An invigorating sea breeze was blowing in from the harbour. It lifted Diana's skirt and caressed her cheeks like a mischievous, invisible fairy.

'Did you enjoy your visit to the art gallery?' she asked Freddy, when they reached the truck and she opened the passenger door for him.

'Yes, Mummy,' he said. 'It was a lot of fun.'

There was ice-cream on Freddy's chin, and she took her handkerchief from her purse and dabbed at it. 'And the orange ice-cream? Was that nice too?'

Freddy nodded. 'It was simply delicious.'

Diana smiled at Freddy's ability to sometimes sound like he was mimicking her when he spoke, although it was always innocent in intention.

'Professor Spencer is very clever, isn't he?' she said.

Freddy climbed into his seat and tilted his head. 'He's more than clever, I think.'

He spoke with such conviction that Diana was surprised. 'Do you mean he's *brilliant*?'

Freddy let out a sigh and stared at his sketchbook. 'He's kind,' he said. 'He is the kindest man I've ever met.'

Diana rubbed Freddy's knee. She, too, longed for kindness. She walked around to the driver's side of the truck and climbed into the seat, then leaned back for a moment and inhaled the harbour's salty air. Laurie was like that sea breeze, she thought, a relief from what she'd been feeling ever since Casper had returned from Europe – an all-pervading sense of dread that followed her everywhere. She longed for a male companion, someone to encourage both her and Freddy. Perhaps Laurie could become a dear friend.

She started up the engine and turned in the direction of home.

# CHAPTER TWENTY-EIGHT

Sabine crouched in the falling gloom of dusk and observed Casper White's house through her binoculars. She would have liked to have sat down but she didn't like the look of those giant ants moving through the crackly leaf litter. She would have to be careful not to make a sound when she got closer to the house. The forest floors of the Dordogne had been soft and mossy, better for sneaking up on your enemy. The day before, when she had been browsing that interior design magazine to understand Australian taste better, and seen Diana White's name in the gardening section, it was as if she had been given a sign that unseen forces were on her side. She'd rung the magazine and pretended to be a French photographer who wanted to send an invitation to an exhibition to the gardening editor and her husband.

'Could you tell me the first name of Madame White's husband, please?' she'd asked the receptionist.

'Casper,' the answer had come without hesitation.

Australians – so trusting, so free to offer information without questioning the caller's intentions.

The article had mentioned the garden in Killara and that had narrowed Sabine's search down to one address in the telephone book. Judging by the size of the neighbours' houses and their sparkling swimming pools, Killara was not a place where the residents had to worry too much about housing shortages, or shortages of anything probably. Sabine gritted her teeth. It seemed the final insult that, after sending so many fine people to their deaths, Casper White had landed on well-heeled feet.

The last remnants of daylight began to fade, and shadows glided silently over the expanse of the darkening sky. Bats. Gigantic ones with five-foot wingspans. Sabine watched their eerie journey with equal parts fascination and horror. Did they eat human flesh? Other strange sounds came from the bushland: squawking birds and hooting owls. Suddenly the tree above her shook, and a growl that sounded like it came from a small lion made Sabine's spine tingle. She looked up to see a grey-furred creature with large eyes and ears like a rabbit's looking down on her. Was it possible such a sweet-looking animal had made such an aggressive sound? Sabine stood up and moved cautiously towards the house. There were vipers in France but nothing like the deadly snakes in Australia that she had read about, ones that had enough venom in a single bite to kill a hundred men. She did not want to be creeping around the bushland at night.

From the garden she had a clear view of the house. There were no curtains and the windows were large, allowing her to see into nearly all the rooms. Casper White obviously felt so safe he didn't expect that anyone would carry out surveillance on him. He must have been very sure that he had got away with his crimes, and didn't fear retribution. That arrogance of his was to her advantage. She could see a young boy sitting at a table, drawing. He had to be Casper's son, Frederick. A woman,

Diana she assumed, was moving about the kitchen. She was not the blonde ice queen Sabine had imagined. Rather, she had a sweet, youthful face with apple cheeks and doe-like eyes. Her hair was a mass of ringlets, like a child's.

Then a man came down the stairs, walked straight to the front window and looked out. Sabine focused her binoculars on his face. At first his features were blurred but then they came into sharp view and once again she saw the handsome face of Christian Vidal. A chasm cracked open in her chest. Her breath came fast and furious. She hadn't realised until then that there was a part of her that still hoped it had all been a mistake, and that it was not Christian who had betrayed the circuit, that somehow this Casper White would turn out to be somebody else. But now that she saw him again, standing alive and well at the window of his charming home, she felt reality shift. Hadn't she seen him shot? Hadn't she grieved for him? Robert had once told her that in traumatic situations, to make sense of what was happening, the brain sometimes registered things that weren't there. It made associations that were pure fantasy. Had she believed that the man she had seen shot was Christian Vidal simply because a Nazi had told her so? Or because they had placed him next to Jacqueline?

Who the poor soul was that the Nazis had convinced her was Christian Vidal did not matter now. She had the traitor in her sights. She would finish the job.

# CHAPTER TWENTY-NINE

*France, May 1944*

Things should have been straightforward in Bergerac, but they weren't now that Christian and Sabine had eliminated Gisèle Babin. They had stayed longer than was safe for them. As she walked back to the hotel room after escorting Gisèle's body to a funeral home, Sabine pondered the fragility of life. That morning Gisèle had been alive. She had woken up, dressed and gone about her day with no idea that strangers were plotting her death. Now all that remained was her pale, lifeless body lying in a coffin. There were other strangers out there hunting Sabine and Christian down. Would they be alive tomorrow?

'You look dead on your feet,' said Christian when she walked into the hotel room.

He didn't look well himself. His face was grey and there were purple circles under his eyes as if he had lost a boxing match. Perhaps the expression of coldness she had seen on his face earlier had simply been exhaustion.

'This stupid business,' she said, her regret about Gisèle giving way to anger. The woman had caused so many problems and brought her demise on herself. 'We should leave now.'

'Let's sleep for a few hours. It's curfew now anyway,' Christian said. 'We'll go first thing in the morning. Before sunrise.'

Sabine didn't like that idea. Despite her exhaustion, she felt jumpy. But she lay down fully dressed next to Casper on the bed. Instead of turning his back to her, he put his arm around her shoulders.

'You did well, Sabine. You are a highly disciplined soldier,' he told her. 'But even soldiers must rest.'

Sabine nestled against his side. Despite the danger all around her, she felt safe with Christian, like a baby bird tucked under its mother's wing. If only they could enjoy this closeness for a while, postpone the war and live only in the present, she thought. But that was impossible. There were too many things – too many others – at stake.

★

Sabine's sleep was deep, the deepest it would ever be again. She rested against Christian's shoulder, her friend, her comrade, and dreamed of her apartment in Paris filled with friends and music. The war was almost over. They only needed to be strong a while longer and then they would all be together again – Henri and Madeleine making wine, Sabine teaching Pierre the beauty of music, Lucien poring over his papers and deriving satisfaction from the correct interpretation of the law. Jaqueline would perform her harp recitals and break the hearts of men all over Europe. Christian would bring his wife and child to Paris. Sabine would take her to Le Bon Marché, introduce her to the wonderful dressmakers in the Rue de Rivoli, and show her the beautiful roses and tulips at the flower market. They would walk together with their children in the Parc Monceau and the boys would speak to each other in both English and French. Les Deux Magots would belong to artists again, not Germans and collaborators, and Sabine and Christian's wife would sit there drinking their coffee, and Sabine would tell her about how her husband came from the sky to a village in the Dordogne and helped a small band of patriots fight a formidable foe.

It was the sound of car doors slamming that made Sabine open her eyes. She fought her way back to full consciousness as heavy footsteps pounded on the stairs. She reached for her revolver as the door splintered and someone turned on the light. She and Christian were surrounded by six men pointing guns at their faces, clearly Gestapo. Sabine recognised one of them from the station. He stepped forward and regarded them with cold eyes.

'What's your name?' he asked Christian, while one of the thugs took Sabine's revolver off her.

'Vidal,' he answered, sounding unnaturally calm given the situation. 'How dare you point guns at my wife! What is this all about?'

'Get up!' said the Gestapo man.

While Sabine and Christian stood in their crumpled clothes with guns trained on them, two of the men flung open the armoire and upturned the bedside drawers, looking for contraband.

'Don't take me for a fool!' said the Gestapo leader. 'What sort of married couple sleep in their clothes and carry guns?'

★

Sabine endured her torture with a fierce and impregnable dignity. She was starved in Fresnes Prison in Paris, interrogated at all times of the night at Avenue Foch, beaten, burned and half-drowned in the torture chambers of Rue des Saussaies. She withstood it because her desire to protect the *Pianiste* circuit and the people she loved was far greater than any pain that could be inflicted on her. And because she believed Christian would not break either. He had prepared her for the questions they would ask. How one interrogator would be calm and suave and talk to her like a friend, while the other would yell and scream and hit her with a truncheon. The one who performed the physical torture would be French, he had said. The Germans did this so they could claim they never tortured French citizens.

After a week of this horror, she could have revealed what she knew, as by then the circuit would have heard that she and Christian had been arrested and gone to ground. But refusing to talk had become a matter of principle for her. Then she was taken one more time to Avenue Foch and led up to a room on the fourth floor to find a different interrogator sitting at the desk. He was suavely dressed in a civilian suit, but the guards referred to his rank as '*Sturmbannführer*' and she realised he was a major. It was a warm summer's day, and the window was wide open, giving a view over the treetops of the Bois de Boulogne. Sabine was pushed into a chair, but this time her hands were not tied behind her.

'Your comrade has talked,' he said. 'We know all about the *Pianiste* circuit. He has given us the names of all the members and their addresses. It is pointless for you to remain silent now.'

Sabine said nothing. She doubted Christian would have done that, but if the major had all the names and addresses there would be no need to interrogate her about them.

Seeing that she was unconvinced, the major added, 'We know all about SOE.'

Indeed, as he rattled out details of the organisation's address and structure, how they operated, and threw out names Sabine had never heard of, she realised he knew a great deal about the British operation that could have only come from a double agent. But what he appeared not to know was where the *Pianiste* circuit had stashed their weapons, and that Jacqueline was their long-surviving wireless operator. As long as he didn't know that, Sabine was protecting the circuit by remaining silent.

The major shook his head. 'I don't understand why a woman like you would involve herself with terrorists,' he said. 'Your first duty as a mother is to your son, is it not? What do the British care for you or your family, Madame Brouillette?'

Sabine flinched at the mention of her real name and of Pierre.

The major stood and looked out the window. 'Do you know that while you have been running around in the middle of the night hiding in farmers' fields, there have been beautiful concerts in Paris? Just the other night, I attended a performance of Mozart's piano concertos. The pianist was one of your former students, Colette Cortot. The Germans and the French have so much in common – a love of beauty and refinement.'

The door opened and another man came into the room. He was not as well-dressed as the major, but he was good-looking with dark hair slicked back from his sculptured face. From his stature and his accent when he greeted the major, Sabine realised he was French. Her breath quickened.

The major went to a gramophone sitting on a table in the corner. He switched it on and lifted the needle onto the record. The room was filled with the haunting melody of Schubert's 'Serenade'.

'Do you remember this recording?' he asked Sabine.

She fought back tears. It was a recording of her and Jacqueline playing together, made when they had graduated from the Conservatoire. Their whole future lay ahead of them. It was said the poignant melody came to Schubert when he was among his friends, drinking beer and enjoying their gaiety and conversation. If the major had meant to persuade her to collaborate with him, all he had done was to strengthen her love for her friends and family and make her more determined to rid the world of the Nazis.

'How many hours of your life, of your mother's life, your teachers' lives were dedicated to enabling you to play as beautifully as that, Madame Brouillette? Your touch at the piano could make angels weep. And yet, you did not go on to claim accolades for yourself as a performer. Rather, you had a burning desire to pass on the gift of music to others, so they could experience its sublime beauty too.'

The major went back to his desk and sat down. He leaned forward and said in almost a whisper, 'If you give me the information I ask for, you can go back to what you are meant to be doing – looking after your son and teaching at the Conservatoire. I will spare your family. You have my word as an officer.'

'Your word means nothing to me,' she said. 'Your army has committed atrocities.'

The major paled at the insult. 'I am sorry you are taking that attitude,' he said.

He nodded to the Frenchman. The guards held Sabine while he took her left hand and splayed it on the desk.

'Now,' said the major, going back to the gramophone and replaying Schubert's piece, 'I am going to ask you some questions. Each time you refuse to answer, your fellow countryman here is going to break one of your fingers. For the last time, I want the locations of the stores where you are keeping the weapons the British supplied.'

Sabine shook her head. The Frenchman took her middle finger in his grip. Sabine looked out the window to the trees of the Bois de Boulogne as pain wracked her body. Her soul lifted out of her and glided towards the treetops, spinning and circling in the summer air, Schubert's beautiful music resonating in her ears.

\*

Something was happening. Sabine had been in solitary confinement for weeks, left in the dim silence with no breaks in the exercise yard and no one to keep her informed of what was going on in the outside world. But this morning she heard an explosion. She sat upright on her bunk and listened. Another explosion sounded. She did not hear planes. Were the Germans blowing supply factories up so they would not fall into enemy hands? Or was it the Resistance coming out for battle? For the past few days she had smelled smoke drifting from the courtyard, but her windows were barred and frosted and she could not see out. The Allies must have landed, and were coming to liberate Paris. A smile of jubilation spread across her face, but her elation was short-lived.

Later that morning, the light was turned on in Sabine's cell and a guard brought her a few sheets of paper and a pencil. 'Write to your family,' she urged her. 'I will make sure they get the letter.'

At first Sabine thought it might be a trick to get her to reveal the address of where Henri and Madeleine were staying with Pierre. But the guard looked frightened, and she wondered if she was hoping that Sabine would put in a good word for her once the prison was liberated. Sabine did as she suggested, writing letters for Lucien and Pierre, her in-laws and Jacqueline. Her left hand throbbed when she tried to hold the paper steady so she could write. She had tried to keep her fingers straight but she had no splint, and she could see now under the light that her ring-finger was bent.

Sabine gave the letters to the guard, who shut the door to the cell again. She could hear the metal clang of doors being opened and footsteps on gangways. Then a while later she heard a volley of gunshots coming from the courtyard – a firing squad.

'My God!' she thought. 'They are shooting the prisoners!'

The door to her cell swung open and two male guards stood there looking grim. She realised her end had come and that she would never see her family again. All they would know of her was those final letters. She stood with as much dignity as her broken strength allowed. She had fought with honour and courage and she would die the same way.

The bright summer day dazzled her when she was taken outside. She squinted and tried to get her bearings. Three German soldiers appeared, one in a major's uniform. She recognised him as the man who had interrogated her.

'You brought this upon yourself,' he said, sounding petulant.

Sabine realised that the fact that the Allies had moved so quickly towards Paris suggested that the weapons the *Pianiste* and other circuits had supplied to the maquis could not have all been discovered by the Germans. If so, she and Christian may have been caught, but the work they had done had not been in vain. She would die with that triumph in her mind.

There was a commotion as two other prisoners were dragged out into the courtyard, both in even far worse condition than Sabine. They were pushed down onto their knees. The man was blindfolded, and the face that Sabine could see below it was distorted by bruising. The woman's nose had been smashed to a pulp and she was whimpering. Her eyes were bruised and almost closed over. She barely looked human. Even with her own demise imminent, Sabine felt compassion for the woman, and horror at what the Germans had done. She wished she could do something to comfort her.

'*Vive la France*,' she called out to her. 'Have courage. God knows what you have done.'

The major shoved Sabine. 'Say goodbye to your friends.'

When Sabine shook her head, not understanding, he smiled cruelly. 'Christian Vidal and Jacqueline Bonnet. You could have saved them, but you did not.'

Her eyes opened wide, struggling to comprehend. She stumbled frantically towards the pair, but before she could cry out one of the soldiers took out a pistol and shot first Jacqueline and then Christian in the back of the neck. They fell on their faces, blood streaming from their bodies and flowing over the cobblestones. Sabine's scream pierced the air and she looked at the soldiers, their expressions cold towards her suffering. Her chest rose up and down in rapid breaths and she couldn't hold herself up anymore.

As she collapsed to her knees and the world turned to fog, she heard the major say, 'Take her back to her cell.'

## CHAPTER THIRTY

Diana made her way through the polished granite foyer of the Hotel Australia to the grand staircase, famous for its Carrara structural glass. At the top, she walked through the stainless-steel doors that led into the wintergarden.

Phyllis was already seated at a table by one of the octagonal columns that were encased in the same Carrara glass as the staircase. She was studying a newspaper, and was wearing a royal purple dress with enormous padded shoulders. On top of her head she wore a bicorn hat that gave Diana the impression she might be lunching with a matador. Like the hotel itself, there was nothing understated about Phyllis.

'Hello, Phyllis,' Diana said cheerfully.

She waved the newspaper at Diana. 'A crime wave is coming.'

'What do you mean?'

Then Diana's eyes fell to the page Phyllis had been reading. She'd seen the column that morning too and had thrown the offending publication away.

*The returned servicemen are a menace to civilised society. Trained in the use of deadly weapons, driven by their animal natures,*

*ready to take a life at the slightest provocation … Young Annie*
*Docker was raped by such a man. Now his lawyer pleads for*
*leniency, claiming that his client, Simon Reynolds, has been*
*left disturbed by his war experiences. He may have had terrible*
*experiences, but he doesn't have a right to rape an innocent girl.*
*What about her? What about justice for Annie Docker?*

Diana had shut herself in the bathroom after reading the article
and cried. It seemed the men who had gone away to war had
returned as monsters.

She looked away now and noticed a woman a few tables from
them. She was slim and strikingly elegant, with raven-black
hair and fine features. She was studying the menu, but Diana
had the distinct feeling that the woman had been watching her.

'Diana?'

She turned back to Phyllis and saw that the waiter had arrived
at the table and was looking expectantly at her. Flustered, she
picked up her menu and ordered the first thing she set her eyes
upon.

'Fillet of snapper and half a dozen oysters,' she said, handing
the waiter the menu.

When he left, Phyllis looked Diana up and down carefully.
'How is Casper, by the way?' she asked. 'You've barely said a
word about him.'

Diana took a sip of water. 'He's taking things slowly …'

But Phyllis's attention was already elsewhere. There was a
flurry of excitement at the door to the wintergarden as a stocky
man in a pinstriped suit and white tie walked into the room.
He was followed by two eye-catching women wearing dresses

that moulded to their curves. The man seemed to recognise Phyllis. His eyes crinkled as he smiled and headed straight towards them.

'Oh fiddlesticks!' cursed Phyllis under her breath. 'He's seen me.'

'Who is he?' Diana whispered across the table.

'Don Morris, an architect I went out with briefly, years ago. He's a hack. No taste. Not like Harry.'

'Hello, Phyllis,' Don said, reaching the table. 'You're looking easy on the eye as always.'

His voice was well-oiled and his suit impeccably tailored, but there was something unpalatable about him. Diana thought that with his flat nose and short neck he could be a wrestler. Phyllis must have been having an off time when she went out with him.

'Thank you,' replied Phyllis, looking like she'd just sucked a lemon. 'This is my gardening editor, Diana White.'

Don took Diana's hand in his clammy one. 'I'm an old friend of Phyllis's. Don Morris,' he said. 'Say, aren't you the little lady Harry has conjured up to do the garden plans for that proposal out west?'

'She's a professional landscape designer, not "a little lady",' Phyllis told him. 'And please don't tell me you have your eye on that land too. Don't you and your property-developer friend have your hands full evicting people for your city developments?'

'The west is the future,' Don said. 'And gardens are foolish, sentimental things. Concrete is what a modern society wants. Practical, clean …'

'Ghastly!' Phyllis finished the sentence for him.

Diana bristled. She knew Don Morris's type. There were plenty of them – people who destroyed every piece of bushland to build concrete jungles.

'Harry and I are going to design beautiful suburbs for families to live in,' she told him. 'Places any person would be proud to call home.'

Don smirked. 'My mother reads your quaint column, Mrs White. Say, don't you have a small child to care for? How are you going to do that and take on such a big project?'

It wasn't the first time Diana had been attacked for being a mother with a career. No doubt Don Morris would use the fact that Harry had partnered with a woman to try and win the job for himself.

'It's for my son that I want to create a beautiful city – for his generation and generations to come,' she said calmly. 'If you clear the greenbelt, those bushlands can't be brought back. It's foolish that human beings destroy nature the way we do. It's as if we have been given a gift and, instead of valuing it, we smash it to the ground.'

Don Morris reached into his jacket and took out a cigarette, which he then flipped into his mouth before lighting it. 'Do you think the people who are going to live all the way out west are even going to understand what the hell you're talking about?'

'All human beings understand beauty. Especially natural beauty,' Diana answered. 'It's got nothing to do with money. The government is moving people out of the slums in the city so they don't have to live in terrible conditions and you'll be creating even worse ones for them out west. You'll give them a desert.'

Don's eyes narrowed. He wasn't playing Mr Charming now. 'Do you know what I think, Mrs White? I think you don't know a thing about the people who are going to live out there. You, with your private school accent and your peaches-and-cream skin. I bet you've never bet on the dogs or even stepped into a pub. The average Australian doesn't want your kind of beauty. What he wants is a cleared block of land and a square house just like his neighbour's, with a dunny and washing line out the back and a straight cement path to his door. You and Mr Fancy Pants Architect don't have a clue about how most Australians live.'

'Don't you dare call Harry that,' Phyllis snapped. 'He's a world-class architect. He has a vision to make this city great, not suck everything out of it for himself.'

The waiter came out of the kitchen with their food. He stopped halfway across the floor when he saw the unpleasant argument taking place.

Don nodded. 'I don't want to interrupt your meal.'

He left to join his party on the mezzanine like a spider scurrying back to its hole. Once the waiter had served Phyllis and Diana and returned to the kitchen, Phyllis rolled her eyes.

'There's nothing like an encounter with Don Morris to put me off my food. Don't worry, my dear, I'm sure you and Harry will succeed for all the reasons you explained and Don is too stupid to understand.'

'The man is a creep. I can't imagine the two of you ever going out together.'

Phyllis didn't seem keen to continue the conversation about Don Morris. She patted her lips with her napkin. 'Have you followed up with Professor Spencer, by the way? I'm thinking we could feature his garden transformation in the Christmas issue.'

'Yes, I went to see him. The house is lovely.'

'Oh, how did you find him?' Phyllis asked.

Diana blushed and Phyllis noticed. A look of amusement came to her face. 'He's rather fetching, isn't he?'

'Yes, I suppose he is,' said Diana, trying to sound nonchalant. 'But I can only look. Not touch. I'm married.'

Phyllis took a sip of her champagne and chuckled. 'While I believe in monogamy in principle, I've found it impossible to practise in real life.'

Diana shifted uncomfortably in her seat and Phyllis reached out and patted her hand. 'I'm only joking,' she said. 'I'm sure it's all very chaste for you. I've known you long enough, Diana. You have a way of falling in love with people's minds and leaving it at that.'

Diana wondered who Phyllis was talking about. Harry? Was her chaste little crush on him that obvious?

'How are things at home, *really*?' Phyllis asked. 'You haven't looked happy since Casper returned. Are you sure everything is all right?'

Diana took a bite of her snapper then put down her knife and fork. 'He's changed, Phyllis. It's as if one man went to war and another returned. He barely talks to me or Freddy. Sometimes I think he'd prefer to still be in France than here at home with us.'

Phyllis waited for Diana to say more and, when she didn't, she said, 'People change. Nobody stays the same, war or not.

The papers are full of stories about women like you – wives who waited faithfully for their husbands to return but now find themselves living with a stranger, or worse. They say the applications for divorce are now outweighing those for marriage.'

'Divorce!' Diana said, almost choking. 'I'm not talking about divorce.'

'The stigma is going out of it,' Phyllis said, watching Diana carefully, 'with so many taking place. I know it's not easy, but leaving my first two husbands were the best decisions I ever made. It's a waste of life, living with a man who doesn't respect you. The fact that society encourages women to sacrifice themselves that way is a crime.'

Diana felt the air go out of her. She looked around at the glittering décor and for the first time she began to think the unthinkable. Tears came to her eyes. When she had stood in that little chapel in Paris, Casper by her side, she was sure that nothing but death could ever separate them. Casper had said he would try, but was he trying enough? She was desperately unhappy. What kind of future could they possibly have?

Phyllis cut a piece of her steak. 'The other thing you must consider is that there might be someone else, someone he met when he was over there. Men are not made of the same stuff that we are. We can survive with each other for company. Men cannot.'

Diana shook her head. 'No, Casper is not the type to be unfaithful.'

But even as she said it, Diana wasn't sure she believed it. What she'd said was true of the former Casper. But how could she assume that about him now that he refused to talk to her about the war? He might do anything now, this man she no longer knew.

She turned in the direction of the elegant woman she'd seen earlier, but she was gone, and her table had been cleared and reset. Diana frowned. It was as if the woman had never been there at all. As if she had been a figment of her imagination.

# CHAPTER THIRTY-ONE

Sabine paced the lurid green carpet of her hotel room and chewed at her thumbnail. She could not forgive herself for attracting Diana White's attention at the Hotel Australia. It was the role of an agent not to avoid being seen but to avoid being *noticed*. Robert had always praised her ability to change her walk or her height with the slightest adjustment of her spine, and within seconds appear to be a different person. She could take on a new persona simply by lowering or raising her voice a pitch or changing her rate of breathing. But Australia was too unfamiliar to her, so of course she stood out. She stopped pacing and tried to walk the way Australian women did. They were not like Parisian women, who were self-aware and poised. They meandered, gently swinging their hips, like little farm animals returning to the barnyard.

She stared at the painting above the bed of trees with white trunks on the edge of an ochre landscape. The humiliating thing was that in every other respect, Diana White and her son were easy targets. They left the house at the same time every morning and walked to school together by the same route. Such regular schedules were an agent's dream. Casper also left the house every morning at the same time and caught a train in the direction of the city. But Sabine was so familiar to him she could not trail him. She was sure he would sense her presence.

She lay on the bed, her arms stretched above her head. Robert had told her to eliminate Casper then leave the country as soon as possible. That wouldn't be difficult to do, given his house was so secluded. He'd come out on his veranda and she would aim and shoot. But she couldn't – she had to know the details of what he had done and why. He might be responsible for more deaths than only the members of her circuit. How much did Diana know about what her husband had done during the war? Very likely nothing at all. He'd die and be hailed as a wonderful husband and father and a war hero. Sabine couldn't allow that. Diana had to be made aware that her husband was a monster and she needed to learn that from Casper's own lips. Sabine would make him confess in front of Diana. He deserved to suffer as much as Lucien and Pierre and all the others had.

# CHAPTER THIRTY-TWO

*Paris, August 1944*

It was the kind of sunny August day that, before the war, Sabine and Lucien would have spent on vacation by the coast. But now Sabine stood with the other women from her prison block in the courtyard of Fresnes, shivering despite the heat. They were a mixed bunch – young, old, adolescent – but all of them wore torn, soiled clothing. Their hair was matted, and a collective rancid smell rose from them that reminded Sabine of spoiled milk. Some of the women were in the advanced stages of pregnancy, their legs nothing more than skinny sticks from starvation while their stomachs jutted out like giant moons.

A convoy of buses waited with their motors rumbling. They were the green and yellow municipal buses that Sabine used to catch to the Place de l'Opéra or to visit friends on the outskirts of the city. They had been requisitioned by the Germans, who were taking the prisoners that they hadn't executed somewhere. But where? Sabine searched among the women's faces for someone she knew, fearing she might see Madeleine or Josephine, the baker's wife, for seeing them would have meant that all was lost and the *Pianiste* circuit had collapsed completely. But she didn't find anyone she recognised.

Further along down the line, the male prisoners were assembling before the buses too. They looked in even worse condition than the women, staggering and limping as the soldiers organised them into groups. Sabine stared at them as if she might find Christian, even though she knew he was dead, but they were too far away for her to see their faces clearly. *Christian!* She could barely bring herself to think about what she had witnessed the previous day. Her heart felt as fragile as an eggshell, and she had to be strong for whatever was to come. He would have wanted her to be that way.

German soldiers pushed the prisoners towards the buses. Some of the women brazenly jeered at them. One old woman spat at an officer's feet. Sabine's breath caught in her throat, waiting for the moment the officer would pull out his revolver and shoot the woman between the eyes. But he did nothing.

The woman next to Sabine grabbed her arm. 'The Germans have lost,' she whispered. 'You can see defeat in their faces.'

But Sabine was not so confident. Something ominous hung in air. The Germans were proud even in defeat, and she suspected a more sinister motive. Perhaps they knew the fate that awaited the prisoners and could bide their time for revenge.

A tall and trim SS officer, a perfect specimen of the Aryan race, addressed the group in German. One of the male prisoners, a Dutchman who spoke the language, was designated to translate for him.

'We will be taken by the buses to the train station,' the

interpreter told them. 'From there, we will go to our next destination.'

The prisoners fell into frantic murmurings. 'Where are we going?' they asked. 'What does this mean?'

The SS officer said something else. The interpreter hesitated, as if he couldn't believe what he had heard. The officer indicated impatiently for him to pass the message on. With an expression of despair, the Dutchman translated for the prisoners. 'He says that if anyone tries to escape, that person will be shot and a grenade thrown into the bus they came from.'

The statement was met with utter silence.

\*

As the convoy of buses made its way through Paris, Sabine looked out at the streets of the city that had been hers. The plane trees were in full summer leaf, offering shade to the pedestrians on what was turning out to be a hot day. There was a woman walking with a poodle, and another wearing an elegant straw hat with a voluminous bow tied at the crown. Sabine's eyes drifted to the people taking their morning coffee at the sidewalk cafés. It seemed to her that she had slipped into some other dimension of life, and she was gazing at the world with the longing of a street urchin salivating over the fancy cakes in a patisserie window. Once she too had sat in cafés, sipping coffee and discussing art and music. Now she was trapped in a nightmare, travelling in slow motion towards her doom.

Her mind drifted to her student, Colette Cortot. She had lowered herself by performing for the Nazis, the rapists of

Europe. Sabine could barely breathe at the shame of it. Colette had been her least talented pupil, but at the insistence of Colette's mother, Sabine had put years into helping the arrogant girl acquire a performer's technique. Colette didn't have the driving passion required to master the piano. She was merely a pretty girl who liked the attention that playing well brought her. Sabine's heart ached with the memory of Jacqueline. Her friend had been a beautiful spirit, a far superior musician with not only virtuoso technique but also the ability to embrace all the emotion, joy and fearlessness that made a magnificent performer. Now Jacqueline was dead, her loveliness burned up in Fresnes's crematorium.

They approached the Gare de l'Est and the prisoners gasped when they realised what lay ahead. They were going to be sent east, most likely to Germany. Their trepidation increased when the convoy passed by the passenger terminal and headed to the freight station where a string of wagons – usually for the transportation of cattle – was waiting at the platform. The soldiers ordered the prisoners off the buses and herded them towards the wagons. In the panic, women shrieked and clung to each other. Red Cross volunteers bobbed like driftwood in the turbulent sea of people, attempting to hand out food packages. Sabine nearly had her ribs broken in the crush. It was in the midst of this new nightmare that she spotted Lucien. Her heart lifted and broke at the same time. Up until that moment she had maintained the hope that he was still free. Their eyes met and they struggled to reach each other. Lucien grabbed her and pulled her tightly to him as they were buffeted by the storm of humanity around them.

'Dearest one, they caught you too?' she said.

'We were all caught, Sabine. We fell like dominos. Every last one of us.'

A soldier turned in their direction, but two women, seeing a man and woman spending a moment together, perhaps their last, deliberately blocked them from his view.

Sabine couldn't bear to hear any more terrible things. 'Pierre?'

'I believe he is safe with my parents,' Lucien replied. 'But I don't know for how long.' He took her firmly by the shoulders. 'We did all we could for France, my darling. Now you must be courageous and live for our son. I will try to escape to go back for him. You must promise me that, no matter what, you will survive, so that Pierre has at least one of us.'

Sabine thought back to what the German officer had said about anyone trying to escape. Lucien's chances were slim and yet she needed to believe escape was possible, for his sake. She pressed herself tightly against his chest, pouring every last vestige of courage and strength she had in her heart into him.

'Be brave, my love,' she said.

'You too.'

Before they could say more, they were ripped from each other's arms by the pressing crowd. Sabine looked around for Lucien but all she could see was his back disappearing into the throng.

The women were loaded into their designated wagons first. One pregnant woman was kicking at a guard who had knocked her to the ground and was beating her with the butt of his rifle. Sabine wished she could die on the spot and not witness any more barbarity. But she remembered what she had promised Lucien. She had a duty to Pierre to survive. She was shoved into one of the dirty wagons and found herself pressed against the back of it by the crush of bodies.

Once the wagon was packed, the guards shut the door. The stifling heat sent the women inside panicking.

'There's no water,' one woman cried out. 'For God's sake, give us water! My mother is eighty. She'll be dead within the hour.'

Another woman tried to comfort her. 'Be calm. There are no toilets in here, so they can't be expecting to take us far.'

Sabine closed her eyes. When she was a child, she had been outraged by the way cattle and pigs were treated – packed onto trucks and trains without water, and then slaughtered in front of each other while those waiting to die trembled and shrieked in fear. Now the same thing was happening to people. Most likely they were going to Germany and that was days away. Many of the prisoners were bound to die in this heat.

A woman with a burn scar down one side of her face nudged her. 'The Nazis shot an angel yesterday. A woman who saved Jewish children. That's all she was guilty of – hiding children. *Babies*. Tell me, are people like that going to worry if we have water or not?'

The women were left in the stifling wagon for the rest of the day without food or water. Sabine sank down onto the tiny piece of floor she occupied, her mouth so dry it felt like she had a thousand cuts on her gums. A rumour spread among the women that the railway workers had joined the Resistance and the Germans were finding it difficult to get an engine to drive the train. Sabine knew that if Lucien was going to escape, he had to do it while the train was still in France. It would be too difficult once they were in Germany, where the people would be hostile and he didn't speak the language.

Just before midnight, the train began to move out of the station at a snail's pace. Sabine waited for it to speed up but it never did. The journey was going to be even more torturous than she'd anticipated, but the slow pace might be Lucien's best chance. Some of the women had collapsed into catatonic states and lay with their heads back and their mouths gaping open. Sabine slept in snatches. She was almost delirious with thirst.

Sometime in the early hours of the morning the train screeched to a sudden stop. Women toppled over each other. The tins they were using to urinate in spilled, and the contents splashed across the floor, so that everyone was covered in the sickly ammonia stink.

Sabine was alert to every sound outside the train. She could hear footsteps on gravel and then the rustle of bushes. Searchlights flashed through the gaps in the wagon. Soldiers shouted to each other in German.

'What are they saying?' Sabine asked the women in the wagon.

'Some prisoners have escaped,' replied the woman with the burned face.

Sabine held her breath and clenched her fists. She used all her will to mentally send Lucien into the night, to help him disappear into the trees and beyond the reach of the soldiers' lights and guns. After an agonising hour, in which no shots were fired, the train began to move sluggishly forward again.

Sabine dared to hope that Lucien had been successful in his escape. With the Allies bombing trains during the day, the Germans had no choice but to make the most of the cover darkness offered and press onwards.

As dawn broke, the train stopped again. Sabine's cheek ached from resting it against the splintery wood of the wagon. The doors to all the wagons were flung open and the prisoners ordered out. Many of them could barely stand and collapsed to their knees as soon as their feet touched the ground. Before them lay a field of golden wheat. A group of farming women were harvesting it, slashing at the crops with old-fashioned scythes. When they looked up and saw the state of the prisoners, they gathered buckets and containers of water and offered them to the prisoners before the guards shooed them away. But it soon became apparent that this stop was not for the welfare of the prisoners.

The SS officer who had addressed them before they left Fresnes called them to attention again now. The same Dutch prisoner was ordered to interpret. He stood next to the officer, looking the worse for wear. His eyes were bleary, and he seemed confused by his surroundings. Sabine's pulse quickened when she saw two soldiers mounting a machine gun on a tripod in one of the fields. Were they all to be shot? Then three men were marched out to the field, their hands clasped behind their heads, their shirts red with blood. They had been beaten. One of the men turned slightly and Sabine's stomach dipped to her feet. *Lucien!* He'd been caught.

The sound of the interpreter's voice was drowned out by the pounding in her ears. 'The officer warned us that any escapees would be shot,' he said.

Sabine wanted to shout, but she had no voice. She pushed her way to the front of the prisoners. Some of the women had started whispering prayers. Others began singing 'Le Chant des Partisans' under their breaths. Sabine reached the front of the prisoners and would have started running if a man had not held her back. 'They'll kill you too,' he told her.

On the officer's order the machine-gunner fired. The three men shuddered as the bullets hit them, then toppled to the ground. Sabine fell too. The man pulled her to her feet.

'Savages!' he muttered. 'The Germans are savages!'

The prisoners were forced back into the wagons. Sabine lay on the floor and the other women gave her as much space as they could. But in Sabine's mind she was still falling, spinning into an abyss of pain. She could not fathom that Lucien had been killed so brutally. No priest, no last rites. She had not been able to hold her husband's hand as he left this world, the final act of duty for any loving wife.

Everything she had left to live for was gone now, except Pierre. No matter what, she had to stay alive for him.

# CHAPTER THIRTY-THREE

It was a perfect autumn day, sunny with a slight breeze, when Diana met Harry at his office so they could drive out to see the land they were hoping the government would acquire and develop according to their proposal. She was wearing the long-sleeved shirt, trousers and straw hat she put on when she went bushwalking. Harry was all matching in blue pressed trousers, shirt and fedora hat. It was as if she was going out west with Cary Grant.

When they drove along the highway, the depressing sight of tents and shacks set up in the fields on either side of the road brought home the extent of Sydney's housing crisis. Clothes hung on washing lines strung between trees and women cooked meals over open fires. Building had been on hold since the Great Depression and young couples were starting out life in their in-laws' garages while families were crammed into slum apartment blocks in the inner city. Diana's home was small but she was thankful to have it.

After an hour of driving, they turned down an arterial road that led them past market gardens and chicken farms, then down a dirt track. Harry pulled up next to an expanse of bushland.

'Here it is,' he said, turning the engine off.

Diana climbed out of the car and took in the landscape as if she was studying a painting. It was not the Sydney Sandstone Gully Forest she was used to, with its deep gorges, rivers and creeks. Gone were the peppermint gums, blueberry ash and prehistoric tree ferns. The bushland before her was open and grassy. She'd studied the plant species found in the Cumberland Plain Woodland, and recognised the forest red gums from their smooth bark and perfectly straight trunks. A yellow and black regent honeyeater flew past her and into the tree canopy. There were tiny birds everywhere – warblers flitting around the ground, yellow and turquoise parrots feeding on the grasses, dozens of finches hopping up and down tree branches. The place was brimming with life.

This was all the beauty that would be destroyed if people like Don Morris got their hands on it. She stepped up to a tree and put her palm against its furrowed bark.

'Did you know that the trunk of the ironbark is like this because the bark is not shed but accumulates and then becomes impregnated with sap?' she said, turning to Harry. 'It creates a kind of armour against fire and protects the tree's living tissue so that it can recover quickly after a burn.'

'I see you do your research,' said Harry, looking impressed.

They walked on a narrow trail through the grass and Diana took in every detail. The soil was heavy clay, which was going to be a challenge for establishing gardens, but it was the perfect argument for using local species. The story she would write for *Australian Home and Garden* once the project was done ran through her head.

*The homes are nestled in beautifully landscaped gardens brimming with Australian bluebells, native indigo and pink rice flowers. Robins and finches take refreshment at the birdbaths hidden among the native raspberry. The gardens blend seamlessly with the woodlands that surround them. A stone pathway weaves through the bush and back to a common pathway so no wanderer or curious child need ever fear not finding their way home again, as long as they follow it. It is the perfect place for children to breathe the healthy fresh air that nature provides and to stare at the sky through the bird-filled trees and wonder—*

'Diana, look!' said Harry, pointing to something at the top of a tree. She raised her eyes to see the grey rump of a koala perched in a fork of the branches.

They moved around the tree and caught a glimpse of the koala's broad face. The fluffy ears, black nose and teddy bear eyes were familiar to her as an iconic image of Australia, but she'd never seen a koala in the wild. Then she spotted one in a tree not far from the first – a mother koala with her young joey on her back. The koala chewed on a gum leaf and regarded them with sleepy eyes. There was a noise in the grass and Diana and Harry turned to see another koala climbing a tree, using its strong claws to lift its substantial weight.

'As far as we know this is the only koala colony left in the area,' Harry told her. 'According to the koala sanctuary, it's important they don't get cut off from the wider bushland so they can interbreed.'

For a moment she was tempted to tell Harry he ought to get a male landscape designer for the government proposal. She was sure Don Morris would do everything in his power to use her sex against her and this place was too precious to lose.

But then Harry turned to her and said, 'You know, Diana, I can't think of anyone else who would know exactly how to create harmony between bushland and a housing development. You are one of a kind.'

Diana thought that was probably true and drew up faith in herself. Everyone else was planting imported species after land had been cleared; no one looked at what was already there.

While Harry surveyed the land, Diana collected seeds and leaf specimens and wrote down her ideas for gardens. She planned to use different shades of green for cooling effects. The gardens would be serene and beautiful, and because they would be small and easy to care for, fathers wouldn't be spending their Saturdays mowing lawns and trimming hedges. You didn't need a large garden when you had the beautiful outlook of the woodlands right on your doorstep.

When it was time to make their way back, Diana put her hand on the side of the car and quickly withdrew it. Her skin stung with the burn.

'It's hot out here,' she said.

'There's no coastal breeze or southerly buster to give relief,' Harry said. 'That air from inland can feel like an open oven door when the wind gets up.'

'All the more reason to keep as much natural vegetation as possible,' she said, taking one last look at the woodland before getting into the car. She noticed another koala in the tree above where she and Harry were standing. It was looking directly at them as if it wanted to speak.

'I'll do everything I can to save your home and family,' she promised it.

*

The day out in the countryside had been an adventure, but now the familiar knot of dread returned to Diana's stomach as she steered her truck in the direction of home. It pulled tighter as she turned off the highway and into her street. She'd felt it once before, the first time she returned to Killara after Aunt Shirley's death. Her aunt had never told her that she'd kept the land where Diana's family home had once stood. Diana had assumed she must have sold it. So she'd been surprised to discover that it had been bequeathed to her, along with a personal note from Aunt Shirley explaining why she had chosen to keep it for Diana.

Apart from some new fences and a few extra garages, on that first visit Diana had found that the street was mostly unchanged. The Federation houses and street trees had stood the test of time. Still, the horrific thing that had happened there had destroyed any pleasure in nostalgia. She grew more apprehensive as she neared the place where her family's house once stood. She pulled up at the end of the street and willed herself to look in the direction of the lot. The house was gone, of course, but the wrought-iron fence remained. Beyond it, where the garden had once been, stood a mess of box elders, whiskey grass and knotweed. Madeira vine hung over the half-collapsed pergola and the pond was a dustbowl of asparagus fern. A great wash of sadness overcame her. She felt an emptiness around her.

But then a different sensation began to warm her skin. It was like breathing in the scent of a gardenia flower, velvety and creamy. Other smells rose in her memory – damp earth, sunshine, fresh rain on leaves. She looked back to the lot and realised that somewhere underneath that mess, her mother's garden was still there, and she would only have to uncover it and coax it back to life. The words Aunt Shirley had written for her sounded in her ears: *It was your mother's legacy to all she loved. You must restore it. In healing beauty, you will heal yourself.*

That was when Diana decided she would take the challenge Aunt Shirley had set her. She would build a home here for her family, and in doing so she would defeat the demons that haunted her.

But the dread that Diana felt as she pulled into the driveway now had nothing to do with the past and everything to do with the present.

Marilyn was halfway down the garden when Diana brought her truck to a stop and climbed out. She waved to her, and Marilyn waved awkwardly back, not quite meeting her eyes. Something was wrong. Diana turned towards the veranda and stopped short. Her desk was there along with her oak swivel chair and low bookshelf.

'What?'

She rushed into the house. In place of her desk stood an upright piano, blocking half the light from the window. Anger rose from the base of her spine to the top of her head. *Janet!*

Marilyn arrived at the door. She took off her boots and stepped inside. One look at Diana's face and her eyebrows rose in alarm. 'You mean you didn't want it? The movers said they had instructions to put it there. I thought you must have arranged it.'

Diana was speechless. She glared at the piano with its macabre bronze candlestick-holders and carved columns down the sides. It looked like a coffin. The back of it was high, which indicated a large soundboard. Could anything be worse?

'I take it you didn't order it then?' said Marilyn.

'It's my sister-in-law's doing. She mentioned giving us the piano, but I thought she'd forgotten about it. I told her I didn't want it because we don't have room.'

Marilyn wiped her hands down her pants. 'Well ...' she said, as if trying to find something positive to say about the situation but utterly failing. She knew that there were few people as particular as Diana about where things were placed. 'Freddy might like it?'

Diana was so furious she considered getting an axe from the shed and smashing the instrument to pieces. 'He's never shown the slightest interest in playing anything. Not even in the school band. All he wants to do is his art,' she said.

'Hmm,' said Marilyn sitting down on the stool and contemplating the piano. 'It's quite fancy. The wood is walnut, I'd say.' She opened two sliding doors on the upper panel to reveal a roll of paper music. 'Oh look, it's a pianola!' she said. 'It can play by itself.' She felt under the keyboard and found a lever. A door on the bottom panel slid aside to reveal two foot pedals. Marilyn leaned over and unfolded them. 'Let's have a go then, shall we?'

Diana watched as Marilyn pedalled and the paper started to roll. The keys moved up and down in a way that struck Diana as spooky, as if a ghost were sitting at the keyboard. Despite being moved, the piano was in tune. It had a big sound, like a grand piano, no doubt due to the oversized soundboard. The whole house shook with it.

Then Diana's blood froze. She recognised the tune.

# CHAPTER THIRTY-FOUR

*Sydney, March 1926*

Diana saw the echidna when she came home from school. The spiny ant-eating creature was lumbering along on its short legs, its stocky body catching the afternoon light filtering through the trees. Whenever wildlife visited the garden, Diana felt time slow down and her heart lighten. Could there be any more magical creature than an echidna? It had spines like a porcupine, a bird-like beak, a pouch like a kangaroo, and laid eggs like a lizard. She'd seen echidnas in the bush, but never in the garden before. She ran inside the house.

'Mummy, come see the echidna!' she called.

Her mother took off her apron and followed Diana out into the garden. As soon as she laid eyes on the animal, the care-worn look on her face dissipated and a sparkle came to her eyes.

'Isn't he wonderful?' she said.

Together they crouched down and watched the echidna digging up leaf litter and examining everything with its nose.

'Look, Diana,' said her mother. 'He's turning the soil over and aerating the garden for me.'

The thing that surprised Diana most about echidnas was that their rear feet pointed backwards. She figured it had something to do with their ability to dig burrows quickly.

The echidna went about its business, paying no attention to the two humans who were under its spell. It found a fallen branch and began to stick its tongue into the crevices, searching for termites to eat.

A twig broke and they turned to see Diana's father standing behind them. One corner of his lip was curled up in distaste. Diana's stomach twisted. She knew that look. It always preceded one of his rages. He'd toy with them slowly first, in that detached, superior manner of his, before his anger would explode and he'd spiral out of control, like a tornado pulling everything around it into its vortex before spitting it out again, broken and shattered.

'Don't you two have better things to do than crawl around on your hands and knees?' he said.

They jumped to their feet. Neither dared mention the echidna. Diana hoped the animal would move on and that her father would think they'd been looking for gumnuts on the ground. Once Diana and her mother had been watching a duck with her ducklings wander through the garden and her father had got his gun and shot it. Diana still trembled at that memory.

'You're home early, Bill,' her mother said. 'Would you like a cup of tea? I baked some biscuits.'

His eyes moved from her to Diana. 'All right,' he said.

She dusted off her skirt and took Diana's hand, but her father reached out and grabbed Diana's arm. 'I want to talk to her. We'll come in later.'

Her mother hesitated, looking nervously at her daughter. This wasn't how things normally went. It was usually Diana who was sent away.

'She's got some sewing she needs to do,' she said. 'Perhaps the two of you can chat after dinner.'

'If she has things to do, why is she crawling around in the dirt with you?'

His tone was chilling. Her mother hesitated, not sure what to do. Would it be better for her to insist? Or would crossing him make things worse? This was their constant torture. The rules of his abuse constantly changed, and they could never tell exactly what caused the rages. He could have a bad day at work and be calm at dinner. He could win a game of golf and nearly beat the life out of Diana's mother after celebrating with his mates. They lived on their tiptoes.

'I said go into the house, Margaret! I've got things to say to the girl.'

Diana and her mother exchanged a glance. She knew her mother would have to obey or things would get worse. Slowly she backed towards the house as if keeping her sights on Diana for as long as she could.

Diana despised herself for letting her father talk to her mother the way he did. One day she would get her away from him, but she'd have to be bigger and stronger than she was now. He loomed over her, and she backed away.

Finally, and very slowly, Diana lifted her eyes to look at him. His gaze was narrow and unfocused, and his chest heaved up and down like a pump.

'Stay there,' he said. 'If you move there will be trouble.'

He left her by the tree and went into the house. He hadn't wanted to talk to her at all. It was part of the strange game he seemed to always be playing: Saying he wanted her to do something and then ignoring her when she did it. Suddenly loud and syncopated trumpet, clarinet and trombone music sounded from the gramophone in the living room. The jazz singer warbled the upbeat tune, 'I'll See You in My Dreams'. Then came the sounds of her mother screaming as Diana's father smashed into her with his fists. Diana ran to the house. The front door was locked and so was the kitchen door. She banged furiously at the windows. Anything to make him stop. But he did not stop.

*

'It's enough now, Mags,' said Aunt Shirley, passing her another cold washcloth to hold against her bruised cheeks. 'The next time he's going to kill you.'

Diana stood in the doorway of the kitchen, watching. When her father had finally let her in the house the previous night, he'd refused to let her go to her mother. But she saw her huddled on the floor when she passed by the kitchen. She wasn't even sure she was still alive until she heard her moving about the house later that night.

Her father came to Diana's room sometime in the early morning, turning on the light and looking at her a long time before sitting on the edge of her bed.

'Your mother can be irritating sometimes,' he said. 'She's got to learn.'

Diana had never known a kind word from her father. Her mother might have had better memories of him, but she'd only ever known him as a monster. Sometimes he'd speak to her as if he were trying to win her over to him. As if by doing so, she might forget that he'd beaten her mother up only a short while before. He touched her shoulder and she cringed.

Infuriated by her rejection, he stood up. 'Breathe a word about anything and I'll burn the house down with you and your useless mother in it.' Then he'd slammed the door behind him.

'The man isn't normal,' said Aunt Shirley, pacing the kitchen. 'There's something wrong with him that's never going to be fixed.' She looked from Diana to her sister. 'It's never going to get better, Mags. He's a sadist who tricked you into marrying him to get hold of your money. He changed the instant you had Diana because he knew you wouldn't leave him then.'

Diana felt the truth of every word her aunt spoke. She could no longer believe that if she did something differently her father would change or leave her mother alone.

'What time is he coming back?' Aunt Shirley asked.

Diana's mother's lips were so swollen she spoke as if she had marbles in her mouth. 'He'll come back from the bank at four thirty sharp. Then he'll have his tea and a nap before going to the men's bible study group from seven o'clock until nine.'

Aunt Shirley nodded. 'All right,' she said. 'That should give us enough time.' She turned to Diana. 'As soon as your father is gone, you telephone me, all right? I'll be waiting for your call. Then both of you pack a bag each, something you can carry easily to the station.'

Diana wondered how they were going to escape on foot. Her mother could barely walk after her father's attack on her. But she understood a taxi would draw too much attention from the neighbours.

When Aunt Shirley was ready to leave, Diana went out with her into the garden.

'He's got a gun,' she told her aunt. 'He keeps it in the hall cupboard.'

Aunt Shirley's face hardened. She rubbed her chin as she thought something over. 'Show me.'

Diana swung open the creaky door of the cupboard as if she were about to reveal a bogeyman hiding there. She hated the idea of touching the gun. Her father had once tried to make her shoot tin cans with it, but she had deliberately missed the targets, even though he boxed her around the ears and called her stupid for doing so. She knew if she mastered shooting, the next thing he'd do was make her kill a bird. Her father sometimes shot animals that came into the garden, because he could, and because he knew it would upset Diana and her mother.

'He checks it every night after dinner,' Diana said. 'It's a Lee-Enfield, like the army uses.'

Aunt Shirley's eyes flickered. 'They rejected him from the army. He never got to go to war, and some woman handed him a white feather for it. Now your mother pays for his shame.' She turned to Diana. 'Is it loaded?'

Diana shook her head. 'But there's a cartridge on the shelf,' she said. 'It can be loaded quickly.'

'Is it heavy? Can you lift it?'

'It's quite heavy but I can lift it.'

Diana was too ashamed to admit to her aunt that she could fire the bolt-action rifle if she wanted to.

Aunt Shirley closed the cupboard. 'This is what I want you to do, Diana. After you telephone me, take the gun and throw it in the creek.'

She took Diana in her arms and held her in a tight embrace. 'Everything will be all right,' she said. 'You and your mother are going to live with me and then I'll get your garden back. It was all bought with Mags's inheritance anyway.'

Diana watched Aunt Shirley walk out the gate. She'd promised Diana they could make a new life. She had to believe it because if she did anything to her father's gun and he caught her, she'd be dead, that much she was sure of. She shivered and realised why her father took that gun out every night. He wanted to make sure she understood that in this household, he had power over life and death.

# CHAPTER THIRTY-FIVE

Sabine was back on top of her game. She smiled at her reflection in the mirror in her hotel room. It was quite a transformation – the loose pale-blue shirtdress, the beige sandals with a medium heel, the dark blonde wig. She had been careful to present herself in the most nondescript manner and it had worked. She had blended in outside the school in Killara without anybody paying her any particular attention, even though she didn't have a child with her.

She had observed that Diana had been in a hurry that day and had rushed Frederick through the gate.

'Come on, Freddy,' his teacher had called out to him. 'Class is about to start.'

*Freddy.*

Sabine hadn't drawn Diana's attention like she had at the Hotel Australia. She'd softened her intensity. She had been a moth not a butterfly. Robert would have been proud of the rapid progress she had made with her surveillance. Four days a week after school, Freddy walked to the house of a woman named Eleanor Dalton, a widow in her seventies. It was a small, well-kept house on the less fancy side of the highway. At half past five, sometimes a bit later but rarely earlier, his mother would come to collect him, driving her dark green Holden Chevrolet utility. On Wednesday afternoons, Diana picked Freddy straight up from school and they went to the art gallery for an hour or so and then had afternoon tea in the Botanic Garden's Refreshment Room. Diana had a woman of formidable stature who worked with her as an assistant, but luckily she did not go everywhere Diana went, otherwise it could have been a problem.

Sabine pulled off her wig and fingered her hair. She didn't feel nervous at all. She had performed far riskier missions during the war when the enemy and their collaborators had been everywhere. She had a car now, a black Ford Mercury that resembled almost every other car in Sydney, and she only had to remember to drive on the left-hand side of the road because the last thing she needed was to attract the attention of a policeman. Once she found a suitable place for her operation, she would rehearse her steps until they were perfect, the way Casper had drilled her for successful missions during the war.

*

Mrs Dalton, it turned out, adhered to a routine even more predictable than Diana's. She did her washing on Monday, ironing on Tuesday, and went shopping at the local greengrocer and butcher on Wednesday. She sat in her front garden for at least an hour every morning, and in the afternoons when Freddy stayed with her, she baked while the boy played with her fox terrier in the back garden. Mrs Dalton didn't bake simple scones and sponge cakes. Her creations were sweet-smelling tarts, buns and pies. The whole street would be enveloped in the scent of sugared fruits and vanilla when she was busy baking. She baked generously too, sending Freddy and Diana home with cake tins filled with pastries, and handing over plates covered in tea towels to drooling neighbours.

From peeking in Mrs Dalton's letterbox, Sabine had learned that she corresponded with family in Queensland but seemed to spend most of her time alone, despite being so generous with her baking. Agents liked lonely and generous people. They were easy targets.

★

The ringer on Mrs Dalton's door emitted a feeble 'zing' when Sabine turned it. She straightened the jacket of her dress suit and waited on the freshly swept doormat, hoping she hadn't overdone it with the pin curls and expensive perfume. A shadowy figure emerged from behind the frosted glass panel of the front door. Mrs Dalton's eyebrows rose in surprise when she saw Sabine.

'Madame,' Sabine said, mustering all her Parisian charm. 'Forgive me for intruding on you, but I was passing by when I noticed the sublime aroma coming from your kitchen. My late husband and I owned a patisserie in Paris before the war, but I have never encountered such fragrant pastry. Tell me, is that nutmeg, lemon and a touch of cinnamon I can smell?'

Mrs Dalton's expression transformed from surprise to delight. She wiped her hands on her apron then patted her hair. 'Yes, nutmeg and lemon but not cinnamon.'

'Ah,' said Sabine. 'You are making a tart.' She paused as if she was about to ask something else but decided against it. 'Well, thank you, madame. I must …'

'I use sour cream as the fat for the crust,' offered Mrs Dalton.

Sabine turned and placed her hand on her heart. 'Ah, is that so?'

'Yes, the dough is easy to roll out and it makes the pastry nice and flaky. Would you like the recipe? If you come in, I can write it down for you.'

Sabine was so astonished that she almost forgot herself and refused. Ingratiating herself with Mrs Dalton was so easy she felt ashamed of herself for doing it, as if she were stealing an ice-cream from a child. French people did not like visitors turning up without an invitation, and they certainly never welcomed complete strangers into their home. It was remarkable where flattery could get you in Australia.

'I would be delighted,' she said.

She followed Mrs Dalton down a long wood-panelled corridor, past a hall table covered with framed photographs of a man Sabine took to be Mrs Dalton's late husband, and on to a kitchen with a scrubbed oak table and glass cabinets full of patterned Cornishware. Through the window above the sink, she could see the fox terrier asleep in the garden.

'Have a seat,' Mrs Dalton told Sabine. 'I'll put the kettle on and we can have some tea while you wait.'

'Oh, please, don't put yourself to that trouble,' said Sabine. 'I did not mean to intrude on you.'

'Nonsense, it's nice to have company. So, where are you living? Close by?'

'I have an apartment near the station,' Sabine said. She didn't, but she had seen one up for rent. 'I've just moved here and I was taking a walk around the neighbourhood when I smelled your delicious cooking.'

The ringer on the door sounded.

'Ah, that will be Freddy,' said Mrs Dalton, rushing to the front door.

Sabine held her breath as Mrs Dalton came back into the kitchen. She hadn't seen Freddy up close yet. He had Casper's square face and green eyes. But while his father had looked about the world with a sharp eye, the boy had the wistful, soft expression of a dreamer.

'What a charming boy. Is he your grandson?' Sabine asked.

'No, but I wish he was,' replied Mrs Dalton, putting her arm around Freddy's shoulders and squeezing him against her side. 'Freddy, say hello to Mrs ...'

'Allard.'

'Mrs Allard,' repeated Mrs Dalton.

Freddy gave Sabine a smile that was radiant and full of trust. 'Good afternoon, Mrs Allard,' he said.

Sabine slipped off her seat and crouched down so that she was eye level with him. 'Good afternoon, Freddy. It's a pleasure to meet you.'

'The tart will be ready soon,' Mrs Dalton told Sabine. 'Why don't you stay and try it? Freddy always has such interesting things to say about his day at school.'

'Thank you,' replied Sabine, not taking her eyes off the boy. 'I would love to hear all Freddy's stories.'

# CHAPTER THIRTY-SIX

While Diana waited for Freddy to finish his breakfast, she looked out the window at Marilyn turning over soil for a garden bed. Blossom was sitting on her haunches next to her, alert like a loyal dog. Diana considered that she might take Marilyn with her as a kind of chaperone when she went to see Laurie with the garden plan. Then she dismissed the idea. Marilyn was busy enough and it would look absurd for Diana to take her assistant with her at this stage. But ever since that afternoon at the art gallery she had been thinking about Laurie and the way he had looked at her. It may have been nothing on Laurie's part, but something had loosened in Diana. She knew it when she used hair cream on her unruly curls and dabbed apple blossom perfume behind her ears – she only did that when she was dressing up to go somewhere special, which wasn't often.

'You smell nice,' Freddy told her as they walked together to school. 'Are you wearing perfume? Mrs Dalton's new friend wears perfume.'

Diana straightened his collar. 'I think it's the soap I used to wash my blouse. It's very sweet-smelling.'

They reached the school gate. 'All right, hurry to your class, Freddy,' Diana said. 'The bell is about to ring.'

But Freddy was keen to tell her about Mrs Dalton's new friend. 'Mummy, Mrs Allard is French. Do you think you could teach me something in French to say to her?'

Diana's mind was on getting to Laurie's on time. She did not want to give him the impression she was a woman who was always rushing, even though she was often doing exactly that these days.

'Well, start by calling her "Madame Allard". She'll appreciate that,' she told Freddy, 'But hurry along now, darling. I'll think about something you can say to Mrs Dalton's friend later.'

★

'Diana!' exclaimed Laurie when his housekeeper showed her into the study. 'How nice to see you!'

'Good morning!' Her reply was a note higher and a touch brighter than she would have liked.

Laurie stood and shook her hand. 'Won't you sit down?'

His hair was standing up in tufts as if he'd been running his fingers through it while reading. That air of intellect about him was enchanting to Diana. Phyllis was probably right – Diana had a crush on his academic mind.

She lowered herself into the chair he indicated and placed the garden plans on her lap.

'There was a chill in the air this morning,' he said, looking out the window before sitting down himself. 'And the chance of a spot of rain tomorrow, apparently, according to the paper.'

'Yes, the mornings and evenings will get much cooler this month,' Diana said. 'But it can still be quite warm in the middle of the day.'

They were more awkward with each other than they'd been the afternoon at the Refreshment Room. The informality of calling each other by their Christian names seemed to have had the effect of making them even more formal. They chatted about the dust storms in Broken Hill, about bushfires in Victoria, and about how rough seas were affecting potato exports in Europe as if they were two strangers talking at a bus stop.

'You've done something with your hair,' he said, as if he'd suddenly noticed it. 'Very nice.'

'Oh yes,' she said, patting her curls. 'I'm afraid it gets a bit unruly. I put some cream through it this morning.'

'My hair is dead straight,' he said. 'At school it was always flopping into my eyes.'

'It doesn't flop now,' she said.

'No, I oil it back.'

'Indeed.'

They looked at each other for a moment and then Diana remembered the plans in her lap. 'Here are my drawings,' she said, passing the folder to him. 'I hope you like them.'

Laurie took out the plans, which were divided into garden sections. 'These look splendid,' he said. 'Your drawings convey not just the placement of the plants but the ambience of the garden.'

Diana sat up a bit straighter at the compliment, the same way Freddy had when Laurie had taken an interest in his art.

'I've given a cost estimate,' Diana told him, trying to sound businesslike. 'I accept a deposit of twenty per cent and the rest on completion.'

Laurie studied her cost sheet briefly and took out his pen to sign it to show his agreement. He went to pass it to Diana but noticed something else in the folder. He pulled it out and studied it. His face instantly brightened.

'Is this me? It is, isn't it?'

He held up the picture Diana had sketched of him sitting in his fernery drinking tea and reading a book on Botticelli.

'It's very charming,' he said, looking at the picture and smiling. 'May I keep it? You did say that you like to give your clients something to frame.'

Diana was mortified. She had thought she'd put the sketch in her desk drawer, but clearly it had got caught up among her papers. She laughed as if she had meant to give it to Laurie. 'Oh, that was just for fun,' she said. 'I'll do a watercolour painting of the finished garden plan for you.'

'I should like that very much,' he said, passing the plans back to Diana but keeping the sketch of himself.

'I have one final request,' said Diana, doing her best to compose herself again. 'The garden should not only be beautiful when you're standing in it but should be lovely when viewed from the house. Do you mind if I look at the garden through your upstairs windows to see if I need to make any adjustments? If your housekeeper would be so kind as to show me which rooms I can enter ...'

'I shall take you myself,' said Laurie, pushing back his chair. 'And all the rooms are open to you. Once again I'm impressed that you think of every detail.'

As Diana mounted the stairs with Laurie, she wondered if it might have been better if she had brought Marilyn with her. He was being perfectly chivalrous, walking one step behind her like a gentleman to catch her should she trip. But there was something intimate about going upstairs to the bedrooms of the house with him.

They reached the landing, and she immediately created distance between them by stepping towards the bay window. 'Oh, this is wonderful,' she said. 'You'll have a full view of the garden from here!'

The upstairs rooms were much like the ground floor ones, with beautifully carved timberwork and decorative ceiling cornices.

'If ever there was a house designed to be built with a garden, it was the Federation house,' Diana said, looking around.

Laurie opened the door to the master bedroom. It was a pleasant room with an oak bed, wardrobe and writing desk. Diana kept her eyes averted from the bed and went straight to the window to see the garden.

'You look down on the fernery from here,' she said.

She turned back to Laurie, who was standing in the doorway, and caught sight of a framed photograph on the bedside table. It was a picture of a blonde woman. Diana's gaze was drawn to it but then she quickly looked away. Still, Laurie saw that she'd noticed it so he felt obliged to say something.

'Is that your wife?' she asked, as casually as she could.

'My fiancée.'

Diana remained outwardly composed but her mind did a spin. Hadn't Phyllis said Laurie was a bachelor? It had never occurred to her that her editor could have been mistaken. If there was anybody who got their facts straight about the love lives of the men she met, it was Phyllis.

Laurie took the photograph from the table and gazed at it with a sad smile then showed it to Diana. The woman had large mesmerising eyes, set wide apart, and arched eyebrows. Her platinum blonde hair made Diana think of Jean Harlow. She shimmered from the picture.

'She's very beautiful,' Diana said.

Laurie sat down on the bed as if all the air had been knocked out of him. 'Lisa was killed by a bomb.'

'Oh,' said Diana, her hand flying to her mouth. 'That's awful. I'm so sorry.'

Laurie appeared so frail and sad that she would have liked to have taken his hand and squeezed it, to offer some comfort. He looked at her with a forsaken expression, but it was as if neither of them had any idea what to say next.

'My husband,' Diana said finally, 'I think he's been very damaged by the war. He isn't quite the person I knew. War is terrible.'

Laurie nodded sympathetically, and Diana realised this situation could go in a direction neither had intended and from which there would be no return. She should not be with an attractive and bereaved man in his bedroom. Strong emotions were often the lead-up to poor decisions.

'Let's go and have a look at the view from the other rooms,' she said.

He stood and straightened his shirt, as if he understood her attempt to break the intensity of the moment perfectly.

★

When Diana returned home, she saw Janet and Alfred's car in the driveway.

'Oh, sugar!' she muttered.

That Janet might have telephoned first was too much to expect. Diana parked the truck and noticed that her desk and chair were no longer on the veranda. Where had they been put now? In the pig pen?

She scanned the garden for Marilyn but there was no sign of her. Most of the beds were marked out with pegs and baling twine, except one that had been half done. Marilyn had probably slipped off as soon as she saw Janet and Alfred arriving. Diana didn't blame her, but tonight she could have done with her backup.

The sound of the pianola starting up with 'Pop Goes the Weasel' floated from the house along with Janet's high-pitched singing. Alfred joined in with a shaky baritone that made Diana think of the tugboat horns on Sydney Harbour. She clenched her fists, readying herself for an unbearable evening of sing-alongs. Then Freddy's purer voice weaved in with the first two. She stopped in her tracks and sighed. Did it matter so much if Freddy enjoyed it? While she was tempted to give Janet a piece of her mind about dumping the pianola on them, she was also aware that Janet and Alfred were all the family she and Casper had, and if something should happen to the both of them, she was relying on Janet and Alfred to take care of Freddy. That was the main reason Diana put up with Janet's shenanigans.

She stepped into the house to see Janet seated at the instrument with Alfred and Freddy on either side of her. Casper, to her surprise, was there too. Not singing but sitting in one of the armchairs and looking relaxed.

Janet stopped playing and flashed Diana a victorious smile. 'We've been having such a merry time,' she said, putting her arm around Freddy's shoulders. 'Haven't we?'

Freddy beamed. 'We sang "Here We Go Looby Loo" and "She'll be Coming Round the Mountain",' he said. 'And Aunty Janet taught me a French song – "Frère Jacques".'

'Ah,' said Diana, patting his shoulder. 'Very good. You'll be speaking French as well as your father soon.'

She took the seat next to Casper and he leaned in close to her. 'I moved your desk into the library,' he whispered. 'You may as well use it. It's a lovely room. I know you meant it for me, but I was thinking that I'd be of more help to you in the garden.'

It was a sweet gesture. Exactly the kind Casper would have made in the past. Diana smiled to show her appreciation, but her heart wasn't in it. She couldn't help thinking anything Casper did now would not be enough. His kindness was a temporary bandage over a wound. She realised it was not only Capser who had changed, but she had too.

# CHAPTER THIRTY-SEVEN

'So where would you like to go?' Sabine asked, opening the doors of her car for Mrs Dalton and Freddy to get inside.

'You are brave, Hélène,' said Mrs Dalton, climbing into the passenger seat and perching her handbag on her lap. 'I was never game to drive, although my dear late husband offered to teach me.'

Freddy bounced into the backseat and looked around the car's interior with awe. He wound the window up and down.

Mrs Dalton ran her hand over the upholstery. 'It's all in very good condition, isn't it? The previous owner took good care of it.'

'Can we go to the National Park, Mrs Allard?' Freddy asked. 'I'd like to look at the ducks on the river.'

'Not that far, Freddy,' said Mrs Dalton. 'Madame Allard can only stay half an hour and your mother is coming to pick you up at half past five. What about the local park? You can show Mrs Allard how high you can go on the swing.'

'Yes, please!' replied Freddy.

Sabine pulled away from the kerb, and then glanced back at Freddy over her shoulder. 'I'll have to bring Monsieur Rouge one time,' she told him.

'Who is Monsieur Rouge?' asked Freddy, leaning over the front seat.

'My pet parrot,' Sabine replied. 'He is very clever. I don't keep him in a cage. He likes to sit on my shoulder and sing French songs.'

'Oh Freddy would love that,' said Mrs Dalton. 'He loves animals. Don't you, Freddy?'

'I do! We have two pet pigs at home. The older one is called Blossom and we just got a new piglet named Dolores.'

Sabine smiled. She didn't have a parrot called Monsieur Rouge, but the way that Freddy's voice brightened at the idea that she might told her exactly what she needed to know.

# CHAPTER THIRTY-EIGHT

Diana was excited. The beauty she'd envisioned for Laurie's garden was now going to be realised. Although it would take a while for the plants to settle and for the trees to grow, a piece of living art was about to unfold.

When she arrived at the house in Wollstonecraft, the two garden hands she'd hired to help Marilyn had already marked up the lawn. The glass repairman was fixing the broken roof of the glasshouse, while his assistant cleaned the hazy panes.

'Well, we have started,' Laurie said, stepping out onto the veranda and surveying the activity around him.

'We certainly have!' agreed Diana.

They watched the garden hands sharpen their spades and begin to slice the lawn where it was to be dug up for the garden beds.

'They are probably cursing me under their breath,' she told Laurie. 'It would have been much easier if I'd allowed them to poison the grass first, but I avoid anything that might affect the quality of the soil in the future.'

'What are you planning to do with the rest of the day?' he asked, indicating the bushwalking trousers and long-sleeved shirt she was wearing.

'I'm going out to Berowra. There's a wildflower nursery there and they are holding some Sydney rock orchids for me. I want to make a day of it by going for a bushwalk afterwards, to get some inspiration.'

'You aren't going walking alone, are you?' asked Laurie, raising his eyebrows.

'Marilyn usually comes with me, but she can't today.' Diana chuckled at his concerned expression. 'Please don't worry, I'm quite an accomplished bushwoman.'

'I have no doubt about that,' he said. 'But I've heard the Australian bush can be formidable.'

Diana glanced at Laurie's slip-on shoes and wondered what sort of bushman he would make. An idea popped into her head and she voiced it before she'd thought all its implications through.

'Why don't you come with me?' she asked. 'If you're free, that is. The track I take is a well-known one and we don't have to go far.' She smiled mischievously. 'It will help me ascertain which kind of person you are.'

'Which kind of person I am?'

Diana nodded. 'I've always thought people can be divided into two categories – those who have an affinity with nature, and those who don't. The first view every bird, animal and plant as fascinating. The others seem to find nature frightening, something to be tamed and dominated or avoided. It's those people who aren't comfortable with the natural world that tend to attract noisome visitations from it. They're always the ones getting stung by insects or swooped by birds.'

'Good Lord, you have thrown down the gauntlet,' Laurie said, a smile tickling the corners of his mouth. 'Your challenge is accepted. I'll have you know I was a King's Scout back when I was a boy.'

'Let's go then,' said Diana. She pointed to his shoes. 'But first you need to change into something suitable.'

* 

Diana brushed off the passenger seat of her truck. Grass seeds were stuck in the grooves of the upholstery as usual. In the wetter weather they sometimes sprouted. She placed a clean burlap sack down so Laurie wouldn't dirty his trousers. He cut a dashing figure in his plaid breeches and trilby hat. He climbed into the passenger seat and didn't make any mention of the loamy smell of soil or the little gnats flitting over the dashboard. She hoped the huntsman spider – large and hairy but not dangerous – that lived in the front grille wouldn't suddenly make a dash across the windscreen once they got going.

'My truck isn't the most stylish mode of transport,' Diana said to Laurie. 'But I need the space in the back for the plants, otherwise we could have gone in your car.'

'Oh, so you noticed my new acquisition in the garage? The ubiquitous Ford sedan. It's not an exciting sportscar but it gets me from A to B.'

'It's probably more comfortable than this old truck.'

'I'm looking forward to the trip,' Laurie replied, resting his hands on his knees, 'And this truck is charmingly rustic.'

Their eyes met and they laughed.

As they drove north, Laurie marvelled at the spread of suburbia. 'I had no idea Sydney was so large,' he said. 'It's so new and fresh.'

'Did you know that Japanese submarines shelled Sydney Harbour?' Diana asked.

He lifted his eyebrows. 'Yes, I read about it in *The Age*. It must have been terrible.'

'The Japanese struck in the early hours of the morning,' she said. 'The sound was horrendous and we heard the defence guns firing. At first, everybody thought we were being bombed from the air. The air-raid warden of our building ordered us all to the basement. I picked up Freddy and followed the others. It should have been terrifying but it only felt surreal. Fortunately, most of the shells failed to explode, so any damage they did was due to their weight. The following morning, when the papers reported the attack, it dawned on everyone how complacent we'd all been. Many people had ignored the air-raid sirens when they realised there were no planes, and gone out into the street to watch. Too many of us had left our lights on. A week before, three mini-submarines had come into Sydney Harbour and one had sunk a naval depot ship, killing twenty-one men. It wasn't Pearl Harbor, but it was distressing. The war was something we thought of as happening far away.'

'I like Australian people,' Laurie said. 'They are charmingly naïve ... and they seem to trust each other.'

'We have differences of opinion regarding religion and politics, to be sure,' Diana replied. 'But, yes, in general Australians pull together when they must. The British did too, during the Blitz ...' She stopped herself, horrified that she'd stumbled onto a sensitive topic. 'Oh, I'm sorry,' she said. 'I didn't think before I spoke.'

'I don't mind talking about it,' he said. 'In fact, it's nice to talk to you about Lisa. Men will buy you a drink and slap you on the back. But women are sympathetic listeners.'

'Tell me about her then. Where did you meet?'

'We fell in love during a performance of *Tristan and Isolde*. Our eyes met across the auditorium and that was it.'

'How romantic!'

'Lisa was a performer. A dramatic soprano.'

'Really?' said Diana, turning the truck onto the dirt track that led to the nursery. 'So she was on the stage when you first saw each other?'

'She was.' He paused and looked uncertain for a moment before saying, 'She died on the stage. It was the way she always said she wanted to go.'

Diana had heard that some concerts continued in London even during the Blitz. The entertainers thought it was important to keep people from falling into despair and gloom, or to not let the Germans think they had got the better of British pluck.

'So heroic and so tragic at the same time,' she said.

'Her father and I still stay in contact,' Laurie said. 'I think we are both lost without her. We feel guilty we weren't there when it happened.'

'There was nothing you could have done. Is Lisa's mother still alive?'

'No. She died when Lisa was a child. She and her father were very close.' He shook his head. 'To honour her I try to live by her favourite proverb: "One today is better than ten tomorrows."'

'How very true,' said Diana. 'We never know what's coming. It's best to be as happy as we can right now.'

She brought the truck to a stop before the nursery gate, so Laurie could see the view across the range. The air was strangely silent of birdsong, and then Diana realised why – a trio of wedge-tailed eagles glided over the ridge and soared across the valley, searching for prey.

'Good Lord!' said Laurie when he saw the birds. 'They're gigantic.'

'With a wingspan of more than two yards, they're powerful enough to snatch young kangaroos, sometimes lambs, and rumour has it, even human babies. But their main diet is carrion. They are the cleaners of the bush.' She turned to Laurie. 'This is wilder than my place and a million times wilder than yours. Is this really your first trip out to the bush in Australia?'

'Yes,' he answered. 'And looking at the size of those raptors, I'm glad I have you to guide me.'

*

Laurie helped Diana load the last of the orchids onto the back of her truck. She fingered one of the rubbery leaves. 'Marilyn is going to plant some in your fernery. In spring they'll put on a show of magnificent lemon-cream flowers.'

'Where to now?' asked Laurie.

Diana hung her water canister over her shoulder. 'The track starts at the bottom of the nursery.'

They followed the track down into the bushland and reached a bubbling creek. Laurie crossed over the moss-covered stepping stones first to check they were secure and then held out his hand to help Diana cross. Once over, the track began to rise again, and Diana lifted her eyes to the towering eucalyptus trees on either side, the bottoms of their blue-grey trunks hidden under a valley of emerald-green ferns. The air was alive with the trills of king parrots and the tinkling chime songs of the bell miner birds. Somewhere in the vicinity, a whipbird was making a whistling call. She cast her eye over the undergrowth of deep green foliage, and at the blueberry ash and lilli pilli trees.

'This is Blue Gum High Forest,' she said in a hushed, reverent tone, as if she were standing in a cathedral. She turned to Laurie. 'There's so little of it left. It's being cut down to extinction but it's wonderful rainforest woodland. The blue gums themselves can grow to over a hundred feet, which makes them some of the tallest trees in Australia. The trunks can sometimes measure thirty feet around the base. When I walk here, I feel there's an invisible door to an ancient world nearby. It would be a terrible shame to lose this forest.'

Laurie turned his face upwards to the towering tree canopy. 'I can appreciate that I am standing on the oldest landmass in the world. It feels prehistoric.'

A wallaby appeared from the bush. Its large ears twitched as it looked at them with its brown eyes fringed with thick lashes. Then it bounded across the track before vanishing into the bush on the other side.

'Goodness, what was that? A kangaroo?' asked Laurie.

'A swamp wallaby,' Diana told him. 'They're smaller than kangaroos and live in the rainforests.'

'Are they dangerous?' he asked.

Diana didn't want to laugh at him but as hard as she tried she couldn't suppress a chuckle. It was absurd to think anything as sweet as a swamp wallaby could be regarded as dangerous, but how could Laurie know that?

'To ferns maybe,' she said. 'That's their favourite food.'

Laurie threw his head back and laughed too. It was a good sound and Diana was glad he didn't take himself too seriously.

'Look at this,' she said, kneeling down to examine a small orchid plant. 'My mother always called this type of orchid 'pixie cap' because the curved heart-shaped leaves look as if they would be the perfect headwear for a tiny mythical creature. She looked around her. 'I wish I'd brought my sketchpad,' she said.

Laurie's gaze followed the length of a blue gum from the base to the canopy. Dappled sunshine danced on his face like magic lights.

'"I think that I shall never see, a poem lovely as a tree,"' Diana proclaimed, reciting her favourite verse by Alfred Joyce Kilmer.

*A tree whose hungry mouth is prest,*
*Against the earth's sweet flowing breast;*
*A tree that looks at God all day,*
*and lifts her leafy arms to pray—*

To her surprise, Laurie knew the poem too and recited the rest of it along with her in his rich, mesmerising voice:

*A tree that may in Summer wear*
*A nest of robins in her hair;*
*Upon whose bosom snow has lain;*
*Who intimately lives with rain.*
*Poems are made by fools like me,*
*But only God can make a tree.*

As they finished the poem, it seemed to Diana that everything around her came into sharp focus. The trunks of the trees glistened and the yellow wildflowers blazed like the sun. Beauty of any kind had that effect on her – whether it was nature, or art or words – it made everything hyper-real.

She looked at Laurie and could feel a flush work itself up from her neck to her temples. She fought to recover her equilibrium, at least outwardly, but couldn't. She wondered what it would be like to kiss him, and in one crazy moment she almost leaned forward to press her lips to his. But then her muscles tensed in horror at the thought of being unfaithful to Casper.

'Gosh, I feel quite giddy,' she said, sitting down on a rock and rubbing her forehead.

She had shocked herself by coming so dangerously close to overstepping a line. It was as if the magic of the trees had made her nearly forget herself. Perhaps if they had been standing in one of Don Morris's hideous housing developments, she wouldn't have thought of kissing Laurie at all.

'Do you mind if I pick up something to eat on the way back?' she asked as she stood up, 'Marilyn and I made an early start this morning and I didn't have breakfast.'

She was inventing an excuse to cut their time in the forest short, but Laurie didn't move. He regarded Diana in a way that looked like he was reading every thought in her head.

'Diana—'

He gently lifted her chin and his gaze settled on her lips.

She felt sick, dizzy and happy all at once. That she and Laurie might share similar feelings was both exciting and terrifying. It was like looking over the side of a precipice to catch a view of something both breathtaking and dangerous. *I'm enchanted,* she thought, *like those people who climb up a mountain and have a sudden suicidal urge to jump off.*

'I can't,' she said, recovering herself and quickly stepping away from him. 'You know that.'

Laurie flinched and Diana was immediately sorry. She would have rather done anything than hurt or confuse him, but whatever was happening between them needed to be stopped.

'I'm so sorry,' she said. 'I've been very foolish.'

He smiled kindly at her. 'You really haven't. I'm as much to blame.' He turned towards the track back to the creek. 'I'll drive us home. You can be the one to admire the view this time.'

★

Neither of them spoke on the drive back to the highway. The road had some tight turns and Laurie had to concentrate. Diana watched the sun dance between the trunks of the magnificent trees that lined both sides of the road. The mood between them was very different to the high spirits in which they had set out for the day. They were both in deep thought, brooding over the same thing.

'Hornsby is on our way,' Diana said, trying to sound casual. 'There's a bakery there that I like.'

When they arrived at the strip of shops on Peats Ferry Road, Laurie parked the truck but didn't look at Diana. 'I'll wait here,' he said. 'Take your time.'

Having attempted to make distance between them, Diana was suddenly drawn to having him close to her again. She felt in control of herself finally. The moment of madness seemed to have passed now they were back in civilisation.

'Come inside with me,' she said, nodding towards the bakery with its window display of plastic wedding cakes and bride-and-groom toppers. 'They make lots of nice things. I'll get you something for dinner.'

Laurie hesitated, then stepped out of the truck and followed Diana into the bakery. The bell on the door tinkled as they entered. The bread racks behind the counter were already empty but there was an assortment of savoury pies, jam tarts and coffee spice cakes under the counter. The air was sweet with the smell of pastry. Jazz was playing on the radio in the background. The atmosphere reminded Diana of being on honeymoon in Paris with Casper. She pushed away the prick of guilt that the association caused. Her eyes settled on a homity pie, Freddy's favourite – an open wholemeal pastry filled with potatoes, onions and cream.

'I'm going to get one of these for dinner at home tonight and I'll buy one for you too,' she told Laurie. 'You can tell me if it's as good as the ones made in England. And I'll get some petticoat tails for us to eat with Marilyn when we get back to your house.'

'That sounds superb,' Laurie said. 'But I insist that this is my treat.'

The shop assistant came out and Laurie stepped towards the counter to order, accidentally bumping into Diana as he did so. He reached out as if to steady her and for a second his hand rested on her arm. A warm feeling of pleasure tingled over her skin and she realised she hadn't regained her sanity at all. Then he let go again and took out his wallet.

While the shop assistant packed the pies and shortbread in boxes, Diana looked on and remembered what Phyllis had said about monogamy: that it was impossible to practise in real life. Then she thought about what Marilyn had said about needing to admit to yourself when you were unhappy. She wondered why she was resisting Laurie. Perhaps she would find happiness in his arms. Perhaps Casper wouldn't even care if—

Her thoughts were interrupted by the bell on the door tinkling. From the corner of her eye, Diana saw two women come inside and stand behind her. Laurie paid the assistant and he and Diana turned around to leave. She stopped in her tracks when she recognised one of the women.

'Janet!' she cried.

She couldn't comprehend how her sister-in-law could be in a bakery in Hornsby. She lived over the other side of the bridge.

'Diana!' said Janet, looking equally astonished. 'What a surprise to see you here!'

Janet turned from Diana to Laurie. She smiled pleasantly at him but then her gaze went straight to his hand, her hawk-like eyes searching for a wedding ring. Diana could see Janet's mind working at one hundred miles a minute.

'This is Professor Spencer,' she said hastily, sounding like a child who had been caught with her hand in the sweets jar. 'He is a client of mine. I took him to the wildflower nursery to choose plants for his garden.'

Laurie extended his hand to Janet. 'I am very pleased to meet you—'

'Mrs Pinkerton,' replied Janet, continuing to hold her purse primly. 'I'm Diana's sister-in-law.'

She stared at Laurie as if she was waiting for some sort of reaction, as if he were a criminal who had been nabbed by the police. But he simply smiled in his usual gentlemanly manner and turned to the middle-aged, ruddy-complexioned woman with Janet.

'I'm Mrs Greyson,' the woman said. 'My daughter is turning twenty-one in a few months and Mrs Pinkerton suggested we come and have a look at the Pacific Cabaret as a possible venue for the party.'

'The places in the city are so expensive,' explained Janet, not taking her eyes off Laurie. 'We were thinking of getting the bakery to do the catering.'

Diana saw Janet's remark as an opportunity to escape. No doubt her sister-in-law would take over the entire planning of Mrs Greyson's daughter's coming-of-age celebrations.

'Oh, we mustn't keep you then,' she said, nudging Laurie ahead of her out the door. 'You two will have a lot to discuss. The pies here are the most delicious in Sydney.'

When she and Laurie returned to the truck, Diana collapsed into the passenger seat and pressed the heel of her hand against her forehead. She knew Janet would make something out of her being at the bakery with Laurie, and that she would tell Casper.

'Goodness me, Diana,' said Laurie, looking concerned. 'You are as pale as a sheet. What's the matter?'

Diana dropped her hand and took a deep breath. 'My sister-in-law is the world's biggest troublemaker.'

# CHAPTER THIRTY-NINE

When Diana and Marilyn turned into their street after leaving Laurie's house, Janet's car was at the intersection. She was heading back in the direction of the city.

*Janet couldn't wait to rush to Casper*, thought Diana, clenching her teeth. *She couldn't wait to tell him about Laurie.*

She parked the truck and Marilyn went to feed the pigs. Diana scanned the garden and saw Casper pulling down what was left of the crumbling pergola, using a pruning saw to cut away the thick vines that enveloped it. He was frowning. Was it the effort or because of something Janet had told him? She took a breath. A moment was needed to calm herself and digest what had happened that afternoon with Laurie. They had come close but they hadn't gone too far. The next time they saw each other it might all be a forgotten folly and no harm done.

She walked back to the letterbox and took out the mail. Among the bills and garden catalogues was an envelope stamped 'International Mail' and addressed to Casper. The handwriting was familiar. She flipped it over to see the return address; it was from Peter Todd, Casper's friend in England. She went into the house and straight to the kitchen. After placing the pie in the refrigerator, she took a glass from the cupboard, filled it with water and added a slice of lemon. When she approached Casper, he turned to her with an odd, half-angry expression, but when he saw that she had brought water, he reached out and took it from her with a smile.

'Thank you,' he said, and then drank thirstily.

Diana looked at the old pergola, rotted and listing to one side. She could remember when it had been elegant, with its pristine white columns and balustrade, and wisteria climbing its latticework. Perhaps everything beautiful was doomed to rot away with time.

Casper handed the glass back to her and picked up the saw again.

'Janet was here a short while ago,' he said. 'She was on her way home from Hornsby with her neighbour. She said she saw you at the bakery on Peats Ferry Road.'

Diana tried to sound matter-of-fact but she could hear the guilt in her own voice as she said, 'Yes, I'd taken my client to the wildflower nursery to choose native plants for his garden. On the way home I picked up a pie for dinner.'

Casper didn't say anything and continued to cut up the vine. She swallowed. Was that the only reaction she was going to get? No reaction?

'A letter came from your friend, Peter,' she said. 'I suspect he wants to know how you are.'

Casper continued to work without looking at Diana. Was he angry with her – or not?

'Do you want to come inside?' she asked him. 'I'll make you a cup of tea and you can tell me what Peter said in the letter.'

He shook his head. 'Let's do it later. I've got my mind set on finishing this.'

'All right,' she replied, stung by his refusal. If only he would talk to her the way he used to, maybe she wouldn't feel such confusion. She glanced at the crepe myrtle tree and saw that it was losing its leaves now that the weather was turning cooler. She shivered when she remembered her mother tiptoeing around her father's moods.

'Did Janet say anything else?'

'About what?' he asked.

'About anything.'

He turned to her, his face strained. 'I wasn't going to mention it, but she did say it looked like this client of yours was keen on you. You need to be more careful with men, Diana. Their motives may not always be as honest as yours. You have your professional reputation to think of.'

His comment tore her up inside. He didn't look in the least bit put out. Was it possible he really thought that she was above having an affair – or so naïve?

'Why are you looking like that?' Casper asked. He frowned. 'Is there something I should be worried about?'

Before Diana could answer, Marilyn came out of her cottage and strode towards them.

'I thought you could do with some help,' she said to Casper, holding up a hand saw. 'It will be dark soon and I reckon between the two of us we can get it done.'

*Poor Marilyn*, thought Diana, *she's walked into a tense moment between me and Casper without realising it.*

'I'd better go and pick up Freddy,' Diana said.

As she walked back to the truck, she could hear Marilyn talking to Casper about Laurie's garden. She felt her husband's eyes on her back the whole way. Perhaps it was a good thing Janet had seen her with Laurie at the bakery and made insinuations to Casper. A dose of jealousy might be what he needed to wake up and be a proper husband to her again.

# CHAPTER FORTY

Sabine clicked open the locks on her suitcase. She felt the familiar rush of emotions that came whenever she was about to embark on a mission: a mix of cold fear and exuberance that eventually gave way to a razor-sharp focus. She made a mental note of the suitcase's contents and checked the rope and wiring. Then she sat down at the table and poised her pen over the piece of manuscript paper. The haunting dirge-like rhythm of 'Le Chant des Partisans' rose in her mind.

Sabine could have taken Casper White by surprise, but she had decided it would be better to unnerve him first, to put him on guard but not let him know from which direction the attack was coming. She wanted him to be aware that someone was watching him. She thought of Freddy White, so sweet, so dear, and so very much like her own Pierre. But she understood the importance of the advice Robert had given her before she left Paris about not developing sympathy for targets. Freddy's welfare was not her concern. Nor was Diana's. They were simply a means to an end.

Sabine wrote out her cryptic message in thick letters, then looked up at her reflection in the mirror. She would unhinge Casper White first by attacking what he held dear … and then she would kill him.

# CHAPTER FORTY-ONE

Diana, Laurie and Marilyn wandered around the curving gravel pathway of the fernery with a sense of satisfaction. Now the ferns and trailing plants were in, the rockeries had taken on the appearance of natural stone formations. The effect was pleasing to the eye but didn't calm the unsettled feeling in Diana's heart. She was aware of how close Laurie was walking next to her. She could feel the heat of his skin. He had been polite and formal with her when she'd arrived, yet it all seemed in vain to break the magnetic pull that was drawing them to each other.

'I've adjusted the roller blinds to let in the optimum light for the plants, but in summer they should be rolled down during the afternoon to provide shade,' Marilyn told Laurie.

In the centre of the fernery was a circular paved area with wicker furniture. Laurie sat down on the chaise longue and mimicked holding a book in one hand and a cup of tea in the other.

'Is this how you pictured it?' he asked Diana.

'Exactly!' she said, forcing herself to look at him.

Marilyn stretched. 'I'll start loading the tools into the truck.'

'I'll come and help you in a minute,' Diana said.

When Marilyn left, she turned back to Laurie. He sat up and indicated the chair next to him. 'What's wrong?' he asked. 'You don't look happy. Was everything all right when you got home?'

She shrugged and sat down on the edge of the chair. 'My husband seemed fine, but he bottles up a lot these days.'

Laurie watched her for a moment. 'Has your husband always frightened you?'

Diana gave a start at the question. 'Frightened me?' She shook her head, but frightened was exactly what she'd been feeling, and she knew it. Still, admitting it to Laurie would feel like a betrayal of Casper.

The clanging sound of Marilyn loading tools onto the truck made her turn towards the driveway. 'I'd better go and help. Marilyn must be bone tired. The rest of the work will be completed in the next few days, and you'll be able to enjoy your lovely garden in peace.'

'You'll come again?' he said, standing.

'David and Sam will be here to maintain the garden. I'll be back in a month's time to check how everything is settling in.'

Laurie took her arm. 'Diana, I have feelings for you, and I know you have feelings for me too. Yesterday—'

'Don't, Laurie,' she said. 'Yesterday was a mistake.'

But he grabbed her more firmly. 'You're frightened of your husband, whether you will admit it to yourself or not, Diana. I can see it in your face every time he comes up in conversation. And I'm frightened for you too. I want to protect you. I want you to know that whatever happens, I am your friend. You can always confide in me.'

He pulled her close to him, and kissed her on the forehead, then on the cheek, moving down her face until his lips brushed her own.

'Please, Laurie, it's not right,' Diana protested. 'I'm married. I have a child.'

But it was too late. His arms were around her, and he was kissing her ardently. Diana kissed him back. All the dormant desire that had lain in wait for Casper seemed to rise up. Her skin tingled and her blood warmed. She felt as though she was melting.

The sound of Marilyn's footsteps approaching made her break away from him as quickly as if they had caught on fire. 'Well then,' she said, struggling to compose herself as Marilyn stepped into the fernery to pick up a bucket. 'That's all from me for now, Laurie. I'll see you in a month's time.'

He straightened himself. 'Thank you, Diana,' he said, his voice husky. 'I look forward to seeing you then.'

Diana and Marilyn walked back to the truck together and climbed in. On the way home, Marilyn talked about Laurie's garden and the jobs she was going to complete. It was an ordinary day for Marilyn, thought Diana, much the same as yesterday. But Diana could still feel the sensation of Laurie's kiss. She no longer felt certain of her future. It seemed to have become lost somewhere, like a mountain covered with mist.

★

When they returned to the house, Marilyn headed straight towards her cottage to feed Blossom and Dolores.

A cold wind was blowing up from the gully and sent an icy chill through Diana. Casper wasn't in the garden. Perhaps he'd decided it was too cold to remain outside.

When she stepped into the living room an unsettling feeling crept up her spine. The house was silent, and she had a sense there was something different about it.

'Casper!' she called up the stairs.

There was no answer. Her eyes travelled over the living room. Everything was exactly as she'd left it in the morning – the cushions on the sofa plumped; the books on the side-table tidy; the vase of grevillea blossoms on the mantelpiece hadn't been disturbed. She looked towards the dining room and beyond it to the library, but nothing seemed out of place.

She was about to climb the stairs when a glimmer of late afternoon light drew her attention to the pianola. The lid was up, yet she had deliberately left it down to prevent dust settling on the keys. Freddy hadn't been home all day, so he hadn't touched it. Had Casper played it? Then she saw it – the slip of paper on the music rack. She walked to the pianola and picked it up. It was a half-page of ledger lines torn from a music composition book. On the ledger lines someone had handwritten a melody, though Diana had no idea what the notes were and there was no title on the piece. Had Janet come to the house again?

The shrill ring of the telephone made her jump. She went to the kitchen and picked up the receiver, still holding the piece of music in her hand.

'Diana? It's Grace.'

Her former neighbour sounded breathless and anxious. Not at all like her normal sunny self.

'Grace? Is everything all right?' Diana asked, worried that something may have happened to Howard or one of the children.

'I'm sorry it's taken such a long time to get back to you, but Howard wanted to be sure.'

For a second Diana held her breath, as her mind travelled back to the day at the milk bar. She remembered she'd asked Grace to see if Howard knew what might have happened to Casper's squadron. Now that Grace obviously had something to tell her, Diana felt rooted to the spot, as if she'd forgotten how to move.

'Are you sure Casper said he flew with the RAF?' Grace asked.

'Yes, he wrote me letters before he went on sorties,' replied Diana, puzzled by the question. 'He was shot down over France and taken prisoner.'

Grace was silent.

'What is it?' asked Diana.

Grace spoke slowly, giving emphasis to each word. 'It's true he went to Britain with the RAF but there's no record of him having flown on any missions. It seems that he simply disappeared.'

Diana swallowed. 'That doesn't make sense. It was the RAF that discharged him after the war. He must have been doing something with them, otherwise they would have tried him for desertion.' She stared at the wall where Freddy had hung the picture he had drawn the day that Casper came home. To her shock, standing next to her in the picture was the figure of Laurie. She quickly took the drawing down, hoping Casper hadn't noticed it. If he had lied to her about the RAF, then she would lose her last precious remnant of hope. Howard had to have made a mistake.

'You mentioned that Casper had been in hospital and then in a convalescent home for almost a year recovering from typhus,' Grace continued. 'That made me think back to my nursing days. I couldn't recall a patient ever taking that long to recover. Not unless there were serious complications. I consulted my nursing books … about the long-term effects of the disease.'

Diana sucked in a breath before asking, 'What are they?'

'Some are physical, and it sounds like Casper has recovered from those,' Grace said. 'But typhus that isn't treated early can lead to psychiatric disorders such as paranoia.'

Diana managed to pull herself out of the fog she was slipping into. Her voice faltered. 'Is there anything I can do?'

'You have to urge him to see a psychiatrist,' said Grace. 'Otherwise …'

'Otherwise what?' Diana was whispering now.

'Otherwise paranoia can make patients aggressive and violent towards people they suspect of lying to them.'

Both women were silent for a moment as the gravity of the situation sank in. Laurie had been concerned about her, Diana thought. Was it apparent to him but not to her that she was sitting on a time bomb? Memories flashed across her mind – the evening sun glinting off the roof of her father's car, the squeak of his boots on the floorboards, her mother's cry.

'Diana?'

Her hands trembled as she hung up the telephone while Grace continued to urge her to get Casper psychiatric help. It was only then that she realised she was still holding the piece of music in her hand. By some compulsion she turned over the paper and her eyes fell to the word written in angry red letters on the back.

*Traitor!*

# CHAPTER FORTY-TWO

Dinner that evening was excruciating. Diana forced herself to swallow her food. She regarded Casper warily. His face was flushed, and she didn't know whether that was from being outdoors all day or from bottling up his anger. Marilyn had joined them for dinner for the first time that evening, and she and Casper kept up a long conversation about the joys of manual work. If there was something that frightened Diana more than aggression, it was passive-aggression. She considered the latter more dangerous because you often didn't see it coming, but when it exploded it was as if a demon had been unleashed to wreak as much carnage as possible. She'd feared it as a child, when her father could be courteous with a guest but fly into a fury at Diana and her mother the minute the visitor had left.

Why leave that strange note and accuse her of being a traitor? Diana fumed. What had he been doing if he hadn't been flying with the RAF? He owed her an explanation. Then she thought back to the conversation they'd had the day before, when he'd asked her whether he should be worried or not about Laurie and she hadn't answered. Maybe things had festered in his mind. They were both keeping secrets from each other; they were both at fault for ruining their marriage.

When they readied for bed, Diana glanced furtively at Casper, wondering whether to bring up the note or to confess to him about Laurie. She decided she shouldn't mention that rash moment with Laurie until Casper was in a psychiatrist's care. It might be dangerous for her and Freddy. But she did need to confront him about the note and ask him what had happened with the RAF.

'Casper—'

But his eyes were already closed, and his chest rose and fell with deep sleep. Did he feel better now that he'd upset her with the note? She lay awake, staring at the ceiling and feeling as though she was sitting on top of a volcano.

*

After a fitful sleep, Diana woke as the dawn light was making its way into the room. She slipped off the bed and looked out the window in the direction of Marilyn's cottage. The light was on and she could see Marilyn standing over the stove, cooking porridge. Diana wanted to get out of the house, and away from Casper. She wouldn't be able to think clearly until she did.

She went downstairs and quickly called Mrs Dalton to ask her to take Freddy for the day. Then she crept into Freddy's room. 'Come on,' Diana whispered, gently shaking her sleeping son. 'I've got to go to work early. I'm taking you to Mrs Dalton's for breakfast. She's going to make you pancakes and then take you to school.'

His eyes flickered and then he rolled over. 'Daddy can take me,' he said sleepily.

Freddy was not usually stubborn but it was as if he could sense her desperation and was deliberately resisting it.

'If you go to Mrs Dalton's this morning,' she said, 'I'll take you to the art gallery early today. I'll pick you up from school straight after lunch.'

At first she thought her bribe had been unsuccessful. Freddy remained still, his face firmly pushed into his pillow. Then as she was about to give up, his muffled voice emerged from the bed linen. 'All right, Mummy.'

*

In the truck on the way to Mrs Dalton's house, Diana ran over in her mind what she would say to Casper. She would tell him that he needed help and, if he refused to get it, he would have to go and live with Janet and Alfred because she couldn't be under the same roof as him anymore.

'*Nous n'irons plus a bois,*' Freddy began singing.

Diana recognised the French nursery rhyme about appreciating the beauty of nature. She'd learned it when she studied French at school.

'*Si la cigale y dort, ne faut pas la blesser.*' Freddy stopped singing. 'What does it mean?' he asked.

'It means if you find a cicada in the woods, you mustn't hurt it,' Diana told him. 'Who taught you that song? Aunty Janet?'

'No, Madame Allard,' replied Freddy. 'You know, she has a parrot named Monsieur Rouge? She said she'll introduce me to him.'

Diana stopped in front of Mrs Dalton's house and kissed Freddy on the forehead. 'That's lovely, darling,' she said. 'Now go on to Mrs Dalton. She's expecting you. And remember that I'll come to your school early to take you to the art gallery.'

Diana watched him climb out and run to Mrs Dalton's front door. His French accent was very good. Children picked things up so easily. She thought that Casper should be teaching him French now, not leaving it until later, and that he should be teaching him other things too, like how to build a model boat and fly a kite. Then the anxious feeling in her stomach reminded her that there were far more urgent things to think about, and soon Casper might not be in their lives at all.

★

When she returned home, Casper was in the garden, cutting the wood for the new pergola. Diana watched him from the veranda. The profiles and stringlines he had made to form a rectangle were perfect. She couldn't have asked more of Marilyn. Perhaps outdoor work would be good for him, but it wouldn't be enough.

'Casper,' she said, when she approached him. 'Why did you put this note on the pianola? Why would you do such a hurtful thing? What if Freddy had found it?'

Casper looked startled when she thrust the note at him.

'I don't even read music,' she said. 'What does it mean?'

Casper's eyes travelled over the musical notes. He hummed the tune. Then he frowned. 'Diana, where did you say you found this?'

'Please don't play games with me, Casper,' she told him. 'There was no one else who could have left it on the pianola. It wasn't there the day before, so it couldn't have been Janet, and nobody else was at home yesterday.' Her voice trembled. 'I waited for you for six years. I didn't go on one dance date even when you were declared missing in action. Yes, I flirted a little with Laurie Spencer, but I wouldn't have done that if you had paid me more attention.'

He looked at her aghast. 'Diana—'

She raised her hand to stop him. Now she had confessed about Laurie, she didn't intend to be derailed. 'I've taken Freddy to Mrs Dalton's,' she said. 'I'm going in to the magazine to help with the layouts and then I'm taking Freddy to the art gallery and Refreshment Room early. When I get back, you and I must talk. If you don't go see someone … a psychiatrist … then our marriage can't go on, Casper. Do you understand? I've tried to be patient …'

'Diana!'

But she was not prepared to listen to any excuses or denials. 'I have to go,' she said. 'We'll talk about it more when I return.'

⋆

The Refreshment Room at the Botanic Garden was quiet now that lunchtime was over, and Diana and Freddy had the place almost to themselves. The other diners were nothing out of the ordinary – a businessman reading the newspaper while sipping tea, a pair of elderly ladies with Mark Foy's shopping bags at their feet. The waitress led them to a table by the window and took their order for orange ice-cream for Freddy, and tea and scones for Diana.

Diana took Freddy's sketchpad from her bag and gave it to him. She needed to gather her thoughts before she spoke to him about his father. When she'd married Casper, she'd loved him with all her heart and soul. Even now, she couldn't hate him. The war was not his fault.

Freddy began to sketch in earnest and Diana watched absent-mindedly until she realised that his subject was the old 'Wishing Tree' in the Gardens. The legend was that those who walked around the Norfolk pine three times forwards, then three times backwards, would have their wishes granted. As Freddy brought the symmetrical branches of the tree to life, Diana remembered she'd told him the story of her and Casper walking around the tree in the prescribed manner, holding hands, and wishing *for him*.

Diana was lost in her thoughts and didn't notice Freddy was licking his bowl, something he was allowed to do at home but not in public. She reached out to take the bowl away from him, but then her heart filled with tenderness and she couldn't rebuke him for such a tiny pleasure.

'Finished!' said Freddy, proudly showing her the empty bowl.

'Let's go for a walk,' she said. 'There's something I need to tell you.'

When she paid the bill, the cashier handed Freddy two bread rolls. 'They're stale now,' the woman said. 'You can feed them to the ducks.'

Diana normally didn't encourage feeding bread to wildlife, but she indulged Freddy on this occasion. He was always drawn to the pond, but not because of the ducks. It was the eels that fascinated him. The first time they had knelt together beside the pond and peered into its green murk, the water had swirled and from the muddy depths several eels appeared. Freddy recoiled at the sight, thinking they were some sort of slimy snake, but changed his mind and became captivated by the creatures when Diana told him their story.

'Those eels were born far away from here in the warm waters of New Caledonia. They travelled as larvae across the treacherous Pacific Ocean until they found their way into the harbour and then through tiny canals leading to the pond in this park. When they reach forty years of age, their spirits and the moon tell them to travel all the way back to their home in order to breed, and then die. The eel has a purpose, and it knows that journey must be fulfilled at whatever cost or danger.'

Freddy looked at the pond and then at the low stone wall that stood between it and the harbour. 'But how do they make their way back from here to the sea?' he asked. 'They have no legs. They can't walk.'

'Yes, some do become landlocked, I'm afraid,' Diana replied. 'But eels show endurance in the face of extraordinary obstacles. On rainy nights, they will leave their ponds and rivers and wriggle across land to the next body of water – even a drain.

Some have been known to swim up dam walls. That's how strong the call of the heart is, my sweet.'

'What about the landlocked eels?' Freddy asked, a look of concern on his face.

She winked and remembered the story her mother used to tell her. 'All that power stays within them and they grow and grow ... and grow. What do you think the Loch Ness Monster is, but a giant eel?'

Diana sat down on a bench and watched Freddy throw pieces of bread to the eels. She wondered if he would understand if she told him that his father needed a purpose, and he might have to go away to find it, as the eels did. From somewhere behind her, a man's voice called her name.

'Diana!'

She turned to see Harry approaching her from the path that ran behind the pond. He had a briefcase in his hand and rolls of blueprints tucked under his arm.

'I'd wave if I had a free hand,' he said, walking to where she sat on the bench. 'What are you doing sitting here by yourself?'

'I'm not by myself,' she replied, nodding towards Freddy, who was now at the opposite end of the pond near a thick clump of palm trees, sketching. 'I come here every week with my son. We go to the art gallery and then wander around the gardens for inspiration.'

'My goodness he has grown since I saw him last,' said Harry. 'And he's the image of his father.'

'You think so?' asked Diana, trying to recall when Harry had last seen Casper. Then she realised it was at his and Phyllis's engagement party – before the war that changed everything.

'I submitted our proposal to the minister for planning,' Harry told her. 'And I've heard back that we're in with a fighting chance.'

'That's wonderful!' said Diana, sincerely pleased that at least her career, unlike her marriage, wasn't an abysmal failure.

'I've made plans for more elaborate houses for a development in the northern suburbs,' he told her. 'Would you like me to show you?'

'By all means,' said Diana, keen for any distraction from the apprehension she was feeling. She glanced at Freddy, who was still absorbed in his sketching.

Harry opened one of the rolls and spread the plan over his and Diana's laps.

'In this design, the central courtyard will make the building feel open and linked,' he explained. 'But at the same time it allows for acoustic separation when needed.'

Diana admired how in Harry's plan the kitchen, living and dining rooms all looked inwards to the courtyard as well as outwards to the main garden. 'What a perfect way to let in natural light,' she said.

She listened with interest as he explained the building materials for the interiors, including off-white mountain ash and natural stone.

'How would you landscape the courtyard?' he asked.

Diana thought for a moment. 'It should feel like an oasis without blocking the light. I'd suggest medium-sized, leafy plants like elephant's ear and Silver Lady ferns with devil's ivy or native viola for groundcover, and maybe crimson bougainvillea for colour.'

Talking about plants was a salve to her heart. Diana looked on as Harry showed her further designs for open-plan houses, and she imagined beautiful, verdant gardens to go with each one.

She turned back to the pond and frowned when she saw Freddy was no longer sitting there. She scanned the lawn but couldn't see him anywhere. She leaped to her feet.

'Freddy!' she called.

When there was no answer, she hurried towards the pond and looked around the trees and the pathway to the harbour. There was no sign of him.

'He was there only a few minutes ago,' said Harry, stepping up beside her.

How long had they been talking? Diana had lost track of time. But surely it hadn't been long – ten or fifteen minutes at most. It was unlike Freddy to wander off without telling her where he was going. She ran down the pathway to the harbour, looking left and right. The garden was thickly planted in stands of lush foliage. It was impossible to take in any sizable section of it in a single sweep. She heard Harry's voice booming out Freddy's name. Two women pushing prams appeared on the pathway, coming towards her.

'Have you seen my son?' Diana asked them. 'A blond boy in a school uniform?'

The women looked at each other and then with sympathy at Diana. 'No, we didn't pass anyone.'

Harry enlisted the help of one of the gardeners, a burly man, who picked up a long fishing net and began poking around the pond, checking the water.

Diana's stomach somersaulted. *No, not there*, she told herself firmly. *Freddy would not have fallen in – he's too careful, and I would have heard a splash or a cry.* But even if Freddy had fallen in without a sound, the pond was shallow and he could swim. She'd taught him herself at the Rushcutters Bay Baths.

Then she thought of it – the Wishing Tree! Freddy must have gone to look at the pine. It would be like him to want to refine the detail of the scaly bark and the exact curve of the leaves. She ran in the direction of the tree. But when she arrived at the place and there was no sign of Freddy, her knees buckled.

Then she spotted a policeman walking through the palm grove. 'I've lost my son!' she called out, running towards him. The words sounded surreal in her head.

'Where?' the policeman asked.

'I was sitting near the pond, only a short distance away from him. I was talking to a friend, and the next minute he was gone.'

'How old is he? Could he be playing hide and seek?'

'He's seven years old. And no, he would never do that to me – not once he heard me calling for him.'

The policeman rushed into action. Diana hurried along beside him. It was after three o'clock now and boys from St Andrews Cathedral School were walking through the park. The policeman enlisted their help to find Freddy.

'I want you to split up into groups,' he told them. 'We have a missing boy in the gardens.' He turned to Diana. 'What does your son look like?'

The blood was humming so loudly in her ears, Diana could barely hear herself. 'He's blond. He's wearing his school uniform – it's grey with a blue shirt.'

The policeman told the boys to search by sections and to look under every tree and shrub. 'Someone might have frightened him, and he might be hiding, or he might have tripped and hit his head.'

Diana thought of the pervert she'd seen hanging around the art gallery but pushed any further images from her mind. The park was swarming with boys in uniform looking through the bushes and garden beds, calling out for Freddy. The world was closing in on her. The palms and giant Moreton Bay fig trees, and even the harbour, seemed to have a sinister haze floating over them.

She returned to the pond. Harry looked at her hopefully but when she shook her head, his face turned grim.

'He couldn't have gone far,' Harry said, trying to shield her from the sight of the gardener leaning over the seawall and peering into the harbour.

Diana forced herself to be brave, to think straight, but she couldn't breathe. She couldn't swallow. Her whole body was trembling. With a mother's instinct, she sensed Freddy's absence. They wouldn't find him in the gardens now, she was sure of it.

The realisation hit her like a shockwave. Freddy was gone.

# CHAPTER FORTY-THREE

Sabine glanced at Freddy, unconscious on the seat next to her. He looked peaceful, with an untroubled brow. His mouth was slack, but his lips were rosy and that was reassuring. Chloroform wasn't quick-acting, like it was in the movies. It had taken a few minutes to subdue him and he had fought. It had made Sabine feel like a monster. She regretted the use of the drug, but she needed Freddy to be quiet until she could get him out of the city, and she was not going to take the risk of knocking a child unconscious by physical force. She had nearly been tripped up because Diana had taken him to the art gallery earlier than usual, and Sabine had almost missed them. The arrival of the man with plans under his arm had been a godsend.

Turning her attention back to the road, she bit her lip. She hadn't liked that moment when the excitement on Freddy's face had turned to uncertainty and he'd realised something was wrong – that they weren't looking for Monsieur Rouge as she'd told him and he was being led away from his mother. It was obvious that she had not only been successful in gaining Freddy's trust during her visits to Mrs Dalton's, but also that he seemed to have a special regard for her. It reminded her of how Hélène

Rosenfeld had been when she'd turned up for her piano lessons before the war. Both children had treated her as if she were a fairy godmother, one capable of transporting them to the realms of fun and magic. Everything she did and said was fascinating to them. Hélène's mother used to say that after her piano lessons, Hélène would talk about nothing but Sabine for hours.

The exit sign to the eastern suburbs loomed up ahead and Sabine took the turn-off. When Freddy came to, he would be nauseous and his head would ache. But she had the room set up in the fancy house she'd rented — no shortage of houses at the rich end of town if you could feign the possession of money — and she would give him ice-cream and comic books to keep him occupied.

She pulled up at a set of lights and looked at Freddy again. He had hair like Pierre, camomile blond and thick. The thought of her son made her heart ache. The lights turned green again and she continued towards the suburb with the French name, Vaucluse. She relaxed her shoulders, remembering how much she had practised and drilled herself. As long as Casper did everything as she'd instructed, Freddy wouldn't suffer.

## CHAPTER FORTY-FOUR

Detective Robertson was a large man with a ring of fat around his middle and the kind of slow gait that made Diana suspect he had a heart problem. He sat down in the wingback chair she offered him and spilled over the sides of it like pastry in a pie dish. Diana wondered if she was expected to make tea. Is that what a woman in her situation would normally do? But she couldn't worry about what was normal now. It was not normal for your child to vanish. All she cared about was finding Freddy.

The detective began to ask the same questions he had when she'd gone to the police station as soon as she realised Freddy was not in the Botanic Garden. He was asking them again because Marilyn had finally been able to locate Casper and he was now sitting beside Diana, his face pale and anguished. Detective Robertson seemed to be one of those policemen who believed that you'd get better, more rational answers, if the husband was present.

'Freddy did not go with a stranger,' Diana told the detective, barely able to contain her frustration. 'He's too smart for that. I've warned him about strangers. It was someone he knew, otherwise he would have put up a struggle and Mr Scott and I would have heard it.'

'Those sick people can be very clever,' the detective replied, rubbing his broad hand over his chin. 'They sometimes pretend that they've lost their puppy and ask the child to help them find it, gradually leading them further and further away.'

'He was gone in ten minutes.'

Detective Robertson sighed. 'Children can be taken in seconds, often in plain sight. Just last year a girl was enticed by a stranger while her mother was trying on shoes. Deviants take advantage the moment a mother's attention is on something else.'

Casper reached out to take Diana's hand, but she flicked it away. Detective Robertson noticed.

Diana wondered why Casper hadn't been in the garden when Marilyn frantically raced home after receiving the call at Laurie's house? Where had he gone? Grace had told Diana that long-term typhus could lead to psychosis. Casper must have been furious that morning when she'd told him that their marriage would be over if he didn't get psychiatric help. She couldn't discount that he had taken Freddy to get back at her.

She glanced out the window at the policeman questioning Marilyn on the veranda. Her assistant's tanned skin had turned ashen. She was hunched over as if someone had punched her in the gut. Then Diana saw Janet and Alfred's car pull up in the driveway. Nobody had informed them. They must have heard the news on the radio.

'Is everything all right at home?' Detective Robertson asked carefully. 'Nothing that would make Freddy want to run away?'

'Of course it is,' said Casper, with a tone of indignation. 'Freddy is a happy child and we're a happy family.'

Diana stared at Casper as if she'd never seen him before in her life. Who was this man who could lie so convincingly? Well, convincing enough for Detective Robertson, whom she'd already concluded was well-meaning but ineffectual. She couldn't risk telling the detective about her suspicions regarding Casper, sure that he would bungle the situation in some way that might result in Freddy's ordeal being prolonged. She would have to figure out a way to approach Casper herself.

★

Nobody felt like eating the ham sandwiches Janet had insisted on making for supper, least of all Diana, who understood how much the sight of the pink flesh wedged between two slices of bread would have upset Freddy.

'Oh, my poor brother,' Janet said, clasping Casper's arm. 'What a terrible thing to have happened! You know, while you were away, I was practically a mother to Freddy. I would never have let him wander off on his own!'

Marilyn's eyebrows shot up and Alfred sent a warning look to his wife.

'How dare you!' Diana glared at Janet. 'Taking Freddy to the movies once a month is what an aunt does, not a mother! You were never there for his nightmares or his illnesses—'

'They'll find him,' Alfred said, patting Diana's hand in an effort to stop a full-blown argument between her and his wife, although it was a long time overdue. 'I have faith in the police.'

Janet pouted sulkily, unhappy that Alfred was taking sides with Diana.

Marilyn looked pointedly at Diana. 'Why don't we go upstairs? You can lie down for a bit. I'll keep you company, and if you fall asleep I promise to wake you up if there is any news.'

Diana frowned. It was an odd thing for Marilyn to suggest. For a moment, she wondered if Marilyn, like Alfred, was trying to keep her and Janet from tearing each other apart. But then Marilyn lifted her eyebrows and she realised that she had something to tell her.

They went to Freddy's room and Diana sat on the bed. She could smell her son on the bedcovers, a mix of the oily residue of crayons and the natural honey-sweetness of his skin. She took his pillow and pressed it to her chest as if she were hugging him.

Marilyn closed the door and sat down next to her.

'You mustn't let Janet get to you,' she told Diana. 'When Freddy comes back, you are going to have to set stronger limits with her.'

Diana nodded, but she knew Marilyn hadn't insisted that she come upstairs to talk about Janet. Marilyn reached into her pocket and pulled out an envelope.

'Professor Spencer gave this to me as soon as I told him what had happened,' she said. 'I've been trying to give it to you all evening.'

Diana opened the envelope and pulled out the note inside. Her eyes ran over its contents.

*Come and see me urgently. I know who took Freddy.*
*Laurie*

Diana stared at the words. How could Laurie possibly know? She looked up at Marilyn, who was watching her expectantly.

'He said he's sorry about Freddy and wishes me well in finding him,' she lied.

Marilyn nodded. 'He's a very nice man. I think he cares for you a lot.'

Diana turned away. She realised that Marilyn had noticed the attraction between her and Laurie. She probably thought the note was a letter of support from a man to his lover. But this was something else, and Diana needed to find an excuse to see Laurie as soon as possible.

The telephone rang downstairs and she heard Janet take the call.

'The *Daily News*, did you say?' Janet said. 'No, I'm afraid you can't speak to the mother, she can barely speak to us … Of course she's upset … I'm his aunt. I practically brought him up when his father was at war and his mother was working … Yes, *working*. She's the gardening writer Diana White … She was speaking with a gentleman friend when Freddy went missing … Yes, that's right. Harry Scott. The husband of her editor.'

Diana gritted her teeth. She could imagine what was going to be printed in the morning papers. But she wasn't going to waste any more time worrying about what Janet did or said.

'It's already ten o'clock,' she said to Marilyn. 'I don't think the police are going to tell us anything more tonight. I need to get out of here. I need to speak to Laurie.'

Marilyn seemed surprised that Diana would leave the house in the circumstances, but true to her form she didn't ask questions. 'I'll take you,' she said. 'I'll tell the others we're going for a short drive to settle your nerves.'

★

Neither Laurie nor his housekeeper answered when Diana rang the doorbell. The house was quiet and seemed deserted. She rang the bell again and glanced around the garden, silvery now that the moon had risen.

She returned to Marilyn, who was waiting in the truck. 'There's no answer. I think I'll see if he's around the back.'

'No rush,' Marilyn said. 'I'll be waiting here.'

Diana went around the side of the house, towards the fernery. She stopped short when she saw Laurie standing under one of the garden lights and smoking. At least, she thought it was him. She'd never seen him smoke before, and he seemed taller and more angular in some way.

'Laurie?'

He turned at the sound of her voice. He stared hard at her through the dark, and then his face softened with recognition.

'Diana!'

He stubbed his cigarette out and came rushing towards her, grabbing her arms as if he was trying to hold her up. 'You got my note?'

'Yes. Who do you think took Freddy? Casper?'

'Come inside and I'll explain everything,' he said. 'How did you get here?'

'Marilyn brought me,' she replied, letting him lead her to

the house by the arm. 'We told the others she was taking me for a drive to settle my nerves.'

Laurie turned the lights on as they made their way down the hallway. He ushered her into the drawing room and indicated for her to take a seat by the fireplace.

'I want to know why you think Freddy was taken by Casper?' he asked her.

'Freddy would not have gone off with someone he didn't know,' she said. 'The only person he would have trusted, and who had a reason to take him, was Casper.'

She told him about the note she'd found on the pianola, the gun that Casper had hidden somewhere, and what Grace had said about untreated typhus leading to paranoia.

Laurie ran his hands through his hair, his face pinched with distress. 'I'm so sorry, Diana,' he said. 'If I had any idea that Casper would do such a thing, I would have acted sooner to protect you and Freddy.'

'How could you have known?' Diana asked. 'I didn't know myself.'

One of the logs on the fire flared, lighting the room with a flash, and then died down again. Diana thought she saw the remnants of burned documents twisting in the fire. She turned to Laurie and registered something odd in his expression. A thought stirred in her mind, as if a fact was trying to make its way to the surface, one of vital importance that she'd failed to comprehend before.

Laurie knelt beside her and took both her hands in his own. 'I am going to tell you something that is going to sound quite impossible, but I need you to believe it,' he said, clasping her hands tightly. 'I need you to trust me and to do exactly what I tell you to. If you follow my instructions, I'll be able to get Freddy back for you.'

Her eyes did not leave his face. 'What is it, Laurie? What's going on?'

'I'll explain everything,' he said. 'But first I must tell you that my name is not Laurie Spencer. I'm Peter Todd. Casper's friend from London.'

# CHAPTER FORTY-FIVE

Diana's mind was in turmoil. Peter watched her patiently, waiting for the confusion he had caused her to settle.

'You are Peter?' she asked feebly. 'But you sent a letter from England recently. How can you be here?' She was surprised at how weak and frail she sounded, like a frightened child. But since the previous day, she had received one shock after another, all crammed together without a break.

'I wrote it before I left England,' he said. 'My colleague posted it. It was important that Casper didn't suspect he was under surveillance.'

'Surveillance?' The word sent jangles up Diana's spine. 'Why on earth would Casper be under surveillance?'

'The British government considers him a traitor.'

Diana's mind plunged deeper into chaos. She shook her head. 'What do you mean he's a traitor?' she asked.

Peter's shoulders sank as if a great weight was pressing down on them. He went to the drinks cabinet and poured two glasses of Scotch. Diana watched him as if he might suddenly snap back into Laurie again and what he'd told her would turn out to be some strange hallucination. But that didn't happen. He placed her glass on the side table next to her and sat down on the sofa opposite.

'I had better explain from the beginning,' he said. 'When the war broke out I was asked to join the Special Operations Executive, SOE – a top-secret organisation charged with aiding the resistance movements in occupied countries. It was my job to assist with agents sent to France. I knew Casper was in Britain, training with the RAF, so I arranged for him to be secretly transferred to work for SOE while maintaining his rank of Squadron Leader. He was the ideal candidate for undercover work – fluent in French and German, and he had first-hand knowledge of France as well as the discipline that came from his flight training.'

Diana tried to follow what Peter was telling her. 'Are you saying Casper was some sort of spy?'

'Not quite a spy, but on his first mission into Marseille he did gather some intelligence that was passed on to MI6, which was why he was held in high regard by all. But his main role was to train and arm local groups of French citizens who were proving to be effective in making life difficult for the Germans.' Peter's face clouded and he hung his head. 'Unbeknown to me, Casper had German sympathies. While I trusted him completely, he was passing on important Allied information to the enemy. As a result, the entire circuit he was supposed to be helping was captured by the Gestapo. The members met terrible deaths in concentration camps or in front of firing squads, including women and children.'

Diana recalled the newsreel she'd seen about the extermination camps. The images of starving people had shocked her. Whatever it was he had done during the war, she couldn't bring herself to believe Casper would support a regime that committed such atrocities. He had been fascinated by the German language and culture for years, but that didn't make him a Nazi.

She stared at the fire and the realisation hit her. Everything Peter had told her about himself was untrue. His name wasn't Laurie Spencer, he wasn't a professor at Sydney University, and he'd probably never even been to Melbourne let alone spent the war there.

'How do I know any of this is true?' She looked about the room and came to a shocking conclusion. 'This isn't even your house, is it? You fooled me into coming and creating a garden for someone else's home!'

Peter's expression darkened. 'You'll be well compensated. And who knows, when the owner returns from the United States with his new wife, he might even like it.'

She flinched at the sharpness of his tone. Laurie wouldn't have spoken to her that way. She realised how duped she had been. Even those kisses had been false. He'd been keeping her close so he could find out about Casper.

'Spies, saboteurs, secret organisations,' she said, fiercely. 'I don't know how you can live with yourself! Is anything you do real? Don't you have a conscience about the games you play with people?'

Peter sighed as if he was watching an unruly child have a tantrum. 'Espionage keeps ordinary people like you, Diana, safe. It wasn't generals and soldiers who won the war; it was the intelligence agents and the codebreakers.'

'You are trying to justify yourself. I've never heard of a spy being awarded a medal for courage.'

Peter grimaced. 'That's true. You can't be a spy and care about accolades. But you do have to be a patriot to put your life on the line for your country. It's spies who must risk torture and death to obtain accurate information for their governments and military. Don't you know that we live in the most dangerous time in history? One where we now have weapons that could see humankind wiped off the face of the planet.'

Diana was losing her patience. 'What has any of this got to do with Freddy?' she asked.

Peter nodded towards the glass of Scotch next to Diana. 'Take a sip first,' he said. 'This isn't going to be pleasant to hear.'

Diana glanced at the Scotch as if it was poison. 'No,' she said. 'Just tell me what all this is about.'

'All right,' he said, taking a sip of his own drink before commencing. 'A double agent by the name of Sabine Brouillette has convinced the French secret service that she is here to assassinate your husband for what he did during the war, when in fact she has already recruited him to spy for the Soviets. In return for the information he provides, the Russians will give him asylum so he can never be brought to trial for his war crimes.'

Diana sat perfectly still. Her heart slowed to the point she feared it might stop.

'They have a rather strong attraction for each other, Sabine and Casper,' said Peter. 'They were lovers during the war.'

'Lovers?'

Diana felt that her mind was a pond whose waters Peter kept stirring. Just as the confusion settled, he'd agitate her and her thoughts would become muddy again.

Peter went to the bureau and took out an envelope from the drawer. Inside it were some photographs, which he placed on the coffee table in front of her. They were pictures of Casper and a dark-haired woman. Diana's heart jumped when she recognised her as the woman she had noticed at the Hotel Australia. That woman was Sabine Brouillette. In the first picture, Sabine and Casper were sitting together in a café, gazing into each other's eyes; in the next, leaning against a barn and laughing; in another, coming out of a house, arm in arm. The intimacy between them was obvious. The last glimmer of hope she held for her marriage flickered out.

'I spent a long time debriefing Casper in England while he was recuperating from typhus, determined to prove the suspicions about him were not true,' Peter continued. 'We had no concrete proof, so eventually we let him return to Australia. But then the French discovered a file in Bergerac, proving Casper was working for the Germans. We received further intelligence that he was in contact with the Soviets, so I was sent here to gather evidence before MI6 had him arrested.'

Diana sat very still. She wondered if it was truly possible to be married to someone, and to have a child with them, and yet not know them at all.

'My husband is unfaithful and has done terrible things,' she said. 'But I still don't see how all this relates to Freddy's kidnapping ...' Then it dawned on her. 'Madame Allard! Mrs Dalton's new friend. That was Sabine!'

Peter levelled his eyes at her. 'I believe Sabine has Freddy and that she and Casper intend to use the boy as a front when they leave the country. A young family is often regarded above suspicion compared to a single man.'

Diana stood up from her chair in horror. 'They intend to take Freddy to the Soviet Union!'

Peter nodded. 'That's how it looks to me.'

Diana was on the verge of being sick. She didn't know what to do. She couldn't think straight. They were going to take Freddy away. She sank back down into the chair and pressed her fist to her mouth.

'Help me,' she said. 'I don't care who you are or what you do. Please help me get my son back!'

Peter's expression softened and for a moment he looked like Laurie again. 'I know everything I've told you has been shocking, and I'm not the man you thought I was, but believe me, I do care for you and Freddy and I will do everything in my power to get him back for you.' He put his hand on her shoulder. 'But you must trust me absolutely. You must do everything I tell you to, exactly as I tell you. You may not like the idea of being a spy, but you must be as astute and calm as one if you want to get your son back.'

# CHAPTER FORTY-SIX

It would have been impossible for Diana to pass the night under the same roof as Casper without scratching his eyes out if Peter hadn't drummed into her the necessity of staying calm if she wanted to get Freddy back. His plan was to park his car in the street and follow Casper when he left the house in the hope of discovering where he and Sabine were keeping Freddy. Diana was to put a vase in the window near the front door. If it wasn't there it would be a sign to Peter that she was in trouble.

After she said goodnight to Marilyn, she headed for the house. The awful secret Peter had revealed sat like a rock in her stomach. The light was on in the living room and through the window she could see Casper's legs stretched out from where he was sitting in an armchair. She steeled herself before going inside.

Casper looked up at Diana with bloodshot eyes. Peter's warning rang in her ears: *Under no circumstances reveal what you know. Casper is dangerous. He has the ability to turn into somebody else in the blink of an eye. He'll have no qualms about killing you if you get in his way.*

'I'm glad you're back,' Casper said, blinking as if he was disorientated. 'I was beginning to worry. Alfred had to go home but Janet is still here. She's asleep in Freddy's bed.'

Janet sleeping in Freddy's bed should have infuriated Diana. Of all the insensitive things to do when someone's child was missing, taking over their room was certainly near the top of the list. Instead, Diana found herself studying Casper with shrewd eyes. How could it be that he could mimic all the emotions of a distraught father when he knew perfectly well where Freddy was being held? She thought back to when she'd first met him in London and how he seemed to be a different person depending on whether he was speaking English or French. Perhaps he was a different person when he spoke German or Russian as well. Casper lifted his hand to his forehead and the wedding ring on his finger glinted in the lamplight. It occurred to Diana that their marriage had probably always been a sham as far as Casper was concerned. According to Peter, he'd switched from being a Nazi sympathiser to a communist with ease. *What an actor you are, Casper,* she thought. *Well, I can be a good actress too, and I will be because I want my son back.*

'I'm exhausted,' she said, swaying on her feet. 'Do you mind sleeping on the sofa tonight? I'll rest better alone.'

She put her handbag on the side table and placed the truck keys next to it. Normally she'd have put them away, but she wanted to give Casper the opportunity to go to wherever Sabine and Freddy were so that Peter could follow him. Peter was already in his car in the street, armed with binoculars and a flask of coffee. Diana moved the vase from the side table to the windowsill to show him that, so far, she was safe.

'Diana,' said Casper, rising and stepping towards her. 'I've let you down in so many ways. But I promise you I'll do everything possible to find Freddy.'

It seemed to her that Casper was now resembling his former self – the erect posture, the lifted chin, the determined look in his eye. If she didn't know better, she would have believed his declaration to be sincere. If she had not gone to Peter, she would have trusted that the man in front of her was going to step up to the plate at last and find their son. She had to bite her lip to stop herself from screaming at him. How could he do this to her and Freddy? They had waited for him for years only to be treated like commodities for him to use.

It was only her love for Freddy that gave her the strength to lie through her teeth. 'I know you will,' she said. 'I know you'll do everything in your power.'

★

The moon was shining brightly in the bedroom and Diana expected to be awake all night when she sat down on the bed fully clothed. But she couldn't keep her eyes open and eventually succumbed to a restless, feverish sleep. She dreamed of Freddy. He was ahead of her on the pathway that led through the Botanic Garden to the Wishing Tree. He was walking quickly on his thin legs and Diana was struggling to reach him. She tried to call out but she had no voice. Each time she almost caught up to him and stretched her hand out to touch him, he would disappear, then reappear further along the pathway.

When she woke up, the moon had given way to the sun and she sat up with a jolt, convinced she was running late and should be up getting Freddy off to school. Then piece by piece what had happened came back to her. With a pain in her chest, she realised that she'd woken from one bad dream into another.

She could hear Janet and Casper talking downstairs. Cupboards were being opened and shut, and dishes and cutlery were being laid out noisily. Diana could picture Janet bustling about 'making herself useful'. She lay back down and closed her eyes, too exhausted to move.

'Come downstairs and have breakfast, Diana!' Janet called from the bottom of the stairs. 'It's nearly ten o'clock! I've made my special scrambled eggs with cream *and ham*!'

\*

'It's all right if you can't eat the eggs,' Casper whispered to Diana when she finally made it to the table. 'Have some toast and black tea with sugar. You need to keep your strength up.'

She met his eyes. They were weary but full of concern. The hand he pressed against her arm was warm and reassuring. It was the touch of a husband determined to protect his wife. Diana swallowed. Casper really could feign anything, she thought. He could sit there pretending he loved her in a manner so convincing she was in danger of succumbing to it, even after all that had happened. Those unfortunate people in France hadn't stood a chance against Casper's ability to win a person's trust. But he couldn't fool her anymore.

'Casper's going on radio this evening to appeal to the public,' Janet told Diana, barely hiding her annoyance as she placed a cup of tea in front of her. 'I'm going with him to support him. I can see you're in no condition to do so.'

'Janet!' said Casper. 'Please!' He turned back to Diana and squeezed her arm again. 'Phyllis will come over to stay with you. I'll drop Janet home on my way back from the radio station.'

Diana nodded but didn't answer, convinced he was angling to have the truck to himself. When she'd suggested to Peter that she should ask Mrs Dalton where 'Madame Allard' lived, he'd told her that Sabine would have given a false address and that she and Casper would not be holding Freddy somewhere close by where someone might recognise him.

While Janet was clearing the breakfast dishes, Detective Robertson arrived to give them an update on the search.

'We've got a hundred detectives and metropolitan police on the case. There'll be a doorknock operation this afternoon. And' – he lowered his voice and averted his eyes from Diana – 'police divers will be searching the harbour.'

Diana pushed her thumbs against her forehead so she could hold in the frustration threatening to burst out of her brain. Freddy would not be found because he hadn't been taken by some run-of-the-mill monster. He'd been taken by people who had been in a clandestine organisation during the war – one who was a French secret service agent, and the other who was the boy's own father. Between them they'd been able to make Freddy disappear into thin air. Without Peter's help, she'd never see her son again. Everything depended on him.

★

When it was time for Casper and Janet to leave, Diana watched Casper straighten his tie in the hall mirror. She saw them to the door, anxious for them to leave so she could be alone with her thoughts. Casper bent his head to kiss her on the lips, but she turned so he had to peck her on the cheek instead.

'Stay strong, darling,' he told her.

Janet, radiating the self-importance the drama was affording her, bustled past Diana. 'You could be a bit kinder to him,' she hissed. 'You're not the only one who's suffering.'

Diana watched the truck turn out of the driveway. A minute later she saw Peter follow in his car, his hat pulled low. Diana took a deep shuddering breath. The race was on to find Freddy.

★

Phyllis arrived a short while later, carrying a pile of newspapers under her arm.

'I thought we could look through them together and write down anything the press mentions that the police haven't told you about.'

Although their efforts would be token at best, Diana nodded in appreciation of Phyllis's thoughtfulness. Her editor knew her well enough to understand that she was best distracted when given something practical to do. They sat down at the dining table and took a newspaper each. Diana stared at the headline on the front page of the *Daily News*: *Boy Vanishes from Botanic Garden in Front of Mother.*

At first it made her feel irresponsible, as if she were to blame for Freddy being taken. But then she inhaled a slow, steady breath. No, it was not that she'd been careless but that the people who took her son were skilled at kidnapping. Professionals, in fact.

From the article that followed, Diana learned that radio stations were giving details of Freddy's disappearance in every bulletin. Church congregations were praying, and the boy scouts were putting up posters on street poles. It seemed nearly every person seen with a child of Freddy's description was being reported to the police. Diana glanced at Phyllis, who was absorbed in taking notes. The public had taken Freddy's abduction to heart, and it occurred to her that they were being manipulated by dark, covert forces, as she had been. The forces Peter claimed kept ordinary people safe.

Diana reached for the *Sydney Morning Herald* and her eyes focused on another headline, nothing to do with Freddy's disappearance.

*Don Morris Buys Up Big in the West*
*Infamous Sydney architect Don Morris announced yesterday that in cooperation with an unnamed property developer, he has obtained 7000 acres of privately owned land west of the city with a view to creating a new suburb to be named Morristown. The State Government had hoped to include the land in the Cumberland Greenbelt Plan for a new type of bushland suburb with designs submitted by innovative architect Harry Scott and landscape designer Diana White. However, they were outbid by Morris's offer and it is doubtful any hopes for a new 'green' suburb will be realised.*

*When asked what he intended to do with the land once
the contracts were exchanged, Morris replied that he planned
to clear the entire area and subdivide it into lots of 700 square
yards in order to maximise profits ...*

Diana felt the air go out of her as if she had been punched in
the stomach.

Phyllis noticed what she was reading. 'Oh dear, I didn't
think they would announce it so soon.'

'Why didn't you tell me?' asked Diana.

'Harry and I only learned about it last night. You have
enough to worry about and I didn't want to upset you further.
The minister was keen to push the project through, but
unfortunately Don Morris approached the landowners privately.
That "unnamed property developer" mentioned in the article
is an underworld criminal Don is in cahoots with, and they
used some underhanded tactics to persuade the landowners to
sell to them instead – not only money but other "incentives",
like not having their legs broken.'

The loss of the land seemed like the final demise of all the
good things Diana had been planning – from having a happy
family, to encouraging people to appreciate nature, to creating
a beautiful city for the future. It was as if Casper's return had
set in motion a series of disasters, and she was left standing in
the wreckage.

★

Marilyn arrived with Blossom and Dolores. The pigs' expressions were forlorn, and they flopped listlessly on the floor at Marilyn's feet. 'They miss him,' she said, her own eyes watering. 'I haven't been able to get them to eat all day.'

Diana bent down and rubbed the pigs' heads. Everyone, including the animals, was suffering because of Casper.

At six o'clock Diana turned on the radio. 'Apparently Casper goes on straight after the news,' she told Phyllis and Marilyn. The women sat down next to each other on the sofa. Blossom rested her head on Phyllis's lap, pressing her chin to Phyllis's white linen skirt. To Diana's surprise, her editor didn't push the pig away but stroked her behind the ears as if Blossom were a cat. She was glad they could find comfort in each other. Diana felt terribly alone with her secret.

After a blast of tinny music, the news came on. Diana listened to the events of the day with a numbness that felt like frostbite. The fact that a man had fallen off the Manly Ferry and drowned failed to move her as it normally would have, and she certainly couldn't care less that Sydney's traffic problem was growing worse now petrol-rationing was coming to an end.

She imagined Casper at the ABC studios, surrounded by the detectives from the Crimes Investigation Bureau, continuing to act as the distressed father. They would have given him notes, she imagined, coached him in exactly what to say to the 'person or persons unknown' who'd taken Freddy.

The newsreader announced that the divers who'd searched the waters around Farm Cove that day had discovered an unexploded depth charge from the Japanese submarine that had attacked the city in 1942, but no sign of Freddy.

Diana sighed. So much effort was being wasted because of a pair of traitors.

Then the announcer introduced Casper on the broadcast. Her husband's voice was measured, with the right amount of tremble in it to pull on heartstrings as he addressed the nation. She had once loved the sound of Casper's voice; now it made her wince.

'I appeal to the person who took our son to return him safe and sound. He's a good little chap who is dearly missed by his distraught mother. We are praying hard for Freddy's return and hope the efforts of the police and public will bring him back home soon.' Then Casper's voice cracked, and he added, 'Freddy, if you hear this, know how much your mummy and daddy love you and miss you. Be a good boy for whoever has you. If they return you to us safe and sound by tomorrow, I give my word we will ask no questions or seek any retribution.'

Marilyn choked back a sob. Phyllis took a handkerchief from her sleeve and patted her eyes. Diana was about to get up and turn off the radio, when Casper announced he'd like to read out one of Freddy's favourite poems. Diana frowned as Casper read out a verse that she was sure Freddy had never recited and that she had never heard before.

*The fox went out on a chilly night,*
*He prayed to the Moon to give him light,*
*For he'd many a mile to go that night ...*

An idea besieged her. He was sending Sabine a secret message in the poem. She rushed to the kitchen and grabbed a pencil and piece of paper from a drawer. She tried to write down as much of the poem as she could recall, although she couldn't make head nor tail of the meaning. Had Peter heard it? She had no idea if he had a radio in his car. She prayed that he did.

★

It was late when Phyllis stood and collected the newspapers. 'I'll come back tomorrow,' she said. Then looking from Marilyn to Diana she added, 'For goodness sake, get some rest, the both of you. The best way to help Freddy is to help yourselves. You must stay strong.'

After Phyllis left, Marilyn returned to her cottage with the pigs. Diana felt light-headed but couldn't have eaten if she'd tried. She had a bath and washed her face before going downstairs and collapsing into one of the wingback chairs. No doubt Janet would delay Casper by forcing him to eat something at her place, and Peter would be left outside, watching for hours. The worst thing was going to be the waiting. She leaned her head back and closed her eyes. Before she knew it, she was asleep.

★

'Don't make a sound!'

Diana opened her eyes and tried to focus. Standing before her was a tall, dark-haired woman with a gun in her hand. She sat up when she realised it was Sabine Brouillette. At least, she thought it was her. Sabine's appearance was different from when Diana had seen her at the Hotel Australia. Without make-up and with her hair loose about her shoulders, she appeared younger. However, now dressed in a black jacket and sweater over grey slacks, she looked the part of a secret agent. Diana focused on the hole at the end of the gun's barrel, from where the deadly bullets would explode if she didn't do as she was told.

'Where is Freddy?' she asked, coming to her senses. 'Is he all right?'

Sabine's expression remained impassive. She gave the impression of being measured and controlled like a panther, confident in her power and able to take her time to size up her prey, which was exactly what she was doing now.

'I know who you are,' continued Diana, surprised at her own boldness. 'You have my son. Please give him back to me, unharmed. That's all I want. After that, I don't care what you and Casper do.'

'Your husband told you about me?' Sabine asked.

Diana could see the mantelpiece clock from where she sat. It was two o'clock in the morning. Where was Casper? Surely not still at Janet's. Had Sabine left Freddy alone somewhere or was Casper with him?

'I know that you're a French agent,' Diana said, 'And I know that you befriended Freddy through Mrs Dalton.'

She tried to stay calm, but each word was tainted with anger.

Sabine's cat-like eyes flickered. She reached into her pocket and pulled out a piece of rope that had been tied into loops. She tossed it to Diana. 'Put your hand through one of the loops,' she said.

It was clear she was about to be tied up, but Diana had no choice but to obey. As soon as she put the loop around one hand, Sabine leaped towards her and in seconds had twisted both hands behind her back and secured them.

'Now, do everything I tell you and I will take you to your son,' she said. Diana felt the gun poke into her neck. 'If you cause me any trouble, I will shoot you and then I will shoot your son. Do you understand?'

Sabine had gone from calm to terrifying in a second. Diana had no reason to doubt her ruthlessness. 'Yes,' she replied, trembling.

Reaching into her pocket, Sabine took out a piece of music composition paper and placed it on the pianola. Diana thought of the note she had found. The one that had read: *Traitor.* She realised it had been left there by Sabine for Casper. There must have been some message between the lines in that song. But coded messages, invisible ink and dead-letter drops were things she'd seen only in movies. She wasn't sure how they worked in real life.

'We are going for a drive now,' Sabine said, yanking Diana so hard that her shoulder felt like it might come out of its socket.

As they moved through the front door, Diana tried to knock the vase off the windowsill, but Sabine had too firm a hold of her and she missed it. Wherever Casper was, Peter would be there too, so there was no hope of rescue. She looked in the direction of Marilyn's cottage and a terrible thought occurred to her.

'You didn't hurt my assistant, did you?' Diana asked.

Sabine led her around the corner of the house to a black car.

'She's all right. But she won't be awake any time before morning.' She pushed Diana into the backseat. 'Keep your mouth shut and I won't gag you,' she told her. 'But if you scream or draw attention to yourself, you'll be sorry. Do exactly what I tell you and you'll be with your son soon enough.'

Sabine tied Diana's feet together. She tugged a hood over her head and then covered her with a blanket. The car dipped as Sabine got in and started the engine. Diana heard the crunch of the gravel under the tyres as they travelled down the driveway then out onto the road. She tried to keep track of where they were going by guessing if they were turning left or right, going down a hill or up one. But soon the flashes of streetlights stopped, and everything was pitch black. All she could tell was that they were driving in a straight line.

Somewhere on the journey they stopped and Sabine got out. She was gone for what seemed liked a quarter of an hour. What was she doing? Leaving another message for Casper?

Sabine got back in the car and they drove on. 'So, tell me, what else do you know about me?' she asked.

Diana realised it would have been wiser if she'd pretended not to know who Sabine was. There could be consequences for knowing too much, but it was too late now.

'I know that my husband is a traitor and that you are his mistress.'

Sabine didn't answer and Diana assumed she wasn't going to reply.

Then, after a few minutes, Sabine said, 'You are right that your husband is a traitor, and for that he is going to die.'

Diana shuddered. Sabine had made the statement with such vehemence that it seemed impossible that she and Casper could be working together. Peter must have been on the wrong track when he'd thought they were planning to leave the country together and use Freddy as a cover. If that was the case, there would be no reason to take Diana as a hostage as well. She thought of the note Sabine had left on the pianola. Perhaps Casper hadn't come home because Sabine had sent him on a wild goose chase with false clues so that she could kidnap her.

Her stomach flipped. She had no idea what Sabine was planning, but it was obvious that she and Freddy were in even greater danger than she had imagined.

# CHAPTER FORTY-SEVEN

Sabine brought the car to a stop a second time. She opened the back door and untied Diana's feet before hoisting her up by the front of her blouse. Diana could feel the freshness of dawn on her skin. She tried to guess where they were. Galahs were screeching in the sky and the sweet smells of yellow box gum and wild grass lingered in the air. The earth was rough beneath her shoes and dry. They had to be somewhere out in the country.

'Walk!' Sabine commanded.

She guided Diana up a couple of wobbly steps and into a room that stank of old wood and bird droppings.

'Mummy!'

Diana's heart leaped at the sound of Freddy's voice.

'Darling!'

Sabine removed the hood and Diana saw Freddy in the corner of the room near a blackened fireplace. He was sitting on a rug, tied by one wrist to a post.

'Mummy!'

Diana lowered herself so she was kneeling next to him and pressed her cheek to his. He smelled lemony, like he'd recently had a bath, and he had a comic book in his lap.

'Madame Allard told me that she'd lost Monsieur Rouge, and I tried to help her find him,' Freddy whispered.

He seemed more astonished than frightened by his circumstances. An oil lamp hanging from a roof beam was still burning, so at least Sabine hadn't left him alone all night in the dark.

Diana whispered back, 'It's all right. Mummy is here now.'

Freddy wasn't wearing his school uniform but a pair of pants with front pleats and a submariner jumper. His hair had been brushed to the side and oiled down. He looked oddly French. Diana glanced around the rundown farmhouse. The rough-sawn timber walls were weathered grey. Scraps of dirty fabric that were once curtains flapped in the windows, which were devoid of glass. A rear door slumped outwards, held only by its bottom hinges, while the front door was non-existent. Freddy couldn't have been here the whole time since Sabine had kidnapped him. He was too clean. Then her eye settled on two chairs set back to back and she shivered. There was something sinister about the way they were placed, as if they were about to duel with each other.

'Why don't you let my son go now you have me?' Diana asked. 'He's only a boy.'

Sabine's face hardened. The change in the Frenchwoman's mood was ominous. She hoisted Diana back up and placed her in one of the chairs, grabbing her arms and lifting them over the back of the chair and securing her to it. Then she tied Diana's feet to the chair legs with rope. Diana watched hypnotised, the way an audience is enthralled by the performance of an acrobat or magician. Sabine was dexterous but Diana noticed she favoured her right hand more than even right-handed people normally did. The left was covered by a glove. But before she could think further on it, Sabine had released Freddy and brought him over to the second chair. She tied him to it in the same manner she had Diana.

'Please don't do that to him,' Diana pleaded.

She wanted Freddy to fight Sabine, to kick her and run for his life. But he was in no position to resist. It would have been impossible to escape anyway. Out the front door she could see a dirt track with bushland on either side of it. What must have once been the front garden was now overgrown with wattle and banksia trees. The place had been abandoned for years. She didn't get the impression that anyone would be passing by anytime soon. Sending Freddy out into unknown bushland wasn't an option.

'Please,' Diana said to Sabine. 'I beg you. Please, don't harm my son.'

Sabine opened a canteen of water and gave it to Freddy. Then she offered it to Diana, who took a sip and tried to steady her breathing. *Surely you don't offer water to a woman and child you intend to kill, do you?* she wondered.

Sabine pulled a scarf from her pocket and rolled it into a gag. Diana turned her head away.

'No!' she protested. 'I need to be able to speak to Freddy. He's scared.'

Sabine grabbed her by the chin and forced the gag into her mouth, tying it so tightly Diana thought it would amputate her tongue. Freddy yelped when Sabine gagged him. Then she placed something in a suitcase under Diana's chair and rolled

out a piece of wire from it. She laid the wire across the floor
and out of the front door, where she attached what looked
like a trigger to the end of it. Diana's heart rose to her throat.
Sabine was going to blow them up! She began to weep for the
first time since the ordeal had started. She was helpless to save
her son.

'Now we wait,' said Sabine, sitting down on the front step
of the veranda, her canteen next to her, the trigger in her hand
and her gun in her lap.

Diana could see what Sabine's plan was now. She had set a
trap for Casper, and she was using her and Freddy as bait.

*

It wasn't until the early afternoon that Diana heard the rumble
of her truck in the distance. It appeared through the trees,
Casper at the wheel. He pulled up at the end of the track and
looked at the house and Sabine through the windscreen. Sabine
turned a lever on the trigger and Diana heard a 'click' that sent
a chill through her.

Casper brought the truck closer and stepped out of it,
disbelief written on his face. 'Sabine?'

From where he stood, he had a direct view past Sabine
into the farmhouse to where Diana and Freddy were being
held hostage over the bomb. He looked back to Sabine with an
expression of utter confusion.

'It's a dead man's switch,' she warned him, holding up the
trigger. 'Remember how good I am with explosives? You
taught me.'

After a pause that seemed interminable, Casper swallowed and said, 'I don't understand.'

Sabine gave a bitter chuckle. 'Of course you don't. You think I died in Ravensbrück. But I didn't. I survived.'

Diana looked at her husband. He did seem at a loss to understand Sabine's actions. But then who could tell what Casper was really thinking? Perhaps it was the performance of a lifetime to save his own skin. That didn't matter to Diana, as long as he saved her and Freddy's skins too.

'Throw your gun onto the veranda,' Sabine told him. 'And put your hands behind your head.'

For one tense moment, Diana prayed that he didn't have the gun with him. Perhaps then Sabine wouldn't despise him so much because he'd come to see her unarmed. But when Casper reached into his jacket and pulled out his pistol, Diana's stomach swooped with dread. He tossed it onto the veranda. It landed just out of Sabine's reach. She left it where it lay. He'd be a fool to try and get it back with the bomb trigger in her hand.

'I only brought the gun because I didn't know who'd sent the message. I wouldn't hurt you, you know that, Sabine,' he said.

Sabine watched him dispassionately. 'Get down on your knees!' she said. 'Do you expect me to believe that lie, like I believed all your others?'

Casper opened his mouth to say something, but Sabine fired at his feet. He jumped back as a puff of dust rose around him. He realised Sabine meant business and dropped down on his knees and put his hands behind his head.

'Please,' he said, a tremble in his voice. 'Whatever it is you have to settle with me, let my wife and son go. They have no idea what this is about.'

'No, your wife and son don't have any idea what you have done,' Sabine said. 'Which is precisely why they need to hear it from your lips. Confess everything before I kill you and I'll let them go. I'm someone who keeps her word. You know that. That's why I was so easy for you to deceive.'

'Confess to what?' asked Casper.

'Tell them about how you passed on information about the *Pianiste* circuit to the Nazis and betrayed us all.'

Diana felt Freddy shivering with terror. Casper had brought this disaster on them and he clearly couldn't fix it. She squinted into the distance for any sign of Peter. He was their only hope now.

'But before the interrogation begins, let me tell you about my own son, Pierre,' Sabine continued. 'Do you remember him? I'll tell you the cost of your treachery.' She regarded Casper with a steady eye before continuing. 'You know very well that many of us from the circuit ended up in concentration camps, where we were subjected to unspeakable brutality. Stripped of all dignity, even our names, we were worked like slaves and starved. Then those who were too weak to go on were killed in gas chambers or shot. Even as the Allies approached, the Nazis wouldn't let us go. They marched us away from the advancing armies. The prisoners who couldn't keep up were shot. The only reason I survived was because I had to. I'd promised Lucien I would not leave Pierre an orphan.' Her voice turned bitter and low. 'My son was the only reason I had to go on in the world. He was the only thing I had left.'

In all the years she'd known him, Diana had never seen such an expression of anguish on Casper's face. Her heart broke. In that look she finally understood why he'd changed so much, and why he was not her Casper anymore. He loved Sabine. Her pain was his pain. He loved the woman who was going to kill his wife and child, the woman who was holding him at gunpoint.

Sabine's gaze drifted over to Diana and Freddy. 'The same day I was taken from Fresnes, the Waffen SS arrived in the village where Henri and Madeleine had gone with Pierre. They surrounded the village and forced the inhabitants out of their houses and into the square. Henri and the other men were lined up in front of the town hall and shot, then the women and children, including Madeleine and Pierre, were herded into the church. Grenades were thrown inside and the church set on fire. People from surrounding villages heard the screams from miles away. After the Germans left, the maquis went to the town and found the charred and mutilated corpses of the women and children. Madeleine was lying on top of Pierre. She had tried to protect him with her body.'

Casper let out a sound that was something between a gasp and sob. Diana's stomach clenched. Sabine had lost a child. The scales of everything tipped. The Frenchwoman was a wounded creature, capable of anything. Diana understood it because she would have been too. Unless Casper could convince Sabine of his innocence, they were all doomed.

'You are going to cry fake tears?' Sabine asked Casper. 'If you had betrayed us under torture, I could understand at least.

But you came to France with the intention of betraying us. When you sat in my family's kitchen and Madeleine served you soup, you already had plans for our destruction.'

'I would never have done such a thing,' Casper said, his face drawn with misery. 'I would never hurt you, Sabine.'

'You came here with a gun,' she said with disgust. 'You intended to kill the last witness to your treachery.'

'How can you accuse me of such things?' he said. 'You of all people should know it's not possible. I was arrested with you. I was sent to Fresnes too—'

'Where you remained until the Allies arrived!'

Casper shook his head. 'I don't understand it myself. I was arrested as an agent but I wasn't tortured or deported. I was given books to read and was allowed to exercise in the yard. My food was rationed but acceptable. I caught typhus because the place was riddled with lice, but so did many of the guards.'

'You got those privileges because you were a double agent,' Sabine spat. 'Keeping you in prison stopped you from being executed as a collaborator and a traitor! The Germans felt they owed you that! It was your reward!'

'No!'

The more Casper denied Sabine's allegations, the more unhinged she seemed to become. Diana scanned the bushland. Then it occurred to her that even if Peter turned up with a hundred policemen, they wouldn't be able to do anything with Sabine holding that trigger. Her only hope was to appeal to the woman's humanity – to speak to her as a mother of a young child. She began to work at the gag, rubbing her chin against her shoulder to try to loosen it.

The sound of another gunshot made her jump. Sabine had fired above Casper's head. 'If you continue to lie to me, the next one won't miss.'

Freddy was sobbing. A trickle of water ran across the floor and Diana realised he had wet himself. She pushed her tongue against the gag to work it off. Her mouth was dry and the material felt like sandpaper.

'I know you betrayed us,' Sabine said to Casper. 'Have the dignity to say why. To declare yourself before you die.'

Sabine pointed her gun directly at Casper's head this time. The air rushed out of Diana's lungs. Casper turned to her with red-rimmed eyes. She pleaded silently that he would confess and save her and Freddy. But he looked back to Sabine, even more determined to defend himself.

'How can I tell you something that didn't happen?' he said. 'I did not betray the circuit. I did not deceive you. I was pulled out of the RAF to work for SOE. I was told I had a fifty per cent chance of coming back from France alive. It turned out the odds of an agent surviving were even less the longer they stayed in the field, and I went into France twice. I did it because I wanted to stop the Nazis, to make the world free for my wife and son. What possible reason could I have for betraying a cause I'd been prepared to sacrifice myself for?'

In every word Casper spoke, Diana heard the truth. The man before her was the man she had married: brave, noble and courageous. The realisation sent a searing regret through her. Her husband was not a traitor; he was incapable of such a thing. She was wrong to have ever doubted him.

'We recovered the file in Bergerac,' Sabine continued, unconvinced. 'You were the only SOE operative in the circuit. Your codename was "the Black Fox".'

'I'm not "the Black Fox",' Casper replied. 'My codename was "Monet", after my wife's favourite artist—'

His mouth opened and he winced as if someone had shot him. At first Diana thought Sabine had. But he remained upright, his mind ticking over. At the same time, a realisation dawned on Diana. Peter's note about knowing who had taken Freddy had been a trick to make her run to him so he could keep track of Casper. He'd lured her like a fox to his den.

*Like a fox to his den.*

Bits of information that had made no sense at the time began to form a picture in her mind. That opera music she'd heard the first time she went to see him. It was Wagner – the Nazis' favourite composer. The names of his boat in London were those of German girls. And Lisa, with that startling Aryan blondeness. Their eyes had met during a performance of *Tristan and Isolde* – a German opera. Lisa had not died in London – Diana had assumed that, and Peter had simply not corrected her – she'd died in the bombing of Berlin. Diana was sure of it now. It was Peter who was the Nazi.

With renewed vigour, Diana struggled to push the gag out of her mouth. It felt like she was about to dislocate her jaw, but she managed to work it over her chin.

'Peter Todd is the Black Fox,' she gasped at Sabine. 'He's here in Australia.'

Sabine looked at Diana over her shoulder and her eyes narrowed. Casper stared at Diana in disbelief.

'Laurie Spencer is Peter Todd,' she told him. 'He used me to spy on you. He said he was with MI6.'

Casper looked from Diana to Sabine. 'When you said the codename "the Black Fox", that's what I thought too. Peter's last name is Todd. *Tod* – a male fox. It wasn't his SOE codename of course, that was "Professor". He was my contact at SOE headquarters. All the information I gathered about the circuit was passed on to him. He knew everything that I did.'

Sabine kept her gun pointed at Casper, not buying any of it.

'Don't you see that Peter hopes you'll kill Casper to cover any suspicion that may fall on him?' Diana said to her. 'A dead man can't defend himself.'

Still, Sabine did not move. Diana had a terrible feeling that, having come this far, Sabine might see Casper's execution through anyway.

'I can prove it to you,' she said, frantically. 'I'll show you where Peter Todd is staying. You can interrogate him yourself. If you kill Casper and then find out he's telling the truth, what will you have achieved? Justice?'

Sabine kept her gun on Casper but spoke to Diana.

'Casper will take your place here with Freddy,' she told her. 'You and I will go back to see if what you are telling me about this Peter Todd is true. But if you are lying, I will kill you and then come back here and deal with them.'

'Don't move!'

Diana froze at the sound of Peter's voice. He was out of her vision, somewhere to the left of the house.

'Throw down your gun,' he shouted at Sabine. 'And put your hands in the air.'

Nobody had seen him approach, and Sabine, standing on the veranda, was in his direct line of fire. She had no choice but to do what he said. She dropped the gun and raised her hands. Diana kept her eye on the trigger switch. With her hands up Sabine wouldn't be able to disengage it. Peter had clearly been listening to their conversation and knew that.

'Move!' Peter said, indicating to Casper to stand near Sabine. When he had done so, Peter inched closer to the house. Diana could finally see him. His golden eyes had a cruel look in them and the lines around his mouth were harsh. He looked diabolical.

'What a mess,' Peter said, through gritted teeth. He glared at Sabine. 'Your own superior told you to get in and out quickly to avoid this sort of thing.'

'You set Sabine up to come and kill me and make me look like the traitor,' Casper said to Peter. 'You came to Australia to make sure she went through with it.'

'It was a brilliant plan,' said Peter, with a shrug. 'Fortunately, it's still salvageable.' He glanced at Diana and Freddy. 'Although it's a pity an innocent woman and child will go along with you both when you die. That wasn't my intention. But I didn't expect someone as focussed as Agent Brouillette to make such a melodrama of it.'

The hairs on the back of Diana's neck stood on end. She realised he intended to kill them all and make it look as if it was Sabine's doing. She tried to think quickly about what she could do. Appealing to Peter's conscience would be futile. He didn't have one. She spotted Casper's gun lying on the veranda and realised that Peter hadn't seen it but it was near Casper's foot. Would he be able to grab it and shoot Peter?

'How could you, Peter?' Casper said. 'I thought we were friends.'

Peter looked affronted. 'I was your friend,' he replied. 'I'm the reason you weren't executed at Fresnes or sent to a concentration camp. It seemed to be the decent thing to do after all the valuable information I obtained from you.' He shrugged. 'I fully intended for you to go back to Australia and continue your life without having any idea of how much you had helped the Nazi cause. But, as it turns out, MI6 has offered me one of their top roles.' He nodded at Sabine and sneered. 'We could all have got on with our lives if the French had let the matter of war crimes go. But unfortunately, before I can accept that role with MI6, I have a little cleaning up of the past to do.'

'You can kill us,' Casper said, his voice full of disgust. 'But we die with pure consciences. You are nothing but a dirty traitor. You'll be found out sooner or later.'

'Traitor?' Peter laughed. 'Let me clear up that delusion for you. What I did, I did for the love of Britain. Germany was our friend. What was the British government thinking in making alliances with Stalin? It wasn't fascism that was a threat to the world order, but bolshevism. And I was right. Who is threatening us with oblivion now?

'All the Germans wanted was for the human race to be purer, more refined than it was,' he continued. 'There was no better race to lead by example than theirs. I learned that from the man who would have been my father-in-law, Hans von Mayer, the head of German intelligence in Paris. And he was right. Britain, Germany, France: we are all friends now against the real enemy.'

'It doesn't stop you from being a war criminal,' Sabine told him. 'Your means did not justify your end.'

He sent her a look of spite. 'What I did made no difference to what happened to your circuit. You were all doomed anyway. It was British intelligence that played SOE like a puppet in the game of deception. All those supply drops and acts of sabotage in 1943 were to make the Germans think an Allied invasion was imminent. Why? Stalin insisted that a new western front be opened to take pressure off the east, but Britain didn't have the resources, so it created the illusion of a planned landing months before the real one took place.'

He turned to Casper. '*They* sacrificed the SOE agents and the French Resistance members to make Stalin happy. All I did was help put the Germans in a position where both our intelligence agencies would be able to join forces against the Soviets after the war.'

'You're evil!' spat Casper.

'Maybe,' Peter replied with a glint in his eye. He aimed his gun at Sabine. 'But let's get on with it, shall we? *Au revoir tout le monde!*'

'Villain!' screamed Sabine.

She made a swoop for her gun and managed to fire a shot from a prone position. It hit Peter in the arm, but he had already discharged his gun. The bullet struck Sabine in her side. The trigger switch tumbled from her fingers. Peter made a run for the bushes to take cover from the coming explosion. 'Freddy!' Diana called out as she braced herself to die. Seconds passed and all she could hear was Freddy's muffled sobs. She opened her eyes again and realised that there hadn't been any explosives. Sabine had never intended to kill her and Freddy.

Sabine was lying on her back, clutching her side and struggling for breath. Blood was oozing from between her fingers.

'Sabine!' Casper cried, falling to his knees beside her. He tore the bottom of his shirt off and pressed it to her side. 'Sabine!'

'Go!' she told him, giving him her gun.

Tears filled his eyes. He shook his head. 'Sabine—'

'Go!' she said again through gritted teeth. 'Finish this thing. For Pierre. For all of us.'

A bullet whizzed past them and hit the wall near Diana's head. Peter was firing from the bushes, still determined to kill them. With one last agonised glance at Sabine, Casper took cover against the building and fired back at Peter.

Sabine picked up Casper's pistol and crawled towards Diana. She took a knife from her belt to cut the ropes around Diana's hands. Once she was free, Diana sliced the ropes from around her own feet.

'Stop moving,' Diana told Sabine. 'You lose more blood when you do.'

'If the Black Fox kills Casper, he'll come back to get you and Freddy,' Sabine said. 'Take my gun and hide. Do you know how to use it? You point it and then *squeeze* the trigger.'

Sabine was growing paler by the minute. The wad Casper had made from his shirt was soaked with blood.

'I can't leave you,' Diana said.

Sabine shook her head. 'Take Freddy and go!'

Realising she had no choice if she was to protect Freddy, Diana freed him and pulled the gag out of his mouth. He was deathly pale with shock, and mumbling, but there was no time to comfort him. Diana peeked out the rear door. There was a patch of dirt before the bush began.

'I've got you,' she told him, grabbing the back of his jumper and pushing him ahead of her towards the trees. When they reached them, she crouched low and pulled Freddy close to her. Diana could hear the men continuing to exchange fire. She looked around for somewhere to hide Freddy, and then she spotted a wombat burrow, deep and wide enough for a small boy to squeeze inside.

'Don't move or make a sound unless Daddy or I come back and get you,' she said. 'Everything will be all right. I'm here to protect you.'

Freddy gave her a look of trust that broke her heart, before he crawled backwards into the burrow and lay down flat.

Diana steadied her breath and moved forward through the bush, peering through the trees to see what was happening. She glimpsed a figure with his back towards her and recognised it was Peter retreating. Casper was still trapped at the side of the house. He'd have nowhere to go if he ran out of bullets. She steadied her breath when she realised Peter was moving in the direction of her and Freddy. There wasn't much blood on his sleeve so the bullet wound must have been superficial. She trained the gun on him, waiting for him to move closer so she could get a clear shot. She couldn't afford to miss and hit a tree instead. A memory of her father flashed in her mind. His eyes were bloodshot and spit was flying from his mouth. He was screaming at her because she'd deliberately missed the tins he'd set up for her to take aim at with his shotgun.

Peter stepped back into Diana's line of fire, but as he did, he turned. Their eyes met. He pointed his gun but she fired first, hitting him square in the chest. Peter's eyes rolled and he fell backwards, his body twitching. Diana rose and made for his gun. But Peter was not going to get up again, that much was certain. Blood trickled from between his lips. He tried to say something, but whatever it was she didn't hear it. Her world had gone silent. Peter stopped moving and Diana couldn't hear anything at all.

# CHAPTER FORTY-EIGHT

From the kitchen window, Diana watched Freddy and Marilyn playing fetch with Blossom and Dolores in the garden. Freddy laughed as he threw the ball. The pigs were enjoying themselves too, playfully grunting and wiggling their tails.

Freddy's smile appeared genuine. But could he really be as happy and carefree as he seemed? She wondered. Tears threatened to spill from her eyes, and she struggled to hold them back. It had been her heartfelt desire to give him the perfect childhood, where he always felt safe and where he never had to witness any sort of horror. She'd failed miserably.

Her mind travelled back to those years in Aunt Shirley's flat, and the endless parade of artists who'd complimented Diana on her maturity and her air of sophistication that was well beyond her years. She had survived, hadn't she? Perhaps she needed to have faith that Freddy would too, even if he'd witnessed his mother kill a man, someone they both had been fond of.

'Professor Spencer wasn't the person he pretended to be,' she had explained to him, after the police interviews were over and they were finally back home. 'He wanted to do bad things to us.'

'I know, Mummy,' Freddy had replied, with the same complete trust he had shown when she'd told him to hide in the wombat burrow. 'You would never do anything bad. You were protecting me and Daddy. And Sabine.'

*Sabine.*

Despite how grim the wound in Sabine's side had appeared on the day, the bullet Peter had fired had missed her vital organs and she was already on her way to a full recovery.

A dramatic flourish of piano notes from the living room snapped Diana's mind back to the present. The music that followed was so sparkling and bold that she could hardly believe it was flowing from Janet's old pianola. Since Sabine had come to stay after being discharged from hospital, she had been surprising them like that. She played marvellously, despite the problem with her left hand.

When Sabine finished playing, Diana walked into the living room. 'What was that piece of music?' she asked her. 'It's lovely.'

'Chopin's "Ocean" etude,' Sabine replied. 'It was one of my favourites to teach to students. The rolling semiquavers mimic the sound of waves.' She studied her left hand for a moment. 'I've adapted it slightly.'

Sabine's suitcase stood at the bottom of the stairs. She was sailing back to France that afternoon and, although their friendship had begun in the strangest of ways, Diana already knew that she would miss her. It was in Sabine's company that Casper had finally come out of his shell. He was reading again, and Diana had heard him tell Sabine he was thinking of returning to teaching. Sabine was a bearer of beauty, Diana thought. She filled the house with music and arranged native flowers artistically on every available surface. She had even tamed Janet, who seemed intimidated by her savoir-faire and kept her opinions to herself, perhaps so as not to appear gauche in front of her. It was the war that had warped Sabine's spirit.

But it was the Frenchwoman's relationship with Freddy that most astonished Diana. Despite what had happened that day at the farmhouse, he wasn't afraid of her. If anything, he seemed to be in awe of her. At random moments he would come out with one her favourite phrases, *Ça va être genial!* (It's going to be wonderful!), and rub his palms together the way she did when she said it. Other times, in imitation of her, he'd pout and say '*Bof!*' with a shrug to show his indifference to something. On several occasions, Diana had caught Sabine and Freddy playing a game together. They would hold each other's chin and stare into each other's eyes. The one who could resist bursting into laughter the longest would be the winner. Freddy always lost, but it did nothing to dampen his enthusiasm for the game.

Despite the traumatic incident that had brought the two women together, Sabine's presence had turned Diana's little cottage with its pretty garden into the relaxed, happy place she'd dreamed it would be.

'Have you seen Casper?' Diana asked her.

Sabine nodded towards the garden. 'I saw him heading towards the creek.'

Ever since the end of the inquest into Peter's death, Casper had been spending a lot of time by the creek. Diana and Marilyn's efforts to stop erosion and eradicate the weeds had paid off. It was a tranquil place to sit and contemplate life. Diana followed the stone steps towards the bottom of the garden. Casper had built them and had skilfully integrated them into the plantings. They looked as though they'd been formed by nature.

Diana found him sitting on a rock ledge and staring out at the water. He looked up when she approached.

'Does he still weigh on your mind?' she asked, sitting down next to him.

It must have been a difficult thing for Casper to process that his friend was a traitor who'd tried to kill him and his family. She understood perfectly. Peter had done a number on all of them. She had almost fallen for Laurie, but he'd never actually existed. He was one of Peter's many illusions.

'If he was a fascist, I didn't realise it at university,' said Casper. 'But it's what he said about British intelligence that makes me lose sleep. So many good agents from SOE died in terrible ways, all believing they were sacrificing themselves for Britain.' He glanced at her. 'Do you think that it is even possible that their own country deliberately sent them to their deaths in some sort of intelligence game?'

Diana thought back to the night Peter had revealed himself and to their conversation about the nature of intelligence. Whether his claim that intelligence-gathering kept the world safe was right or not, in her eyes it was amoral and about power, not people.

'I suspect there's no black and white answer to that question,' she said finally. 'War is not a simple thing. *Life* is not a simple thing.' She glanced at her hands and then back up again. 'I kissed him once. I was under the illusion that I rather liked him.'

Casper turned to her with pain in his eyes. 'You were lonely and trusted him. That's my fault. Peter could charm people and then drop them without so much as a goodbye when it suited him.' He rubbed her arm and smiled sadly. 'I was fooled by him too, Diana. I thought he was being kind to me by visiting me every day at the convalescent home, but I now suspect he was drugging me to make me appear sicker than I was, and to get information out of me.' He stood up, his hands on his hips, and walked to the edge of the water then back again. 'You had to shoot him. I can't forgive myself for putting you in that position.'

Diana couldn't deny that the incident had been shocking. But she'd shot Peter to defend herself and Freddy and to protect Casper. The inquest had cleared Sabine and declared Peter's death as 'justifiable homicide'. No doubt MI6 had been influential in getting the investigation over with quickly to cover up the actions of one of their agents. Diana saw no reason to torture herself over killing Peter. He had made his choices, and when a man threatens a woman's family, he shouldn't be surprised if she fights to the death. It happened in the wild. Bear sows, lionesses and vixens all made formidable foes when their young were threatened.

'Good people sometimes have to do terrible things,' she said.

They fell into silence and watched fish flick the surface of the water, sending tiny ripples outwards to the reeds.

Diana turned to Casper. 'You know that land Harry and I were trying to save out west? It's all been cleared now. I saw the photographs in the newspaper. The woodcutters moved in and everything we tried to preserve is gone now. All the animals that lived there are dead. When I read about it, my heart broke and I wondered if darkness and greed will always win.' She paused for a moment to gather herself before continuing. 'All my life I've tried to protect beauty because it's the best antidote I know to evil, and when evil wins and vanquishes beauty, we must get up and revive her again. That's what I've been trying to do with the garden – to make the evil that happened here go away and restore the beauty my mother created.'

Casper grimaced. 'I'm sorry about what happened to you and Harry with the development. I've lost my faith in people,' he said. 'That's the worst of it. I've seen what people can do. It's people who create horror. We inflict it on each other, on nature … on everything. You can't imagine how much I despise myself for bringing that horror back with me from Europe, for sullying the beautiful life you were trying to create for me and Freddy. When I look at you, well, you've always been so pure. So perfect. I forced you to kill a man to protect me and Freddy.'

Diana drew a breath. She couldn't believe she was going to say it. She'd buried it for years because it was what Aunt Shirley had convinced her was the right thing to do. All Casper knew of her past was that her parents had died in a house fire, and that Diana would have died too, if Aunt Shirley had not been there to save her.

'Casper,' she said, 'there's something I've haven't told you.'

# CHAPTER FORTY-NINE

*Sydney, March 1926*

Outside, dark clouds were spreading over the twilight sky. Through the window, Diana watched the shadows fall over the garden as she helped her mother wash the dishes. Her swing, strung from the sturdy branch of a liquidambar tree, rocked in the rising breeze. The young crepe myrtle they'd planted was leaning against the stake supporting it. She wondered where the echidna she'd seen was now. Echidnas couldn't run from their predators. Their defence was to burrow quickly into the ground.

She glanced at her mother. Her face was frozen and her hands trembled. If they were leaving, it wasn't going to be tonight. Diana's father hadn't gone to his men's bible study group after dinner as they'd expected. She could see him now through the doorway to the living room. He sat in the lounge chair gripping the arm rests tightly. He wasn't reading or listening to the radio. The fixed look on his face and the tension in his jaw were a study in brewing rage. Diana felt a lump of fear in her stomach as heavy as a stone. A storm was coming and no amount of soothing and compliancy could stop it now.

She glanced at the telephone. Aunt Shirley must be

wondering what was happening. Perhaps she would come anyway, thinking Diana had forgotten to call. That would be even worse. Diana pictured the gun, hiding in the cupboard like a vampire in a coffin. Her father hadn't gone to check it after dinner as was his habit. And until he did, she couldn't throw it in the creek like Aunt Shirley had told her to.

'Everything will be all right,' her mother whispered. 'Tomorrow is a new day, and we can go then.'

Diana took a cup of tea to her father and put it on the side table, forcing herself to smile at him. But he sensed the falseness in it. He was a man with eyes in the back of his head. He knew that something had changed in the atmosphere of the house.

'She's been here, hasn't she?' he snapped at Diana. 'I could smell her fancy perfume when I walked in the door.'

'Who?' she asked.

'That troublemaker.'

Diana knew better than to deny that Aunty Shirley had been at the house. 'She came to see the garden,' she lied. 'She needed some roses for an art show opening.'

'She came all the way here to get roses?'

Diana averted her eyes. That was the way it was with her father when you answered his questions. It was like being caught in a net – the more you twisted and turned, the more you found yourself trapped.

She returned to the kitchen, her skin tingling. She had an urge to flee, to grab her mother's arm and make a run for it. Perhaps they could go to a neighbour's house and telephone from there.

'I think we should go,' she whispered to her mother. 'I think we should go now. Don't worry about taking anything.'

She shook her head. 'The mood will pass. It always does. Go to bed and you'll see things will be better in the morning.'

Diana was torn between doing what her mother told her and what her instinct was screaming at her. Her father's moods usually 'passed' after he'd destroyed something – or someone. She looked at her mother's face, blue and swollen like a plum. There wasn't anywhere else on her body that he could leave a new mark. Whatever was festering inside him that night, it was more malevolent than anything she had seen before.

\*

Diana woke when she heard a noise. She sat up, straining to listen. At first, she thought it was the wind outside, then she heard the sound again. Something was being dragged along the floor. She slipped out of bed and turned the knob of her bedroom door slowly. The house was dark, except for a light coming from the kitchen. Diana stayed close to the wall and crept down the corridor. From somewhere in the living room she could hear another sound, like water gurgling down a sink. An eerie feeling engulfed her. She moved towards the light and looked into the kitchen. Her mother lay slumped over the kitchen table. Her neck was twisted at a strange angle. Her eyes were open, but she wasn't moving.

'Mummy?'

A figure appeared before her and blocked out the light. Her father loomed over her. It was only then she noticed the sharp smell of gasoline. She backed away, horror creeping up her spine when she realised what he'd done and what he intended to do.

She turned and ran back down the hallway. The window in her parents' room was large and she made a run for it, slamming the door behind her and locking it. She fiddled with the window latch, her fingers trembling. Her father was kicking at the door. She could hear it coming loose at the hinges. Then it splintered down the centre. She flung the window open and scraped her shin as she tried to lift herself through it. But before she could get her leg over the windowsill, her father burst into the room and grabbed her. Diana wanted to scream but her voice stuck in her throat. She clawed at her father as he tried to get his hands around her neck. He threw her against the cupboard and for a moment she saw stars.

Before she had a chance to make sense of what was happening, he opened the cupboard door and tried shoving her inside. Her terror reached a crescendo. He said that he'd burn the house down with her and her mother in it, and that's what he was going to do. She kicked and yelled although she knew no one would hear her. Then she heard a shrill cry and the light went on. Aunt Shirley was standing in the doorway.

'You killed Margaret!' Aunt Shirley screamed.

Her father let go of Diana and lunged at Aunt Shirley, grabbing her by the collar of her dress. Aunt Shirley knew that Diana's father hit her mother, but she'd never seen how bad he got and what he was capable of when he was in a rage. Aunt Shirley's eyes grew wide as he slammed her into a wall. He grabbed her chin and pushed it backwards, as if her head were a walnut he was determined to crack.

Her father had murdered her mother and now he was going to kill Aunt Shirley too. Seized by blind fury, Diana fled into the hallway and wrenched open the door to the cupboard where her father kept his gun. She loaded it and ran back into the bedroom. Her father turned as she aimed. There was no fear on his face as he watched her pull the trigger, only a sneer of indignation. The shotgun was heavy, and the recoil smacked into Diana's ribs when she fired it, but she'd hit her mark. Her father fell back on the bed, his arms splayed out and his legs trembling as if he were one of the rabbits he had shot. Then he stopped moving and the room was silent, except for the rasp of Aunt Shirley's breathing.

It had all happened so quickly that Diana's mind was blank with shock. She sank down to the floor and clasped her hands over her head as if to protect herself from invisible blows.

'I killed him.'

Her declaration sent Aunt Shirley into action. 'No, you didn't! He killed himself,' she said, rising to her feet and holding Diana by the shoulders. 'He killed your mother then turned the gun on himself. But not before setting the house on fire so we would perish too.'

'We?'

'Yes,' said Aunt Shirley, her voice firm. 'I was staying overnight, remember? I smelled the smoke and dragged you through the window.'

Aunt Shirley took the rifle and placed it between William Buchanan's legs. Then she turned to Diana, her expression firm.

'Go!' she ordered.

Diana climbed out the window and Aunt Shirley followed her. Then, without another word, her aunt lit a match and threw it inside the house.

# CHAPTER FIFTY

Diana looked at Casper. He'd been listening intently, never taking his eyes from her face.

'Dear God,' he said, his brow furrowed. 'I never knew. I never even imagined something like that had happened.' He put his hand on her shoulder. 'It doesn't change anything as far as I'm concerned. Everything you did was justified.'

'The law doesn't say that. The church doesn't say that.'

'To hell with the law and to hell with the church,' Casper said vehemently. 'Why should an innocent girl have gone to jail for slaying a monster? The Allies mobilised thousands of men and women to effectively do the same thing.' He shook his head. '*I've* killed people too. Most of them soldiers, but some civilians. Never in my life did I imagine that I would be capable of it. Sometimes you have to do terrible things to prevent a greater evil.'

Diana rubbed her legs. 'That's what Aunt Shirley must have thought, although we never discussed what happened after that night. In fact, I'm sure that Aunt Shirley came to sincerely believe my father had shot himself. By sticking to our story, it became the truth.' She turned to him. 'I didn't get away with it completely. After the house went up so quickly, some ashes fell on my nightdress and burned right through it. That's how I got those scars on my stomach. Most of the time I forget they're there, but when I undress, I see them, and I remember.'

Casper leaned closer and looked into her eyes. 'Why didn't you tell me this before? I would have understood completely.'

She shrugged. 'I thought it was too big a burden to place on another human being. Especially one I loved. I didn't want to sully you with it.'

Casper nodded. 'The same reason why I didn't want to tell you about my time in France.' He slipped his hand into hers and squeezed it. 'We must be honest with each other from now on,' he said. 'There can be no more secrets.'

Diana took a breath – now came the hard part. Casper was right. There could be no more pretending.

'Do you believe you can be happy here in Australia with me and Freddy?' she asked. 'I need you to be truthful with yourself and with me. Would you prefer to return to France with Sabine?'

'Good God, Diana!' said Casper, looking hurt and shocked. 'It's not like that. It never was. Sabine and I were bonded by a common cause, that's all.'

'I know,' Diana persisted. 'But that bond is very deep. I had the same with Aunt Shirley. You see, I can't live with only half of you. I know you tried but it wasn't enough, not for me and not for Freddy. And he needs stability and attention more than ever now, after what's happened. Please don't think that I don't love you. I love you very much. That's why I'll let you go if that's what you want.'

Casper's eyes opened wide. But he didn't say anything further.

'Anyway,' she said, trying to sound braver than she felt. 'I need you to decide. If you want to go, then go this afternoon with Sabine. I don't want to have to watch you leave again. But if you stay, then I need you to put your whole heart into your life here. I know things have changed, I know *we* have changed, but there is no other way forward.'

A sense of peace buoyed Diana. She'd spoken her truth, and wherever the chips fell she would have to be satisfied with that.

'We'll be back earlier today. At four o'clock,' she told Casper. 'If you're not here then, I'll understand. I'll explain it to Freddy.'

They looked into each other's eyes. There was no attempt to make light of things or to hide away from the truth now. She could see that he was taking her seriously. They'd fallen in love when life was good, but it took something else to stay together when the world turned dark.

*

Diana returned to the house to find Freddy and Sabine standing on the veranda, playing their absurd chin game together.

'I hope you have a good journey back to France,' Diana told Sabine. 'I will miss your beautiful music.'

Sabine clasped Diana in a fierce embrace and kissed her on both cheeks. 'Thank you for all you have done to help me.'

They held each other's hands firmly as if to cement their friendship, and then let each other go.

Diana went to her truck and opened the passenger door for Freddy. Harry had asked her to see him at his office, and she planned to drop Freddy at school along the way. They waved again to Sabine as Diana drove the truck around the turning circle.

'Are we going to see Sabine again?' Freddy asked when they headed out onto the street.

'Darling, I don't know,' she said. 'She lives very far away. In France.'

'Do they have art galleries in France?'

'They do,' she replied. 'Very nice ones. And a lot of artists too.'

'So, we will go?'

Diana swallowed the lump that always seemed to be in her throat lately. She couldn't escape the bitter irony. It seemed that she was going to lose both the men in her life to the charms of Sabine. Freddy would grow up and one day get on a ship and sail for Europe, as his father once did, and leave her forever.

Tears stung her eyes. 'It's possible,' she said.

*

Diana was surprised to see Phyllis with Harry when his receptionist showed her to his desk. Phyllis was smiling like the cat that had swallowed the canary.

She stood and hugged Diana. 'You are too thin!' she told her. 'I'm taking you to the Hotel Australia tomorrow for a good fattening up. You've been through that dreadful inquest but now that's all over, you can get on with your life.'

Diana didn't argue with Phyllis. She might need her friend's shoulder to cry on the following day.

'Well, let's look at what Harry has got to show you,' Phyllis said.

'I hope you'll be as excited about this as I am,' Harry told Diana. 'Please have a seat.'

The three of them sat down around the desk. Harry opened a plan and flattened it out on the table. Diana expected he was going to show her more housing designs for the property development in the northern suburbs. But when she examined the drawings, she saw the houses were smaller and simpler than she had been expecting, although elegantly designed with clean lines and large box-frame windows.

'These are lovely, but I thought you had multi-level houses and inner courtyards in mind for the new development.'

Harry exchanged a look with Phyllis before addressing Diana. 'These are plans that anybody can order when they subscribe to *Australian Home and Garden.* That way the average person can build a well-designed house without the expense of engaging a master architect. A couple of my colleagues are offering plans now, but what I intend to include with mine is a garden plan designed by you, along with a list of plants suitable for different areas – that way the house and the garden will work together on small lots of land.'

'And I intend to publish suggestions for the interiors – the types of finishes to use and light fixtures that will offer beautiful illumination and not depressing garishness,' Phyllis added.

'Oh,' said Diana, so moved that tears sprang to her eyes.

'What a wonderful idea!' She took a breath. 'How beautiful. How very beautiful.'

Harry beamed. 'Indeed. These houses won't be Don Morris's ugly little boxes on barren patches of lawn. They will be appealing homes that work with the natural environment, like the ones you and I were hoping to have built out west.'

'We can't do much about bad taste,' Phyllis said, 'or greedy developers, but we can influence open-minded people, one house at a time.'

Diana's heart lifted. Harry and Phyllis weren't willing to give up. Maybe Sydney could still become the city with the most beautiful suburbs in the world.

'Can you put something together for me right away?' Phyllis asked her.

Diana smiled through her tears. Phyllis always seemed to know when she needed a new project.

★

Diana parked her truck outside Mrs Dalton's house and took a moment to collect herself. As the day had gone on, she'd become more certain that Casper wouldn't be there when she and Freddy returned home. It was an inexplicable sense of something having shifted, of things changing. A clearing of the old so the new could begin.

The front door to Mrs Dalton's house swung open and the old lady came out with Freddy.

'I don't let him out of my sight these days,' Mrs Dalton said, opening the passenger side door and helping Freddy into the seat. She passed Diana something warm wrapped in waxed paper and smelling of ginger and burned sugar.

'Thank you, Mrs Dalton,' Diana said.

As they drove home, she glanced at Freddy. It had been just the two of them for so long and now it would be again. She felt a surge of protective love.

'Freddy, I'm very proud of you. You are a special boy.'

He looked at her with that knowing smile that was appearing regularly on his face these days. 'When will we be going to the art gallery again, Mummy?'

Whether he'd meant it to or not, the remark hit a bull's-eye in Diana's heart. She hadn't taken Freddy to the art gallery since the afternoon he'd gone missing. But it wasn't because she associated it with what Sabine had done, but because of Peter Todd and the way he had betrayed her trust. It had opened a wound that had been there since childhood, caused by the way her father treated her and her mother while showing the world a congenial face. She couldn't tolerate that kind of deception.

'The eels might be going home soon,' Freddy added with a serious look in his eyes. 'And I'd like to tell them goodbye.'

Freddy's second arrow hit even more painfully than the first. She realised that in her effort to protect her son she'd deprived him of a chance to say goodbye to his father. But it was too late for that now.

As if to confirm her assumption, the house was quiet when Diana pulled the truck up in front of it. The windows were closed, and the door was shut. It wasn't until that moment that she realised she'd been holding her breath.

*He's gone*, she thought.

She reached into her purse for her key and gave it to Freddy. 'Go wash your face and change out of your uniform,' she said. 'We'll go for a walk. There's something I want to tell you.'

She watched Freddy disappear inside the house and drew a steadying breath before stepping out of the truck. She needed a moment to herself before breaking the news to him about his father. The afternoon sunlight sparkled over the garden. Gone were the tangled morning glory vines, the woody lantana and the Madeira vines that had almost strangled the trees to death. In their place was the enchanted garden Diana's mother had started, with its winding stone paths that disappeared under lush canopies of trees. It was a garden that made you pause and ponder which direction to take first, and yet gave you confidence that around each bend something wonderful would appear.

Diana sat down on the bench that Marilyn had repaired and remembered the many times when she and her mother had sat on it together. She would rebuild herself again, like she had restored the garden. It was better not to think about what you'd lost, but about the wisdom you had gained. She still had Freddy and Marilyn. She had friends like Phyllis and Harry to spur her on. The world she lived in was a good place, with or without Casper.

'Diana.'

She looked up, and had to steady herself. Casper was standing next to her with Freddy by his side.

'Apparently you told Freddy we're going for a walk,' he said. 'And there's a trail that goes from the bottom of the garden through the bush that he's been wanting to show me for some time. Fairies live there.'

Diana's heart beat quickly. She searched Casper's face and it told her all she wanted to know. He was staying.

She looked to Freddy. 'You've seen fairies?' she asked him. 'You never told me.'

'They've been waiting,' he said. 'They wanted you to finish the garden first before introducing themselves.'

Casper took Diana's hand and helped her up. They smiled at each other, a moment of perfect accord. She knew then that they, like the garden, had every hope of blossoming again.

She turned to Freddy and touched his cheek. 'Well, your father and I had better go and meet them then.'

Together the three of them walked through the garden and crossed over the creek. The bushland was alive with birdsong. The air around them shimmered with light and winged insects.

Diana squeezed Casper's hand as she remembered what he'd told her when they were courting. *À coeur vaillant rien d'impossible.* For a valiant heart, nothing is impossible.

# ACKNOWLEDGEMENTS

Thank you very much to the talented team at HarperCollins Publishers Australia for helping to bring *The French Agent* to fruition. I would particularly like to express gratitude to my enthusiastic publisher, Anna Valdinger, and hardworking senior editor, Scott Forbes.

I also appreciate the support of my intrepid agent, Catherine Drayton, and everyone at Inkwell Management in New York.

Thank you to Dianne Blacklock for her insightful feedback during the editing process, and to my first reader, Roslyn McGechan, for her attention to detail. Also thank you to proofreaders Bronwyn Sweeney and Melinda Hutchings for dotting my i's and crossing my t's.

Special thanks goes to Paul Wesley for helping me construct the fighting and kidnapping scenes. I'd also like to express appreciation to Carmen Maravillas for her assistance with my art questions, Lily Testa for her technical expertise, and Tom Branighan of Ku-ring-gai Wildflower Nursery for his advice regarding Australian native plants.

Last but not least, I would like to sincerely thank my friends and family, including my three beloved cats. Although it may not be immediately apparent on the pages, your love and support for me are always there, woven between the words of the story.

With love and thanks,
Belinda
XX

# SAMPLE QUESTIONS FOR BOOK CLUBS

1. Did you find Sabine a sympathetic character? Why or why not?

2. After the Second World War, the responsibility for helping returned military servicemen settle back into society was put largely on the shoulders of their wives. Do you think that was a fair burden considering some of the veterans were clearly traumatised? Do you think veterans and their families get the support they need today?

3. The main characters in *The French Agent* are all keeping a secret of some sort. Whose secret surprised you most when they revealed it?

4. Nature plays an important part in the novel. Diana says that natural beauty is the best antidote to war and other horrors. Do you agree with her?

5. What did you think of the 'green suburb' that Harry and Diana hoped to create? Would you like to live in such a suburb?

6. Australia is among the worst eleven countries for deforestation and has the highest rate of wildlife extinctions. What does Australia need to do better to meet the needs of a growing population while at the same time taking care of its natural environment?

7. What themes and recurring motifs did you notice in the novel?

8. What do you see in store for each of the main characters? What would you like to see happen to them in the future?

# Discover the world of Belinda Alexandra ...

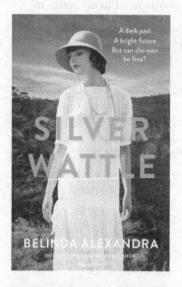

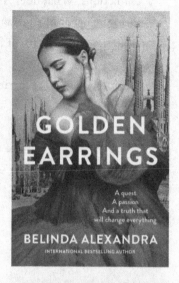

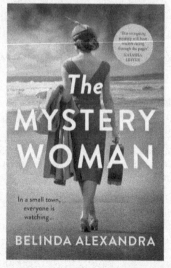